They were bright kids, he reflected. In fact, he estimated they probably had at least a five or ten percent chance of actually pulling off their rebellion. Of course, their chances would have been one hell of a lot better if they'd actually been dealing with Manticore.

Well, you can't have everything, "Talisman," Damien Harahap, one time Solarian Gendarme, more recently agent of the Mesa System government, and currently in the employ of the Mesan Alignment, thought dryly. *And at least they're a lot closer to sane than that maniac Nordbrandt!*

He smiled and shook his head. He actually had nothing at all against "Talisman" and "Magpie," when it came down to it. In fact, he wished them well, not that he actually expected things to turn out that way. Still, it was nothing personal. Only business.

He watched the ground car disappear through the drooping gate and checked his chrono. Seven and a half minutes, he decided. That ought to be a sufficiently random interval before he headed off in the opposite direction himself.

To purchase these and all other Baen Book titles in e-book format, please go to www.baen.com.

SHADOW OF FREEDOM

DAVID WEBER

This is a work of fiction. All the characters and events portrayed in this book are fictional, and any resemblance to real people or incidents is purely coincidental.

Copyright © 2013 by Words of Weber, Inc.

All rights reserved, including the right to reproduce this book or portions thereof in any form.

A Baen Books Original

Baen Publishing Enterprises
P.O. Box 1403
Riverdale, NY 10471
www.baen.com

ISBN: 978-1-4767-8048-1

Cover art by David Mattingly

First Baen mass market paperback printing, May 2014
Second Baen mass market paperback printing, September 2015

Library of Congress Control Number: 2012047564

Distributed by Simon & Schuster
1230 Avenue of the Americas
New York, NY 10020

Pages by Joy Freeman (www.pagesbyjoy.com)
Printed in the United States of America

SHADOW OF FREEDOM

This is a work of fiction. All the characters and events portrayed in this book are fictional, and any resemblance to real people or incidents is purely coincidental.

A Baen Books Original

Baen Publishing Enterprises
P.O. Box 1403
Riverdale, NY 10471
www.baen.com

ISBN: 978-1-4767-8048-1

Cover art by David Mattingly

First Baen mass market paperback printing, May 2015
Second Baen mass market paperback printing, September 2017

Library of Congress Control Number: 2012047561

Distributed by Simon & Schuster
1230 Avenue of the Americas
New York, NY 10020

Pages by Joy Freeman (www.pagesbyjoy.com)
Printed in the United States of America

SHADOW OF
FREEDOM

"It'll be easier the next time . . . and there *will* be a next time. There always is."

—Frinkelo Osborne,
    Office of Frontier Security,
    Loomis System.

Chapter One

THE WINGLESS, SAUCERLIKE DRONE drifted through the wet, misty night on silent counter gravity. The fine droplets of rain sifted down in filmy curtains that reeked of burned wood and hydrocarbons and left a greasy sensation on the skin. Despite the rainfall, fires crackled noisily here and there, consuming heaps of wreckage which had once been homes, adding their own smoke and soot to the atmosphere. A faint, distant mutter of thunder rolled through the overcast night, though whether it was natural or man-made was difficult to say.

The drone paused, motionless, blacker than the night about it, its rain-slick, light-absorbent coat sucking in the photons from the smudgy fires which might otherwise have reflected from it. The turret mounted on its bottom rotated smoothly, turning sensors and lenses towards whatever had attracted its attention. Wind sighed wearily in the branches of sugar pine, crab poplar, and imported Terran white pine and hickory, something shifted in one of the piles of rubble, throwing up sparks and cinders. A burning rafter burned through and collapsed and water dripped from rain-heavy limbs with the patient, uncaring persistence of nature, but otherwise all was still, silent.

The drone considered the sensor data coming to it, decided it was worth consideration by higher authority, and uploaded it to the communications satellite and its operator in far distant Elgin City. Then it waited.

The silence, the rain, and the wind continued. The fires hissed as heavier drops fell into their white and red hearts. And then—

The thunderbolt descended from the heavens like the wrath of Zeus. Born two hundred and sixty-five kilometers above the planet's surface, it traced a white line from atmosphere's edge to ground level, riding a froth of plasma. The two-hundred-kilo dart arrived without even a whisper, far outracing the sonic boom of its passage, and struck its target coordinates at thirty times the speed of sound.

The quiet, rainy night tore apart under the equivalent of the next best thing to two and a half tons of old-fashioned TNT. The brilliant, blinding flash vaporized a bubble of rain. Concussion and overpressure rolled out from its heart, flattening the remaining walls of three of the village's broken houses. The fury of the explosion painted the clouds, turned individual raindrops into shining diamonds and rubies that seemed momentarily frozen in air, and flaming bits and pieces of what once had been someone's home arced upward like meteors yearning for the heavens.

❖   ❖   ❖

"Thank you used a big enough hammer, Callum?" the woman in the dark blue uniform of a lieutenant in the Loomis System Unified Public Safety Force asked dryly.

She stood behind the drone operator's comfortable chair, looking over his shoulder at the display where the pinprick icon of the explosion flashed brightly. The operator—a sergeant, with the sleeve hashmarks of a twenty-T-year veteran—seemed to hesitate for just a moment, then turned his head to look at her.

"Unauthorized movement in an interdicted zone, Ma'am," he replied.

"And you needed a KEW to deal with it?" The lieutenant arched one eyebrow. "A near-deer, do you think? Or possibly a bison elk?"

"IR signature was human, Ma'am. Must've been one of MacRory's bastards, or he wouldn't've been there."

"I see." The UPS officer folded her hands behind her. "As it happens, I was standing right over there at the command desk," she observed, this time with a distinct bite. "If I recall correctly, SOP is to clear a KEW strike with command personnel unless it's time-critical. Am I mistaken about that?"

"No, Ma'am," the sergeant admitted, and the lieutenant shook her head.

"I realize you like big bangs, Callum. And I'll admit you've got a better excuse than usual for playing with them. But there are Regs for a reason, and I'd take it as a personal favor—the kind of favor which will keep your fat, worthless, trigger-happy arse in that comfortable chair instead of carrying out sweeps in the bush—if you'd remember that next time. Do you think you can do that for me?"

"Yes, Ma'am," the sergeant said much more crisply,

and she gave him a nod that was several degrees short of friendly and headed back to her station.

The sergeant watched her go, then turned back to his display and smiled. He'd figured she'd have a little something to say to him, but he'd also figured it would be worth it. Three of his buddies had been killed in the first two days of the insurrection, and he was still in the market for payback. Besides, it gave him a sense of godlike power to be able to call down the wrath of heaven. He'd known Lieutenant MacRuer would never have authorized the expenditure of a KEW on a single, questionable IR signature, which was why he hadn't asked for it. And if he was going to be honest about it, he wasn't really certain his target hadn't been a ghost, either. But that was perfectly all right with him, and his intense inner sense of satisfaction more than outweighed his superior's obvious displeasure.

This time, at least, he amended silently. *Catch her in a bad mood, and the by-the-Book bitch is just likely to make good on that reassignment.* He shook his head mentally. *Don't think I'd like slogging around in the woods with those people very much.*

❖　　　❖　　　❖

"Confirm impact, Ma'am," Missile Tech 1/c George Chasnikov reported. "Looks like it drifted fifteen or twenty meters to planetary west of the designated coords, though." He shook his head. "That was sloppy."

"Was the problem at their end, or ours?" Lieutenant Commander Sharon Tanner had the watch. She also happened to be SLNS *Hoplite*'s tactical officer, and she punched up the post-strike report on her own display as she spoke. "I'm not real crazy about 'sloppy' when we're talking about KEWs, Chaz."

"Me neither, Ma'am," Chasnikov agreed sourly. "Reason I brought it up, actually." He shook his head, tapping a query into his console. "I hate those damned things," he added in a mutter Tanner knew was deliberately just loud enough for her to hear.

She let it pass. Chasnikov was an experienced, highly valued member of her department, a lifer who would stay in SLN uniform until the day he died, and every TAC officer he ever served under would be lucky to have him. That bought him a little extra slack from someone like Sharon Tanner.

Not that he didn't have a point, she thought bitterly, reflecting on all the things *Hoplite* and her small squadron had been called upon to do over the past few weeks. Compared to some of those, expending a single kinetic energy weapon on what had probably been a ghost target was small beer.

"Their end, it looks like, Ma'am," Chasnikov said after a moment. "It didn't miss the designated coordinates; it missed the *amended* coordinates. They sent us a correction, but it was too late to update the targeting queue."

"And did they happen to tell us what it was they wanted us to kill *this* time? Or if we got it?"

"No, Ma'am. Just the coordinates. Could've been one of their own battalions, for all I know. And no strike assessment, so far." *And there won't* be *one, either . . . as usual*, his expression added silently.

"I see." Tanner rubbed the tip of her nose for a moment, then shrugged. "Write it up, Chaz. Be sure to make it clear we followed our checklist on the launch. I'll pass it along to Commander Diadoro. I'm sure he and the Skipper will . . . reemphasize to Groundside that little hiccups when you're targeting KEWs can have major consequences. And emphasize that they didn't give us a clear target description, either. We can't go around wasting the taxpayers' KEWs without at least knowing what we're shooting at."

And I hope Captain Venelli uses that little memo to rip someone a new asshole, she added silently. *Chaz is right, we've done too damned much of this kind of shit. I don't think there's anything* left *down there that's genuinely worth a KEW, and anything that discourages those bloodthirsty bastards from raining them down on some poor damned idiot with a pulse rifle schlepping through the shrubbery all by himself will be worth it.*

There were many things Sharon Tanner had done in her Frontier Fleet career of which she was proud; this wasn't one of them.

❖   ❖   ❖

Back in the shattered ruins which had once been a village named Glen mo Chrìdhe, the sound of rain was overlaid by the heavier patter of falling debris. It lasted for several seconds, sparks bouncing and rolling through the wet as some of the still-burning wreckage struck, and then things were still once more. The crater was dozens of meters across, deep enough to swallow an air lorry...and more than enough to devour the cellar into which the thirteen-year-old boy had just darted with the food he'd been able to scavenge for his younger sister.

❖   ❖   ❖

"They got Tammas." Erin MacFadzean's voice was flat, worn and eroded by exhaustion and gradually swelling despair. She looked across the dingy basement room at Megan MacLean and her expression was bitter. "Fergus just reported in."

"Where?" MacLean asked, rubbing her weary eyes and clenching her soul against the pain of yet another loss.

"Rothes," MacFadzean replied. "The Uppies stopped the lorry on its way into Mackessack."

"Is he alive?" MacLean lowered her hands, looking across at the other woman.

"Fergus doesn't know. He says there was a lot of shooting, and it sounds like he was lucky to get away alive himself."

"I see."

MacLean laid her hands flat on the table in front of her, looking down at their backs for a moment, then inhaled deeply. It shamed her to admit it, but she hoped Tammas MacPhee hadn't been taken alive, and wasn't that a hell of a thing to be thinking about a friend she'd known for thirty T-years?

"See if we can get in touch with Tad Ogilvy," she said after a moment. "Tell him Tammas is ... gone. He's in charge of whatever we've got left outside the capital now."

"On it," MacFadzean acknowledged and quietly left the room.

As the door closed behind her, MacLean allowed her shoulders to sag with the weariness she tried not to let anyone else see. Not that she was fooling anyone ... or that everyone else wasn't just as exhausted as she was. But she had to go on playing her part to the bitter end. At least it wouldn't be too much longer now, she thought harshly.

It wasn't supposed to be this way. She'd organized

the Loomis Liberation League as a *legal* political party seven years ago, during one of the Prosperity Party's infrequent bouts of façade democracy. She hadn't really expected to accomplish anything—this was Halkirk, after all—but she'd wanted MacMinn and MacCrimmon to know there were at least some people still willing to stand up on their hind legs and voice their opposition. The LLL's candidates had actually won in two of the capital city's boroughs, giving it a whopping four tenths of a percent of the seats in the Parliament, which had made it the most powerful of the opposition parties. It probably wouldn't have won those races if the Prosperity Party hadn't been putting on a show for the Core World news crew doing a documentary on the silver oak logging camps, of course, but two seats were still two seats.

Not that it had done any good. And not that either of the LLL's members had won reelection after the news crew went home. President MacMinn hadn't even pretended to count the votes in the next general election, and that was the point at which Megan MacLean had listened to Tammas MacPhee, the LLL's vice chairman, and MacFadzean. She'd maintained her party's open organization, its get-out-the-vote and lobbying campaigns, but she'd also let MacFadzean organize the Liberation League's thoroughly illegal provisional armed wing.

It had probably been a mistake, she thought now, yet she still couldn't see what other option she might have had. Not with the Unified Public Safety Force turning more and more brutal—and worrying less and less about maintaining even a pretense of due process—under Secretary of Security MacQuarie.

Except, of course, to have given up the effort completely, and she simply hadn't been able to do that.

And now this. Seven years of effort, of pouring her heart and soul into the liberation of her star system, and it ended this way, in death and disaster. It wasn't even—

She looked up again as the door opened and Mac-Fadzean walked back into what passed for their command post.

"I got a runner off to Tad," she said, and her lips twitched in a mirthless smile. "Somehow I didn't think I should be using the com, under the circumstances."

"Probably not a bad idea," MacLean agreed with what might have been the ghost of an answering smile. If that was what it was, it vanished quickly. "It was bad enough with just the Uppies tapping the coms. With the damned Sollies up there listening in..."

Her voice trailed off, and MacFadzean nodded. She understood the harsh, jagged edge of hate which had crept into MacLean's voice only too well. They had Frinkelo Osborne, the Office of Frontier Security's advisor to MacMinn's Prosperity Party, to thank for the for Solarian League Navy starships in orbit around the planet of Halkirk. Officially, Osborne was only a trade attaché in the Solarian legation in Elgin, the Loomis System's capital. Trade attachés made wonderful covers for OFS operatives assigned to "assist and advise" independent Verge star systems when their transtellar masters felt they stood in need of a little outside support. And if an "attaché" required a certain degree of assistance from the SLN, he could usually be confident of getting it.

We could've taken MacCrimmon and MacQuarie

on our own, MacFadzean thought bitterly. *We could have. Another few months, a few more arms shipments from Partisan and his people, and we'd have had a fighting chance to kick the LPP straight to Hell. Hell, we might have pulled it off even now, if not for the damned Sollies! But how in God's name are people with pulsers and grenade launchers supposed to hold off orbital bombardments? If I'd only been able to get word to Partisan—!*

But she hadn't. They hadn't been supposed to move for a minimum of at least another four months. Partisan had been supposed to be back in Loomis to lock down the final arrangements—the ones she hadn't yet discussed even with MacLean—and there hadn't been any way to get a message out when the balloon went up so unexpectedly.

She glanced across the room again, wondering if she should have told MacLean about those arrangements with Partisan. She'd thought about it more than once, but secrecy and security had been all important. Besides, MacLean wasn't really a revolutionary at heart; she was a reformer. She'd never been able to throw herself as fully into the notion of armed resistance as MacFadzean had, and the thought of relying so heavily on someone from out-system, of crafting operations plans which *depended* on armed assistance from a foreign star nation, would have been a hard sell.

Be honest with yourself, Erin. You were afraid she'd tell you to shut the conduit down, weren't you? That the notion of trusting anybody from outside Loomis was too risky. That they were too likely to have an agenda of their own, one that didn't include our best interests. You told yourself she'd change her mind if you could present a finished plan that covered all the contingencies you could think of, but inside you always knew she still would have hated the entire thought. And you weren't quite ready to go ahead and commit to Partisan without her okay, were you? Well, maybe she would've been right . . . but it wouldn't have made any difference in the way things've finally worked out, now would it?

She looked up at the command post's shadowed ceiling, her eyes bitter with hate for the starships which had rained down death and ruination all across her homeworld, and wished with all her exhausted heart that she *had* been able to get a messenger to Partisan.

Chapter Two

"HOW MUCH LONGER DO you expect this crap to go on?" Captain Francine Venelli's tone was harsh. "I've got better things to do with my time than sit here in orbit killing a bunch of backwoods ground-grubbers, and my people don't like it." She glowered at the neatly dressed civilian on the other side of the briefing room table. "They don't like it at all. For that matter, neither do I. And it's not like there aren't enough wheels coming off at the moment that I can't find plenty of other more worthwhile things to worry about!"

"I don't know how much longer, Captain," Frinkelo Osborne replied as calmly and reasonably as he could. "I wish I did. And, while we're being so frank with each other, *I* wish you weren't here doing this, either." He shook his head, his expression even more disgusted than Venelli's. "It's like using a hammer to crack an egg. Or maybe more like spanking a baby with an ax!"

Venelli's blue eyes narrowed and she sat back in her chair. She'd dealt with more Office of Frontier

Security personnel in her career than she could have counted—certainly a lot more of them than she could have wished! Too many of them, in her experience, were entirely in favor of using hammers on eggs, if only to discourage the next chicken from getting out of line. Of course, as a mere advisor to President Ailsa MacMinn's Loomis Prosperity Party administration, not a full-fledged system or sector commissioner, Osborne might still be far enough down the food chain to believe there were more important things in the universe than his own bank balance.

Or maybe he's just smart enough to realize what KEWs are likely to do to the source *of his bank balance,* she reminded herself. *I wonder how many hectares of silver oak we've turned into cinders so far?*

She kept her mental grimace from reaching her expression and glanced at the spectacular live feed from the exterior view projected on the briefing room's smart wall while she considered that depressing question.

Her "squadron"—the battlecruiser *Hoplite*, the light cruiser *Yenta MacIlvenna*, and the destroyers *Abatis* and *Lunette*—had been improvised on very little notice when Loomis' request for assistance came in. Now her ships orbited the planet Halkirk, the Loomis System's primary inhabited planet, and the direct visual of the smart wall was magnificent. Indeed, under other circumstances, the captain, who was something of a connoisseur of planetary oddities, would probably have enjoyed her visit to the star system. Unlike the majority of systems, Loomis had two planets smack in the middle of the G7 primary's liquid water zone. In fact, Halkirk and its sister planet, Thurso, were not only in the liquid water zone but orbited a common center of mass seven light-minutes from the star as they made their way around it. Yet while they might be sisters, they were far from twins.

Halkirk was all greens and browns—especially browns—with far less blue than Venelli was accustomed to seeing, since sixty percent of its surface was dry land. Some of it, like the continental interiors, was *very* dry land, as a matter of fact, although the smaller, mountainous continents of Stroma and Stronsay were quite pleasant. In fact, *they* were actually on the damp side, thanks to ocean currents and prevailing wind patterns, and even "small" continents were very large pieces of real estate. Hoy and Westray, which between them accounted for better than seventy percent of Halkirk's total land area, were another story entirely, of course. Venelli understood exactly why the LPP had established its reeducation camps on Westray.

Thurso was a very different proposition—a gleaming, gorgeous sapphire of a world. Over ninety percent of *its* surface was water, and the widely scattered archipelagoes which were nominally dry land had to cope with tidal surges that reminded the captain more of tsunamis than anything most planets would have called tides. Not too surprising, she supposed, when Thurso's "moon" was three percent more massive than Old Earth herself. Weather was...interesting on Thurso, as well, and it wasn't too surprising that the planet's population was tiny compared to Halkirk's. On the other hand, Thurso's gargantuan fisheries produced a startling tonnage of gourmet seafood which commanded extraordinary prices from Core World epicures. Probably not extraordinary enough to have attracted Star Enterprise Initiatives Unlimited's attention to Loomis by itself, but enough to have made the star system a worthwhile trading stop even without Halkirk. The asteroid resource extraction industries and the gas mining operations centered on the star system's trio of gas giants undoubtedly helped cover SEIU's operating expenses, too, but the real treasure of the Loomis System lay in Halkirk's groves of silver oak.

Francine Venelli was a professional spacer, accustomed to compact living quarters aboard ship or orbital habitats. She didn't think in terms of planetary housing, or the kinds of huge, sprawling domiciles wealthy dirtsiders seemed to think were necessary. For that matter, she didn't really understand the fascination "natural" materials exercised on some people's minds. Durability, practicality, and appearance were far more important to her than where the materials in question came from, and wood was a pretty piss-poor construction material where starships were concerned.

Despite that, even she had been struck by the sheer beauty of Halkirk silver oak. The dense-grained, beautifully colored, beautifully patterned wood was like a somatic holo sculpture, deliberately designed to soothe and stroke the edges of a frayed temperament. Something about its texture—about the half-seen, half-imagined highlights that gleamed against its dark cherry wood color, like true silver deep inside the grain—was almost like the visual equivalent of barely heard woodwinds playing softly at the back of one's mind or a gentle, relaxing massage. Just sitting in a room paneled with it was almost enough to make a woman forget why she was so pissed off with people like the Loomis System government. She supposed she shouldn't be surprised that the price it commanded in

Core World markets, as a medium for sculptors and furniture designers as well as a building material, was truly astronomical.

Between them, Loomis' resources would have been more than enough to provide the system's population a comfortable standard of living...except, of course, for the tiny problem that the system population didn't control them. Not anymore, anyway. For the last forty-five T-years, that control had belonged to Star Enterprise Initiatives Unlimited, headquartered in the Lucastra System, only seventy light years from Sol. SEIU had secured the typical transstellar hundred-year leases from the LPP, and that, by one of the tortuous and circuitous paths with which Venelli and Frontier Fleet had become only too familiar, explained why she and her ships were in orbit around Halkirk at this particular moment.

Her gaze swiveled back from the visual display to Osborne, and she pursed her lips.

"How the hell did it get this bad?"

Her own question surprised her, because it wasn't the one she'd meant to ask. It wasn't exactly the most tactful way she could have phrased it, either but the disgust in Osborne's answering grimace wasn't really directed at her.

"It wasn't hard at all," he said. "Not with an idiot like Zagorski calling the shots."

"I thought we'd been called in by President MacMinn and Secretary MacQuarie," Venelli said sardonically.

"President MacMinn is so far past it by now that I doubt she seals her own shoes in the morning." Osborne reply was caustic enough to dissolve asbestos. "MacCrimmon's the one who really calls the shots inside the LPP these days. He'd probably retire MacMinn to a nice, quiet geriatric home—or an even quieter cemetery—if he could, but she's still the Party's Beloved Leader. One of those little problems that arise when politicians encourage personality cults."

Venelli nodded. Ailsa MacMinn and her husband had been the leaders of the Prosperity Party when it seized power in a brief, bloody coup, but Keith Mac-Minn had been dead for over twenty T-years, and by now Ailsa was well past seventy—without the benefit of prolong. Vice President Tyler MacCrimmon was less than half her age, but although he was widely acknowledged as her inevitable successor, she was still the Party's public face. He might be the power behind the throne, yet he needed her to give him legitimacy.

And he also needed Senga MacQuarie and her Unified Public Safety Force to prop up the entire Prosperity Party edifice. Fortunately for MacCrimmon, MacQuarie was still a relative newcomer to the cabinet (her predecessor and mentor, Lachlan MacHendrie, had been one of MacMinn's "old comrades" until his recent death due to unspecified "medical problems"). She needed him as much as he needed her, at least for now.

"Part of the problem," Osborne continued, "is that the LPP didn't make a clean sweep of the MacRorys after the Revolution. A miscalculation on the Mac-Minns' part, but it's a little hard to blame them for that one, really." He grimaced. "Tavis III probably meant well, but he'd never been a strong king, and most people didn't really seem to mind when he 'voluntarily' abdicated in the Party's favor. I expect Keith and Ailsa didn't want to risk generating sympathy for the dynasty after the fact by having him assassinated, since as near as I can tell he died of genuinely natural causes shortly after the Revolution. But they didn't prune back his family, either, probably because Clan MacRory had so many relatives scattered around the system. Oh, they banned them from politics—such as they were and what there was of them—and kept a close eye on them, but they didn't really go after them or 'encourage' them to emigrate. And as long as things went reasonably well, that didn't matter all that much, but after SEIU moved in and started turning the screws on the locals, a lot of people started remembering the good old days and 'Good King Tavis.' Of course, by that time he was safely dead, but his son was still around."

"And he started conniving to regain power, did he?"

"No." Osborne shook his head. "Or not as far as I've ever been able to discover, anyway. There were enough people who *wanted* him to by then, but it looks to me like he was smart enough to realize he wasn't going to accomplish anything through any sort of open reform process and that he'd only get a lot of people killed if he tried something more ... energetic. Unfortunately for him, that didn't prevent MacQuarie's predecessor from arranging a fatal 'traffic accident' for him fifteen years ago. Got his older son in the same 'accident,' too. The bad news from their perspective was that they missed his younger son, Mánas. The good news was that he's no idiot. He understood exactly what had happened to his father and his brother, and he stayed as far away from politics as he could for as long as he could. Which was working out just fine ... until SEIU promoted Zagorski to System Manager."

He grimaced, and Venelli felt herself grimace back. As a general rule, her sympathy for Frontier Security's minions was distinctly limited. In this case, however, she'd had the dubious pleasure of meeting Nyatui Zagorski shortly after her arrival in-system, and she hadn't enjoyed the experience.

"What *is* his problem?" she asked.

"Disappointment," Osborne replied. "He expected better than he got, and he wasn't happy with the consolation prize."

"Seems like a pretty sweet deal for him to me," Venelli observed, waving one hand at the planets on the smart wall. "Of course, I'm only a naval officer. My perspective may be a bit more limited than his— him being such a mover and shaker of the universe, and all."

Osborne's lips quirked at her ironic tone, but he shook his head.

"That's part of his problem, really. I think he sees himself as exactly that—a mover and a shaker—and he feels . . . deprived of a platform worthy of his profound talents. Unfortunately for him, SEIU's not one of the major transstellars. It's more of a middleweight, and Loomis is worthwhile, but it isn't in the same category as one of the real pot-of-gold propositions, and Loomis isn't the top rung of even its ladder. Worse, Zagorski was assistant system manager in Delvecchio, which *is* SEIU's crown jewel, for ten years. I'm pretty sure he expected to move up to system manager there when his boss got recalled to the home office, which would finally have made him a really big fish in his own personal pond. Only somebody with better family connections got Delvecchio, and *he* got Loomis as a consolation prize. I think that really pissed him off, and he arrived in get-rich-quick mode. He wants to squeeze as much as he can out of Loomis as fast as he can, partly for what he can skim off the top, but also—I think—because he's hoping that a spike in system revenues on his watch may still get him promoted to something even better."

"Great." Venelli snorted harshly. "If I had a credit for every time one of these assholes screwed the pooch out here trying to look good for the home office I could buy *Hoplite* as my private yacht and retire!"

"You probably could," Osborne agreed. "In this case, he decided to raise the quota on silver oak. In fact, he doubled it. Then he raised it *again*. There's a lot of timberland on Halkirk, but it's not unlimited, and the Halkirkians know it. He's basically clearcutting their most valuable planetary resource, and they don't like it. He doesn't care, of course. Even at the rate he's going through them, there are enough stands of silver oak to keep him in business for another ten or twenty years, and he plans on being long gone by then."

Venelli felt as disgusted as Osborne looked. Slash-and-burn tactics like Zagorski's were entirely too common in the Verge, and they accounted for at least half of the Solarian League Navy's headaches.

"When the new logging policies came in, a lot of people who'd been willing to keep their heads down rather than attract the UPS' attention started remembering Good King Tavis a lot more affectionately," Osborne continued. "Mánas MacRory may not have cherished any political ambitions, but his nephew Raghnall—his older brother's son—knew MacCrimmon and MacQuarie weren't likely to take his word for it. So, without mentioning it to anyone—including

Mánas—he started organizing the 'MacRory Militia.' As far as I can tell, it was supposed to be a purely defensive move on his part. I think he just wanted to put together something tough enough to make MacQuarie think twice about assassinating his uncle the way MacHendrie assassinated his father and his grandfather. Unfortunately, it didn't work out that way.

"The level of unhappiness really started spiking about two years ago, and MacQuarie began seeing conspirators under every bed in Elgin. I'm pretty sure she was deliberately exaggerating in her cabinet reports as a way to suck in more resources for UPS, but that didn't mean she was completely wrong, either. In fact," he sounded like someone who disliked what he was admitting, "my own sources indicate that someone here on Halkirk had actually begun some serious organizing and established some out-system contacts for small arms and some heavy weapons. It's a fairly recent development, and I still haven't been able to nail down exactly whose idea it was. It wasn't the MacRorys, though; I do know that much. By now, three or four different groups have come out of the woodwork under the umbrella of MacLean's 'Loomis Liberation League's Provos,' but that happened later, after MacQuarie realized there really *was* someone here in Loomis who was genuinely interested in shooting back and decided she'd better nip it in the bud. She leapt to the conclusion that it *had* to be the MacRorys, unfortunately, and she tried to take Mánas into 'protective custody.' And that, Captain Venelli, was when the shit hit the fan and I put in a call for someone like you."

"You couldn't find a smaller sledgehammer?" Venelli asked caustically, and the OFS officer shrugged.

"I didn't want a sledgehammer at all. Unfortunately, Zagorski didn't leave me much option. He wants results—*fast* results—and he's got a big enough marker with somebody further up the chain than me to get them."

"I guess what I object to the most is how frigging *stupid* this all is," Venelli said. "On the other hand, I suppose I should be used to stupidity by now."

"There's enough of it lying around, anyway," Osborne agreed. "I don't recall seeing a more spectacular example of it lately, though."

He shook his head, and Venelli realized there was more than just disgust in his eyes. There was anger... and even regret.

"I've assisted in—even officiated over—some pretty ugly things in my time, Captain," the OFS officer told her. "It comes with the territory, and I've got to admit the pay is pretty good. But sometimes... sometimes it isn't *good* enough, and this is one of those times."

❖   ❖   ❖

Innis MacLay lay on his belly, peering cautiously out of the sixtieth floor window. For Halkirk, that made his present perch a tall building, although the gleaming ceramacrete towers SEIU had constructed in the heart of the city dwarfed it. Two of those towers were far less pristine than they had been, marked by the dark scars of multiple missile strikes and streaked with smoke from the fires which had consumed whole floors of their interiors, and MacLay showed his teeth briefly as he remembered watching the explosions ripple up and down their flanks. That had been when he thought the Provos had a real chance.

Now he knew better. They'd had the damned Uppies

on the run for the first couple of weeks, and maybe as many as a third of the smaller cities and towns had come in on the LLLP's side, or at least declared their neutrality. But that had been before they found out the frigging OFS had called in the Solly navy.

His eyes went bleak and hard as he recalled the first kinetic strikes. MacCrimmon and MacQuarie hadn't seemed interested in taking prisoners. Maybe they'd just wanted to avoid the expense of building bigger reeducation camps on Westray, or maybe they'd been scared enough they struck out in panic. Or maybe they were just such bloody-minded bastards they'd decided to eliminate as many of the opposition as they could while the eliminating was good. MacLay figured he'd never find out for sure which it had been, and it didn't much matter, anyway. There'd been no warning, no call to surrender, no threats of orbital strikes at all. There'd been only the terrible white lines streaming down through the skies of Halkirk to pock the planetary surface with brimstone.

That was what had broken the Resistance's back. The first wave of strikes had taken out a dozen towns and the regional city of Conerock, whose city council had been the first to go over to the Liberation League when the Provos seized the local UPS stations and the hub airport. No one knew how many had been killed, but Conerock's population had been over eighty-five thousand all by itself, and there'd been precious few survivors.

So now they were left with this, he thought grimly. There was no surrender—not for the Provos, not for the hard-core, like Innis MacLay. They wouldn't last long in the camps, anyway, even assuming they'd live long enough to get there, and he was damned if he'd give MacQuarie and General Boyle the satisfaction. Besides, his wife and kids had been in Conerock, so they could just drag him out of his last burrow when the time came, and his teeth and claws would savage them the whole way. When he got to Hell, he'd walk through the gates over the souls of all the Uppies he'd sent ahead to wait for him.

It wasn't much for a man to look forward to, but he'd settle for what he could get, and—

He stiffened, eyes narrowing. Then his jaw clenched and he reached for the old-fashioned landline handset. The sound quality wasn't good, but it was a lot more secure than any of the regular coms, and not even Solly sensors could localize and identify it against the background of the city's power systems.

"Yes?" a voice at the other end answered.

"MacLay, on the roof," he said tersely. "They're coming. I've got eyes on at least a dozen tanks and twice that many APCs headed down Brownhill towards Castlegreen." He paused for a moment. "I think they've figured out where we are."

Silence hovered at the far end of the line for seconds that felt like hours. Then—

"Understood, Innis. I expect you'll see a couple of missile teams up there in a minute or two."

"I'll be here," MacLay replied, and put down the phone.

He moved from his observation post to the French doors that gave access to the apartment's small balcony. The protective sandbags piled just inside them weren't visible from ground level ... and neither was the heavy, tripod-mounted tribarrel behind them. The field of fire wasn't perfect, and MacLay was under no illusions about what the Uppies' heavy weapons teams would do to his improvised perch once they located his position. But a man couldn't have everything, and he expected he'd probably get to add at least a round dozen of them to his family's vengeance first.

❖   ❖   ❖

"It's time for you to go, Megan," MacFadzean said flatly as she hung up the phone. "They're headed straight for us, and we don't have a prayer of stopping them."

"And where do you expect me *to* go, Erin?" MacLean asked almost whimsically. "You want me to go hide in the logging camps? Put other people at risk for helping hide me?" She shook her head and reached for the pulse rifle leaning in the corner behind her. "I think not."

"Don't be stupid!" MacFadzean's voice was sharper and she glared at the other woman. "You're the League chairwoman—the one who can speak for us! Get the hell out of here, lie low, and then find a way to get off-world."

"And do *what?*" MacLean demanded. "We're *done*, Erin—we've lost, and nobody else in the entire galaxy gives one single solitary damn what happens here on Halkirk!"

"That's not true," MacFadzean said. MacLean stared at her in disbelief, and she shook her head. "I . . . didn't tell you everything," she said after a moment, looking away rather than meeting her friend's eyes. "Our supplier for the weapons . . . he offered more than just guns, when the time came."

"What are you talking about?" MacLean's eyes had narrowed.

"He told me he could get us naval support." Mac-Fadzean turned back to face her fully. "When we were ready, if I got word to him, he was going to arrange things so *we'd* be the ones with starships in orbit."

"That's crazy! How was he supposed to do that? And why didn't you *tell* me about it?!"

"I didn't tell you about it because you already didn't trust him," MacFadzean's voice was flatter than ever. "You may even have been right. Probably he and his friends *were* only helping us for their own ends, but he told me he wasn't really a freelance arms dealer after all. That that was just his cover, a way to provide deniability if the wheels came off. He told me he was actually speaking for his own government, that his queen was ready to come into the open to support us if it looked like we might pull off our end of it, and I believed him. Hell, maybe I just *needed* to believe him! But if you can get off-world, find a way to contact him, maybe—"

She broke off, tears spangling her eyes, then shook herself savagely.

"Goddamn it, Megan! It's all we've got *left!* You're our chairwoman, if anyone can speak for us, you can! At least get out there and see to it that someone hears *our* side of what happened here. Don't let the bastards just sweep us and Conerock and all the rest of this shit under the rug like it never even happened!"

MacLean stared at her for a moment, shaken to the marrow of her soul by the raw appeal in Mac-Fadzean's last sentence.

"I wouldn't even know how to contact him," she said finally. Something exploded in the near distance, the sound muffled but clear through the apartment building's walls. "And that's assuming I could get off-world in the first place."

"Here." MacFadzean tossed her a data chip. "The contact information's on there." She smiled crookedly. "It's in my personal cipher, but you've got the key."

MacLean caught the chip. She looked down at it for a moment, then clenched her fist around it.

"I'm not running out and leaving you and everyone else behind, Erin. I'm just not doing it."

"Yes, you are," MacFadzean told her as more explosions began to shake the command post. "You *owe* it to us."

She locked eyes with the other woman, and it was MacLean's gaze that fell.

"Jamie will get you out through one of the tunnels," MacFadzean said then. "If the two of you can get out of Elgin, head for Haimer. I think our cell's still secure there. Lie low for a few weeks, and Tobias MacGill—he's the cell leader in Haimer—will fix you up with new papers. Then he and Jamie will get you onto one of the timber shuttles. From there . . . from there you'll have to play it by ear, but you can do it, Megan. You *have* to."

"I—"

MacLean tried to find one last argument, but she couldn't, and there wasn't much time. She looked at her friend, the friend she knew was about to die with all those other friends, and she could hardly see through the blur of her tears.

"All right," she whispered. "I'll try."

"Good." MacFadzean stepped around the table and enveloped her in a brief, crushing hug. "Good. Now go!"

MacLean hugged her back for an instant longer,

then nodded, grabbed her pulse rifle, and headed for
the door. MacFadzean watched her go, then picked
up the handset again and pressed the button that
connected her to every other handset simultaneously.

"Blàr Chùil Lodair," she said simply. "Let's buy
some time for the tunnel rats."

"No fucking around this time!" Colonel Nathan
Mundy snarled over the battalion communications
net. "And no excuses, either! Get in there, kick their
asses, and bring me their fucking heads!"

Acknowledgments came back, and he smiled savagely
as he settled deeper into his seat while his ground
effect command vehicle slid around the final corner
and his direct vision screens showed him the apartment building the rebels had taken over. It didn't
look any different from half a dozen other buildings
they'd occupied across the capital, but this one was
special. *This* was the one that was going to break
the rebels once and for all, because this was their
central command post. He'd thought for a while that
MacPhee wasn't going to break, but the UPS had a
way of convincing even the most recalcitrant. Maybe
MacPhee *wouldn't* have broken if they'd had only him
to work on, but when they brought in his daughter...

I suppose he still might've lied, the colonel thought
harshly. *Of course, if he did, he'll think what we
already did to the bitch was nothing.*

"Get closer!" he barked at his driver.

"Sir, I—"

"Get me *closer*, goddamn it!"

"Yes, Sir."

The tanks were Solarian surplus, at least two generations out of date, but some tank was always better than no tank, and their armor shed pulser fire with contemptuous ease. They moved forward steadily, pounding the apartment building and the two structures to either side with fire from their main guns—fifty-millimeter hyper-velocity weapons with the firepower of a pre-space hundred and fifty millimeter cannon. Gouts of dust and smoke erupted, spewing showers of splintered ceramacrete, and coaxially mounted tribarrels spat thousands of explosive darts at their targets. It was impossible for anything to survive under that pounding, and the tank crews knew it.

But the tank crews were wrong.

The first antitank missile struck like hell's own viper. The superdense penetrator impacted on its target's frontal armor at just over ten thousand meters per second, and that armor might as well have been made of paper. The tank erupted in a thunderous fireball, and an instant later there was a second fireball. And a third.

"Christ!" someone yelped over the command net. "Where the fuck did they get *that?!* Break right! Alfie, *break ri—!*"

The voice cut off abruptly.

Innis MacLay bellowed in wordless triumph as the first UPS tanks exploded. Then a pair of APCs encountered one of the improvised explosive devices the Provos had buried in the sewers under Brownhill Road. It wasn't powerful enough to destroy them outright, but the blast was more than enough to cripple them, and he watched their vehicle crews bail out, the Uppies scattering like blue-uniformed maggots.

The grips of the tribarrel were comfortable in his hands as he peered through the holographic sight, and he squeezed the trigger stud.

❖   ❖   ❖

Nathalan Mundy stared at his readouts in disbelief. That bastard MacPhee! He hadn't said a single word about weapons *that* heavy! And the rebels hadn't shown anything like that kind of firepower here in Elgin! How was he supposed to have realized—?

❖   ❖   ❖

Another tank exploded, but this time one of its companions got a firm lock on the third-floor window from which it had come. A turret swiveled, a tank gun flashed, and half the floor behind that window disintegrated in a deafening explosion.

❖   ❖   ❖

MacLay couldn't feel the shock of the explosion from his lofty perch. Or, at least, he couldn't feel it clearly enough to separate it from all the other shocks and vibrations whiplashing through the building. He saw the tank fire, though, and it wouldn't have if it hadn't had a target.

He wondered who'd just died, but it didn't matter. They could hurt the bastards, but they couldn't *win*, and he'd already heard the reports from the other side of the building. The Uppies had to know exactly where they were; they were closing in from every direction, and MacFadzean was right. Only those closest to one of the escape tunnels had any chance at all of getting out alive.

Assuming someone else kept the Uppies occupied, that was.

He selected another target, slamming his heavy

caliber darts through the thinner top armor of one of the APCs. The twenty-five-man personnel carrier staggered to a stop, then exploded, and his bloodshot eyes glittered with satisfaction. It was only a matter of time before someone spotted his firing position, but at the moment they were more preoccupied with the missile teams than mere tribarrels, and he swung his weapon's muzzle towards fresh prey.

❖   ❖   ❖

"Fall back!" Colonel Mundy snapped at his driver. "Get us further back—*now*, damn it!"

The driver snarled something that could have been an acknowledgment, and the command vehicle curtsied on its ground effect cushion as he spun it around. The sensor cluster kept the apartment building centered in Mundy's display even as the vehicle turned away, and a cursor flashed on the screen, highlighting a balcony on the sixtieth floor. An icon appeared beside it as the command vehicle's computers identified the energy signature, Mundy's eyes widened as he recognized the data code.

Tribarrel! a corner of his brain gobbled. *That's a tri—*

❖   ❖   ❖

The GEV erupted in a boiling cloud of red and black. It tore apart, incinerating its crew, and Innis MacLay howled in triumph. It was brief, that triumph, no more than seconds before one of the surviving UPS tanks put a round from its main armament right through the balcony's French doors, but it was enough.

❖   ❖   ❖

"This way, Megan!" Jamie Kirbishly said hoarsely. "We're almost there."

Megan MacLean nodded, wading through the ankle-deep water at her guide's heels, trying not to think about what was happening behind her. There were perhaps twenty more people in the tunnel with her, stretched out in a long, grim-faced queue, most of them people who still had—or might still have—family somewhere on the other side of holocaust. People who knew their friends—friends who no longer had anyone waiting for them—had chosen to stay behind and cover their escape.

She put her hand into her pocket, feeling the hard edges of the chip folio, wondering who the man who had called himself "Partisan" really was. If he'd told MacFadzean the truth about his official status or if it had all been a lie. And if it hadn't, what had he and the star nation who'd sent him really intended? Why had they offered to help the Liberation League? Whatever MacFadzean might have thought, it hadn't been out of the bigness of their hearts. MacLean was certain of that, and God knew they had enough problems of their own at the moment. Had they simply been looking for a way to distract their enemies? That might well make sense, she supposed. But it was also possible it hadn't *all* been cynical, pragmatic calculation on their part. They had a reputation for standing up for lost causes; maybe they even deserved it. And if they did, and if she really could get off-world and reach them somehow, maybe this nightmare slaughter wouldn't have been entirely in vain after all. Maybe—

"*Down!*" Kirbishly screamed.

MacLean responded instantly, throwing herself down on her belly in the icy water even before she realized she'd moved. She landed with a splash, hearing shouts behind her, and raised her head just in time to see the heavily armored UPS troops plummeting down the ladder from the manhole above with their pulse rifles flaming in full automatic.

It was the last thing she ever saw.

◇　　◇　　◇

Frinkelo Osborne stood on the landing platform of SEIU Tower, his face hard and set as he watched fresh smoke billow up to join the dense, choking cloud hovering above the Loomis System's capital. Over twenty percent of Elgin's buildings had taken at least some damage, he thought disgustedly. MacQuarie insisted it wasn't that bad, and it was possible his own estimate was high because of the revulsion and fury boiling through his brain, but he didn't think so. She was a liar trying to cover her own arse, and she was going to have plenty of covering to do now that the shooting was over. Just what he could see from his present vantage point was going to cost billions to repair, and the damage here in Elgin was nothing compared to what Captain Venelli's KEWs—not to mention the UPS' kill teams—had done to the *rest* of the planet. He remembered his conversation with Venelli in *Hoplite*'s briefing room and his right hand rose, touching the hard angularity of the holstered pulser under his left armpit.

Tempting, *so* tempting. He could walk into Zagorski's penthouse office and no one would think twice about admitting him. And once he got there...

He took his hand away from the pistol again and grimaced bleakly. The thought might be tempting, but he wasn't about to act on it, and he knew it. Just as he knew the real reason he wanted to paint Nyatui Zagorski's office walls with his brains.

Osborne had served OFS well, for longer than he liked to remember, but this was the worst. Somehow he'd always managed to avoid the details like this one, but now he'd climbed down into the sewer with the worst of them, and he'd never be clean again.

And the worst of it, he thought in the cold, cruel light of honesty, *is that now that I've done it once, it'll be easier the next time. And if I stay with it long enough, there* will *be a next time. There always is.*

He stood for another few minutes, gazing at the blazing apartment building, wondering how much longer it would stand before its skeleton collapsed into the inferno, wondering if there was anyone still alive inside that furnace, praying for death.

Then he turned and walked silently away.

It was still and dark in the smoke-choked sewer under the city of Elgin. There was no light, no movement...no life. Not any longer, and a data chip folio settled slowly, slowly through the bloody water into the sludge below.

MARCH 1922 POST DIASPORA

"Trust me, the hole would've been a hell of a lot deeper!"

—Ensign Helen Zilwicki,
Royal Manticoran Navy

✦ Chapter Three

"JUST A SECOND, GWEN," Captain Loretta Shoupe said as she followed Lieutenant Gervais Winton Erwin Neville Archer out of Admiral Augustus Khumalo's office space aboard HMS *Hercules*.

Gervais had just finished delivering a late-hour briefing to Khumalo and Shoupe, his chief of staff. There'd been a lot of those briefings over the last three weeks, and it didn't look like getting better anytime soon. The entire Spindle System was still somewhere between astonishment and euphoria over the devastating defeat Admiral Gold Peak's Tenth Fleet had inflicted on the Solarian League Navy, but the Navy remained too busy to celebrate as it scrambled frantically to deal with the enormous flood of POWs it had so suddenly and unexpectedly acquired. Despite which—or perhaps because of which, given the exhaustion quotient of her crew—the ancient superdreadnought flagship of the recently created Talbott Station was quiet around them.

"Yes, Ma'am?" Gervais replied, turning to face her.

"You know Ensign Zilwicki pretty well, don't you,

Gwen?" Shoupe's tone made the question a statement, Gervais thought, and wondered where she was headed.

"Yes, Ma'am," he said again. Despite the monumental rank disparity between a mere ensign and a senior-grade lieutenant, he'd come to know young Zilwicki, Sir Aivars Terekhov's flag lieutenant, *very* well, as a matter of fact.

"I thought you did," Shoupe said now. She actually looked a bit uncomfortable, but she went on steadily. "The reason I ask is that—like everyone else, I suppose—Commander Chandler and I are trying to get some kind of handle on this story coming out of Mesa. I don't want to intrude on her or pressure her, but the truth is that we really need any insight she could give us about this."

Gervais nodded respectfully, despite a quick flare of anger. Commander Ambrose Chandler was Khumalo's staff intelligence officer, and like Captain Shoupe, he was usually on Gervais' list of good people. And Gervais even understood exactly why they were looking for any "insight" they could get. The horrendous 'fax stories about what the Solly newsies had dubbed the "Green Pines Atrocity" had reached Spindle the day after the battle—less than nineteen hours after Admiral O'Cleary's surrender, in fact—and he didn't envy Admiral Khumalo or Baroness Medusa (or, for that matter, Lady Gold Peak) when it came to dealing with *this* one's implications. None of which made him any happier about where he was pretty sure Shoupe was headed.

"Yes, Ma'am?" he said in as neutral a voice as he could manage.

"I don't want you to *grill* her, Gwen," Shoupe replied

with an edge of sharpness. "But it's obvious just from what we've heard from home that this story's already making problems—*big* problems—where Solly public opinion is concerned. For that matter, the local Solly newsies are starting to ask the Governor and the Prime Minister for their reactions to 'Manticoran involvement in the atrocity,' as if anyone out here would have a clue even if the Star Empire *had* been behind something like that!" She snorted in disgust. "What makes them think we could know more than *they* do, given the communications loop, or that we'd've been briefed in on a black op like this—assuming anyone back home could've been stupid enough to sanction it—completely eludes me, but there it is."

She shrugged. It was an angry, frustrated gesture, Gervais noted.

"On top of that, we're less than two hundred and sixty light-years from Mesa," she went on. "No one expects the Mesans to launch some kind of retaliatory strike at us, but they're for damned straight going to play it for all it's worth in the League. And given how far they've already gone to destabilize the Quadrant, there's no telling how else they might try to capitalize on it. For one thing, I think we can be pretty damned sure they're going to be flogging their version of what happened to every independent star system in hopes of keeping any more of them from siding with us or being 'neutral' in the Star Empire's favor. It looks like the Solly newsies are fully prepared to help them do it, too, to be honest, and we need to be able to knock that on the head. While I doubt Ensign Zilwicki's in a position to shed any light on what actually happened in Green Pines, any window into what her father might have been doing—*really* doing, I mean—to lead Mesa to make this kind of claim could be extraordinarily useful."

"I haven't discussed it with her, Ma'am," Gervais said. "I haven't seen her face-to-face since the story hit Spindle, and, to be honest, it wasn't something I wanted to discuss with her over the com. My understanding is that it's been months since she actually saw her father, though, and frankly, I doubt she'd be able to add anything much to what we already know."

"I understand your feelings, Gwen." Shoupe's tone was a bit cooler. "I'm afraid this comes under the heading of doing my job, however. In fact, there's a part of me that's inclined to invite her in to personally discuss anything she might know, think, or suspect in my office. I'm trying to avoid turning this into some sort of formal interrogation because I don't doubt for a moment that she's even more worried—and with a lot better personal reasons—than anyone else in the Quadrant."

Gervais looked at her for a moment longer, then sighed mentally.

"It's only about twenty-one hundred local in Thimble, Ma'am, and I was planning on having a late dinner. I suppose I could see if she'd be free to join me."

$\diamond \qquad \diamond \qquad \diamond$

Ensign Helen Zilwicki followed the waiter across the mostly empty restaurant with an expression she hoped gave no sign of her inner feelings. Gwen Archer's last-minute, late-notice invitation had come at a good time, in many ways. Commodore Terekhov had been keeping her busy, but there was a limit to how many hours of legitimate duty time even the most inventive flag officer could find for his aide. And, unfortunately, she'd gotten too efficient. She kept running out of things to do before she ran out of hours to sit around and think about the hideous lies about her father.

At the same time, she suspected Gwen's invitation hadn't simply materialized out of thin air. Countess Gold Peak was keeping him even busier than Commodore Terekhov was keeping Helen, and she doubted he had a lot of time to visit groundside. Given his druthers, he would have been spending any time he did have with Helga Boltitz, too, which suggested someone further up the military food chain had asked him to get her take on Green Pines.

She couldn't blame him for that, and she was grateful, if her suspicions were correct, that he'd at least picked as comfortable a venue as possible.

She'd never eaten in this restaurant, and she wondered if that, too, was something Gwen had deliberately arranged. The food smelled good, and the subdued lighting projected a welcome she found soothing despite the nature of the conversation she expected. Still, she was a little surprised when the waiter led her not toward the main dining area but into a smaller room which contained only half a dozen tables. Only one of those tables was occupied—by Lieutenant Archer and the beautiful, golden-haired Helga Boltitz, Minister of War Henri Krietzmann's personal assistant.

"Helen!"

Both of them stood as the waiter led Helen to the table, and Helga stepped around to give her a brief, tight hug. The embrace took Helen slightly by surprise—Helga wasn't usually that demonstrative in public—but she hugged the other woman back, then looked at Gervais.

"Gwen," she said in greeting, and smiled faintly. "I appreciate the invitation...even if Helga *is* thinking of me as a third wheel!"

"Never," Helga said firmly. Her sharp-edged Dresdener accent gave her Standard English a harsh edge, but her tone was firm and she shook her head for added emphasis.

"Helga, I love you," Helen replied, "but you shouldn't go around telling whoppers like that one!" Her smile flashed into a grin for a moment. "I know how busy Gwen's been, and I don't imagine it's been any calmer in Minister Krietzmann's office."

"I didn't say I wouldn't like to have more time with him. I only said I'd never think of you as a 'third wheel,'" Helga pointed out.

"Yeah, I heard you. But you hang out with all those diplomats and politicians now," Helen observed. "I think it's corrupting that Dresden directness of yours."

Helga chuckled and shook her head, and Helen turned back to Gervais.

"But however gracious and diplomatic our Helga's become, Gwen, I have to say I've nurtured a few suspicions about just how you happen to have time free to invite me to dinner. Especially when you could have been spending that time doing...something else."

She let her eyes flip sideways to Helga for a moment, and both of the others chuckled. Then Gervais' expression sobered.

"Unfortunately, you've got a point," he said. He waved the waiter aside, pulled out her chair, and held it. "And I'm not going to try to pretend this is the purely social occasion I'd prefer for it to be. Both of us really are glad to see you, though."

"I know."

Helen allowed him to seat her, despite the difference in their ranks, then turned and accepted the menu from the waiter and gave him her initial drink order. She watched him disappear before she turned her attention back to Gervais.

"I know you're glad to see me," she repeated. "And I'm pretty sure I know who suggested you and I have a little talk. All the same, I don't expect the conversation to do wonders for my appetite."

"It wasn't Admiral Gold Peak, if that's what you're thinking," Gervais replied, and she shook her head.

"Didn't think it was. She's a pretty direct person, and she's had the opportunity to talk to me about it herself if she wanted to. For that matter, she probably would've gone through Sir Aivars if she was the one asking the questions. Same for Captain Lecter. Nobody on Admiral Khumalo's staff, on the other hand, really knows me or enjoys the opportunity to just slip questions into a casual conversation. Which leaves us with 'the usual suspects,' doesn't it?"

"I guess it does." Gervais leaned back in his chair, regarding her across the table. "Frankly, though, I think the reason they asked *me* to talk to you about it was that they figured it'd be less stressful for you. Less of a formal inquisition, you might say."

Helen snorted, but it made at least some sense. And she supposed she was grateful they were trying to avoid stepping on her feelings.

"All right, then," she said, "as Duchess Harrington would say, 'let's be about it.'" She smiled tightly. "What certain unnamed senior parties would like to know is whether or not I think there's any truth in the reports that my father and his lunatic terrorist cronies were responsible for detonating multiple nuclear devices—probably with the Star Empire's knowledge and direct connivance—in the town of Green Pines. Nuclear devices which, according to the Mesan authorities, killed thousands of people, and one of which was detonated in the middle of a crowded park on a Saturday morning, incinerating every child present. Is that about the gist of it?"

Gervais winced internally. Helen Zilwicki had one of the sturdiest personalities he'd ever met, and that acid tone was very unlike her.

"More or less." He sighed. "That's not exactly the way anyone put it, of course. And I don't think it's the way anyone would describe it if they were asked to. What I think they're really interested in is any insight you might give them as to why the Mesans might've gone about it the way they did. Claiming your father was involved, I mean."

"I'd think that was pretty obvious!" Helen planted her forearms on the table and leaned forward over them. "Daddy's been a pain in their ass ever since Manpower kidnapped me in Old Chicago when I was thirteen. Trust me, you do *not* want my dad pissed at you—not the way *that* pissed him off—and having him get together with Cathy Montaigne only made bad even worse from Mesa's perspective. Then there was that little business on Torch. You remember—the one where my sister wound up queen of a planet populated by liberated slaves, every single one of whom hates Mesa and Manpower on a—you should pardon the expression—genetic level? If there's anyone in the entire galaxy whose reputation they'd like to blacken more than his, *I* don't know who it might be! And if you throw in the opportunity to saddle Torch with responsibility for something like this, and then claim Daddy's involvement means the Star Empire was behind it, as well, it can only get even better from their viewpoint. Just look how they're using it to undercut our credibility when we claim *they've* been involved in everything that's been going on out here in the Quadrant! Obviously we've invented all those nasty, untruthful allegations out of whole cloth as another prong of whatever iniquitous plot we've hatched against them! Doesn't the fact that we're enabling Ballroom terrorists to nuke their civilian population *prove* we're only targeting them as a way to distract all right-thinking Sollies' attention from our own evil, imperialist agenda?"

The anger in her tone wasn't directed at Gervais, and he knew it. It wasn't even directed at the "unnamed senior parties" who'd asked him to have this conversation with her. It was, however, an indication that she was more worried—and hurting worse—than she wanted anyone to suspect. And it didn't do a thing to make him feel any better about dragging her into this conversation in the first place, either.

"I think they've already figured that part out," he said after a moment. "What they're really asking about is whether or not you have any idea what really happened. What could have transpired to suggest the idea of blaming your father and the Ballroom to them in the first place."

"You mean they're wondering what Daddy could've been doing that might've gotten him involved in whatever happened, whether he was *responsible* for it or not, don't you?"

"I think that's probably a fair enough way to put it," he agreed.

"Well, I'm afraid I can't help you out with any specifics," she said a bit tightly. "Daddy understands operational security pretty well, you know. And he's always been careful not to put me in an awkward position by telling me things a Queen's officer ought to be reporting to ONI. If he had been up to something, he wouldn't have discussed it with me—definitely not *before* the fact, anyway. And there's no way he would have sent me any letters that said 'Oh, by the way, I'm off to Mesa to nuke a city park.'"

Her scorn was withering.

"Helen, I don't think anyone thinks you've been deliberately 'holding back' anything that could help them get a handle on this. And I'm sure everyone's fully aware your father wouldn't be sending you chatty messages about clandestine operations, whether they were his or the Ballroom's or Torch's. They're looking for... deep background, I guess you'd say."

"I don't have a lot of that for them, either," she said in a more normal tone. "Anything they don't already have available, I mean. That exposé Yael Underwood did on him a while back did a pretty good job of blowing his cover and pasting a great big target on his back. Underwood did get most of his facts right, though, and I doubt I could add a lot to his history. The short version is that ever since he resigned his commission after he tangled with Manpower for the first time, he's been directly involved with the Ballroom. He's never made any secret of that, or of the way he's been directly involved with Torch, as well, ever since its liberation. He's more of an analyst than a 'direct action' specialist, and I don't doubt he's helped the Ballroom plan the occasional operation. I'm not saying he's not *capable* of a more . . . hands-on approach when it seems appropriate, either, because he damned well is. But I think pretty much everyone realizes that's not really what you might call the 'best and highest use' of his talents. Of course, that's subject to change if you go after somebody he cares about. When that happens, he gets *very* hands-on."

She paused, looking steadily into Gervais' and Helga's eyes across the table, then shrugged.

"He's pretty tight with the Royals, too, since that business with Princess Ruth, although he's been a lot more focused on Torch and the Congo System since Berry got crowned Queen. And he and"—the hesitation was so slight that only someone who knew her as well as Gervais did would have realized she'd changed what she'd been about to say—"the Torches have certainly been looking for every way they could possibly hurt Mesa. Hell, Torch has declared *war* on them! And let's not forget what those bastards tried to do to the entire planet five months ago.

"So, on the surface, there's a certain plausibility to Mesa's claims. He hates Manpower's guts; they've tried more than once to kill him—or me, or Berry, or Cathy; and I wouldn't be surprised if he'd managed to turn up at least some evidence Manpower was about to use those StateSec stumblebums to hit Torch. Trust me, if he'd seen *that* coming, he would've done anything he could to prevent it. But he wouldn't have tried this way. If nothing else, he'd've known it wouldn't work, and he's spent enough time with Cathy to know exactly how disastrous something like this could be politically—not just for Torch, but for the abolitionist movement in general."

"Not even if he thought the attack on Torch was going to work?" Helga asked quietly, and Helen looked at her. "I mean, if he found out about the attack and didn't know Admiral Rozsak would be able to stop it? If he figured your sister and all his friends on Torch were going to be killed?"

"No way." Helen shook her head firmly. "Daddy doesn't think that way. Oh, I'm not saying he wouldn't have made Mesa and Manpower pay big-time if they'd managed to pull something like that off, but he wouldn't have done it before he *knew* they'd pulled it off. And he wouldn't have gone about *this* way it even if they'd managed to turn Torch into a cue ball. It's not the way he thinks, not the sort of thing he'd involve himself with."

"Grief and hatred can make someone do terrible things," Gervais pointed out gently, and Helen surprised him with a snort of laughter.

"You don't have to tell me that. Remember what happened to me on Old Terra? Or what happened to my mom? Or the way I *met* Berry and Lars, for that matter? But Daddy is a very...guided weapon, Gwen. He's got really good target discrimination, and he's just as good at holding down the collateral damage. Besides, nuking a *park*? A park full of *kids*?" She shook her head. "He'd die first. Or, for that matter, kill anybody else who thought that would be a good idea! I'm not saying my daddy's a saint, because he's not. I love him, but nobody who knows him would ever claim he's an angel. Or, if he is, he's one of those *avenging* angels with a really sooty halo, anyway. And I could see him not worrying a whole lot about the tender sensibilities of a bunch of slave-trading Mesans. I could even see him using a nuke against some kind of hard target, the kind that wouldn't kill a stack of civilians when it disappeared in a mushroom cloud. But not this. Never a park."

"You're sure?"

"Gwen, I'm *damned* sure Daddy didn't plan and carry out this strike. I don't know where he is, and I don't know why he hasn't spoken up yet. And, yeah, I'll admit that scares the shit out of me. He's got to know how Mesa's using Green Pines as a club to beat both the Star Empire and the Ballroom, and he'd never let them go on doing it if he could do anything—like surfacing to refute their version—to stop it. But it's not his style. Oh, yeah, if they'd actually managed to genocide Torch, then he might've gone after them on Mesa. He wouldn't have done it until he *knew* they'd gotten through to Torch, though, and he wouldn't have done it this way even then. He'd've been looking for another target, and when he was done, there wouldn't be any question about who'd been responsible for it."

"Why not?" Helga asked, her tone one of fascination despite the topic of the conversation, and Helen gave another, harsher snort of laughter.

"Because if *my* daddy had gone after a target on Mesa, he wouldn't have wasted his time on Green Pines. If he was in city-killing mode, he'd've gone after Mendel and their entire system government, not some lousy bedroom community. And, trust me, the hole would've been a hell of a lot deeper!"

Chapter Four

FINE, MISTY RAIN DRIZZLED down from a dim, gray sky. The brisk wind drove the droplets in billowing waves, almost (but not quite) like fog, and the air was cold, its edge sharpened by the approach of winter. The battered old ground car's side windows had been patched with tape, drafts probed through its interior, and its aged heater's valiant battle against the chill was dwindling toward defeat. Water splashed against the vehicle's underside as it jolted down the potholed surface road, and the passenger side's old-fashioned wiper blade was frozen uselessly in place.

Indiana Graham hunched forward in the driver's seat, leaning over the wheel and bending down to peer through the lower portion of his side of the windshield where the equally old-fashioned fan-powered defroster had actually managed to produce a very inconveniently placed clear patch. His coat was thick and reasonably warm, although it was also badly worn, but he wore neither hat nor gloves. The slender young woman huddled in the passenger's seat who looked enough like him to have been his sister (because she was) *was* wearing gloves, but she had her hands tucked into her armpits, anyway. Her breath steamed slightly, and she looked thoroughly miserable.

The car splashed through a deeper, wider puddle, throwing up wings of water on either side. Some of that water splashed in through the tape-repaired rear side window, and she grimaced as it hit her right cheek.

"Ugh! Do you think you could've found a *deeper* puddle, Indy?" she demanded, wiping the muddy water off her face with a gloved palm.

"Sorry, Max," the driver took his eye off the road long enough to dart a smile at her. "I'll try, but it'll be hard. Would you settle for one that's just a lot *wider*? I only ask because I see one coming up ahead."

"Very funny." Mackenzie Graham leaned over to look through his side of the windshield, and her eyes widened. "Indy, don't you *dare*!"

"Sorry," her brother repeated, perhaps a shade more seriously than before, "but the only way across is through."

She glared at him, but she couldn't seem to produce her customary voltage. Probably because Indiana was obviously correct. This pothole stretched clear across the road, and while the security fences that paralleled the roadway were old and neglected, sagging with age, they were still sufficient to confine the decrepit old ground car to the paved (more or less) surface.

Indiana gave her an apologetic smile and tapped the brake, slowing down as they approached the wind-rippled expanse of muddy water. The front wheels dropped into it with a splash that jolted both of them, and the car's motion took on a distinct floatiness. More water sprayed up on either side, although not so high this time. Then the rear wheels dropped into the same hole and Mackenzie was afraid they were going to lose traction entirely. But they continued churning forward with a lurching, muddy sort of determination, and she grimaced and raised her feet as water found its way in through small rust holes, flooding the floorboards. The incoming tide rose to almost a centimeter in depth, they slowed still further, and she braced herself for the thought of climbing out in the middle of their own private lake when the car finally bogged down. But then—with one last, bouncing sway—they broke free of the pothole and regained solid ground.

"I was really afraid we might not make it that time," Indiana said, as if he'd read her mind and was voicing her thought for her. She gave him a speaking look, and he shrugged. "Hey, I didn't pick the spot for this meeting, you know!"

"Yeah, I *do* know," she agreed.

She didn't look any happier, and it was Indiana's turn to grimace in acknowledgment. She was the organizer, the one who kept track of details, but she was also the voice of caution. He was the natural born point man, the fellow who just had to get out in front, couldn't seem to leave well enough alone or settle for a life of grim, gray obedience to their "betters." Their father had been like that . . . which was how he'd ended up sentenced to a thirty-five-T-year term in Terrabore Maximum Security Prison.

So far, Mackenzie had prevented Indy from joining him there, and he was in favor of keeping things that way. All the same, both of them realized that at least some risks had to be run if they were going to do anything about getting their father (and several thousand other prisoners) out of the none-too-gentle arms of General Tillman O'Sullivan's Seraphim System Security Police.

Among other things.

"I only wish I knew why the meeting got moved all the way out here," Mackenzie went on after a moment. "I don't like how easy it would be for O'Sullivan or Shelton to just 'disappear' us in a place like this without anyone ever noticing."

"Believe me, the same thought's occurred to me," Indiana said. "On the other hand, they don't really need to get us out in the country to do that, do they? In fact, the more I think about it, the more sense it would make for them to do exactly the opposite. Come in with all sirens screaming and bust us in the middle of the capital, I mean. SWAT teams everywhere, scags on the rooftops... Think about the statement *that* would make!"

Mackenzie shivered with more than just the cold as her all too lively imagination pictured the scene her brother had just described.

"Golly gee, thanks, Indy," she said sourly. "That ought to be good for the odd nightmare or two."

"Well, there *is* a counter argument to their doing anything of the sort," he said cheerfully. "If they bust us publicly, they're effectively admitting there's a genuine independence movement cooking away under the surface. I don't think they'd want to do that—especially after what's been going on over in the Madras Sector."

"Which means it really might make a lot of sense for them to get us out in the boonies this way before they pounce, after all," his sister pointed out in an even more sour tone.

"Well, yeah." Indiana nodded. "Come down to it, though, we've gotta take a chance or two if we want to pull this off. Besides, all the codes were right, Max. If O'Sullivan's scags had all of that, they wouldn't have to lure us anywhere. They'd probably already know exactly who we are and exactly where we live, too, and they'd just've come calling in the middle of the night, instead."

"You're making me feel enormously better with every word," she told him with a glare, and he shrugged.

"Just considering all the possibilities. And while I'm at it, what I'm actually doing is pointing out that this almost certainly isn't a trap because there are so many other ways they could have dealt with us if they knew about us in the first place and that was what they wanted to do."

She made a face at him and turned back around to sit straight in her own seat, yet she had to admit he had a point. To her surprise, that actually did make her feel better. Quite a bit, in fact.

"There's the turn," she said, removing her right hand from her left armpit to point through the rain-streaked window beside her.

"Got it."

Indiana guided the ground car through the open, dilapidated gate in the security fence. The rain was beginning to come down harder, turning into distinct drops rather than the fine, drifting mist it had been, and he pulled under the overhead cover of the deserted loading dock with a distinct sense of relief. Not only would it protect the car (such as it was, and what there was of it) from the rain, but it also offered at least some protection against the SSSP's overflights.

The Seraphim System's indigenous industrial and technical base left a lot to be desired, as the use of something as ancient and old-fashioned as asphalt rather than ceramacrete even here in the planetary capital of Cherubim indicated. But that didn't mean better tech was completely unavailable if the price was right, and the scags, as General O'Sullivan's security troopers were universally (and with very little affection) known, tended to get the best off-world equipment money could buy. Even the Seraphim Army had been known to express the occasional pang of envy, but President Jacqueline McCready knew where to invest her credits when it came to "system security." Which meant the SSSP had first call on the treasury...and a large and capable stable of surveillance platforms.

Not even the scags had an unlimited supply of them, however. And serviceability was often an issue, since the Seraphim education system didn't turn out the best trained maintenance techs in the explored galaxy. So the odds were against any of them being used to keep an eye on such a dilapidated and useless stretch of the Rust Belt, as the once-thriving wasteland on Cherubim's perimeter had come to be known. There hadn't been anything worth worrying about out here since the transstellars like Krestor Interstellar and Mendoza of Córdoba had moved in and eliminated Seraphim's once vibrant small-business sector. These days, either you worked as a good little helot for your out-system masters or you didn't work at all. And God help you if you thought you could scrape up a little startup capital and try to change that situation.

That was what had happened to Bruce Graham.

Mackenzie rolled down her battered window and

looked out, peering into the gloomy shadows which had gathered in the corners of the loading dock. It was still only late afternoon, but what with the rain and the onset of winter it looked a lot later (and darker), and she squinted as she tried to make out details.

"I don't see anybody," she said after a moment, her voice more than a little nervous.

"I don't either," Indiana acknowledged. "On the other hand, we're a couple of minutes early. He may still be on his way. Or—"

He broke off as a man stepped out of the dim recess from which he'd apparently been examining the ground car. The newcomer moved calmly and unhurriedly, with his collar turned up against the cold and a soft hat of a style which had once been called a "fedora" pulled well down. He looked like a mid-level manager, or possibly someone a little further down the pecking order from that.

He also looked nothing at all like the man the Grahams had expected to meet, and Indiana's ungloved hand stole into his coat and settled around the grip of the shoulder-holstered pistol.

"*Indy*," Mackenzie said softly.

"I know," he replied, and patted her on the leg with his free hand, never taking his eyes from the stranger. "Stay here."

He drew the pistol from its holster and slid out of the ground car, holding the gun down beside his right leg where it was screened from the other man's sight. Then he stood there, his shoulders as relaxed as he could make them, while his pulse hammered and adrenaline hummed in his bloodstream.

"I think that's probably close enough," he said,

raising his voice against the sound of the rain as the stranger came within seven or eight meters of the car. His tone, he noticed with some surprise, sounded much steadier than his nerves felt.

"Works for me," the stranger said calmly, and shrugged.

His accent was slight but noticeable, that of an off-worlder, and he held his own hands out from his sides and turned the palms towards Indiana, as if to deliberately demonstrate that unlike the Seraphimian he was unarmed. Or, at least, that he wasn't actively flourishing any recognizable weapons at the moment, anyway.

He was a very ordinary, eminently forgettable looking man, Indiana thought. He was of medium height, with medium brown eyes, medium brown hair, medium features, and a medium complexion. In fact, that word—"medium"—pretty much summed up everything about him.

I wonder if all that's natural or if he's disguised? Indiana thought. *Hell of a disguise, if he is. Nobody's going to think twice if they notice him. For that matter, you could look straight at him and never "notice" him at all! Probably something we should bear in mind for future use.*

"Nasty weather for an off-worlder to be out touring the sights," he observed out loud, and the other man chuckled.

"I hadn't expected it to be this lousy," he agreed. "And if you think it's bad now, you should've been standing out here with me waiting for the last hour or so."

"Waiting for what?" Indiana asked.

"I appreciate your caution, Talisman," the other man said, "but if I were a scag my fellow scags would already have pounced, don't you think? And I promise you, if I *were* a scag I'd already have signaled the sniper team to take you down rather than let you stand there with a gun in your hand!"

"I see." Indiana glanced around—he couldn't help himself—then shrugged and holstered the pistol. The other man had a point, after all. Not that the fact that he did proved he *wasn't* a scag playing some sort of complicated game. On the other hand, he obviously did know Indiana's codename, which was at least a tentative vote in his favor.

"I don't know you," he said conversationally, and the stranger nodded.

"I know. To be honest, that's why I set up the meet out here, where there wouldn't be a lot of witnesses if you reacted . . . energetically to the surprise of a new face." He shrugged. "There's been a change of plans, unfortunately, and I'm your new contact."

"What kind of change of plans?" Indiana's voice was tauter than it had been, and the other man smiled slightly.

"I'm afraid I can't be a lot more specific than that," he said. "I have to worry about everyone's security, not just yours and not just my own. I can tell you it doesn't have anything to do with anything that's happened here in Seraphim, though. In fact, I'll go ahead and admit that it's more of a logistic problem than anything else. They needed your previous contact somewhere else, so they sent me in to sub for him."

"They did, did they?"

"Caution is good; I like that. On the other hand, if all we do is stand here and be suspicious of one another we're not going to accomplish a lot except to freeze our asses off. So. I believe the phrase you're looking for is 'It is dearness only that gives things their value.'"

Indiana felt his shoulders relax and drew a deep breath.

"'And it would be strange if an article like Freedom should not be highly rated,'" he replied.

"True enough," the other man agreed, then grimaced slightly. "On the other hand, if we're going to use Thomas Paine, I really would have preferred to get the quotation at least remotely right."

"Maybe." Indiana looked at him for a moment, then smiled. "On the other hand, if the scags were to ... acquire partial knowledge of our recognition phrases, let's say, they might just end up researching the quotation without realizing how much we'd paraphrased it."

"I see." The other man tilted his head to one side, eyes narrowing. "Clambake didn't mention that you were the one who'd chosen the recognition phrase. I thought *he* had." He nodded slowly. "I don't know if it would really have done any good, but it was probably a wrinkle that was worth incorporating. Oh, you can call me Firebrand."

"'Firebrand'?" Indiana repeated, and grinned. "I like it. It's got a more ... proactive feel to it than 'Clambake.'"

"I'm glad you approve," Firebrand said dryly. "And I suppose that's Magpie still in the car?"

"Yes," Indiana confirmed. "You want to sit in the car to talk? The heater's not much, but it's at least a little warmer than standing out in the open this way."

"Actually, I'd rather step inside the warehouse," Firebrand demurred. "No offense, but I prefer a more solid roof and walls between me and any scag surveillance platforms that might happen by."

"I don't have any problem with that," Indiana said and turned to beckon to Mackenzie. She looked at him for a moment, then opened her door, climbed out into the steadily strengthening rain, and joined the two men.

"Step into my office," Firebrand invited, and led the way into the abandoned warehouse.

It was cold, drafty, and dreary. Abandoned stacks of plastic pallets leaned drunkenly, and a derelict forklift—not one of the grav-lifters the transstellars used in *their* warehouses, but a genuine, old-fashioned, pre-OFS forklift—loomed in the shadows. Raindrops drummed on the roof, and Indiana and Mackenzie heard the waterfall sound of runoff pounding down through holes to splash on the warehouse floor. It was a thoroughly miserable venue for a meeting, Indiana reflected, watching the plume of his breath. And it was also a perfect metaphor for what had happened to Seraphim since the Office of Frontier Security had come to the star system's "rescue."

"So you're Clambake's replacement," he said, and Firebrand nodded.

"Like I say, we've had to make a few adjustments. On the other hand, one of the reasons we've done it is that we've been able to accelerate our plans a little bit."

"You have?" Mackenzie asked, eyes narrowing, and he nodded. "How much?"

"To be honest, we're still in the process of establishing that," Firebrand admitted. "The biggest problem is that shipping's scarce enough out this way, except for Krestor's and Mendoza's, that we have to be careful about our arrangements." He chuckled suddenly. "There are some advantages to dealing with that crowd, though—not to mention the simple satisfaction of using their own ships against them! Their freight agents are about as corrupt as they are themselves, after all, and smuggling's always a growth industry in the Protectorates. No one in the League has anything like a reliable estimate of the size of the 'gray economy' out here, but everyone knows damned well that it's huge, so we might as well take advantage of it. Unless things change in the next month or two, what we'll actually be doing is shipping your goodies in covered by Krestor shipping manifests. They'll just sort of wander away from the rest of the queue once they hit dirt-side."

"Isn't that risky?" Mackenzie asked.

"Not really." Firebrand shrugged. "I know we got the first couple of shipments in using the 'tramp freighter' approach, but that's actually a lot riskier than doing it this way. There just aren't enough legitimate tramps visiting your system to cover any kind of volume shipments, Magpie. If you people are going to pull this off we need to move some serious mass and cubage, and, realistically, Seraphim doesn't have enough independent business to attract a genuine tramp. The transstellars have choked your people out too thoroughly for that. So if we want to bring in the weapons and other equipment you're going to need, we've got to get a bit more inventive. And the good news is that if we do it this way, the freight agents who arrange the shipments are going to have every reason to keep them totally off the books without asking too many questions. Frankly, they aren't going to give a rat's ass what's being shipped, even if they realize it's actually weapons, as long as they get paid off and it doesn't come back on them."

Mackenzie looked less than delighted, but Indiana nodded.

"He's got a point, M—Magpie. He's right about how hard it would be to find any kind of legitimate excuse for an independent freighter to drop in out here, anyway." He grimaced. "That's part of the problem, isn't it? The fact that there's nothing to attract anyone to do business with us?"

"Yes," she admitted after a moment. Her expression firmed. "Yes, it is."

"There're going to be some other changes, as well," Firebrand went on. "For one thing, the situation with the Sollies is heating up from our side, as well. To be honest, the distraction quotient you and the other people we've been talking to represent may be needed more badly—and sooner—than we'd been thinking."

"I see," Indiana said slowly while his thoughts raced.

Part of him was delighted by the prospect of accelerating the schedule. Another part of him was unhappily aware of how speeding things up might lead to mistakes, the kind of slip-ups that got people jailed... or killed. And although he'd never had any illusions about the philanthropic selflessness of his allies, Firebrand's announcement had reminded him that he and the Seraphim Independence Movement were just that as far as Manticore was concerned: a distraction for their main enemy.

Well, it's not like it was any kind of a surprise, he reminded himself. *And it always comes down to self interest in the end, doesn't it? I don't doubt the Manties wish us well. Everything I've ever heard about them suggests they wouldn't much care for what OFS has done to us here in Seraphim. But the real reason they made contact with us in the first place is that they're up against the* Solarian League. *Against someone that big you need every distraction you can get, and it'd be unrealistic as hell to pretend that isn't what Firebrand's here to arrange.*

I guess we're just going to have to hope they don't decide they're in such deep shit that—however regretfully—they end up figuring they've got no choice but to use us as an expendable *distraction.*

"I know what you're worrying about," Firebrand said shrewdly. "Don't blame you, either. But look at it this way, Talisman. Sooner or later the fact that we've been helping you—and quite a few other star systems, I might add—is going to leak, no matter how hard we try to keep it a secret. For that matter," he shrugged, "there's not going to be a whole lot of reason to *try* to keep it secret, once it's a done deal. And when that happens, we're not going to be able to afford a reputation as someone who uses, abuses, and betrays allies. That's exactly what Frontier Security's been doing for centuries, and the whole point of our support for you and the others is at least partly to prove we're *not* Frontier Security. What I'm saying is that we're not in such a deep crack that it's going to make sense to us to throw you and the others to the hexapumas, because if we get a reputation for doing that kind of thing, no one's going to trust us enough to work with us after the dust settles."

Indiana nodded slowly, although it occurred to

him that if Firebrand really was planning on "throwing them to the hexapumas" (whatever a "hexapuma" was), that would be exactly the argument he'd use to convince them he intended to do nothing of the sort. On the other hand, it did make sense . . . and if he and Mackenzie weren't willing to take at least a few chances, he hadn't had any business organizing the SIM in the first place.

"I have to admit I'm not as sublimely confident as I'd like to be," he said.

"No reason you should be," Firebrand agreed, then smiled at his expression. "Look, I'm a professional at this kind of thing. By definition, you guys are amateurs. I don't mean to be casting any aspersions by that. I'm just saying that the nature of independence movements and revolutions is that the people in charge are generally getting on-the-job training, since it's something most of them are only going to do once in their lives. And it's not the kind of career that lets you sign up for training courses at most colleges ahead of time, either. Right?"

Indiana nodded, and Firebrand shrugged.

"All right, that means all of this is terra incognita for you, and we're talking about your home star system. If it goes south, you and everyone you care about are going to be utterly screwed, Talisman—that's just the way it is. I understand that. And I understand why you're bound to be nervous. Having to rely on somebody else—somebody whose motives you know perfectly well aren't the same as yours—*ought* to make you nervous. So don't think anybody on our side's going to get his tender sensibilities hurt if you exercise a little caution and . . . creative skepticism, let's say."

Indiana felt himself nodding again, and he was more than a little surprised by how relieved Firebrand's attitude made him feel.

"We'll get the weapons shipped in to you," Firebrand went on. "If I can, I'll try to arrange to get an instructor or two shipped in, as well, but I'll be honest—the odds of my being able to pull that off aren't real high. We're way too strapped for manpower. On the other hand, we'll get you all the tech manuals, and most of the launchers and other heavy weapons come with VR simulator programs.

"The key point, the critical timing, is still going to be up to your people, though. There's no way we can predict from our end when the situation here in Seraphim is going to be right. That's going to be a judgment call on your part, although we'd obviously like it to happen sometime fairly soon, let's say." He smiled crookedly. "We don't expect you to commit suicide by moving too early, though. If for no other reason, because we'd sort of like you to succeed and go right on being a distraction for the Sollies, if you see what I mean."

"Yeah, I can see that," Indiana acknowledged.

"To be honest, one of the things we're still working on is the best way to coordinate your actions with ours. You're obviously going to need some fleet support to keep Frontier Fleet from just securing the planetary orbitals and dropping gendarmes and kinetic weapons on your heads. We're probably not talking about any really heavy units of our own—just something big enough to keep Frontier Fleet off your backs. But we're either going to have to have a firm schedule for when you're going to move, or else you're going to have to have some way to communicate with us to tell us when *you're* ready. And, frankly, providing a communications loop that's both secure and reliable *and* covert is going to require some thought. The good news is we've got some time to think about it before the first big shipments start coming in. If anything inventive occurs to you folks, don't be shy about sharing it. I said you're amateurs, and you are, but sometimes amateurs think outside the box in ways that would never occur to us stodgy old professionals."

"We'll think about it," Indiana promised him. "I don't really expect we'll come up with anything that won't already've occurred to you 'stodgy old professionals,' but if we do we'll certainly let you know.'"

"Good!" Firebrand cocked his head to one side, eyes narrowed for a moment, obviously running back over all they'd said. "I think that's about everything, then," he said finally. "For now, at least. I'll be on-planet for a few more days, and I'll use the channels Clambake set up to get back in contact with you before I leave. I'll also be setting up a message account here in Seraphim—I'll give you the access code so you can 'hack' the account rather than being an official addressee—and we'll use that for me to get you the information on the shipment schedules. I'm assuming you still have that one-time pad Clambake gave you?"

"Yes," Mackenzie said dryly. "I'll agree we're amateurs, but we have managed to hang onto the secret code book, Firebrand."

"I was sure you had." This time, he gave her a dazzling smile, no mere grin. "In that case, though, I think we're through here. And now that we've had a chance to get to know one another, so that you're not likely to be, oh, waving any pistols around the next time we meet"—he darted a humorous look at Indiana—"I think we can probably arrange to get together somewhere a little more comfortable and dryer next time. A nice little mom-and-pop restaurant with tables in the back where no one's likely to overhear a conversation, maybe."

"Sounds like a winner to me," Indiana agreed with heartfelt sincerity.

"Good." The Manticoran agent held out his hand. "In that case, I think we should all be going. And if you don't mind, I'll let the two of you leave first."

"Not a problem."

Indiana and Mackenzie each shook the offered hand in turn. Then they nodded to him, headed back out across the loading dock, and climbed into their battered old ground car.

The man called "Firebrand" watched as the car vibrated to life, backed out of its parking space, and headed off into the rain once more.

They were bright kids, he reflected. In fact, he estimated they probably had at least a five or ten percent chance of actually pulling it off. Of course, their chances would have been one hell of a lot better if they'd actually been dealing with Manticore.

Well, you can't have everything, "Talisman," Damien Harahap, one time Solarian Gendarme, more recently agent of the Mesa System government, and currently in the employ of the Mesan Alignment, thought dryly. *And at least they're a lot closer to sane than that maniac Nordbrandt!*

He smiled and shook his head. He actually had nothing at all against "Talisman" and "Magpie," when it came down to it. In fact, he wished them well, not that he actually expected things to turn out that way. Still, it was nothing personal. Only business.

He watched the ground car disappear through the drooping gate and checked his chrono. Seven and a half minutes, he decided. That ought to be a sufficiently random interval before he headed off in the opposite direction himself.

APRIL 1922 POST DIASPORA

"It's an imperfect universe. *Deal* with it."

—Admiral Michelle Henke

Chapter Five

CHRIS BILLINGSLEY POURED THE final cup of coffee, set the carafe on the small side table, and withdrew without a word. Vice Admiral Gloria Michelle Samantha Evelyn Henke, Countess Gold Peak and commanding officer, Tenth Fleet, Royal Manticoran Navy watched him go, then picked up her cup and sipped. Other people were doing the same thing around the conference table, and she wondered how many of them were using it as a stage prop in their effort to project a sense that the universe hadn't gone mad around them.

If they are, they aren't doing a very good job of it, she thought grimly. *On the other hand, neither am I because as near as I can tell, the universe has gone crazy*.

The first intimation of what looked like it was going to come to be called "the Yawata Strike" because of the total destruction of the city of Yawata Crossing had reached Spindle twenty-six hours ago. At that time, all they'd had was the flash message telling them the Manticore Binary System itself had been attacked and that damage to the Star Empire's industrial capacity had been "severe." Now the first follow-up report, with a more detailed estimate of the damage—and the casualties—had arrived, and she found herself wishing the message transit time between Spindle and Manticore was longer than eight days. She supposed she should be glad to be kept informed, but she could have gone for years—decades!—without this particular bit of information.

"All right," she said finally, lowering her cup and glancing at Captain Lecter. "I suppose we may as well get down to it." She smiled without any humor at all. "I don't imagine any of you are going to be any happier to hear this than I am. Unfortunately, after we do, we've got to decide what we're going to do about it, and I'm going to want recommendations for Admiral Khumalo and Baroness Medusa. So if any of you—and I mean *any* of you—happen to be struck by any brilliant insights in the course of Cindy's briefing, make a note of them. We're going to need all of them we can get."

Heads nodded, and she gestured to Lecter.

"The floor is yours, Cindy," she said.

"Yes, Ma'am."

Lecter didn't look any happier about the briefing she was about to give than her audience looked about what they knew they were going to hear. She spent a second or two studying the notes she'd made before she looked up and let her blue eyes circle the conference table.

"We have confirmation of the original reports," she said, "and it's as bad as we thought it would be. In fact, it's worse."

She drew a deep breath, then activated the holo

display above the conference table, bringing up the first graphic.

"Direct, immediate civilian loss of life," she began, "was much worse than any pre-attack worst-case analysis of damage to the space stations had ever suggested, because there was absolutely no warning. As you can see from the graphic, the initial strike on *Hephaestus*—"

❖   ❖   ❖

"I never realized just how much worse a victory could make a defeat taste," Augustus Khumalo said much later that evening.

He, Michelle, Michael Oversteegen, and Sir Aivars Terekhov sat with Baroness Medusa on the ocean-side balcony of her official residence. The tide was in, and surf made a soothing, rhythmic sound in the darkness, but no one felt very soothed at the moment.

"I know," Michelle agreed. "It kind of makes everything we've accomplished out here look a lot less important, doesn't it?"

"No, Milady, it most definitely does *not*," Medusa said so sharply that Michelle twitched in her chair and looked at the smaller woman in surprise.

"Sorry," Medusa said after a moment. "I didn't mean to sound as if I were snapping at you. But you—and Augustus and Aivars and Michael—have accomplished an enormous amount 'out here.' Don't ever denigrate your accomplishments—or yourselves—just because of bad news from somewhere else!"

"You're right, of course," Michelle acknowledged after a moment. "It's just—"

"Just that it feels like the end of the world," Medusa finished for her when she seemed unable to find the exact words she'd been looking for.

"Maybe not quite that bad, but close," Michelle agreed.

"Well, it damned well should!" Medusa told her tartly. "Undervaluing your own accomplishments doesn't necessarily make you wrong about how deep a crack we're all in right now."

Michelle nodded. The Admiralty dispatches had pulled no punches. With the devastation of the home system's industrial capacity, the Royal Manticoran Navy found itself—for the first time since the opening phases of the First Havenite War—facing an acute ammunition shortage. And that shortage was going to get worse—a *lot* worse—before it got any better. Which was the reason all of Michelle's remaining shipboard Apollo pods were to be returned to Manticore as soon as possible. Given the concentration of Mark 16-armed units under her command, the Admiralty would try to make up for the differential by supplying her with all of those they could find, and both her warships and her local ammunition ships currently had full magazines. Even so, however, she was going to have to be extraordinarily circumspect in how she expended the rounds available to her, because there probably weren't going to be any more for quite a while.

"At least I don't expect anyone to be eager to poke his nose back into this particular hornets' nest anytime soon," she said out loud.

"Unless, of course, whoever hit the home system wants to send his 'phantom raiders' our way," Khumalo pointed out sourly.

"Unlikely, if you'll forgive me for sayin' so, Sir," Oversteegen observed. Khumalo looked at him, and Oversteegen shrugged. "Th' Admiralty's estimate that whoever did this was operatin' on what they used t' call 'a shoestring' seems t' me t' be well taken. And, frankly, if they *were* t' decide t' carry out additional attacks of this sort, anything here in th' Quadrant would have t' be far less valuable t' them than a follow up, knock out attack on th' home system."

"I think Michael's probably right, Augustus," Michelle said. "I don't propose that we take anything for granted, and I've got Cindy and Dominica busy working out the best way to generate massive redundancy in our sensor coverage, just in case, but I don't see us as the logical candidate for the next sneak attack. If they *do* go after anything in the Quadrant, I'd imagine it would be the Terminus itself, since I can't see anything else out this way that would have equal strategic value for anyone who obviously doesn't like us very much. And that, fortunately or unfortunately, we're just going to have to leave in other peoples' hands."

Her uniformed fellows nodded, and Baroness Medusa tilted back her chair.

"Should I assume that—for the moment, at least— you feel relatively secure here in the Quadrant, then?"

"I think we probably are," Khumalo answered, instead of Michelle. He was, after all, the station commander. "There's a great deal to be said for Admiral Oversteegen's analysis where these mysterious newcomers are concerned. And, frankly, at the moment, the League doesn't have anything to send our way even if it had the nerve to do it. That could change in a few months, but for now, at least, they can't pose any kind of credible threat even against ships armed 'only' with Mark 16s."

"Good." Medusa's nostrils flared. "I only hope that

sanity is going to leak out somewhere in the League before anyone manages to get additional forces out our way. Or directed at the home system."

❖   ❖   ❖

"Any change in the escorts' formation, Guns?" Commander Naomi Kaplan asked.

"No, Ma'am." Lieutenant Abigail Hearns replied. "They're maintaining interval and heading."

The slender, brunette lieutenant didn't add that the escorts in question had to have picked up the impeller signatures of the two destroyers overtaking them from astern. Naomi Kaplan had been HMS *Hexapuma*'s tactical officer back when Abigail Hearns had been the heavy cruiser's *assistant* TO, and Abigail had learned a great deal from her. Including the fact that only rarely did the commander need the painfully obvious explained to her in detail.

"I see." Kaplan nodded acknowledgment and tipped back in her command chair, frowning, as she contemplated the current tactical situation as seen from the probable mindset of one Captain Jacob Zavala.

Zavala had originally been the senior officer of Destroyer Squadron 301's second division. He'd inherited command of the entire squadron from Commodore Ray Chatterjee following the massacre of three quarters of DesDiv 301.1 at New Tuscany, however, and reorganized the squadron's surviving five ships into two understrength divisions. As part of that reorganization, he'd shifted his flag from HMS *Gawain* to HMS *Kay* and left *Gawain* in DesDiv 301.2, where her skipper, Captain Frank Morgan, had become the division's new senior officer. At the same time, *Kay* had been detached from DesDiv 301.2 and, along with

Kaplan's own *Tristram*, now constituted a half-strength DesDiv 301.1. They'd been promised enough ships to make up the squadron's losses and bring both divisions back to full strength, but that had been before the Yawata Strike. Now it was anyone's guess how long they'd have to wait . . . or, for that matter, if they'd ever see the promised replacements at all. Frankly, Kaplan didn't think it was likely they would.

In the meantime, it seemed probable the squadron was going to find itself tasked for independent operations. Its *Roland*-class destroyers were big, powerful units, and the devastating, long-range punch of their Mark 16 missiles made them ideal commerce-raiders. They also made excellent convoy escorts, of course, but locating convoys in hyper was hellishly difficult, and the Talbott Quadrant's member star systems were already well protected against raiders once a ship dropped back into n-space. That meant *Tristram* and her sisters could be dispensed with in the escort role, which left them available for other duties. Given the fact that Manticore's confrontation with the Solarian League was likely to get a lot worse before it got any better, and given the further fact that the Madras Sector's star systems were *not* well protected against *Manticoran* raiders, whatever Frontier Fleet might fondly imagine, it wasn't hard to figure out how DesRon 301 was likely to find itself employed in the painfully near future.

Hence the current exercise.

Why do I have a bad feeling about this? Kaplan asked herself. *I mean, there they sit, plodding along at barely forty thousand kilometers per second—slow, fat, dumb, and happy. Sure, they've got a pair of*

*light cruisers to back the destroyers, but that's still
no match for a pair of* Rolands, *damn it!*

She frowned some more, one dark-skinned hand
playing with a lock of bright blonde hair. On the face
of it, there wasn't much the putative Solly escorts
could do to stop *Tristram* and *Kay* from skinning
their convoy like a Sphinxian prong buck. Kaplan's
Mark 16s had over three times the reach of the SLN's
Javelin-class shipkillers, which meant she could destroy
all of those merchies without ever even entering their
escorts' range.

Of course, a *Roland* carried only 240 Mark 16s, and
accuracy would be significantly degraded at maximum
range, even against merchantships. True, the simulation's
parameters assumed the raiders were accompanied by
a missile transport from which they could resupply,
but with the Yawata Strike's catastrophic consequences
for missile production, no one wanted to waste any of
the limited number available. So the logical move was
to get as close to her prey as she could without ever
entering the escorts' powered envelope. That would
maximize the accuracy (and economy) of her own fire
while maintaining her immunity from the defenders.

*Which is exactly what I was planning to do. And
so far I haven't seen any reason to change my mind.
Not one I could put my finger on, anyway. But still . . .*

Her eyes narrowed as she finally realized what was
bothering her. She didn't know Captain Zavala as well
as she wished she did, but he struck her as quite a
different proposition from the larger-than-life, almost
boisterous Commodore Chatterjee. No one who'd
ever served with Chatterjee could have doubted the
commodore's competence, but his enthusiasm and

inexhaustible energy had been the first things to strike almost anyone on first acquaintance, and he'd had a very...direct approach to problems. Not only was Zavala barely two thirds as tall as Chatterjee had been, he was also far quieter, with a thoughtful, almost preoccupied air which she'd quickly realized was deceptive. Chatterjee had been well suited to his nickname of "Bear," but Zavala was a treecat—compact, sleek, and with the confident, composed watchfulness of a patient predator.

She'd also done a bit of quiet research since he'd assumed command of the squadron and found that *Commander* Zavala had been a senior tactical instructor at Saganami Island for four years. He'd been slated for command of a destroyer at the time Oscar Saint-Just had been toppled, but he'd lost that appointment in the Janacek build-down and been sent to the Academy instead. In fact, his Saganami Island stint had coincided almost exactly with Edward Janacek's tenure as First Lord of Admiralty, and being beached by the Janacek Admiralty was a recommendation in its own right, as far as Kaplan was concerned. From the look of things, he'd done a damned good job as an instructor, though, and the *White Haven* Admiralty had given him command with almost indecent haste. He'd posted a pretty good record as a destroyer skipper since, too. In fact, he'd been jumped straight past captain (junior-grade) to captain of the list on the basis of his performance with Eighth Fleet. Well, that was scarcely surprising. All false modesty aside, Kaplan knew the Navy wasn't choosing *Roland* skippers at random, and every CO in the squadron had amply demonstrated his or her capabilities before being selected.

Yet for this exercise, Zavala had relegated himself to the role of a passenger aboard his flagship. He was only there to observe, he'd explained, and *that* was the reason Kaplan's mental antennae were quivering.

An observer, yes, but to observe exactly what, *I wonder?*

She stroked one eyebrow with an index finger, remembering how straightforward the simulation had sounded when she read the initial ops order. In fact, it had gone beyond mere straightforwardness to the absurdly simple, and for the life of her she couldn't remember the last time a *good* senior officer had organized a training sim as a "gimme." The Manticoran tradition was to train its people in exercises which were deliberately *harder* than actual operations were likely to prove. That obviously wasn't the case here, yet someone like Zavala was unlikely to forget the tradition. Which meant there was a nasty hook somewhere inside that tasty-looking bait. But what sort of hook . . . ?

"Abigail," she said.

"Yes, Ma'am?" Lieutenant Hearns looked over her shoulder, one eyebrow raised.

"Do you have those reports on what happened at Torch handy?"

"Such as they are and what we have of them, yes, Ma'am."

"I know we don't have much detail," Kaplan acknowledged, which was unfortunately true. Admiral Luis Rozsak and the Erewhonese were keeping any reports of the actual engagement pretty close to their vests. "But I'm thinking more about ONI's speculations. About the performance of the missiles Mesa equipped those StateSec retreads with."

"We don't have any hard numbers, Ma'am." Abigail's own expression turned thoughtful as she paged through her orderly mental files. "In fact there's nothing specific about the Mesan-supplied missiles at all. But one of the analysts on Admiral Hemphill's staff did suggest they may not have been standard Solly issue. Is that what you were thinking of, Ma'am?"

"That's exactly what I was thinking about." Kaplan nodded. "Refresh my memory."

"Well, as you said yourself, it's all speculative, Ma'am. But stripped of all the statistical analysis, his basic point was that we know Erewhon is building new units for Governor Barregos. We also know Erewhon has multidrive missiles of its own. They're still the big, bulky capacitor-powered model, but they've got plenty of legs, and their warheads and seekers are better than anything the Sollies have. For that matter, Erewhon certainly ought to be able to manufacture the old Mark 13 extended-range missile for smaller launchers, and he suggested Barregos and Rozsak would have held out for at least the Mark 13. Whatever they may or may not be telling Old Chicago, *they're* obviously aware missile ranges have been climbing in our neck of the woods. That being the case, they probably would have insisted on buying the longest-ranged birds they could get."

She paused, as if to be sure her CO was with her so far, and Kaplan nodded again.

"The point he made—the one I'm pretty sure you're thinking about, Ma'am—was that given Rozsak's reported losses and assuming he *had* acquired longer-ranged missiles from the Erewhonese, he must either have fought like a complete and total idiot, which isn't what his résumé would lead someone to expect, or else significantly underestimated his *enemies'* range. If he hadn't, he never would have entered it in the first place. If he did, he may have shaved the margin too tightly trying to get in close enough to maximize his hit probabilities."

"Exactly." Kaplan smiled thinly. "We don't know what the range actually was, but I think your analyst was onto something, Abigail."

"I admit it makes a lot of sense, Ma'am. But we've gotten really good intel on the Sollies' weaponry since Spindle. We haven't found any extended range missiles in any of their magazines. For that matter, there's absolutely no reference to anything of the sort in their tac manuals or the training sims we captured from them. I've been playing with their missile doctrine—offense and defense—ever since we got access, and it's all concerned with really short-range engagements, at least by our standards. And they obviously never saw the range of the Mark 16 or the Mark 23 coming at Spindle."

"I know. In fact, I wouldn't be a bit surprised if whatever the Mesans handed their mercenaries for the attack on Torch was another little toy their good friends and fellow scum at Technodyne whipped up just for them. I'm thinking about those system-defense missiles they surprised us with at Monica."

Their gazes met, and Kaplan saw the same memory in Abigail's gray-blue eyes. The memory of how those system-defense missiles had ravaged Aivars Terekhov's scratch squadron—and damned near killed Naomi Kaplan—from far beyond the threat range Kaplan herself had projected based on known Solarian missile performance.

"Those were awfully big missiles, Ma'am," Abigail pointed out. She wasn't arguing, Kaplan realized. She was simply thinking out loud. "We haven't seen any sign these people have pods on tow, and no Solly cruiser or destroyer could launch birds that size without being virtually rebuilt. Even then, they probably couldn't get more than four or five launchers and forty or fifty missiles aboard something the size of one of their light cruisers. And even completely ignoring the mass and volume penalties of launchers that size, I'd be surprised if one of their tincans could squeeze in more than twenty birds that big. On a good day."

"Agreed. But suppose Technodyne came up with something smaller that still offered a significant range increase over the standard Javelin? They wouldn't have to have the kind of legs we ran into at Monica to come as a nasty surprise to someone who thought she knew exactly what kind of range they *did* have. And somehow I can't escape the suspicion that Captain Zavala may just have read the same reports—and the same ONI 'speculation'—you and I read. In which case, I think we might want to consider the possibility that these foolishly overconfident escorts know something *we* don't know about their missiles."

"I don't have any problem with that, Ma'am," Abigail agreed with a smile.

"Of course, there's the little problem that we don't know just how much of a range extension Captain Zavala might have opted for," Kaplan mused out loud. Several of her other bridge officers were listening in now, and other smiles began to blossom. "I think the simplest way for him to go about it would have been to simply double their effective range," she went on. "Of course, he may have settled on some other multiplier just to be difficult, but their accuracy at any sort of extended range is going to be a lot worse than ours. Unless he's decided to go ahead and give them Ghost Rider, as well!"

It's always possible he's done exactly that, she reflected to herself. *But let's be reasonable here. The idea's to make exercises* difficult, *not automatically suicidal! Well, unless you're Lady Gold Peak pinning back Admiral Oversteegan's ears, at least.*

She chuckled at the thought, but it was unlikely Zavala would have been quite as nasty as Lady Gold Peak. After all, the countess and Oversteegan had something of a history, according to the rumor mill.

"Sixteen million kilometers, you think, Ma'am?" Abigail asked politely, interrupting her thoughts.

"Let's make it seventeen," Kaplan demurred. "It gives us a little more of a fudge factor, and with Ghost Rider, we ought to be able to punch out merchies at that range without wasting *too* many attack birds."

"Yes, Ma'am." Abigail glanced down at her displays, lips pursed, then looked back up at Kaplan. "I'll need five or six minutes to reconfigure my firing plans, Ma'am."

"Well, by my calculations it's going to take us another three hours to get to seventeen million klicks," Kaplan observed dryly. "I think we've got time."

❖   ❖   ❖

"Used up quite a few missiles there, didn't you, Captain Kaplan?" Jacob Zavala inquired testily. "They don't grow on trees, y'know! Especially not now."

"No, Sir, they don't," Naomi Kaplan acknowledged with a mildness which would have raised warning flags with anyone who knew her well. "On the other hand, we did take out every one of the freighters without ever entering the escorts' reach."

"True, but you could've saved at least twenty percent of your ammo expenditure if you'd closed another five or six million kilometers, and that still would've left you outside even Javelin range," Zavala pointed out.

"Yes, Sir, it would have." Kaplan nodded. "On the other hand," she continued in the same mild tone, "it probably *wouldn't* have left me outside the range of the missiles you actually gave the Sollies for the exercise."

"What's that?" Zavala cocked his head, blue eyes narrowed as he gazed quizzically at Kaplan. "Are you suggesting I'd *cheat*, Captain?"

"To quote one of my tac instructors at the Crusher, Sir, if you aren't cheating, you're not trying hard enough." Kaplan shrugged. "Just as a matter of curiosity, how much of a range boost *did* you assign?"

"You, Captain Kaplan, have a disrespectful and insulting opinion of my fair-mindedness," Zavala said severely, then snorted. "As a matter of fact, they had a nominal effective range of twelve million kilometers. A twenty-five percent jump seemed about right."

"Really?" Kaplan smiled. "I figured you'd settle for a nice round number and just double it, Sir."

"Now *that*, Captain, *would* have been underhanded, unfair, sneaky, and generally despicable. Which is why I'll probably do exactly that to Captain Morgan's division when it's his turn in the barrel." Zavala waggled a finger in Kaplan's direction. "And don't you go warning him, either!"

"Me? *Warn* him about it?" Kaplan laughed. "Oh,

don't worry about that, Sir. As a matter of fact, I've already bet him a bottle of Glenfiddich Grand Reserve that he can't match our score on the sim. I've known Captain Morgan for a while, you know. And somehow I seem to've forgotten to mention to him the range at which *we* engaged the convoy. I hate to say it," she assumed a mournful expression, "but under the circumstances, I strongly suspect he's going to decide that if he closes to just outside Javelin range, he'll be able to punch out all of the merchies with a lot fewer missiles than we expended."

She shook her head sadly, and Zavala laughed.

"A woman after my own underhanded, unfair, sneaky, and generally despicable heart," he observed. "I definitely see an admiral's flag in your future, Captain Kaplan!"

Chapter Six

"THIS," YANA TRETIAKOVNA ANNOUNCED, "is booooring."

The tall, attractive, and very dangerous blonde flung herself backward into the threadbare armchair. She leaned back, crossed her arms, and glowered out the huge crystoplast wall at what any unbiased person would have to call the magnificent vista of Yamato's Nebula.

At the moment, she was less than impressed. On the other hand, she had a lot to not be impressed about. And she'd had a lot of time in which to be unimpressed, too.

"I'm sure you could find something to amuse yourself if you really wanted to," Anton Zilwicki said mildly, looking up from the chess problem on his minicomp. "This *is* one of the galaxy's biggest and most elaborate amusement parks, you know."

"This *was* one of the galaxy's biggest amusement parks," Yana shot back. "These days, it's one of the galaxy's biggest deathtraps. Not to mention being stuffed unnaturally full of Ballroom terrorists and Beowulfan commandos, not one of whom has a functioning sense of humor!"

"Well, if you hadn't dislocated that nice Beowulfan lieutenant's elbow while arm wrestling with him, maybe you'd find out they had better senses of humor than you think they do."

"Yada, yada, yada." Yana grimaced. "It's not even fun to tease *Victor* anymore!"

A deep basso chuckle rumbled around inside Zilwicki's massive chest. When Yana had first signed on to assist in his and Victor Cachat's high-risk mission to Mesa, she'd been at least half-frightened (whether she would have admitted it to a living soul or not) of the Havenite secret agent. She'd agreed to come along—mostly out of a desire to avenge her friend Lara's death—and she was a hardy soul, was Yana. Still, the notion of playing the girlfriend (although the ancient term "moll" might actually have been a better one) of someone many people would have described as a stone-cold, crazed sociopathic killer had obviously worried her more than she'd cared to admit. In fact, Zilwicki thought, Cachat had never struck him as either stone cold or crazed, but he could see where other people might form that impression, given his Havenite colleague's body count. As for sociopathy, well, Zilwicki's internal jury was still out on that one in some ways.

Not that he hadn't known some perfectly nice sociopaths. Besides, Zilwicki had observed that who was the sociopath and who was the defender of all that was right and decent often seemed to depend a great deal on the perspective of the observer.

And sometimes the cigar really is *a cigar, of course,*

he reflected. *That's one of the things that make life so interesting when Victor's around.*

Over the course of their lengthy mission on Mesa, Yana had gotten past most of her own uneasiness with the Havenite. And the four-month voyage from Mesa back to the Hainuwele System had finished it off. Of course, the trip shouldn't have taken anywhere near that long. The old, battered, and dilapidated freighter *Hali Sowle* their Erewhonese contacts had provided had been a smuggler in her time, and she'd been equipped with a military grade hyper generator. It wasn't obvious, because her original owners had gone to considerable lengths to disguise it, and they hadn't tinkered with her commercial grade impeller nodes and particle screening, but that had allowed her to climb as high as the Theta Bands, which made her far faster than the vast majority of merchant vessels. Unfortunately, the hyper generator in question had been less than perfectly maintained by the various owners through whose hands the ship had passed since it was first installed, and it had promptly failed after they managed to escape Mesa into hyper. They'd survived the experience, but it had taken Andrew Artlet what had seemed like an eternity to jury-rig the replacement component they'd required.

They'd drifted, effectively motionless on an interstellar scale, while he and Anton managed the repairs, and even after they'd gotten the generator back up, using the Mesa-Visigoth Hyper Bridge had been out of the question. They'd been better than nine hundred and sixty light-years from their base in Hainuwele (and well over a thousand light-years from Torch) but given the . . . pyrotechnics which had accompanied their escape, they'd dared not return to the

Mesa Terminus and take the shortcut which would have delivered them less than sixty light-years from Beowulf. Instead, they'd been forced to detour by way of the OFS-administered Syou-tang Terminus of the Syou-tang-Olivia Bridge, then cross the four hundred and eighty-odd light-years from the Olivia System to Hainuwele the hard way.

The trip had given them plenty of time to hone their cardplaying skills, and the same enforced confinement had given the coup de grace to any lingering fear Yana might have felt where Victor Cachat was concerned. It had also given Cachat and Zilwicki plenty of time to debrief Herlander Simões, the Mesan physicist who had defected from the Mesan Alignment. Well, "plenty of time" was probably putting it too strongly. They'd had *lots* of time, but properly mining the treasure trove Simões represented was going to take years, and it was, frankly, a task which was going to require someone with a lot more physics background then Zilwicki possessed.

Enough had emerged from Simões' responses and from the maddeningly tantalizing fragments which had been proffered by Jack McBryde, the Mesan security officer who'd engineered Simões' defection, to tell them that everything everyone—even, or perhaps *especially*, the galaxy's best intelligence agencies—had always known about Mesa was wrong. That information was going to come as a particularly nasty shock to Beowulf intelligence, Zilwicki thought, but Beowulf was hardly going to be alone in that reaction. And as they'd managed to piece together more bits of the mosaic, discovered just how much no one else knew, their plodding progress homeward had become even more frustrating.

There'd been times—and quite a few of them—when Zilwicki had found himself passionately wishing they'd headed towards the Lynx Terminus of the Manticoran Wormhole Junction, instead. Unfortunately, their evasive routing had been more or less forced upon them initially, and it would have taken even longer to backtrack to Lynx than to continue to Syou-tang. And there'd also been the rather delicate question of exactly what would happen to Victor Cachat if they should suddenly turn up in the Manticore Binary System, especially after the direct Havenite attack on the aforesaid star system, word of which had reached the Mesan news channels just over two T-months before their somewhat hurried departure. It had struck them as unlikely that one of Haven's top agents would be received with open arms and expressions of fond welcome, to say the least.

For that matter, exactly who had jurisdiction over Simões (and the priceless intelligence resource he represented) was also something of a delicate question. Their operation had been jointly sponsored by the Kingdom of Torch, the Republic of Haven (whether or not anyone in Nouveau Paris had known anything about it), the Audubon Ballroom, the Beowulf Biological Survey Corps, and Victor Cachat's Erewhonese contacts. There'd been absolutely no official *Manticoran* involvement, although Princess Ruth Winton's contributions hadn't exactly been insignificant. She'd been acting in her persona as Torch's intelligence chief, however, not in her persona as a member of the Star Empire of Manticore's ruling house.

Bearing all of that in mind, there'd never really been much chance of heading straight for Manticore. Instead, they'd made for Hainuwele, on the direct line to Torch.

It was the closest safe harbor, given the available wormhole connections, and they'd hoped to find one of the BSC's disguised commando ships in-system and available for use as a messenger when they got there. They'd been disappointed in that respect, however; when they arrived the only ship on station had been EMS *Custis*, an Erewhonese construction ship which had just about completed the conversion of Parmley Station into a proper base for the BSC and the Ballroom to interdict the interstellar trade in genetic slaves.

Artlet's and Zilwicki's repairs had been less than perfect, and *Hali Sowle* had limped into Hainuwele on what were obviously her hyper generator's last legs. *Custis'* captain been out of touch for two or three months himself while his construction crews worked on Parmley Station, but he'd been able to confirm that as far as active operations between Haven and Manticore were concerned, a hiatus of mutual exhaustion had set in following the Battle of Manticore. Both Anton and Victor had been vastly relieved to discover that no one had been actively shooting at one another any longer, given what they'd learned on Mesa, but it had been obvious the good captain was less than delighted at the notion of finding himself involved in the sort of shenanigans which seemed to follow the team of Zilwicki and Cachat around. He'd apparently suspected that his Erewhonese employers wouldn't have approved of his stepping deeper into the morass he was pretty sure *Hali Sowle* and her passengers represented. They might have convinced him to change his mind if they'd told him what they'd discovered on Mesa, but they weren't about to break security on *that* at this point. Which meant the best he'd been willing to do was to take his own ship to Erewhon (which, to be fair, was the next best thing to twenty light-years closer to Hainuwele than Torch was) to fetch back a replacement generator for *Hali Sowle*. In the process, he was willing to take an encrypted dispatch from Victor to Sharon Justice, who'd been covering for him as the Republic's senior officer in the Erewhon Sector, but that was as far as he was prepared to go.

Zilwicki didn't try to pretend, even to himself, that he hadn't found the captain's attitude irritating. Fortunately, he was by nature a patient, methodical, analytical man. And there were at least some upsides to the situation. Neither he nor Cachat wanted Simões out of their sight, and while they had no particular reason to distrust *Custis'* captain or crew, they had no particular reason to *trust* them, either. If even a fraction of what Jack McBryde and Herlander Simões had told them proved true, it was going to shake the foundations of star nations all across explored space. They literally could not risk having anything happen to him until they'd had time for him to tell his tale—in detail—to their own star nations' intelligence services. Much as they might begrudge the month or so it would take *Custis* to make the trip to Erewhon, they preferred to stay right where they were until Justice could arrange secure transport to Torch. They'd both breathe an enormous sigh of relief once they had Simões safely squirreled away on Torch and could send discreet dispatches requesting all of the relevant security agencies send senior representatives to Torch.

No one expected it to be easy, and he knew Cachat was as worried as he was over the possibility that the

Star Empire and the Republic might resume combat operations while they waited, but both of them were aware that they'd stumbled onto the sort of intelligence revelation that came along only once in centuries. Assuming it wasn't all part of some incredible, insane disinformation effort, the Mesan Alignment had been working on its master plan for the better part of *six hundred* T-years without *anyone's* having suspected what was happening. Under those circumstances, there were quite literally no lengths to which Victor Cachat and Anton Zilwicki wouldn't go to keep their sole source of information alive.

Which was why they were all still sitting here aboard Parmley Station's moldering hulk while they awaited transportation elsewhere.

"You know," Yana said a bit plaintively, "nobody told me we were going to be gone on this little jaunt for an entire year."

"And we haven't been," Zilwicki pointed out. "Well, actually, I suppose we have, depending on the planetary year in question. But in terms of T-years, it's been less than one. Why, it's been barely ten T-months, when you come down to it!"

"And it was only *supposed* to be four," Yana retorted.

"We told you it might be five," Zilwicki corrected, and she snorted.

"You know, even Scrags can do simple arithmetic, Anton. And—"

The powered door giving access to the combination viewing gallery and sitting room was one part of Parmley Station which had been thoroughly refurbished. Now it opened rather abruptly, interrupting Yana in mid-sentence, and a dark-haired man came through it. Compared to Zilwicki's massive musculature and shoulders, the newcomer looked almost callow, but he was actually a well-muscled young fellow.

"Ah, there you are!" he said. "Ganny El said she thought you were in here."

"And so we are, Victor," Zilwicki rumbled, and raised an eyebrow. "And since we are, and since you're also here at the moment, may I ask who's babysitting our good friend Herlander? Unless I'm mistaken, it *is* your watch, isn't it?"

"I left Frank sitting outside his door with a flechette gun, Anton," Cachat replied in a patient tone, and Zilwicki grunted.

The sound represented at least grudging approval, although one had to know him well to recognize that fact. On the other hand, Frank Gillich was a capable fellow. He and June Mattes were both members of the Beowulf Biological Survey Corps, part of the original BSC team which had discovered the Butry Clan here on Parmley Station and brokered the deal that left the Butrys alive and turned the station into a BSC/Ballroom front. Most people, or most people who didn't know Victor Cachat, at least, would have considered Gillich and Mattes about as lethal as agents came, and Zilwicki was willing to concede that Gillich could probably be counted upon to keep Simões alive for the next fifteen or twenty minutes.

"I thought *I* was the hyper-suspicious, paranoid, obsessive-compulsive one," Cachat continued. "What is this? Are you trying to claim the title of Paranoiac in Chief?"

"Hah!" Yana snorted. "He's not trying to do anything. He's just been hanging around *you* too long. That's enough to drive anyone—except Kaja…maybe—around the bend!"

"I don't see why the entire universe insists on thinking of me as some sort of crazed killer," Cachat said mildly. "It's not like I kill anyone who doesn't *need* killing."

He said it with a completely straight face, but Zilwicki thought it was probably a joke. *Probably.* One could never be entirely certain where Cachat was concerned, and the Havenite's idea of a sense of humor wasn't quite like most people's.

"May I assume there's a reason you left Frank playing babysitter and asked Ganny El where you might find us?" Zilwicki asked out loud.

"Actually, yes," Cachat replied, dark brown-black eyes lighting. "I think I've finally found the argument to get you to agree to take Herlander straight to Nouveau Paris, Anton."

"Oh?" Zilwicki crossed tree trunk arms and cocked his head, considering Cachat the way a skilled lumberjack might consider a particularly scrubby sapling. "And why should we suddenly depart from our agreed on plan of parking him on Torch and inviting all the mountains to come to Mohammed?"

"Because," Cachat replied, "a dispatch boat just came in from Erewhon."

"A dispatch boat?" Zilwicki's eyes narrowed. "Why would anyone in Erewhon be sending a dispatch boat out here?"

"Apparently Sharon decided it would be a good idea to let anyone from the Ballroom or the BSC who checked in with Parmley Station know what's going on," Cachat replied. He shrugged. "Obviously, she didn't know *I* was going to be here when she sent the boat—she sent it off about three weeks ago, and the earliest *Custis* could get to Erewhon is tomorrow."

"I'm perfectly well aware of *Custis*' schedule," Zilwicki rumbled. "So suppose you just go ahead and tell me 'what's going on' that's so important your minions are throwing dispatch boats around the galaxy?"

"Well, it happens that about three months ago, Duchess Harrington arrived in Haven orbit," Cachat said. "The news got sent out to all of our intelligence stations in the regular data dumps, but it still took over a month to get to Sharon, and she sent the dispatch boat out to distribute it to all our stations in the sector. It stopped off at Torch, too, according to its skipper. We were the last stop on the information chain." He shrugged again. "I imagine the only reason it got sent here at all was Sharon's usual thoroughness. But according to the summary she got from the home office, Duchess Harrington is in Nouveau Paris for the express purpose of negotiating a peace settlement between the Republic and the Star Empire."

Anyone who knew Anton Zilwicki would have testified that he was a hard man to surprise. This time, though, someone had managed it, and his eyes widened.

"A peace settlement? You mean a formal *treaty*?"

"Apparently that's exactly what she's there to get, and according to Sharon's summary, President Pritchart is just as determined as the duchess. On the other hand, after twenty years of shooting at each other, I doubt they've already tied it all up in a neat bow. And since Duchess Harrington actually believed both of us before we ever set out for Mesa, I don't see any reason she wouldn't believe us if we turned up with

Simões in tow. For that matter, she'll have her treecat with her, and he'll *know* whether or not we're telling the truth. Or whether or not Herlander is, when you come down to it."

"And if there's anyone in the Star Empire who could convince the Queen to listen to us, it's Harrington," Zilwicki agreed, nodding vigorously.

"Exactly. So my thought is that we leave the recordings of our interviews with Herlander here on our station to be picked up by the next BSC courier to come through and taken on to Torch. Redundancy is a beautiful thing, after all. In the meantime, though, you and I commandeer Sharon's dispatch boat, load Herlander on board, and head straight for Haven." Cachat grinned. "Do you think finding out about the Alignment's existence might have some small impact on the negotiations?"

✦ Chapter Seven

VICE ADMIRAL GOLD PEAK stood in the late-night quiet of her day cabin in a pair of comfortably worn sweats and fluffy purple treecat bedroom slippers. Her shoulders were hunched, her hands were shoved deep into her sweat shirt's pockets, and she glowered—undeniably, she glowered—at the outsized holographic display. One side of that display showed a detailed, if small-scale, schematic of the Spindle System; the other side showed a breakdown of her current fleet strength. If she'd cared to turn her head and look at the smart wall behind her, she would have seen a star chart of the entire Talbott Quadrant, as well. At the moment, however, she was concentrating fairly hard on *not* looking at that chart, since she found herself rather in the position of someone with insufficient icing to cover the birthday cake she'd just been given.

Hell of a birthday party, she reflected morosely, although to be fair it wouldn't be her birthday—her *sixty-fourth* birthday, to be precise—for another two days. Given the amount of time she'd spent trundling around the universe at relativistic velocities, her *subjective* age was a good three years less than that, but no one worried about that when it came time to keeping track of birthdays. And the Royal Manticoran Navy used its own calendar, not someone's subjective experience, to determine relative seniority, as well.

She considered that last point for a moment, then grimaced as she thought about the rank insignia sitting in the upper drawer of the desk behind her. The ones she would be allowed to officially pin onto her uniform collar in two days.

I can just see Beth grinning all over her face when she saw the official date of rank. Hell, for that matter I'll bet she damned well had the original date changed to make sure it fell on my birthday! Just the sort of thing she'd do.

There could be disadvantages to being the Empress of Manticore's first cousin and next in line for the crown after Elizabeth Winton's two children and her brother. Especially for someone who'd spent her entire career aggressively fighting even the appearance of nepotism. She remembered the day her best friend had ripped a strip off of her for the way her avoidance of anything which could have been construed as preferential treatment had slowed her career, and the memory made her snort in amusement.

Well, I've made up for it since, haven't I, Honor? Forty-one years from the Academy to vice admiral, then only eleven T-months to full admiral! Talk about a career catching fire. Of course, her amusement faded, *it would have been nice if the rest of the galaxy hadn't decided to catch fire right along with it.*

She shook her head as the weight of those waiting

admiral's stars ground down upon her. She wondered sometimes if perhaps the real reason she'd so zealously avoided favoritism was because she'd feared the responsibilities that came with exalted rank and hadn't wanted to admit it to herself. She'd certainly found herself wishing over the last year or so that she could have handed the ones currently bearing down on her to someone else.

She imagined there was a lot of that going around, too.

She inhaled deeply and gave herself an impatient shake. Brooding about the unfairness of the universe was about the least effective way of *dealing* with that unfairness she could think of, and she made herself re-focus her attention on the numbers and ship names before her.

While there might be a few people who suspected her rapid promotion was due primarily to who she'd chosen as a cousin, there were undoubtedly a lot more who saw it as a reward for Tenth Fleet's smashing triumph in the Battle of Spindle. For that matter, there was almost certainly a political element in it, as well, since the promotion was yet another way for Empress Elizabeth—Michelle was still working on remembering her cousin was an *empress* these days, not "just" a queen—to demonstrate her approval and support for Michelle's actions. A way to reemphasize to the rest of the galaxy, and especially to the Solarian League, that the Star Empire of Manticore had no intention of backing down before the threat of the League's massive economic and military power.

Michelle was confident her family connections had played the smallest part in the decision. She'd have been even happier if she could have been certain they'd played no part at all, but she happened to live in the real universe, and politics and diplomacy would always be politics and diplomacy. That was one reason she'd chosen the Navy instead of going into politics herself. Yet there was another aspect to it, as well, and she knew it.

If Elizabeth was going to retain her in command of Tenth Fleet (and it would have been impossible to relieve Michelle without looking like Manticore was backing down), Michelle needed the rank to go with the growing strength of her command. No fewer than four vice admirals, all senior to her, had been added to Tenth Fleet over the last month or so. It was always awkward when a junior commanded a senior, so the Admiralty had cut this particular Gordian knot by once again promoting Michelle "out of the zone." Which was why in two days' time she'd be exchanging the pair of stars on each point of her collar for a trio and replacing the three broad rings on her uniform cuffs with four. Which, at the tender age (for a prolong society) of only sixty-four, was a meteoric rise, indeed.

Unfortunately, even with the number of flag officers being added to it, Tenth Fleet remained badly understrength for its obligations. With upwards of a dozen star systems to defend, spread throughout an area of responsibility which stretched over two hundred and thirty light-years from the Lynx Terminus to the Scarlet System and four hundred from Tillerman to Celebrant, she could have wished for at least twice her assigned order of battle. And that would have been if she'd been worried about defending it against any reasonably sized foe, rather than the

Solarian League. But whatever she could have wished, her total strength, after the dust settled, was only seventy-seven hyper-capable combatants. On the other hand, twenty of those were CLACs, which gave her just over two thousand light attack craft, and present-generation Manticoran LACs were nothing to sneer at. Especially against someone whose designs were as obsolescent—or even outright obsolete—as the SLN's had demonstrated themselves to be. The Sollies still might not be prepared to accept that anything as small as a LAC could possibly threaten a capital ship, but if they did think that, and if they attempted to prove it, they'd be sailing into a universe of hurt. The only problem was that what happened to *them* wasn't going to keep a lot of Michelle Henke's spacers from getting killed right along with them.

And not a single Apollo-capable unit in sight, she thought glumly. *Not one. Not that I can really argue with the Admiralty's decisions after what happened to the home system.*

None of the followup dispatches had made any effort to hide the terrifying severity of the blow Manticore's industrial capability had suffered. The sheer scale of the Yawata Strike's loss of life had been horrifying, but to make it even worse, it had been concentrated in the sectors of the Star Empire's labor force most essential to supporting the Navy. Effectively, every Manticoran shipyard was simply gone. Even the production lines which had supplied the fleet with missiles had been destroyed. The ships Manticore had, and the missiles which had already been manufactured, were all the Star Empire was going to have for a long, long time, and the defense of the home system, its population, and what remained of its industrial base (not to mention the wormhole junction which was absolutely essential to Manticore's strategic survival) had to take priority over almost any other consideration. Especially since Solarian strategic doctrine was uncompromisingly oriented around seeking a knockout blow by crushing the capital system of any star nation foolish enough to cross swords with the League.

Under those circumstances, the two squadrons of Keyhole-Two-equipped pod-laying superdreadnoughts Michelle had been promised had been recalled to the home system almost before they'd arrived in Spindle. Only ships with the Keyhole-Two control platforms could fully utilize the FTL telemetry links of the Mark 23-E multidrive missiles which were the heart of the Apollo system, and all of them—and all of the Navy's existing store of Mark 23Es—were desperately needed to defend the Manticore Binary System.

In partial exchange, she'd gotten twenty Keyhole-*One* SD(P)s, and in terms of combat power, that was a pretty impressive consolation prize. No, they couldn't use Apollo, but they could handle more missiles than any Solarian superdreadnought could even dream of firing, their own missile defenses were incomparably better than anything the other side might have, and while they weren't equipped with the Mark 23-E *control* missiles, the standard Mark 23s in their magazines enormously out-ranged any Solarian weapon. Accuracy at extreme ranges was going to be much poorer than it would have been using Apollo, yet the missile storm they could bring down on any opponent would be devastating. And, fortunately, six T-months had passed between Haven's Operation Beatrice and the Yawata

Strike. The tempo of combat had dropped virtually to nothing during that time period, as well, which meant there'd been no real ammunition expenditures to cut into those six months worth of wartime-rate missile production. And *that* meant the Royal Manticoran Navy had a lot of those standard Mark 23s already produced and distributed to the fleet.

It wasn't that Michelle entertained any doubts about what would happen to any Solarian admiral unwise enough to confront her combat power in space. The problem was that she had so *much* space to protect. She couldn't possibly be everywhere she needed to be in sufficient strength to prevent an audacious Solarian flag officer from avoiding her combat power and carrying out devastating (there was that word again) raids on the infrastructure of the systems she was responsible for defending.

Then there was the interesting question of just what sort of reinforcements the Sollies might have en route to the Quadrant. And, for that matter, the even more interesting question (assuming her own suspicions about who'd been pulling the puppet strings behind the current catastrophe were correct) of what Manpower and Mesa might have up their collective sleeve.

And, finally, there was the body blow to the priority she'd been originally promised on the new Mark 16-equipped units.

News of the "Zunker Incident" had reached Spindle aboard a Navy dispatch boat only this morning, and Michelle found herself almost equally impressed by Captain Ivanov's tactics and by the unwonted discretion shown by the Solarian flag officer involved. The confrontation had also confirmed—or reconfirmed, perhaps—the tactical superiority the Mark 16 conferred upon the RMN's lighter units. Unfortunately, Michelle was certain there'd been other "Zunker Incidents" in the three weeks since the original, and every one of them would only increase Admiralty House's demands for additional Mark 16-capable vessels. Especially given the decision to go ahead and implement Lacoön Two.

She could hardly fault the Admiralty for that priority, but Lacoön Two obviously required a lot of relatively fast, relatively well-armed hyper-capable platforms. Which, when she came down to it, was pretty much an exact description of the *Nikes*, *Saganami-Cs* and *Rolands*. Which, in turn, explained why the light combatants she'd expected to see were now going elsewhere at high rates of speed.

It's an imperfect universe, Mike, she told herself tartly. *Deal with it.*

She snorted again, then squared her shoulders, hauled her hands out of her pockets, turned and marched back to her workstation. She picked up the cup of coffee Chris Billingsley had left for her and settled into her work chair. She and Augustus Khumalo were scheduled to meet tomorrow with Governor Medusa, Prime Minister Joachim Alquezar, Minister of War Henri Krietzmann, and the other senior members of Alquezar's war cabinet to discuss her new deployment plan. Under the circumstances, she thought as she started punching up the appropriate files, it probably behooved her to have a deployment plan to discuss.

❖   ❖   ❖

"So that's about the size of it, on the housing side, at least." Henri Krietzmann looked around the Governor's House conference room in the planetary and quadrant capital of Thimble and shrugged. "It's only been seven weeks since O'Cleary's surrender, so despite Admiral Bordelon's protests, we're actually doing pretty damned well, I think. Especially considering the fact that *we're* not the ones who went and invaded *their* star system!"

"Surely you don't expect Bordelon to admit that, do you, Henri?" Baroness Medusa observed tartly.

Most of the people seated around the long table grimaced, but she had a point. With Admiral Keeley O'Cleary's departure for Old Chicago, and the deaths of Admirals Sandra Crandall, Dunichi Lazlo, and Griseldis Degauchy in the Battle of Spindle, Admiral Margaux Bordelon had inherited command of the surrendered personnel of SLN Task Force 496. Judging from her own conversations with Bordelon, Michelle Henke was confident the Solarian officer would have declined the honor if she'd had any choice.

Any impartial board of inquiry would have to conclude that Bordelon bore no responsibility for what had happened to Crandall's task force. She might not have covered herself with glory, but Michelle doubted any Battle Fleet flag officer was likely to have accomplished *that*. As far as the battle itself was concerned, Bordelon had done precisely what she'd been ordered to do, and she'd conducted herself in punctilious accordance with the Deneb Accords since becoming senior officer of the Solarian POWs. None of which was likely to cut any ice where the consequences to her career were concerned. As TF 496's two surviving senior officers, she and O'Cleary could pretty much count on being scapegoated for the deceased Crandall's mistakes, unless their own family connections were lofty enough to avoid that fate.

It seemed unlikely they could be, in O'Cleary's case, since she'd been the one to actually surrender to the handful of cruisers which had ripped Crandall's SDs apart, but there might be some hope—careerwise, at any rate—for Bordelon. After all, *she* wasn't the one who'd "cravenly" (to use what appeared to be the Solly newsfax editorials' favorite adverb, although "gutlessly" seemed to be running a close second and "pusillanimously" was clearly in contention, as well, at least for newsies with impressive vocabularies) surrendered. And she obviously intended to be as inflexible as possible in demanding Manticore meet the Deneb Accords' obligations to properly "house, feed, and care for" prisoners of war. The fact that there were the next best thing to half a million of those prisoners, and that they'd arrived with absolutely no warning, couldn't mitigate those obligations in any way, as far as Bordelon was concerned. She not only repeated her demands for "adequate housing" at every meeting with any of Medusa's or Krietzmann's representatives but insisted her protests against her personnel's "mistreatment" be made part of the official record.

Clearly, she hoped her demands that her people should be properly treated (and the clear implication that they *weren't* being) would produce the image of a decisive flag officer, refusing to buckle before the brutality of her captors, despite the situation she faced through no fault of her own.

Michelle liked to think she would have had more on her mind than career damage control in Bordelon's place. In fairness, though, she had to admit there wasn't a lot else for Bordelon to be worrying about at the moment. Particularly since the Solarian knew perfectly well that Medusa and Krietzmann were doing everything humanly possible to see to her people's well-being. And it wasn't as if any of the Solarians were actually suffering. The islands Prime Minister Alquezar had designated as POW camps were all located in the planet Flax's tropics. With the moderating effect so much ocean exercised on temperature, those islands came about as close to having perfect climates as was physically possible. That might change during hurricane season, but hurricane season was months away, and proper housing and other support facilities were being constructed at an extraordinarily rapid pace. Yes, the majority of Bordelon's personnel were still under canvas, yet that was changing quickly, and not even Bordelon could complain about the food or the medical attention.

"No, I don't suppose I should expect her to *admit* it," Krietzmann said now, in response to Medusa's comment. "Doesn't make me any less tempted to wring her neck every time she opens her mouth, though!"

Krietzmann's Dresden accent was more pronounced than usual, and Michelle wondered if that was intentional. As the Quadrant's Minister of War, he was directly responsible for the coordination, maintenance, and management of the various planetary militias and the Quadrant Guard local defense force organized under the Quadrant's Constitution. It was a new departure for Manticore, but some the delegates to the Constitutional Convention had argued in favor of a locally raised and maintained military force to serve as backup for the Royal Navy, and the Grantville Government had agreed to it. For one thing, it would ease the burden on the Navy and the Royal Marines considerably, The Quadrant would also be responsible for maintaining the Quadrant Guard out of local tax revenues, which would prevent it from becoming a charge on the imperial treasury. And, finally, Grantville's agreement had recognized the unspoken truth that the maintenance of a local force would help Talbotters sleep more soundly at night. Not only would it *insure* that OFS wouldn't come calling while the rest of the Star Empire was distracted elsewhere, but it had been something of a sop to any local fears of "Manty tyranny" from the Old Star Kingdom's direction.

At the moment, however, it was Krietsmann's Guard which had responsibility for security where the POWs were concerned. That was enough to make Bordelon's protests especially irritating to him all by itself, but that particular irritation *wasn't* by itself. For some odd reason, TF 496's unprovoked onslaught on their capital system hadn't made Talbotters in general any fonder of Sollies, and Dresden's hatred for all things Solarian had burned hotter than most to begin with.

"I trust you haven't been as...forthright with Admiral Bordelon as you are with our cabinet colleagues, Henri," Minister of the Treasury Samiha Lababibi said dryly, and Krietzmann snorted a laugh.

"No, I haven't," he said. "Yet."

"Then we all have something to be grateful for," Prime Minister Alquezar observed. Alquezar, by far the tallest person seated at the table, turned to Admiral Augustus Khumalo. "And while Henri's doing his best to leave Bordelon's neck un-wrung, I believe you had something you and Admiral Gold Peak wanted to bring up, Admiral?"

"And which you would prefer to discuss rather than Minister Krietzmann's relationship with Admiral

Bordelon, Mr. Prime Minister?" Khumalo responded innocently.

Khumalo was a full head shorter than Alquezar, but the planet of San Miguel's gravity was only .84 g. For all his height, Alquezar looked almost frail beside the considerably more massive Khumalo.

"Admiral, I'd rather discuss almost *anything* rather than Henri's 'relationship' with Bordelon!" the prime minister said emphatically, and Krietzmann grinned. Then Alquezar's expression sobered. "And all humor aside, the truth is that at the moment the disposition of our naval forces is more important than just about anything else we *could* be discussing."

Khumalo nodded, then glanced at Michelle before he turned back to the other people at the conference table.

"Since Admiral Gold Peak is the commander of our mobile forces, I'll let her address the specifics of your question, Mr. Prime Minister. Before she does, though, I'd just like to emphasize that she and I have discussed the situation exhaustively, both between ourselves and with our squadron commanders, and with Minister Krietzmann and the members of his staff, as well. I don't think anyone's genuinely satisfied with the deployment stance we've come up with, but under the circumstances, I believe it's the best available to us."

He looked around the attentive faces, then back at Michelle.

"Milady?"

"Thank you, Sir," Michelle replied with rather more formality than had become the norm between her and the man who commanded Talbott Station. Then it was her turn to look around the table, making eye contact with the men and women responsible for the Quadrant's governance.

"Essentially," she began, "our problem is that while Admiral Khumalo and I believe we've decisively demonstrated our combat superiority, we simply don't have enough hyper-capable units to cover the entire Quadrant. I doubt anyone back at Admiralty House is any happier about that than we are, although I'll grant our unhappiness has a little more immediacy than theirs does. Unfortunately, I don't see any way the deployment priorities are going to change anytime soon. Given the combination of what's happened to the home system, the fact that we have no reason to believe at this time that the Sollies have an additional force anywhere near the size of Crandall's in our own vicinity, and the activation of Case Lacoön, there simply aren't any more ships for the Admiralty to send our way.

"So we have to make do with what we have, and while neither Admiral Khumalo nor I like that situation, it's one Queen's officers have had to deal with more often than we'd like to remember.

"After careful consideration, we've concluded that the best use of our current forces will be to cover each system of the Quadrant with four or five LAC squadrons for local defense, backed up by a couple of dispatch boats. The LACs should be more than adequate to deal with any 'pirate' stupid enough to come this way, and given what we've seen of SLN technology, they also ought to be able to deal with any Solly raiding force that doesn't include a core of capital ships. Given Crandall's losses, it's unlikely there are enough Solarian capital ships anywhere near the Quadrant to provide that kind of force. Obviously, that's subject to change—possibly without much warning—but even in a worst-case scenario, the local-defense LACs should be able to at least delay and harass any attackers while one of the dispatch boats goes for help.

"I realize there's been some thought of splitting up our own capital ships in order to give our star systems greater protection."

She carefully didn't look in the direction of the two men sitting on either side of Samiha Lababibi. Antonio Clark, from the Mainwaring System, was the Quadrant's Minister of Industry, while Clint Westman, a Montanan cousin of the famous (or infamous) Stephen Westman, headed the Ministry of the Interior. On the face of it, they should have been almost as unlikely allies of an oligarch like Lababibi as Krietzmann once had been, but the nature of their responsibilities gave them a certain commonality of viewpoint. Inevitably, all three were worried—deeply—about what would happen if the Quadrant's star systems were hit by anything like the Yawata Strike. Westman and Clark, especially, had argued in favor of dispersing Tenth Fleet to give every star system at least some protection. After all, they'd pointed out, the decisive superiority of the Manticoran Navy had been conclusively demonstrated, so the traditional risks of defeat in detail for dispersed units must be less applicable than usual.

Lababibi had found herself in the same camp, although she'd been a rather less fervent spokeswoman for their position.

"There are several reasons we're not proposing to do that," Michelle continued. "The two most important ones, though, are that dispersing our capital ships wouldn't provide any appreciable increase in system security against the sort of attack which hit the home system, but it *would* disperse the powerful, concentrated striking forces it's vital to maintain to respond to any fresh Solarian activity in our area.

"At the moment, the Admiralty and ONI are still working on how the Yawata Strike was launched. From the information available so far, Admiral Hemphill is more convinced than ever the attack relied on a new, previously unknown drive technology. In effect, we believe the attackers were 'invisible' to our normal tracking systems. So far, at least, no one's been able to suggest how whatever drive they used might work or how we might go about figuring out how to detect it in the future. In the meantime, however, analysis also suggests the attackers were probably operating in relatively small forces, relying on their cloak of invisibility rather than raw combat power. I realize that may sound absurd, given the damage inflicted, but I assure you that if a single podnought—or even a couple of *Nike*-class battlecruisers—had been able to get into range of the inner system totally undetected, that would have been ample to have inflicted all of that damage.

"My point is that the problem in Manticore wasn't lack of combat power or lack of defenses; it was the inability to see the enemy coming. Scattering wallers around the Quadrant's star systems isn't going to appreciably increase our ability to detect these people. We can deploy enough remote sensor platforms—in fact, we're already in the process of deploying them—to give each of our systems more detection capability than an entire squadron of SDs could provide. The LACs will give us large numbers of manned combat platforms to chase down and prosecute possible contacts; the dispatch boats will be available to send for help in the case of an attack in strength; and we'll be deploying enough missile pods in planetary orbit to provide the long-range missile firepower of at least a pair of SD(P)s in each system. We won't have the sort of *sustained* firepower superdreadnoughts could provide, or the area missile defense they could offer, but we'll have enough to deal with anything short of a Solly battle squadron, assuming we see it coming."

She paused, and this time she did look across the table at Lababibi, Clark, and Westman.

"I believe those deployments will give us at least as much defensive depth as splitting up my wallers could accomplish. In addition, however, it will permit Admiral Khumalo and me to concentrate my hyper-capable units into two striking forces, each with a powerful LAC element of its own. One will be deployed to Tillerman; the other will be based on Montana.

"Obviously, the Tillerman force will be closest to Monica and Meyers, which would normally be the most probable threat axis where any fresh Solarian adventures were concerned. Frankly, though, at the moment I'm not really very concerned about something coming at us out of the Madras Sector, given the fact that we just polished off seventy-plus *superdreadnoughts* that were stationed in that sector. It seems unlikely they have still more capital ships tucked away out here, even with Mesa and Manpower pulling every string they can reach.

"If the Sollies do decide they have anything else

to spare and send it our way, it's more likely to come in direct from the Core. That's why I'm planning on basing the second force at Montana to cover the Quadrant's flank, and the Lynx Terminus picket force will be available to cover any threat that might come in past Asgard. There are some arguments in favor of staying right here in Spindle instead of moving to Montana, given Spindle's more central location within the Quadrant, but so far Admiral Khumalo and I don't find them persuasive. To be honest, our objective is to get sufficient combat power—enough combat *density*—deployed across a broad front to permit me to respond quickly to dispatches from the star systems behind me while simultaneously positioning me to operate *offensively* into Solly and Mesan space, if that should become desirable."

She saw one or two sets of eyes flicker at the reference to Mesa. Not everyone in the Quadrant endorsed her own suspicions of Mesa and Manpower, Incorporated. It wasn't that anyone questioned Manpower's involvement in what had happened at Monica and New Tuscany. Nor did anyone in the Quadrant doubt Mesa's and Manpower's implacable (and thoroughly reciprocated) hostility towards the Star Empire. More than one of the people sitting around that table, though, remained of the opinion that Frontier Security (and possibly other interests within the League) had been using Manpower as a catspaw. Certainly that made more sense, in their view, than the possibility that a single outlaw transstellar corporation was using the entire *Solarian League* as a catspaw!

Most of the others were prepared to grant at least the possibility that Michelle and Khumalo and their staffs might be correct—that Manpower or the Mesa System might indeed have been the prime mover. Might even have provided the "invisible" starships which had carried out the Yawata Strike. Michelle doubted any of them found the notion any less bizarre than she did, but they were at least open to it. And if she was reading the ONI appreciations from home accurately, opinion within the Admiralty and the Grantville Government was hardening in the same direction. There was, however, a vast gap between "prepared to grant the possibility" and "willing to bet the farm on it," and she decided—again—not to go into all the details of the logic behind her proposed deployments.

She'd considered mentioning that she intended to base herself on Montana, closest to Mesa and what she believed was clearly the greater threat, while assigning the Tillerman force to Vice Admiral Theodore Bennington, who'd become her senior battle squadron commander upon his arrival from the home system. Under the circumstances, though, it would undoubtedly be wiser to let that particular sleeping dog lie. She didn't expect Alquezar or Krietzmann to object, anyway, and they were the Talbott decision-makers who really mattered where fleet movements were concerned.

"In addition to the deployment plan Admiral Gold Peak and I are proposing," Khumalo said after a moment, "there are certain other measures we'd like to set in motion. Three of them are especially important.

"First, as Prime Minister Alquezar, Minister Lababibi, Minister Krietzmann, Minister Clark, and I have already discussed, we need to complete our survey of the Quadrant's industrial capabilities as quickly as possible. I suspect our local resources may be able to contribute more materially to our defense here than some people might think. Nobody's going to be building any superdreadnoughts anytime soon, but several of our systems—Rembrandt, San Miguel, and Spindle itself come to mind—have sufficient local industry to provide significant support for both our local defense and striking forces. Obviously, we'll be making technical advisors from Admiral Gold Peak's repair and depot ships available wherever possible.

"Secondly, and possibly even more importantly, Admiral Gold Peak has proposed we begin a vigorous program to expedite the raising and training of naval personnel right here in the Quadrant. The Navy's taken substantial losses in both the Battle of Manticore and the Yawata Strike, and unless I'm sadly mistaken, the emphasis in the home system and Trevor's Star—where the bulk of our more...technologically sophisticated population is concentrated—is going to be on reconstituting our skilled labor force as rapidly as possible. I believe that, especially if we make use of the LAC simulators already available to us and request additional simulators from the home system, we'll be able to produce and train a significant number of naval personnel. To be painfully blunt—and I hope no one will take offense—providing personnel with the *education* level we would expect from the home system or Trevor's Star is going to be beyond our capabilities here for some time to come. Within the next several T-years, the effort being invested in improving the Quadrant's educational systems is going to correct that problem. For the immediately foreseeable future, however, it's going to remain with us. That means the personnel we'll be able to train won't be as *fully* trained as we might hope—won't have as deep a skill set, let's say—but they'll still provide a very useful expansion of our manpower, and the technical aspects of their education can be continued aboard ship.

"The third initiative we'd like to consider very seriously is for us to use the Quadrant Guard as the basis for an expansion of *planetary* combat troops. Manticore has never had a powerful ground combat component and, frankly, a lot of what we did have has become committed to Silesia. Not because there's a lot of armed resistance going on, but because we had to pretty much disband a sizable percentage of the existing Silesian forces when we started weeding out entrenched cronyism and military corruption. With them gone, we had no choice but to provide peacekeeping and law enforcement personnel—and cadre to train and supervise locally raised police forces—out of our none-too-large Marine and Army strength. That situation seems to be well in hand, but it's still going to tie up those Marines and Army personnel for many months to come.

"That diversion to Silesia is also the reason we've seen virtually no Army personnel transferred to the Quadrant. Well, that and the fact that the Quadrant isn't Silesia and—with the exception of Nordbrandt and a couple of other lunatics—we haven't faced anywhere near the same *need* for additional peacekeeping and law enforcement personnel as Silesia, particularly with the Guard in the course of formation. In addition, as we all know, our new-build construction is *very* short on organic Marine detachments, and Tenth Fleet's entire attached Marine strength amounts to little more than a pair of brigades. That's a lot of firepower, given their equipment and training, but it's a very limited total number of men and women. If the situation with the League turns as ugly as we think it may—if we find ourselves forced to carry out offensive operations against the League, for example—that shortage in troop strength is likely to come home to roost with a vengeance.

"Because of those considerations, we believe it would be a good idea to use the Guard as a platform to begin raising, training, and equipping at least several divisions of infantry and atmospheric combat support units right here in the Quadrant. We can teach the technical skills an effective ground force would require much more rapidly than we can train personnel in the sorts of shipboard skills the Navy will need. In addition, our existing infrastructure can produce planetary combat equipment as good as or better than anything we're likely to face out here in the Verge . . . and probably get it into the troops' hands in adequate quantities by the time we can get the necessary recruiting and training programs into place. Frankly, it may turn out that the provision of the ground forces we're almost certain to require may be the most effective immediate contribution to the Star Empire's overall defense that the Quadrant can provide. And, finally, while the skills we'll have to teach our planetary combat forces aren't the same ones the Navy requires, they'll still represent a powerful step upward for a lot of our member star systems here in the Quadrant—one which is going to carry over to their peacetime economies once the shooting ends.

"In addition to the actual increase in manpower and eventual overall education and training levels, however, the sort of programs we're proposing should also contribute to the Quadrant's sense of solidarity and unity and that, after all, is one reason for the Guard's existence in the first place. We all know this is still a new political unit. We're all still . . . settling down with one another, and the threat of outside attack is generating a lot of fully justified anxiety and uncertainty. We believe—*I* believe—that directly involving as many as possible of our citizens in their own self-defense will be the best antidote for that anxiety. We're not proposing this as any sort of placebo. If it succeeds as well as we believe it can, it *will* contribute materially to our ability to defend the Quadrant and probably to the overall defensive strength of the Star Empire *outside* the Quadrant. For that matter, I personally would strongly oppose any dispersal of effort that *wouldn't* contribute to that ability and combat strength. I'm simply pointing out that it could contribute in more ways than one."

There was silence for several seconds, then Prime Minister Alquezar looked at Baroness Medusa.

"I'm inclined to endorse Admiral Khumalo's and Admiral Gold Peak's proposals, Madame Governor. I know Henri's already had considerable input into them, and while I'd like the opportunity to read over the details for myself, I have the greatest respect for both Admiral Khumalo's and Admiral Gold Peak's judgment. With your concurrence, I'd like to suggest we authorize them to begin organizing to deploy Admiral Gold Peak's units as they've proposed and that you and I review those details with an eye towards giving them a firm approval—and requesting the Quadrant Parliament's approval for the necessary funding, of course—within the next two days."

"That seems perfectly reasonable to me, Mr. Prime Minister," Medusa agreed. "And that ought to give everyone else involved"—she allowed her own gaze to slew sideways to Lababibi, Clark, and Westman for a moment—"enough time to review them and put forward any suggestions they might care to make, as well."

"In that case," Alquezar said with a somewhat crooked smile, "I propose we adjourn. I'll see all of you at the War Cabinet meeting Wednesday, I'm sure. By which time, no doubt, the ghost of Murphy will have visited yet another crisis upon us."

Chapter Eight

"YOU KNOW," MICHELLE HENKE said thoughtfully, tipped back in her chair with her feet propped somewhat inelegantly on the coffee table, "these Sollies are beginning to severely piss me off."

"No, really?" Captain Cynthia Lecter raised her eyebrows. "I find that difficult to believe, Ma'am."

Michelle chuckled, although the sound was a bit sour, then glanced up as Chris Billingsley appeared with Lecter's whiskey glass and Michelle's own bottle of beer. Over the years, she'd developed a pronounced preference for Honor Harrington's favorite, Old Tillman. In fact, her friend had actually converted her to the barbarism of drinking it chilled, and she smiled as she accepted the cold bottle from her steward, then made a face as Dicey hopped up into her lap. The cat landed with a pronounced thump, butted her chest twice with his broad, scarred head, then settled down possessively with a deep, rumbling purr.

"This monster is *your* cat, isn't it, Chris?" she demanded.

"Yes, Ma'am," Billingsley acknowledged imperturbably.

"I just wondered," she said, rubbing Dicey between the ears in token of abject surrender. "Thanks for clearing that up."

"You're welcome, Ma'am." Billingsley smiled benignly and withdrew, and Michelle shook her head and returned her attention to Khumalo.

"As I was saying, these Sollies are beginning to get on my nerves. And I wish to hell I understood what Dueñas thinks he's going to accomplish with this."

"Assuming our information about what he's supposed to've done is correct, of course, Ma'am," Lecter pointed out.

"I realize we have to keep our minds open to all possibilities, Cynthia, but say that again with a straight face," Michelle challenged. "Just what mistake have the Sollies passed up making that would encourage that sort of optimism?"

"I can't think of one right off hand," Lecter acknowledged, "but that's not to say they couldn't have avoided at least one somewhere without our noticing."

"Maybe so, but I'm not inclined to believe it was in Saltash."

Michelle's tone was darker, her expression less amused, and her chief of staff nodded in less than delighted agreement.

Michelle nodded back and sipped beer, continuing to rub Dicey's head, as she contemplated the latest unpleasant decision to land on her desk.

I suppose we're lucky Lörscher was on his way to Montana anyway and decided to share the news with us, she thought.

Michelle and her detachment of Tenth Fleet had

arrived in Montana less than three days ago, and she was still in the process of settling down to her new duty station. She'd visited Montana before, on her initial swing through the Talbott Quadrant back before everything had gone to hell in a handbasket, but it had been a brief visit, little more than a quick look in. This time, unless (or, rather, *until*) something else went wrong, she'd be here for a while, and she'd plunged into a round of courtesy calls with the local system government and the local business sector. Along the way, she'd met—briefly—the infamous Stephen Westman. Abbreviated although their meeting had been, she'd recognized a kindred soul in Westman; they were both the sort of people who had a tendency to demolish obstacles with the handiest blunt instrument. Stubborn, too, the both of them.

She was also getting a better feel for the system's economy, and she'd begun to understand why Montana had been one of the more affluent of the old Talbott Sector star systems. Montana beef was among the best Michelle had ever tasted, and the system's location put it within a couple of hundred light years of over a dozen other star systems. For that matter, it was only two hundred and ten light-years from the Mesa Terminus, which had given it direct access to the heart of the Solarian League and the Core Worlds' spoiled, wealthy gourmands even before the Lynx Terminus' discovery. Two light-centuries wasn't all that far for the fast freighters which served the meat packing trade, and Montana shipped literally millions of tons of beef a month. None of which even considered the ranchers' ability to penetrate new markets now that Lynx *had* been discovered.

Always assuming the entire explored galaxy didn't decide to blow itself straight to hell, of course.

What mattered at the moment, however, was that it was Montana's beef production which had brought Captain Li-hau Lörscher, of the Andermani freighter *Angelika Thörnich*, to the star system. He hadn't expected to see a full squadron of Manticoran ships-of-the-wall—not to mention battlecruisers, CLACs, cruisers, destroyers, and supply ships—waiting for him here, but he'd grabbed the opportunity with both hands.

"You know, Ma'am," Lecter said after a moment, "it could all be misinformation."

"I thought about that," Michelle acknowledged, sipping more beer, but then she shrugged. "Lörscher seems to be exactly who he says he is, though. And he's got a half dozen regular suppliers here in Montana who're prepared to vouch for him." She shook her head. "Someone who's been on the same run for over ten T-years isn't likely to be a plant, and he's got a wife and family back in the Empire. It's not as if he could just disappear afterward if he'd decided to sell us a bill of goods. Besides, I don't think Emperor Gustav would be especially happy with him if it turned out he was deliberately passing us false information. It might land not only us but the Andermani in the middle of a fresh manipulated incident with the Sollies, and I sort of doubt Gustav's going to be real eager about joining an anti-League crusade even if he is currently our ally against Haven. For that matter, there's the question of who'd want to 'misinform' us about something like this. I agree healthy suspicion is indicated, especially given everything that's already gone down out here, but still..."

She shrugged again, and her chief of staff nodded slowly. Lecter's expression remained troubled, though, and her eyes were thoughtful as she took a sip of whiskey.

"I agree Lörscher's probably exactly who he says he is, Ma'am, and I'll agree that *I* wouldn't want to be the Andermani merchant skipper who pissed off the Emperor by lying to his allies. That doesn't automatically mean he isn't, though. And what sticks in my mind is that if Manpower or Mesa really has been manipulating things out this way, feeding us something that would draw us into a potential—*another* potential—incident with the Sollies might suit their playbook just fine."

"The thought had crossed my own mind," Michelle agreed.

"Well, if that's what this is, then Lörscher very probably could be telling us the truth...insofar as he knows it, that is. *He* could have been lied to and sent out to lie to us, though. For that matter, if the Saltash System governor's in Mesa's pocket like Verrocchio—or even like New Tuscany was, when you come down to it—Lörscher could be telling us the truth about what actually happened and it could still be a trap designed to draw us into yet another confrontation with the League."

"Agreed." Michelle nodded more grimly, but her tone was firm.

It was one of Lecter's functions to look for the hidden hook inside any potential bait that came Tenth Fleet's way. And God knew there'd been enough skulduggery over the last several months to turn anyone paranoid. In fact, the truth was that despite her own

comment to Lecter, she could readily see how whoever was manipulating the situation might relish the
possibility of piling another incident with the Solarian
League onto the fire. Unfortunately...

"I think we have to assume Lörscher's telling the
truth," she said. "And one of the reasons I'm inclined
to think this isn't deliberate misinformation on anyone's
part is that Montana's where Lörscher was headed all
along, but no one could've known *we'd* be here when
he got here. He'd probably have passed the information along anyway, but it would've taken two weeks for
a dispatch boat to get word back to Spindle even if
Montana had one ready to go on zero notice. If they
wanted to draw us into doing something unfortunate,
I think they would have sent their messenger directly
to either Spindle or Lynx, where they could've been
sure of finding the Navy waiting for them and drawing a quicker response."

"There is that, Ma'am," Lecter acknowledged.

"And, frankly, the bottom line is that it doesn't
matter whether or not this is a set up," Michelle said
in a harsher tone. "Either Dueñas really has started
impounding our merchies, or he hasn't. Whoever we
send is going to have to mind his feet and be sure
he doesn't step on any tender Solly sensibilities if
this *is* some sort of misinformation. But if it's not—if
Dueñas *has* done what Lörscher says he has—then I
really don't care who put him up to it."

Lecter's eyes widened in alarm, and Michelle chuckled coldly.

"I'm not going all berserk on you, Cynthia," she
said. "But the bottom line is that one of our primary
missions ever since there's been a Navy has always

been the protection of Manticoran commerce. Nothing in any orders I've seen has changed that. And they haven't put any limitations on who we're supposed to protect our commerce and our merchant spacers *from*, either. I don't know if this was Dueñas' own brainstorm or if someone put him up to it, and it doesn't matter, when you come down to it. Maybe it *is* an effort to create a deliberate provocation, but even if it is, it's one we can't ignore or back away from. And to be perfectly honest, I don't want to, either." She showed her teeth. "In fact, that's one of the main reasons I haven't already jumped on it. I wanted to make sure I had myself on a short enough leash to give some *thought* to it, first."

"I've known you a while, Ma'am," Lecter observed. "And if you'll pardon my saying so, it sounds to me like you've done most of the thinking you intend to do."

"Yep." Michelle gave Dicey's head another rub and nodded her own. "I think this should be right up Zavala's alley. And a destroyer squadron—especially one that's a little understrength—will be a lot less threatening than a division of battlecruisers."

"Do you think five tincans will be enough to convince a Solly system governor to back down?"

"When they're bigger than most Solly light cruisers, I think the odds are probably pretty damned good," Michelle said. "And I'd prefer to tailor our response to the nature of the mission. I don't want to use any bigger club than we have to, which is one reason I'm thinking Zavala would be a good choice. He won't take any crap, but he's not going to come in throwing around threats until he's at least tried to get them to see reason. And, to be honest, I can't really afford to start slicing off detachments of cruisers or battlecruisers—not when the whole notion is to maintain a concentrated force here in Montana."

And not when I don't know when the next Lörscher's likely to turn up with somewhere else I need to send a detachment, she added silently.

"I follow your logic, Ma'am," Lecter said, which wasn't precisely the same thing as saying she *agreed* with it, Michelle noted. "Should I assume you want to speak to Zavala personally before we send him off?"

"I definitely do." Michelle nodded firmly. "This isn't something you send someone off to do without making damned sure she understands her orders, and that those orders are going to cover her backside if it all goes south on her."

"Understood, Ma'am," Lecter replied, although the chief of staff could think of quite a few flag officers she'd known who would've been more concerned with covering *their* own backsides than that of the officer they'd designated to carry out a mission like this one.

"Good." Michelle took a final pull at her beer, then leaned forward and set the empty bottle on the coffee table. Dicey gave her a disgusted look as her lap moved under him, then relented and gave her a parting head butt of affection before he hopped down. She smiled as the cat meandered out, then looked back at Lecter. "I'd like to have him underway within the next twelve hours."

"I'll see to it, Ma'am." The chief of staff tossed back the last of her whiskey and set the glass beside Michelle's bottle. Then she rose, nodded respectfully to Michelle, and headed for the day cabin's door.

Michelle watched her go, then she climbed out of

her own chair and keyed the holo display above her desk, frowning at the steadily blinking icon of the star called Saltash.

I sure as hell hope *it isn't some kind of set up, Cynthia,* she thought after her vanished chief of staff. *I talk a good stiff upper lip and all that, but I really, really don't want to step into it all over again with the damned Sollies.*

It was like picking her way without a map through a waist-deep swamp she knew was filled with patches of quicksand and poorly fed alligators. There was so damned much treachery, so many crosscurrents of deception, so much Solarian arrogance and resentment, and so many things which could go disastrously wrong. The temptation was to fort up, go strictly onto the defensive to avoid the kind of mistakes which could only make the situation worse. But as she'd told Lecter, that wasn't an option in this case. If Lörscher was right about what was going on in Saltash, Michelle had to act.

And I hope to hell this doesn't go as badly for Zavala's squadron as things went for it in New Tuscany, too, she thought.

✧ Chapter Nine

"I DON'T LIKE IT," Rosa Shuman said, sitting well back in the outrageously comfortable, thronelike chair behind her desk. She was turned half away from her single guest, looking out through her office windows over the capital city which had been named (with dubious humor) "Capistrano" by the colony's original settlers. "I don't like it at all. Those Allenby yahoos have always been too big for their britches."

"*I'm* not going to argue with you about that, Rosa," General Felicia Karaxis replied in the sort of tone very few other people would have dared use with the president of the Swallow System Republic. Felicia Karaxis wasn't "other people," though. She commanded the Swallow System Army, and since Swallow had a unified military, that meant she also commanded the security forces responsible for keeping one President Rosa Shuman seated in that thronelike chair. She also knew where most of the bodies were buried on Swallow... especially given how many of them she'd planted herself.

"I've been telling you for years that we needed to go in there and clean them out," Karaxis continued, leaning back in her own chair and reaching into her tunic's inside pocket for one of the thin cigars she favored. She found one, extracted it, and began peeling it out of its sealed wrap as she continued. "Let me make a sweep through their damned mountains with air cav and infantry. *I'll* sort the bastards out!"

"Believe me, I'd love to let you," Shuman replied, although if she was going to be honest she was a bit less confident than Karaxis about just how simple it would be to "sort the bastards out." She hated the entire Allenby clan with a pure and burning intensity not even Karaxis could match, but she wasn't going to take them lightly.

"I'd love to let you," she continued, "but Parkman and those other bastards over at Tallulah don't want us spoiling the tourist trade."

"Tourist trade!" Karaxis snorted harshly, exhaling smoke. "If I were him, I'd be a lot more worried over what Floyd and Jason might send to visit *him* than over getting out for a little skiing!"

Shuman rolled her gray eyes. Felicia might be a bit short on tact, she thought, but she did have a way of cutting to the heart of things. And if it had been possible for there to be anyone in the entire Swallow System more hated than Rosa Shuman, it would probably have been Alton Parkman, the Tallulah Corporation's system manager. Hell! *Shuman* hated his guts, for that matter! Not that she was in much of a position to do anything about it.

At the same time, she had to admit Parkman did have a point...of sorts, at least. Swallow wasn't a particularly wealthy star system, and the Tallulah Corporation wasn't much as Solarian transstellars went. Of course, even a relatively poverty-stricken star system represented a very large amount of money, and as the system's legal president—duly appointed as vice president by her since deceased husband, Donnie, and his legal successor under the constitution he'd personally drafted—Shuman was in a position to skim off quite a bit of it. Parkman was in an even better position, since Tallulah (like quite a few of the transstellars) was prepared to wink at its managerial personnel's graft, tax evasion, and outright theft as long as they continued to show a healthy bottom line. It was Tallulah's version of an incentive program.

Swallow basically represented a captive market for Tallulah, whose faithful minions Donnie and Rosa Shuman had crafted a tariff policy guaranteed to close anyone else out of the system's economy. Of course, Donnie had gotten a bit too greedy later and tried to insist on taking a bigger slice of the pie, which was how he'd come to suffer that tragic air accident and Rosa had tearfully inherited the presidency. Aside from her husband's untimely demise, however, Rosa had little about which to complain. She knew that, and she was perfectly happy to settle for Donnie's original deal with Tallulah and OFS. A population of over four billion human beings, forbidden the opportunity to trade with anyone else, could produce a *very* healthy bottom line, with plenty to go around, and Swallow had done just that for Tallulah for the better part of fifty T-years. But the "tourist trade" Parkman was worried about added another nice, solid chunk of change to the Tallulah balance sheets.

The Cripple Mountains were among the more spectacular mountain ranges in explored space. Broken Back Mountain, the Cripples' tallest peak, was almost two hundred and fifty meters taller than Old Earth's Mount Everest, and three more of the Cripples' mountains were at least as tall as Everest. The rest of the mountain range was scaled to match, providing superlative skiing, some of the most rugged and towering (and beautiful) scenery in the galaxy, and opportunities for mountaineering, camping, hunting, and fishing in a genuinely unspoiled wilderness paradise. True, that same "wilderness paradise" could kill the unwary in a heartbeat, yet that only added to its appeal for the true aficionado, and Tallulah Travel Interstellar had a complete lock on *that* part of the system's economy, as well.

Unfortunately, the descendants of the people who'd homesteaded the Cripple Mountains were about as hard to tame as the mountains themselves, and Floyd Allenby was a case in point.

"I'm telling you, Rosa," Karaxis said, jabbing the air with her cigar as if it were a pointer or a swagger stick, "sooner or later we're going to *have* to go in to deal with the Allenbys, and the longer we put it off, the worse it's going to be when we do. Let me go in quick and dirty and will see how long this 'Cripple Mountain Movement' of theirs lasts!"

Shuman considered pointing out that it had been Karaxis' security people who'd killed Floyd Allenby's wife eight T-years ago. To be fair, they hadn't meant to. Sandra Allenby's air car had simply happened to be in the wrong place at the wrong time. In fact, Shuman had acknowledged that Sandra's death had been a terrible accident and offered a very generous financial settlement. Unfortunately, Floyd Allenby didn't seem to think a surface-to-air missile came under the heading of "accidents," and he'd wanted blood, not money. A lot of those Cripple Mountains rednecks thought that way. In fact, his entire damned family seemed to agree with him.

"Felicia," the president said, "we can't afford to kill off Allenbys in job lots—especially right now—for a lot of reasons. You know the way they think. If we go in after any of them, we have to go after *all* of them, and the effect of eliminating the biggest, most highly skilled, and most *profitable* group of guides would *not* make our Mr. Parkman very happy. And to be honest, I don't think your people would really enjoy going after them on their own ground. I don't doubt you could deal with them in the end," she continued quickly (and not entirely accurately) when she saw Karaxis' expression, "but it wouldn't be a pleasant experience and I'm pretty sure it would take longer than either of us would believe at this point. Even worse, they aren't exactly the only bunch up in those mountains who'd raise all kinds of hell if you went after them the way you'd have to to make them give up Floyd or the others."

Karaxis growled something unintelligible around her cigar, eyes angry, but she couldn't very well dispute what Shuman had just said.

"Besides," the redhaired president continued, "as near as we can tell, even the Allenbys are still split over whether or not they should be supporting Floyd. All of them hate our guts, but for right now at least a majority of the clan doesn't seem to feel that going up against us openly is a winning strategy."

"Because they aren't all *completely* crazy after all," Karaxis grunted. "If they ever come out in the open where we can get at them, we'll chop them into husky bait!"

"I'm sure that's a factor in their thinking," Shuman agreed. "The problem is that they're so damn bloody-minded. If we step on their toes hard enough, they may just decide they don't care how ugly things could get. Don't forget what old Simon was like!"

That reminder seemed to give even Karaxis pause, and the general nodded soberly.

"At least Floyd never got prolong in time," Shuman continued. "He's—what? Thirty? Thirty-five?—by now. Give him a few more T-years, and he's likely to decide this 'liberation movement' of his is a game for younger men. Looked at that way, time's on our side, wouldn't you say?"

Karaxis gave an unconvinced-looking nod. Shuman suspected the general was thinking about Simon Allenby, Floyd's grandfather. Old-age hadn't slowed Simon up noticeably. According to tradition—and Shuman was pretty sure the tradition was correct—Simon Allenby had fought his last duel at the tender age of ninety.

And he'd won.

Handily.

Hadn't even had to kill his opponent, only crippled him for life.

"Either way, Felicia," the president said with a shrug, "I couldn't greenlight that kind of operation right now even if I were completely convinced it was a good idea. Not with that pain-in-the-ass Luther and his other Nixon Foundation buddies here in the system."

Karaxis' frown turned into an active glower. Shuman understood perfectly, since she, too, would have liked nothing better than to arrange a creative (and hopefully fatal) accident for Jerome Luther and the rest of the Nixon Foundation team investigating all those ridiculous allegations of human rights violations here in Swallow. She would have gone ahead and authorized the accident without hesitation if Parkman hadn't warned her that the Nixon Foundation's expedition was being financed by one of Tallulah's competitors in hopes of turning up something egregious enough to justify Frontier Security intervention. Tallulah was currently involved in a bidding war to buy OFS off, but until that was resolved, they had to be cautious about creating pretexts Frontier Security could use to mandate régime change . . . and hand Swallow (and its cash flow) over to someone else. Or, even worse, turn the entire system into a direct OFS protectorate, which would put the bulk of the system economy straight into Frontier Security's pocket.

"That's why I said I don't like it," Shuman continued. "If we let ourselves be provoked into a large-scale operation in the Cripples, it's bound to get out and that busybody from Nixon will jump right onto it. I think he genuinely believes his foundation can 'make a difference' out here, and if we give him a toehold . . ."

She let her voice trail off and shrugged, and Karaxis glowered some more.

"All right," the general said finally. "I understand your reasoning, and I don't want to upset the apple cart any more than anyone else does. But if these rumors my people are picking up are accurate—if Allenby and the others are genuinely planning to start some kind of active guerrilla campaign—we're going to have to respond. And when we do, it's going to escalate. That's why I'm still convinced it would be better to go in fast and hard now, break as many eggs as we have to to nip this thing in the bud, instead of letting it drag on and turn into something even bigger and messier."

"I agree there's a risk of that happening, and I've pointed that out to Parkman. His theory is that as long as we restrict ourselves to reactions to the other side's provocations, we can pass it off as a standard law enforcement response to criminals, not a military campaign against some kind of political resistance organization. To be honest, I think what he's really hoping is that Luther and those other Nixon pests will get tired and go home before this reaches the messy stage. Once we get them out of here, I'll be a lot more willing to go ahead and turn you loose. We just need to keep a lid on things for a few more T-months. Maybe a whole T-year."

"*I'm* willing to keep a lid on it," Karaxis said sardonically. "The question is whether or not *Allenby* is!"

❖   ❖   ❖

"What do you reckon the odds really are, Floyd?" Jason MacGruder asked.

"Odds of what?" Floyd Allenby hawked up a gobbet of phlegm and spat it into the campfire. "Whether or not it's going to snow? Or what the snow bear hunting's going to be like this year?"

"How 'bout whether or not we're gonna be alive this time *next* year?" MacGruder suggested.

"Oh, that." Allenby shrugged and looked back down at the snowshoe he was mending. "Couldn't tell you that, Jason. Looks to me like there's only one way to find out."

"Figured that was what you were gonna say," Mac-Gruder said gloomily, and Allenby smiled down at his work.

MacGruder was his second cousin, with the same brown hair and brown eyes—not to mention the beak-like Allenby nose—although MacGruder favored the tall and lanky side of the family while Allenby came from its compact, broad shouldered, fireplug side. There wasn't much to choose between them in a lot of ways, but MacGruder did have a positive gift for looking on the gloomy side.

Not that there was all that much of a side that *wasn't* gloomy at the moment.

Allenby finished replacing the broken rawhide lacing, knotted it, and carefully trimmed off the excess length. He set the repaired shoe aside and leaned closer to the fire to pour a cup of coffee from the battered black pot. Then he sat back again, leaning against the flat stone face which helped to both conceal their fire and to reflect its heat back into their tiny encampment.

"You know," MacGruder said in a thoughtful tone, leaning back against his own bedroll and folding his arms behind his head, "our mighty liberation movement's bitten off quite a mouthful here, Floyd."

"Yep," Allenby agreed.

"'Pears to me we're just a tad outnumbered," Mac-Gruder continued. "Something like, what, around three or four thousand to one?"

"'Bout that."

"With air cars, recon drones, sting ships, armored

personnel carriers, tribarrels. Heck, Floyd, they've even got tanks, I hear!"

"Heard that, too," Allenby agreed, sipping the scalding hot coffee.

"Don't think those odds might be a little steep even for an Allenby, do you?"

"Maybe just a *little*."

MacGruder made a disgusted sound, but his lips twitched, and Allenby smiled down into his cup. Then he stopped smiling and looked back up.

"The truth is, Jason," he said much more seriously, "this is probably a losing hand. You sure you want to sit in?"

"You don't want to go around insulting people by asking a man a question like that," MacGruder pointed out, looking up at the huge, brilliant starscape above the Cripple Mountains' thin atmosphere.

"I'm serious, Jason. I think we've got a chance, or I wouldn't be doing this, but having *a* chance isn't the same as having a *good* chance."

"And what does Vinnie have to say about that?" MacGruder inquired politely.

"You *know* what Vinnie has to say about it." Allenby's voice was suddenly harsher and much colder than it had been, and a look of apology filled MacGruder's eyes as they flicked to his cousin's face.

Vincent Frugoni was the brother of Sandra Frugoni Allenby, Floyd Allenby's dead wife. Like Sandra, he'd been born off-world. He'd been ten T-years younger than Sandra when Dr. Frugoni had come out to Swallow after their parents' deaths. Sandra had been in the Tallulah Corporation's employ at the time, but it hadn't taken her long to realize what was going on in Swallow, at which point she'd resigned and set up her own practice in the Cripples. Vincent had been delighted with her decision, and they'd both always felt comfortable around the stubborn, hard-working, bloody-minded folk of the Cripple Mountains. In fact Vincent was even more stubborn and bloody-minded than most of Swallow's clansmen. In a lot of ways, killing his sister had been just as big a mistake as killing Floyd Allenby's wife.

Leave it to that bitch Karaxis to piss both *of them off with one frigging SAM,* MacGruder thought now. *And me, too, come to that.*

Blood and family meant a lot up in the Cripples. Sandra Allenby had been as treasured for who she was as for her medical skills or the fact that she'd married one of their own, and MacGruder was an old-fashioned clansman, just like Allenby himself. He'd have rallied around his cousin even if he'd never met Sandra, but like everyone else who'd known her, he'd loved her. It would have been personal for him, anyway, but he was honest enough to admit to himself that it was even more personal than it might have been.

"What I meant, Floyd," he said in a softer, less bantering tone, "was whether or not Vinnie thinks we can pull it off, not whether or not it's a good idea."

"To be honest, I'm not sure whether or not he thinks we can actually bring Shuman and Karaxis down," Allenby admitted after a moment. "I think he's convinced we can at least make both of them wish they'd never been born, but actually knock off the government?" He shrugged. "That's a lot steeper order. All I can say is he thinks there's at least a chance, and if this contact of his comes through for

us, we may have a lot *better* chance than I thought
we did when we started."

"Makes a man a little nervous counting on 'contacts'
he's never met," MacGruder observed.

"Naw." Allenby shook his head. "Doesn't make a
man a *little* nervous, Jason. Not 'less he's the kind
of idiot couldn't count to eleven without taking his
shoes off, anyway."

MacGruder chuckled, although in his saner moments
he knew Allenby was right about that. At the moment,
their Cripple Mountain Movement consisted of a
grand and glorious total of just under four hundred
volunteers. Given the imbalance between the imported
equipment of Karaxis' military and the civilian weaponry
available to them, angering even that many enough to
step forward had been a monumental achievement on
the Shuman Administration's part. And virtually all of
those four hundred were Cripple Mountains clansmen
and women, which meant that even family members
unwilling to take up arms themselves would greet any
outside pursuers or investigators with hostile, willful
ignorance of the guerrillas' whereabouts.

Some of the CMM's members wanted to open a
large-scale campaign of attacks on the Tallulah Corporation's infrastructure, but for the moment, Allenby was
restricting their operations to keeping their mountainous
stronghold free of the system security forces. There'd
been perhaps a dozen serious clashes between his people
and Karaxis' over the last local year or so, and their
frequency seemed to be accelerating, yet they were
still the exception, not the rule. In fact, most of them
had been the result of accidental collisions between the
two sides, not something either of them had planned.

Things had begun to accelerate in other ways, though—especially since First Sergeant Vincent Frugoni, Solarian Marine Corps (retired) had returned to Swallow. Frugoni shared his dead sister's blond hair and blue eyes, and his face, while undeniably masculine, was an almost painful reminder of Sandra. He was also—as his sister had been—a prolong recipient, which neither Allenby nor MacGruder was. Twenty years older than either of them, he looked more like someone's adolescent brother than the tough, decidedly nasty character he was, and he kept a well honed artfully innocent expression ready for instant use at need.

He'd also spent twenty-seven T-years in the Solarian Marines, rising to the second highest noncommissioned rank available, and under his tutelage the four hundred members of the CMM had attained a level of training and tactical sophistication light-years ahead of the majority of Felicia Karaxis' so-called soldiers.

That wasn't enough to offset the imbalance in the equipment and technical capabilities available to the two sides, of course. Although . . .

"Tell me true, Floyd," MacGruder said finally, his expression unwontedly sober. "You know I'm with you all the way, however it works out. Bastards've got it coming, and I'm ready to give it to them, however it comes out at the finish line. But do you really think these people—these 'Manties'—are ready to help out?"

"I don't know. Not really," Allenby admitted, returning honesty for honesty. "If half the stuff we're hearing is true, they're going to need every edge they can get, though. Makes sense to me they'd want to . . . distract the Sollies' attention, and you know as well as I do how it really works out here. Frontier Security's not backing

Tallulah just because of that asshole Parkman's beautiful eyes! They're getting a cut from every credit Tallulah rakes off from Swallow, and if the League's got a real war on its hands for the first time in its life, it's going to need all the cash it can squeeze out of the Protectorates...and us. So if the Manties can make it hard for them to do that, it's got to help Manticore, right?"

"Even I can get that far," MacGruder said dryly. "What bothers me is whether or not they're going to give a fart in a windstorm what finally happens to *us*."

"Fair enough." Allenby nodded. "And while I'm being fair, why *should* they give a fart in a windstorm? They don't know us, and they sure as hell don't *owe* us anything! But the truth is, it's not going to take a lot of effort on their part to provide us with the guns and the support weapons we'd need to take Karaxis on. It's not like we're going to be some kind of long-term heavy burden on them. In fact, this is about the cheapest way they can get into the Sollies' henhouse, when you come down to it. And if they promise to help us and then don't come through—if they don't provide what they've agreed to and just leave us hanging—it's going to get out. I'm thinking anyone ballsy enough to take on the League isn't going to want the rest of the galaxy to think they just use up allies and throw them away. Might make sense to them in the *short* term, but in the long term it'd do them a *lot* of damage with all the independent star systems. And if they're going to survive facing up to the League, they can't afford to piss off the independents, Jason. They're going to need access to markets out here to replace the ones they're going to lose in the League. And they're going to need allies, not just trading partners. Somehow I don't think someone who goes around screwing people over and then throwing them to the ogre wolves is going to find a lot of people willing to stick their necks out for them against something like the League."

MacGruder's eyebrows rose. Sometimes, listening to his cousin speak, Allenby's rustic mountain accent could fool even him into forgetting the acuity of the brain behind those brown eyes. But then Floyd would come up with a piece of analysis like that and remind him.

"I'm not saying the Manties are going to back us out of the pure goodness of their hearts any more than I think OFS is backing Tallulah because they love Parkman so much," Allenby continued. "I'm just saying we both have reasons to be pissed off as hell at Frontier Security, and if it makes sense to the Manties to go after Shuman and Karaxis—*and* Parkman—here in Swallow, it makes sense to me to let them help us do it."

"Put that way, makes sense to me, too," MacGruder admitted after a moment. He considered for several more seconds what his cousin had said, then he cocked his head.

"So when do we expect to hear back from Vinnie?" he asked.

"Sometime in the next week or so." Allenby refilled his coffee cup again. "I don't think Karaxis even realizes Vinnie's back on-planet, but the only place he could make contact is in Capistrano, so we're not going to know how it went until he's had time to get back here without attracting anyone's attention. So"—he shrugged—"about a week or so."

"And just how are the Manties planning on getting weapons shipments through to us when Tallulah controls all the traffic into and out of Swallow?" MacGruder sounded as much honestly curious as skeptical, and Allenby snorted a laugh.

"Damned if I know!" he admitted cheerfully. "That's up to Vinnie and this Manty super secret agent he's hooked up with." He shrugged. "If Mr. 'Firebrand' can come up with a way to get the guns to us, though, I'm pretty sure we'll be able to figure out what to do with them after he does."

✧ Chapter Ten

"WELL, HOSEA, I HOPE you've completed your homework assignment," Naomi Kaplan said dryly as HMS *Tristram* bored through hyper-space, twelve hours after leaving Montana orbit. "I'd like to sound like I've got *some* clue what I'm talking about for the Commodore's conference."

"I wouldn't say I'm happy about the amount of detail I've managed to turn up, Skipper," Lieutenant Hosea Simpkins, *Tristram's* astrogator replied with a wry smile. "I've pulled everything I could find out of the files, but Tester knows it isn't much."

"Somehow, I'm not surprised." Commander Kaplan shrugged and leaned back in her chair at the head of the briefing room's conference table. "Go ahead and give us what you've got, though."

"Yes, Ma'am." Kaplan's Grayson-born astrogator didn't bother to consult his notes. "Technically, Saltash's an independent star system. Actually, it's been an OFS client for about sixty T-years. The single habitable planet is called Cinnamon. Orbital radius is about nine light-minutes, population's just under two-point-five billion.

Planetary diameter's only point-nine-six Old Earth, but gravity's almost a full standard gravity, so it's obviously a little denser than most. Hydrosphere is right on seventy-three percent, and its axial inclination's only nine degrees, so it sounds like a fairly nice place to live.

"Unfortunately, the local political structure was a real mess sixty or seventy T-years back. The Republic of McPhee and the Republic of Lochore both claimed to be the sole legitimate system government, and they'd fought two or three wars without settling things. They were headed towards another war, and all indications were it was going to be a really ugly affair this time around, when the president of MacPhee called in Frontier Security to play referee."

"Where have we heard this story before?" Lieutenant Commander Alvin Tallman muttered with a scowling expression.

"I hate to say it, Sir," Simpkins told *Tristram's* executive officer, "but in this case OFS really did end up doing one of the things it was ostensibly created to do. I'm not saying it did it out of the goodness of its heart, you understand, but if the League hadn't intervened, McPhee and Lochore were probably getting ready to pretty well sterilize Cinnamon. That's how bitter the situation had gotten."

"Any idea *why* things were that bad, Hosea?" Kaplan asked, her eyes intent, and Simpkins shrugged.

"Not really, Ma'am. Given the intensity of the last war they actually fought, these people were as unreasonable as we Graysons were before we exiled the Faithful to Masada, but it doesn't seem like religion was behind the antagonism in Saltash's case. The only thing I can tell you for sure is that the two sides had obviously hated each other for a long time, and it looks like they'd simply reached the point of being so pissed off, if you'll pardon my language, that they were ready to pull the trigger even knowing there was a pretty good chance they'd wreck the entire planet."

"Well, that sounds promising as hell." Lieutenant Vincenzo Fonzarelli sighed.

"It might not be that bad, Vincenzo," Abigail Hearns said, smiling slightly at *Tristram*'s chief engineer. Fonzarelli looked back at her skeptically, and she shrugged. "We're not really here to deal with the Saltashans directly, so it doesn't matter if they're as crazy as the Faithful . . . or even Graysons." Her smile turned dimpled. "All we have to worry about is the OFS presence in the system."

"*That's* a reassuring thought," Lieutenant Wanda O'Reilly observed waspishly. The communications officer's resentment of Abigail's promotion and (in her opinion) privileged status had abated—slightly—but it still rankled, and no one was ever going to accuse O'Reilly of giving up a sense of antagonism easily.

"I could wish we weren't here to confront the Sollies, too, Wanda," Kaplan said mildly. "Unfortunately, we wouldn't be making the trip if there weren't Sollies at the other end of it, now would we?"

"No, Ma'am," O'Reilly acknowledged.

"So how much system infrastructure is there, Hosea?" Kaplan asked, turning her attention back to the astrogator.

"Not much, actually." This time the Grayson did look down at his notes. "There's some mining in the Casper Belt between Saltash Delta and Himalaya, the system's only gas giant, although the total belter population—work force and dependents, combined—is way under a half million. And there's a gas extraction plant orbiting Himalaya itself. There doesn't seem to be much local heavy industry, though, and the system's only real cargo transfer platform is Shona Station. Which also happens to be Cinnamon's only significant orbital habitat."

"How big a population does it have, Hosea?" Abigail asked with a frown, and Simpkins checked his notes again.

"Almost a quarter million," he said, and Abigail's frown deepened.

"Something bothering you, Abigail?" Kaplan inquired, and Abigail gave herself a slight shake.

"Only that that's a lot of civilians to be potentially getting in harm's way, Ma'am," she said. "I was just thinking about how ugly things almost got in Monica."

Kaplan gazed at her for a moment, then nodded.

"I see your point. Hopefully nobody's going to be stupid enough for us to have to start throwing missiles around this time, though."

"Hopefully, Ma'am," Abigail agreed, and Kaplan turned back to Simpkins.

"Should I take it there's no indication that this Shona Station's armed?"

"Not according to anything in the files, Ma'am."

"Then given the Sollies' well demonstrated ability to screw things up by the numbers, I suppose we'd better hope the files are accurate in this case," Kaplan said dryly.

A flicker of laughter ran around the conference table, and Tallman cocked his head at his commanding officer.

"Do we actually know whether this Dueñas character is likely to be reasonable or not when we turn
up, Skipper?"

"That *is* the million-dollar question, isn't it?" Kaplan's
smile was thinner than ever. "And the answer, I'm afraid,
is that we don't have a clue. Our bio data on him is even
thinner than Hosea's info on the star system. Officially,
he's not the system's governor—legally it's only a 'courtesy title,' it says here—" she tapped her copy of the
squadron's orders from Michelle Henke and rolled her
eyes, "but from what Hosea's said, when he says 'jump'
the only question anyone in Saltash asks is 'how high.'"

"That's about right, from everything I've been able
to find, Ma'am," Simpkins put in. She cocked an eyebrow at him, and he shrugged. "Under the terms of
the Frontier Security 'peacekeeping agreement,' OFS
was assigned responsibility for managing the system's
local and interstellar traffic. Just to make sure no one
was sneaking any warships into position for attacks, you
understand. Of course, it was necessary for Frontier
Security to levy a slight service fee for looking after
Saltash's security that way."

"How big a service fee?"

"Try thirty-five percent . . . of the gross, Ma'am,"
Simpkins replied grimly, and Kaplan's lips pursed in
a silent whistle. That was steep, even for OFS.

"Do you know if that level was part of the original agreement?" she asked. "Or did Dueñas and his
predecessors crank it up to give them a better level
of graft after they were in place?"

"That I couldn't tell you, Ma'am. Sorry."

"Not your fault." Kaplan shook her head. "You've actually done better than I expected, given how small—and

how far from home—Saltash is. I didn't think you'd be able to pull this much out of the files."

Simpkins' smile showed his pleasure at the compliment, and she smiled back at him briefly. Then she returned her attention to Tallman.

"Like I say, Alvin, we don't really have a good enough feel for Dueñas to make any predictions on how he's likely to react when we turn up on his doorstep. Unless he's a fool, he has to've known word of his activities was going to get to the Talbott Quadrant sooner or later, though, so I'm not exactly inclined towards wild optimism about how reasonable he's likely to be. Captain Zavala checked with everybody in Montana who's had dealings with Saltash, but he's only held the governorship for less than a T-year. That's not long enough for anyone to've gotten a real handle on his personality. On the other hand, he was sent out here specifically to replace his predecessor *after* things started going into the crapper between us and the League, and try as I might, I can't convince myself that's a *good* sign."

"Well, I guess there's only one way to find out, isn't there, Ma'am?" Tallman smiled fleetingly. "Just once I wish we could do it the easy way, though."

"Oh, I do, too," Kaplan told him, and then she showed her own teeth in a thinner and far colder smile. "I do, too," she repeated, "but one thing Saltash is *not* going to be, people." She looked around the conference table. "It isn't going to be another New Tuscany. Not this time."

"Any new thoughts occur to anyone since our last meeting?" Jacob Zavala asked.

His squadron was eleven days out from Montana and still four days short of Saltash by the clocks of the galaxy at large, although only eight days had passed by DesRon 301's clocks, and his com display was split into four equal sized quadrants. Each quadrant was further subdivided into thirds to show the commanders, executive officers, and tactical officers of four of his squadron's five destroyers. Commander Rochelle Goulard, Lieutenant Commander Jasmine Carver, and Lieutenant Samuel Turner of HMS *Kay* were physically present in his flagship's briefing room, along with Lieutenant Commander George Auerbach, his chief of staff, and Lieutenant Commander Alice Gabrowski, his operations officer. Now he looked around the faces—electronic as well as flesh and blood—with one eyebrow raised.

"I've got something, Sir," Lieutenant Commander Rützel, HMS *Gaheris*' CO said. He was a heavyset man with a face designed for smiling, but at the moment he was frowning slightly, instead. "Not so much a new thought as an observation, though."

"Observe away, Toby," Zavala invited.

"I've been looking back at the information—such as it is—we've been able to pull together on Shona Station, Sir. I know none of our data suggests the station mounts any anti-ship weaponry, but according to the best info we have, there's an OFS intervention battalion permanently stationed there. I realize it's probably going to have a lot of its personnel deployed as detachments on Cinnamon and elsewhere around the system, but if they've managed to hang on to any significant portion of that troop strength and we have to actually board the station, things could get ugly."

There was silence for a moment. Then Captain Morgan, HMS *Gawain*'s CO and the squadron's senior captain, spoke.

"Toby's got a point, Sir," he said. "Under most circumstances, it probably shouldn't be a problem, but we've already had ample evidence the Sollies are willing to push things way past the point of reason. Especially when we don't have a batch of Marines of our own to send aboard to help them recognize the logic of our argument."

Zavala nodded soberly.

"You've both got points," he agreed. "I'd like to think any responsible officer would recognize the need to stand down when we turn up in strength, but people have different definitions of 'responsible.' And let's be fair here. *I'd* find it difficult to roll over and play dead if a *Solly* squadron came sailing into a star system I was responsible for defending and started throwing around demands."

"And Frank's right about our dearth of Marines, Sir," Naomi Kaplan said a bit grimly. "Holding down crew size is all well and good, and I'm all in favor of the increased efficiency for *shipboard* operations, but not having *any* Marine detachment for moments like this is a pain in the ass."

Abigail Hearns, by far the youngest officer attending the conference, nodded unconsciously in agreement with her CO's observation. She seemed to specialize in being short of Marines when she needed them, Abigail thought wryly, remembering a really unpleasant afternoon on a planet called Tiberian and another, almost as bad, aboard a shattered hulk which had once been the Solarian superdreadnought *Charles Babbage*.

Never around when you need one, she reflected wryly. *Well, aside from Mateo*, she amended, thinking about Lieutenant Mateo Gutierrez.

"There *are* moments when something more . . . flexible than a laser head seems indicated," Zavala acknowledged. "Hopefully this won't be one of them. We do need to be prepared in advance if it turns out it is, however. Now I wonder who among us might be best qualified by experience and training to oversee a little responsibility like this?"

His tone was almost whimsical as his eyes tracked across the com display. He smiled as they came to rest upon one of his officers' faces, and Abigail found herself looking back at him.

"I believe *you've* had some small experience in matters like this, haven't you, Lieutenant Hearns?"

❖   ❖   ❖

"What's this all about, Vice Admiral?" Damián Dueñas demanded a bit testily. He'd been in bed for less than two hours when the emergency com call came in, and he wasn't one of those people who woke up cheerful.

"We've confirmed a significant hyper footprint, Governor," Vice Admiral Oxana Dubroskaya replied from his display. "Gravitics make it five separate point sources."

Dueñas stiffened and felt his face oozing towards expressionlessness. Merchantships didn't travel in shoals like that in Solarian dominated space, and he wasn't expecting any additional Navy visitors. Or not from his *own* Navy, at any rate.

"What else can you tell me, Vice Admiral?" he asked after a moment.

"Less than I'd like to, Sir." Dubroskaya didn't much care for Dueñas, and she'd argued—respectfully— against his plan from the outset, which was one reason she took such care to address him as courteously as possible. "They're headed in-system now, but they made their translation right on the hyper limit, and they're still over nine light-minutes from Cinnamon. It'll be another couple of minutes before we can get any lightspeed sensor reads on them. I can confirm that they're headed for the inner system on a least-time course for a zero/zero intercept with the planet in approximately"—her eyes moved to the time display in the corner of her own com—"another one hundred and seventy-one minutes, however. From their footprints and the strength of their wedges, CIC puts them in the hundred and fifty to two hundred-ton range, but their initial velocity was nine hundred and twenty-six kilometers per second, and they're up to just over thirty-two hundred now. That means they're accelerating at five-point-six KPS squared, Governor."

Dueñas looked blank, and Dubroskaya reminded herself not to sigh.

"Sir, our *Rampart*-class destroyers are only half that big, and their *maximum* acceleration rate, with zero safety margin on the compensator, is only five-point-*zero-nine* KPS squared."

Understanding blossomed in Dueñas' eyes.

"Manties," he said.

"I don't see how it could be anyone else with that accel, Sir," Dubroskaya agreed.

The system governor didn't look very surprised, she thought. Unhappy, yes; but not surprised.

"Damn," Dueñas said mildly after a moment. "I'd hoped to get some additional reinforcements in here before they turned up." Dubroskaya stiffened visibly, and the governor shook his head quickly. "That's no reflection on you or your ships, Vice Admiral, I assure you. But I'd be happier if we had an even greater margin of superiority. One thing these people have already demonstrated is that they're not exactly likely to be reasonable."

Dubroskaya contented herself with a silent nod, although she wasn't sure "reasonable" was a word Damián Dueñas should be throwing around at a time like this. Impounding the merchant vessels of a sovereign star nation and jailing their entire ships' companies without trial or bail didn't strike her as meeting the dictionary definition of that adverb, either, no matter what theoretical justification for it he might have concocted. On the other hand, the decision wasn't hers to make, and she wasn't going to shed any tears about pinning the Manty upstarts' ears back the way they needed.

"Even assuming there's any truth to the rumors about Spindle, Governor," she said, "we're not picking up anything that could be transporting the missile pods they'd need to equalize the odds here in Saltash."

Those rumors were a lot more fragmentary than she would have preferred, but they did seem to strongly suggest that Fleet Admiral Sandra Crandall's visit to the Spindle System hadn't gone very well. The only problem was that no one in Saltash had a clue as to how *badly* it might have gone. The battle (if a battle had actually been fought at all) had taken place little more than two months earlier, and there simply hadn't been time for any reliable account of it to reach a backwoods star system like Saltash.

One thing Dubroskaya was confident of was that the stories they *had* heard—like the ones about what had happened to Josef Byng in New Tuscany—had obviously grown in the telling. There had to be at least some core of truth to the wild tales of disaster, but the destruction of *dozens* of SDs while the Manties got off scot free? Ridiculous! Still, the SLN had clearly taken losses and, presumably, retreated from the system in the face of unexpectedly heavy resistance, and that was more than bad enough for Oxana Dubroskaya. The fact that a Solarian fleet had failed to take its objective for the very first time in the SLN's history was a sobering—and infuriating—thought, and she was determined not to let overconfidence lull her into creating her own disaster, which was one reason she was less than enthralled by Dueñas' strategy. She and her staff had analyzed the badly garbled bits and pieces of information they had as carefully (and pessimistically) as possible, however, and it seemed evident that the Manties must have managed to get more system-defense missile pods into the system than Crandall had realized. They'd probably been longer-ranged than Crandall had expected, too, judging by the limited accounts they had. That was the only explanation they could come up with . . . and as she'd just pointed out to the governor, missile pods in *Spindle* weren't going to help them in Saltash.

"I'm glad to hear that, of course, Vice Admiral." Dueñas nodded. "But I'd like to settle this without an exchange of fire if we can, and having more of our warships in attendance might help assure that outcome."

"I'd just as soon not shoot myself, Sir," Dubroskaya said. "If the Manties are crazy enough to push it, though, they'll soon discover they shouldn't have."

"I don't doubt that at all, Vice Admiral," Dueñas replied. "My concerns have nothing at all to do with your ships or your people. I'm just thinking about the political and diplomatic as opposed to the directly military implications."

"Understood, Governor." Dubroskaya nodded, although the truth was that she was far from certain of exactly what Dueñas' political objectives were in this case. Still, whatever his *intentions*, his *orders* had been clear enough.

He wasn't especially shy about handing those orders out, either, she thought with more than an edge of resentment. She'd been a flag officer for over twenty T-years, and she didn't enjoy being ordered around by the governor of a single star system on the backside of nowhere that wasn't even officially League territory. Unfortunately, her deployment orders made the chain of command clear and unambiguous. And according to Tucker Kiernan, her chief of staff, Dueñas was well-connected back on Old Terra, which suggested that pushing back against his presumptuousness might not be a career-enhancing move, however much the pain in the ass deserved it.

What I'd like to do is squash him like a pimple, she thought. But then she gave a mental snort. *Not like he's the first arrogant civilian you've had to take orders from, Oxana! And at least the Manties only sent along light cruisers. However... questionable his strategy may be, you've got more than enough force advantage to keep a lid on the situation.*

"Thank you for getting this information to me so promptly," Dueñas continued after a moment. "I need to confer with my people here in Kernuish. Please keep us apprised of any additional information that comes your way."

"Of course, Governor."

❖   ❖   ❖

"What do you think, Cicely?" Damián Dueñas asked two minutes later.

"Probably the same thing you do," Lieutenant Governor Cicely Tiilikainen replied from his com, and shrugged. "Dubroskaya's right—they have to be Manties, with that acceleration rate."

"But why haven't they said anything yet?" Dueñas wondered out loud.

"Who knows?" Tiilikainen shrugged again. She'd never shown any particular enthusiasm for Dueñas' plan, and he felt a flicker of anger at her obvious intention to stand back and make it abundantly clear it was *his* plan. "Maybe it's some kind of psychological warfare ploy. They have to've thrown this together pretty quickly to get here this soon, so maybe they figure we don't have any Navy detachment of our own. If that's the way they're thinking, they may figure that letting you worry about them for a while will soften you up for their demands."

"Maybe." Dueñas rubbed his chin, eyes narrowed in thought, carefully taking no note of the second-person pronoun in her last sentence. Then he gave himself a shake and straightened up.

"I'd better get dressed. Meet me in my office as soon as you can."

"On my way now," she said, panning her visual pickup to let him look out the side window of her air car as it sped through the sparse late-night aerial traffic of the city of Kernuish. "I'll be waiting by the time you can get there."

✧ Chapter Eleven

"WE'RE GETTING BACK GOOD data on the forward platforms, Skipper," Abigail Hearns said, and Naomi Kaplan turned her command chair to face the tac section and cocked her head in response to Abigail's tone.

"I'm seeing three merchies in parking orbit with the platform, Ma'am," Abigail said, replying to the unspoken question. "They're not squawking transponders, but we're close enough for good visuals, and at least two of them look Manticoran-built to me. That's not the interesting thing, though."

"No?" Kaplan smiled thinly. "That sounds interesting enough to be going on with to me, Abigail."

"Oh, I agree, Ma'am. But what I thought was *really* interesting were the four battlecruisers lying doggo in the inner system."

A frisson of tension ran around *Tristram's* bridge.

"You're right, that *is* interesting," Kaplan conceded after a moment. "I'm assuming Commodore Zavala has that information, as well?"

"Yes, Ma'am. It's on the distributed feed."

"Good." Kaplan's hexapuma smile was even thinner—and much colder—than before. "I think this little spider may have underestimated the fly."

✧   ✧   ✧

"It's confirmed, Sir," Lieutenant Commander Gabrowski said a half-hour later. "All four of the battlecruisers are *Indefatigables*—older units, from their emissions signatures—and the recon platforms say they have hot nodes. Our platforms've gotten a good look at the entire inner system now, though, and aside from the trio of tincans on the far side of Cinnamon's moon, that seems to be all they've got."

"And still not a peep out of any of them, correct, Abhijat?" Jacob Zavala asked Lieutenant Abhijat Wilson, his com officer.

"Not one, Sir," Wilson confirmed.

"And they have to know we're here . . . and that we sure as hell aren't merchies," Lieutenant Commander Auerbach added. "So I have to wonder *why* they haven't said a word to us."

"Well, at least it makes a pleasant change from the usual Solarian bluster, don't you think?" Jacob Zavala's tone was whimsical; his expression was not.

"What it suggests to me is that there's a *reason* we're not hearing the usual Solarian bluster, Sir," Auerbach replied. The chief of staff liked and respected Zavala, and they usually got along well, but George Auerbach had never been noted for his spontaneity or sparkling sense of humor.

"Fair's fair, George," Zavala pointed out in a more serious tone. "We haven't talked to them yet, either."

Zavala's truncated squadron had been inbound for eighty-five minutes. His destroyers' velocity relative to the system primary was up to 29,400 KPS, and they were barely three minutes from their turnover for a zero/zero intercept with the planet of Cinnamon, still over 88,000,000 kilometers ahead of them. They were also well inside the twelve-light-hour limit where they were supposed to have announced their identities. There was a little leeway in that requirement, especially for ships emerging from hyper—as most ships did—well inside it, but they were still supposed to get around to it in a "timely fashion," and he supposed it could be argued that he hadn't.

Pity about that.

"I know we haven't talked to them yet, Sir," Commander Rochelle Goulard said from the com display which tied Zavala and his staff into HMS *Kay*'s command deck. "On the other hand, I can't see them trying to hide from our sensors if they didn't have something nasty in mind."

"I can think of at least a couple of legitimate— from their perspective, at least—reasons for 'hiding,' Roxy," Zavala told his flag captain. "For one thing, they might've come up with a Frontier Fleet officer bright enough to seal his own shoes. They may not have details on Spindle here in Saltash yet, but it's been five T-months since Byng got himself blown away in New Tuscany. There's been time enough for them to've heard all about *that* encounter, and if they've paid some attention to the reports of our weapons' range from New Tuscany, they may just want to make sure we're inside *their* range basket before they make their presence known. Especially if they buy into the notion that we're the ones who're actually picking this fight, which is exactly how the Sollies spun New Tuscany."

"Agreed, Sir," Lieutenant Commander Gabrowski said. "But there are some other possibilities here, too." Zavala looked at her, and the ops officer shrugged. "We've wondered all along why a system governor might do something as daft as seizing Manticoran merchantmen. What if they were intended from the beginning as bait and these battlecruisers are the trap?"

"I think that's an entirely plausible scenario," Zavala acknowledged. "Mind you, I'm not going to rush in *assuming* it's what's happening, but I'm damned well not going to assume it *isn't*, either!"

"That's a relief, Sir," Gabrowski said earnestly. "Given how gullible and easily taken in you usually are, I mean."

Unlike Auerbach, Gabrowski *did* have a sense of humor, and Zavala grinned at her, then rubbed the tip of his nose thoughtfully.

The Sollies had undoubtedly figured out who—and what—his command was by now. Or they'd at least figured out his ships had to be Manticoran, at any rate, even if they didn't realize something as large as a *Roland*-class destroyer wasn't a light cruiser. On the other hand, it was unlikely anyone in Saltash had detected the highly stealthy Ghost Rider recon platforms fanning out in front of his squadron. Which *probably* meant that—so far, at least—he knew about their battlecruisers and they didn't know that he knew about them.

The problem was what he did with that information.

I know what I'd like to do with it, he thought grimly. *Unfortunately, Admiral Gold Peak made it abundantly clear I'm not supposed to do that if I have a choice. So I guess just blowing them out of space without warning would be just a bit of an overreaction. Of course, if they decide to be unreasonable about this...*

"I suppose we'd better go ahead and talk to them, Abhijat," he said.

"Yes, Sir," Lieutenant Wilson replied, trying hard not to crack a smile at the resignation in his superior's tone. "I'll see about getting hold of someone."

❖   ❖   ❖

System Governor Damián Dueñas' com buzzed discreetly and he tapped the virtual key to accept the connection.

"I have a com request from a Captain Jacob Zavala, Governor," Maxence Kodou, his executive assistant, announced from the holographic display when it materialized above his desk.

"Really?" Dueñas tipped back his chair and frowned. "Took the bastard long enough to get on the com, didn't it?"

"Well, he's coming up on Dubroskaya's projected turnover point," Lieutenant Governor Tiilikainen observed from where she stood gazing out over the lights and air car traffic of the city of Kernuish. She turned to face the governor. "If his intention was to let us sweat, we've had time to start doing that nicely now, so he probably figures it's time he got around to talking to us." She made a face. "From what we've seen out of him so far, I don't imagine he intends to be particularly accommodating about it, either."

"I almost hope you're right, Cicely," Dueñas half-growled. "In fact, I'm looking forward to it. I don't imagine he's going to be very happy when he finds out we're a lot readier for his visit than he expected us to be! I just want to get him farther in-system before he figures out what we've got waiting for him."

Tiilikainen nodded, but Dueñas felt another stir of resentment as she turned back to the window. He couldn't fault her willingness to dig in and make the plan work, despite her lack of enthusiasm, but she'd been the lieutenant governor here in Saltash for over ten T-years, and she seemed far less...engaged than Dueñas would have preferred. Or as engaged as someone with a proper sense of ambition should have been, for that matter. Not too surprising, really, he supposed. The *lieutenant* governorship of a single backwater star system like Saltash wasn't exactly the sort of plum assignment for which a really up and coming OFS bureaucrat would choose to compete. Even a full governorship out here was little more than a stepping stone to something better and more profitable, but Tiilikainen seemed prepared to settle for her current slot. Damián Dueñas, on the other hand, was not. And the system governor who finally managed to bloody the Manties' nose would be bound for bigger and better things.

Hell, if this works out half as well as I expect it to, I'll even take her along with me! he thought. Then he looked back at Kodou.

"Go ahead and put him through to my desk, Maxence," he said.

"Of course, Sir." Kodou nodded courteously and disappeared from the hologram. A moment later, he was replaced by the image of a small, dark featured officer with incongruously blue eyes in an obviously military skinsuit.

"Captain Zavala, I presume?" Dueñas said with a

cool smile, then sat back to wait the ten-plus minutes while the light-speed message zipped to the distant Manticoran's ship and his response came back again.

"Indeed," the man in his display said, barely nine seconds later. "And you, I assume, are System Governor Dueñas?"

Dueñas twitched. He couldn't help that any more than he could help the involuntary widening of his eyes. He turned his head, shooting a sharp glance at Tiilikainen. The lieutenant governor was outside his own com's pickup's field of view, but she'd turned quickly back from the window, her expression as astonished as Dueñas felt.

"Under the circumstances," Zavala went on from the display, "I thought it would probably be a good idea to minimize transmission lags for this conversation, Governor. I *am* speaking to Governor Dueñas, I trust?"

"Yes. I mean, I'm System Governor Dueñas. What can I do for you, Captain?"

Dueñas' voice sounded less firm than he might have wished, almost hesitant, in the face of the Manticorans' demonstration that they *did* have the faster than light communications capability the human race had sought for the last thousand T-years or so, and he willed his face back into impassivity.

"I'm here to inquire into certain reports we've received, Governor," the Manticoran officer responded with that same disconcerting quickness, but then he paused.

"What sort of reports would that be, Captain?" Dueñas asked, then swore silently at himself for allowing Zavala to suck him into filling the silence the other man had deliberately left.

l personnel interviewing and examining the
of the two ships in question."

m afraid that's quite impossible, Captain. Quar-
ie regulations are very strict, you know."

I see," Zavala said for a second time, and cocked his
d slightly. "And just precisely how long do you expect
s quarantine period to continue, Governor Dueñas?"

"That's going to depend on the recommendations
f my medical personnel." Dueñas' smile turned thinner and considerably less affable. "I'm afraid it could
be . . . quite lengthy, however."

"Particularly given the fact that there's no medical
justification for it at all, you mean, Governor?" Zavala's
tone was even colder—and more cutting—then Dueñas' smile had been.

"I'm sure I don't know what you're talking about,
Captain," the system governor replied, his smile disappearing. It was the response he'd wanted, but he was
more than a little taken aback by how soon he'd gotten
it. This Zavala was obviously even more arrogant than
he'd expected!

"I'm almost tempted to believe that, Governor,"
the Manty said levelly. "That you can't give me a time
estimate I mean. I don't suppose anyone ought to be
surprised that someone stupid enough to pull something
like this in the first place is also too stupid to count
weeks on his fingers and toes. Frankly, I'm astonished
he can even manage to wipe drool off his own chin."

Dueñas stiffened. For a handful of heartbeats, sheer
incredulity that anyone would dare to speak that way
to a Solarian-appointed governor held him motionless.
His eyes widened in shock, and then he felt his face
darken with a scalding flush of fury.

"According to information which h[as] Gold Peak," Zavala replied courteou[s] Manticoran merchant vessel *Carolyn* h[as] fully detained here in Saltash." He sho[wed] in a brief flash of white. "I'm certain it's misunderstanding, but Lady Gold Peak sent [me to] get to the bottom of things."

"I see." Dueñas folded his hands together [on the] desk blotter and regarded Zavala's holographic [image] levelly. He was starting to come back on balance n[en-]tally, although the confirmation of the Manties' F[TL] communications ability had been unpleasant. Mostly because it suggested some of the other wild rumors might have some substance in fact, as well.

"Well, Captain Zavala," he said after a moment, "I'm afraid it's not all 'simply a misunderstanding.' I have, indeed, denied *Carolyn* departure clearance and placed her crew in medical quarantine. I'm afraid that's also true of the Manticoran vessel *Argonaut*, in fact."

"I see." Zavala had an excellent poker face, but it was obvious from the glitter in his eyes that he'd echoed the governor's own words with malice aforethought. "May I ask the nature of this medical emergency? And how many other vessels which might have been exposed to it have also been detained?"

"I'm scarcely well-versed in medical matters, Captain. I had no choice but to rely on my own medical personnel to evaluate the risk, and then acted accordingly." Dueñas smiled with immense affability. "As for other vessels having been detained, I'm afraid there's no indication anyone else has been exposed to the apparent contagion's source."

"Then I'm certain you won't object to my own

"I *beg* your pardon?!" he bit out.

"You should," Zavala said. "And you should come up with better lies next time, too, Governor. I doubt this one would fly even back in Old Chicago. And somehow I don't think Permanent Senior Undersecretary MacArtney's going to be very happy with you when this blows up as spectacularly as it's about to."

"What do you mean by that?" Dueñas demanded, his face still dark with rage, and Zavala shrugged.

"I mean there's no medical emergency and your 'quarantine' is as bogus as it is stupid, Governor. You've chosen to unlawfully seize not one but two Manticoran merchantmen in flagrant disregard of several solemn treaties and at least two cardinal principles of interstellar law, and you've done it on a pretext you *know* would never stand up in any admiralty court. Your attempt to cloak your actions under the cover of a medical quarantine might fool a particularly credulous two-year-old, but no one else is going to believe it for a moment. *I* certainly don't, and my orders from Lady Gold Peak are very clear on this point."

"And what might those orders be, *Captain*?" Dueñas' lips curled contemptuously, and Zavala shrugged.

"My instructions are to recover any unlawfully detained Manticoran vessels in this star system and to repatriate them to Manticoran space as expeditiously as possible, Governor."

"And just how do you intend to do that, Captain? Despite your own reckless language and contempt for a legally declared medical emergency, I have no intention of releasing quarantined vessels until I'm thoroughly convinced no health risk will result." Dueñas locked eyes with the Manticoran. "There may be a difference of opinion about the validity of that medical emergency, Captain Zavala, but its *legal* standing is beyond dispute."

"Its legal standing is exactly zero, Governor, so let's not waste each other's time pretending otherwise, shall we? Under the Treaty of Beowulf, you're *required* to grant my medical personnel access in order to determine the legitimacy of your personnel's diagnosis. You've refused to do so, which means your declaration of quarantine has *no* legal standing whatsoever."

"I'm afraid I disagree with your legal interpretation on that point, Captain," Dueñas said inflexibly. "And absent instructions from higher authority, I'm also afraid I'll have to act on my own understanding of the circumstances and the treaty's provisions. I'll be happy to request those instructions, of course, but"—he smiled again, coldly—"it will probably take some months to get clarification from Old Earth."

"That's unacceptable, Governor," Zavala said calmly.

"I'm afraid it's the best I can do, Captain. Under the circumstances, you understand."

"Oh, I understand the circumstances better than you may believe I do, Governor. With all due respect, however, I'm not certain *you* do."

"Meaning what, precisely, Captain?"

"Meaning I'm under orders to repatriate those vessels as quickly as possible by any means necessary. And if you need me to be more specific, Sir, 'any means necessary' *does* include the use of force."

"Are you seriously proposing to commit an act of war against the Solarian League on its own territory?" Dueñas demanded.

"First, the Saltash System is *not* Solarian territory,"

Zavala replied. "It's legally an independent star system, and the Solarian presence in it is—*legally*—solely to serve as a peacekeeping authority to prevent hostilities between the Republic of MacPhee and the Republic of Lochore. Although the Office of Frontier Security does enjoy certain administrative rights as a result of its agreements with MacPhee and Lochore, that doesn't make Saltash Solarian territory, no matter how much cash you squeeze out of it every T-year. Second, I'm not the one who's committed an act of war; *you* are. In the absence of a genuine and legitimate medical emergency to justify your so-called quarantine, your actions amount to piracy. And I might point out to you, Sir, that piracy is a capital offense. And, third, I'm not *proposing* to use force if you refuse to release my star nation's vessels and personnel peacefully; I'm *promising* to use force."

Dueñas stared incredulously at the officer in his display. Zavala looked extraordinarily—indeed, one might almost have said insanely—calm for a mere captain who'd just threatened a Solarian League governor in language like that. Dueñas had anticipated intransigence. In fact, he'd *counted* on it. But he'd never contemplated the possibility that Zavala would step into his trap so quickly . . . and with such obvious contempt for the League in general and Damián Dueñas in particular. It cut deep, that contempt, coming from such a lowly officer in the neobarb navy of a pipsqueak little star nation with delusions of grandeur, and the governor felt his face flushing angrily once more.

"Should you attempt to carry out that outrageous and totally unacceptable threat, Captain, it will be the end of your career! I promise you that! And the consequences for your star nation's relations with the Solarian League will be severe!"

"I doubt my career will suffer in the least, Governor, and even if I didn't, it would take a worse threat than that to prevent me from carrying out my instructions. And as for the Star Empire's relations with the League, I'll take my chances on that, too. To date, the League's been the instigator in every incident between the Star Empire and the League, including this one. And as my Empress and her government have attempted to make clear to Old Chicago, the Star Empire of Manticore is not prepared to allow the Solarian League to kill its personnel, insult its sovereignty, or seize its merchant vessels"—his eyes bored into Dueñas'—"without reaction. If you refuse to respond to an effort to resolve the crisis *you've* provoked by peaceful means, then I'm prepared to assume you prefer a more...bellicose resolution. In which case, Governor, my squadron and I are at your disposal."

"I've heard quite enough of this!" Dueñas snapped. "Be advised, Captain, that in light of the threatening language you've seen fit to use in this conversation, I have no alternative but to consider that your vessels represent a hostile force. If you continue deeper into the star system, I will so regard your presence and I will use all means at my disposal to resist your intrusion into Solarian-protected space."

"And would 'all means at my disposal' include the four *Indefatigable*-class battlecruisers currently approximately five thousand three hundred kilometers this side of Shona Station, Governor?"

Dueñas' jaw tried hard to drop at the Manticoran's level—and undeniably contemptuous—tone. Vice Admiral Dubroskaya had assured him that her vessels would be undetectable until the Manties got far closer than they were. The fact that Zavala already knew they were there was bad enough. The fact that he was prepared to issue such threats *knowing* they were present, though . . .

"You might want to inform the local senior officer that I have complete tactical readouts on his vessels," Zavala continued. "Including the fact that one of them is down a beta node in her forward impeller ring. I'm perfectly aware of their locations, and also of the three destroyers hiding on the far side of Cinnamon's moon. I'm not sure why you bothered to hide *those*, but I'm certain you had a reason that made sense to *you*, at any rate. To use your own turn of phrase, 'be advised' that I'm as well aware of the Solarian forces currently deployed in the Saltash System as I am of the SLN's demonstrated proclivity for firing on unprepared vessels of sovereign star nations with no warning. In light of that demonstrated proclivity, please inform your local commander that I entertain no doubt of my ability to engage and destroy all of his units if I should be forced to do so. And since you've seen fit to threaten my command with attack by 'all means' at your disposal, I have no option but to consider your warships to be hostile units. As such, I require that they stand down immediately. They will power down their impeller nodes and shut down all tracking and targeting systems, and their personnel will immediately evacuate to the surface of Cinnamon. And I should point out, Governor, that my sensor resolution of your vessels is more than adequate to determine their status and whether or not the life pods used to evacuate their crews are actually occupied. Assuming my requirements are met, your vessels will be left unmolested and you may...reclaim them following our withdrawal from the star system."

"And precisely what do you intend to do if this pipe dream of yours fails to come to fruition?" Dueñas demanded furiously.

"If your crews haven't abandoned ship within the next twenty-seven minutes," Zavala said with a flat, implacable calm worse than any shouted threats, "I will construe that as an indication of hostile intent, and I will open fire. The decision is yours, Governor. In either case, my ships will be in orbit around Cinnamon in approximately one and a half hours. Whether or not any of *your* warships are still intact at that time is up to you. Good day."

Dueñas was still staring at the display in disbelief when it went suddenly blank.

✦ Chapter Twelve

"I DIDN'T REALIZE THE Commodore had such a command of diplomatic language, Ma'am," Alvin Tallman observed from his position in *Tristram*'s Auxiliary Control over his private com link to Naomi Kaplan.

"He does have a way with words, doesn't he?" Kaplan replied. "I've always admired a well-turned phrase, and I was impressed by his subtlety, too. And that comment about Tango Three's beta node was a nice touch. But at least nobody on the other side's going to be able to get away with claiming he didn't give them clear warning, now are they?"

"They may not get away with it, but that doesn't mean they aren't going to *try* to, Skipper," Tallman pointed out.

"That much was a given going in. Personally, I'm with the Commodore. Better to be hanged for a hexapuma than a pussycat. Besides," Kaplan smiled coldly, "we tried it their way at New Tuscany. Now *they* can try it *our* way."

✦   ✦   ✦

"He's got to be crazy, Ma'am," Tucker Kiernan told Oxana Dubroskaya flatly. "Five light cruisers against four *battle*cruisers? They've got at most—what? Maybe eight tubes per broadside? Well, we've got *twenty*-eight per broadside!"

"Captain Kiernan has a point, Admiral," Captain Maksymilian Johnson, SLNS *Vanquisher*'s commanding officer, said. "On the other hand, and not wanting to sound alarmist," the flag captain continued, "if they've got the kind of range advantage some of the wilder reports from New Tuscany indicate, they may be planning on opening fire from well beyond our range."

"Are you suggesting a batch of light cruisers is going to open fire at forty million kilometers, Sir?" Captain Kelvin Diadoro, Dubroskaya's operations officer, sounded a little more incredulous than he probably should have speaking to someone with Johnson's seniority, but the vice admiral couldn't really blame him.

"I'm not necessarily suggesting anything of the sort, Kelvin," Johnson replied with a touch of frost. "I would point out that forty million klicks does comport reasonably well with the claimed range at New Tuscany, but whether or not those claims have any relationship with reality is more than I'm prepared to say. What I *am* suggesting, however, is that this Zavala's clearly suggesting he has a significant range advantage and he's planning to make use of it. And if it should happen he really *does* have that kind of range, it doesn't matter how many missile tubes we have and how many he has, since we won't be able to put fire on him without our birds going ballistic twenty or thirty million kilometers before they even reach him, at which point even a light cruiser's countermissiles and point defense will eat them for lunch."

"Maksymilian has a point, Admiral," Captain Meridiana Quinquilleros, SLNS *Success'* CO, said diffidently. All eyes swiveled towards her quadrant of the communications display and she shrugged. "I doubt any shipkillers a light cruiser could launch internally have anything like the range reported from New Tuscany, but they could still have more range than anything we've got. And whether or not it's going to work the way he has in mind, that's clearly what he has to intend to do if he's actually planning on engaging us at all."

"Point taken, Meridiana," Dubroskaya said, and turned her own gaze on Diadoro. "Assume that *is* what he has in mind, Kelvin. Where does that leave us?"

"We're talking about light cruisers here," Diadoro pointed out, "and I don't care *how* 'missile heavy' their tactical doctrine is, light cruisers—even big-assed ones like these—can't have more than two or three hundred shipkillers on board. You just couldn't fit them in, especially if they've got some kind of extended drive system to eat up still more mass and cubage. So call it fifteen hundred birds, each with the warhead of one of our own Spathas." The Spatha was the SLN's new-generation missile for destroyers and light cruisers, with a considerably lighter laser head than the Javelins being issued to heavy cruisers and battlecruisers. "If they could *hit* us with all of them, it'd hurt, no question. But there's no way one of them could put more than eight or nine—ten, max—birds into a single salvo, and at least some of those are going to have to be penaides. Without that, they wouldn't have a prayer of getting through our missile defenses. So say they give up—what? a quarter?—of their total launch capability for penetration aids and electronic warfare platforms. That gives the five of them a maximum throw weight of about thirty-eight lightweight shipkillers per salvo against four *Indefatigables*. I've got to like those odds, Admiral."

"And if they've got any missile pods along?" Dubroskaya asked.

"I know that's what they probably used at New Tuscany—and Spindle, assuming there's any accuracy at all to what we've heard." Diadoro added the qualifier conscientiously, although he was one of the squadron's officers who was confident the rumors about Spindle were wildly inaccurate. "And they could have a few along," he continued, "but they can't have many. They'd have to be tractored to their hulls, or our lightspeed platforms would have picked them up, and you just couldn't fit more than a handful of pods big enough to carry that kind of missiles onto the skin of a light cruiser. Besides, there're still the limitations of their fire control. A light cruiser's only got so many telemetry channels; there's no way they could control pod salvos big enough to get through our defenses. I'm not saying they might not get two or three leakers through, land a couple of lucky punches, and it's possible they could have enough range on internally-launched birds to engage us before we could engage *them*. But they're not going to be able to saturate our defenses heavily enough to let them win, especially with Spatha-grade laser heads. Not when they've got nine hundred thousand tons of warship and we've got three-point-four *million* tons."

"I can't fault Kelvin's analysis, Ma'am," Captain Ham Seung Jee of the *Inexorable* said. "The only problem I have is that the Manties have to be able to figure that out just as well as we can . . . and they're trying it anyway."

"I'd say that's because they've screwed the pooch," another voice said. The others looked at the com image of Captain Borden McGillicuddy, SLNS *Paladin*'s CO, and he waved one hand in a throwing away gesture. "They're committed to coming down our throats," he pointed out. "Even if they went to max decel at this point, they're still going to have to come all the way to Cinnamon orbit before they can kill their current velocity. Whatever their damned range advantage, they're *going* to enter ours, whether they want to or not."

"You're suggesting this is some kind of bluff on their part?" Ham asked.

"All I'm suggesting at this point is that I don't think they got their 'invisible recon platforms' close enough to pick us up quite as early as they'd like us to believe," McGillicuddy replied. "Maybe this Zavala character didn't realize what he was walking into until just before he contacted Governor Dueñas. God knows we've all seen how arrogant Manties can be! Maybe he just came bulling straight in without bothering to scout the inner system. After all, how likely was it that he was going to run into an entire division of battlecruisers in an out-of-the-way system like Saltash? By the time he figured out what he was actually up against, it was too late for him to fall back across the limit and hyper out. So maybe he decided that rather than rolling over he'd try to run a bluff on the strength of what's supposed to've happened at New Tuscany and Spindle."

"And when it doesn't work?" Dubroskaya asked.

"Then he goes ahead and rolls over anyway, probably,

Ma'am," McGillicuddy said, and shrugged. "This time limit of his is going to put him a good thirty million klicks outside our powered missile envelope when it expires. That leaves him plenty of time to change his mind and adopt a more conciliatory tone before we could blow him out of space. If I were in his place, I might figure I didn't have anything to lose throwing my threats around ahead of time. If the other side blinks; I run the table. If the other side *doesn't* blink; I'm no worse off than I was and I can still surrender before he engages me."

Dubroskaya nodded slowly. McGillicuddy's hypothesis made a certain degree of sense, and Diadoro was certainly right about the limited magazine capacity and small broadside of a light cruiser. She wasn't quite as confident as McGillicuddy about the Manties' fundamental rationality, given the fact that they'd been foolish enough to pick a fight with the Solarian League in the first place, but the captain's analysis of the other side's unpalatable tactical situation had a lot to recommend it.

In fact, that was Dueñas' basic plan in the first place, she reminded herself. *The whole object was to draw the Manties into an untenable position—and get them to commit themselves in a way that clearly demonstrated their belligerence—before they ever figured out we were here. Which is basically what Borden's arguing happened, after all.*

The governor might have hoped to have even more firepower available, but four battlecruisers against five light cruisers was an overwhelming mismatch by anyone's standards. And if she and Dueñas pulled it off—if they forced an entire Manty light cruiser squadron to tamely roll over and surrender—Education and Information's talking heads would turn it into an overwhelming triumph. The sort of thing the Solarian public wanted to hear about as an antidote for the rumors of devastation coming out of Spindle.

And let's be honest here. Borden's got a point—Dueñas was luckier than hell I had even four BCs that could get here in time! If we hadn't, he'd be well and truly stuck in orbit in a leaky skinsuit right now.

The rest of Battlecruiser Squadron 491 was either dispersed to other star systems or in shipyard hands, but that was par for the course for Frontier Fleet. Its squadrons were always understrength, and there were always too many places they needed to be at the same time. But in this instance, at least, Dueñas truly had lucked out.

Always assuming Borden's right about the Manties screwing up, of course, she reminded herself conscientiously. Yet even as she did, she knew she didn't really think McGillicuddy was wrong.

Assume Kelvin's estimate is off, or that they really do have more range than we do, and they get a couple of dozen missiles through our defensive basket before we get close enough to hammer them, she thought. *No, make it fifty to be on the safe side. Against four* Indefatigables? *Hell, even* Javelin-*range laser heads would hardly scratch our paint!*

No, even if Borden didn't get everything right, there's no way these bastards can hope to take me on and walk away from it. They're truly and royally screwed, whatever happens, and I think I'll be able to live with being the first Solarian admiral to smack them down the way they deserve.

"Well," she said mildly, "since they know we're here now, I suppose we might as well go ahead and get our wedges up so we can welcome them properly."

❖   ❖   ❖

"They're coming out to meet us, Ma'am," Abigail Hearns announced three minutes later, as the battlecruisers' nodes went fully online and a quartet of impeller wedges appeared on the tactical display and began moving away from their original position between Shona Station and DesRon 301.

"I see them, Guns," Naomi Kaplan replied almost absently, but Abigail knew that tone of voice. *Tristram's* CO was putting on her warrior's face, settling into predator mode while her brain whirred like another computer.

"We'll just have to see how serious they are about this, I suppose," Kaplan added a moment later, and her smile was hungry. For DesRon 301, and especially for HMS *Tristram*, the Star Empire of Manticore's confrontation with the Solarian League was personal.

Very personal.

That was as true for Abigail as for anyone else in the ship's company, and she found herself wondering if that was one of the reasons Lady Gold Peak had picked Captain Zavala's squadron for this operation in the first place.

❖   ❖   ❖

Vice Admiral Dubroskaya's battlecruisers accelerated towards the oncoming Manticoran destroyers at 3.89 KPS squared, eighty percent of their maximum theoretical rate of acceleration. There was no particular hurry, and even at that low accel, they'd move over four million kilometers closer to the Manties before Zavala's twenty-seven-minute time limit expired. Of course, during that same time the Manties would move forty-two million kilometers closer to Cinnamon. The range between the two forces would be down to "only" 36,700,000 kilometers at that point, and the closing speed between them would give the Solarians' Javelin anti-ship missiles an effective powered envelope at launch of better than twelve million kilometers.

Dubroskaya was more willing than Kelvin Diadoro to admit that the Manties tube-launched missiles *might* have more range than hers, but nothing the size a light cruiser could stow internally was going to have a *lot* more, she thought as she watched her ships' icons moving across the display. For that matter, assuming constant accelerations on both sides, it would require only an additional fifteen and a half minutes for her to reach her own powered range of the Manties. Two of her ships—*Success* and *Paladin*—were Flight V *Indefatigables*, with the old SL-11-b launcher, with a forty-five-second launch cycle, but *Vanquisher* and *Inexorable* had the newer SL-13 launcher with a cycle time of only thirty-five seconds, and the Manties could probably do a bit better than that. *Solarian* destroyers and light cruisers certainly could have, given the smaller and lighter missiles with which they were armed, but any internally launched missile with enough range to threaten her squadron at this kind of range was going to have to be at *least* as large as her own Javelins. That was bound to slow their rate of fire, so call it thirty seconds for the other side's launch cycle. That meant they'd have time for roughly thirty-one broadsides before she could range on them, but with no more than eight to ten tubes per broadside, that would be only three hundred and ten missiles, maximum, per platform, delivered in combined salvos of no more than fifty each. And as Diadoro had pointed out, at least some of those missiles were going to have to be configured as penetration aids and electronic warfare platforms. Her four battlecruisers mounted eight counter-missile tubes and sixteen point defense stations in each broadside, which gave the squadron thirty-two CMs and sixty-four laser clusters against a probable threat of no more than forty shipkillers per launch.

She smiled coldly, contemplating the plot. No cruiser-sized missile ever built was going to get through that strong a defense in sufficient numbers to stop her before she was able to bring her own tubes into action, and *her* ships mounted twenty-eight of them in each broadside. Once she got into range, she'd be firing salvos of a hundred and sixteen missiles each... at which point her heavier Javelins would reduce the Manties to drifting wreckage in quick order.

❖   ❖   ❖

"They don't seem to be very impressed, Sir," George Auerbach observed quietly, and Jacob Zavala nodded.

"It's been my observation that the best way to impress a Solly is to shoot him squarely between the eyes," he told his chief of staff, never looking away from the plot. "You wouldn't want to shoot him anywhere else, though. You might hurt him."

Auerbach winced slightly at his CO's idea of humor, yet he couldn't deny that Zavala had a point. Still, he was the squadron's chief of staff, which gave him certain responsibilities.

"We'll be coming up on Point Alpha in about ten minutes, Sir. Are you sure you want to go with Sledgehammer?"

"Doing your job again, I see, George," Zavala said, turning away from the tactical display to smile briefly at Auerbach.

"As you say, Sir, it *is* my job."

"I know, George. I know."

Zavala reached up to put his hand on the taller Auerbach's shoulder and squeezed gently. And, he admitted to himself, the chief of staff had a point. No one in DesRon 301 had been particularly happy with Fire Plan Zephyr, the alternative to Sledgehammer, yet he had to concede that it would be more elegant and might—might!—reduce the severity of the incident which was about to occur here in Saltash.

The problem was that it would also be riskier... and far less personally satisfying.

I wonder how honest I've been with myself about this? Zavala thought. *It would be riskier, but how much have I allowed that satisfaction quotient to color my thinking?*

He made himself stand back and consider the alternatives one more time.

Zephyr would be more in the way of a demonstration of the consequences of unreasonableness than a serious attack: a concentrated salvo of Mark 16s fired from far beyond the Sollies' effective range to penetrate their defenses *without* hitting anything, much as Duchess Harrington had done to the Havenites' Second Fleet with Apollo at First Manticore and Captain Ivanov had done more recently, in Zunker. In theory, a reasonable Solarian commander would realize most of his ships would be pounded into ruin in the fifteen or sixteen minutes it would take him to get into his own range of Zavala's squadron. At which point, that hypothetical reasonable Solarian commander would conclude he had no alternative but to stand down after all.

There was, however, a minor weakness in that logic: it presupposed a *reasonable* Solarian commander. There'd been precious few of those in evidence since Josef Byng had come upon the scene. Worse, if the commander on the other side refused to take the hint, Zavala would have wasted one of his salvos for no return, and a *Roland*'s limited magazine space was its Achilles' heel. With only twenty rounds for each of his tubes, he couldn't afford to "waste" ammunition. And, still worse, even a Solly who wasn't totally unreasonable might decide he could survive whatever DesRon 301 could throw at him for fifteen minutes and still get to grips with the destroyers. Zavala didn't think Dubroskaya could, but his analysis of the only engagement between a Mark 16-armed force and Solarian-designed battlecruisers suggested that they might. Of course, Aivars Terekhov had been equipped with the first-generation Mark 16 at the Battle of Monica, whereas DesRon 301's birds mounted the latest Mod G laser heads. That probably changed the equation considerably, but there was no way for Zavala to *know* that.

Either way, given their closing velocity, the Sollies were going to overfly his own ships before they could decelerate, and any of the battlecruisers which survived the crossing might well escape into hyper after all. Zavala doubted any of them *would* survive, and even if they did get into their own missile range of DesRon 301 before they were knocked out, a *Roland*-class destroyer's missile defenses were actually considerably tougher than an *Indefatigable's*, given the superiority of Manticore's counter-missiles, decoys, and ECM.

But his destroyers were no better *armored* than any other destroyer or light cruiser. If Zavala was wrong about his defenses' ability to fend off incoming missiles, and if the Sollies got lucky, it wouldn't take very many Javelin hits to ruin a *Roland*'s entire day.

Besides, he thought grimly, *we don't owe these bastards a frigging thing, and I'm* damned *if I'm going to put my people at risk trying to keep the arrogant pricks from getting themselves killed!*

It was possible, he conceded, that he wasn't cut from the right material for a successful diplomat. On the other hand, Countess Gold Peak had known that when she sent him out.

"I've thought about it, George," he said. "I really have. But no, we're not going with Zephyr."

"Yes, Sir." Commander Auerbach gazed into the display or a second or two, then shrugged.

"Actually, Sir, I'm fine with that," he said.

❖   ❖   ❖

"Com request from the Manties, Ma'am," Commander Gervasio Urbanowicz said. Vice Admiral Dubroskaya glanced at him, and the communications officer shrugged. "It's that Captain Zavala, Ma'am, and I think his signal's being relayed by whatever he used to speak to the Governor FTL. It's a standard com laser coming from some kind of platform just ahead of us, at any rate."

Dubroskaya glanced at Captain Kiernan.

"Interesting timing, Ma'am," Kiernan said. "Maybe McGillicuddy was onto something after all."

"I suppose we're about to find out," Dubroskaya

said, and nodded to Urbanowicz. "Put it on the main display, Gervasio."

"Yes, Ma'am."

The same officer whose image Governor Dueñas had relayed to Dubroskaya appeared on the master communications display. He looked out of it for a moment, then his eyes narrowed as he saw her image. It had taken less than two seconds for him to react, even though they were still better than two light minutes apart, but at least she'd had enough forewarning to keep her unhappiness at that proof of his FTL capabilities from reaching her eyes or her expression.

"I am Vice Admiral Oxana Dubroskaya, Solarian League Navy," she said coldly. "What can I do for you, Captain Zavala?"

"You might consider standing down and abandoning ship in the next two minutes or so, Admiral Dubroskaya," he replied, and an icy centipede seemed to sidle along her spine as his unflinching eyes and level tone registered. If this was a man who'd just discovered his bluff had failed, he was one hell of a poker player.

"And what makes you think I might be interested in doing that, Captain?" she asked. "I believe Governor Dueñas has made the Solarian League's position abundantly clear. If, however, you'd care to surrender *your* vessels before I turn them into a drifting debris field, feel free."

"You know," Zavala said coldly, "I'm perpetually astonished by Solarian arrogance. My recon platforms picked up your battlecruisers less than forty-five minutes after my alpha translation, Admiral. That's how long they've been all over you. And I knew not just *where* you were but *what* you were better than a half hour before I made turnover, and I've got over two hundred gravities of accel in reserve. Think about that. If I'd been worried about what you might do to me, I could've been all the way back across the hyper limit and headed home before I even spoke to Governor Dueñas."

The centipede seemed to have invited its entire family to keep it company, Dubroskaya reflected.

"That's a bold statement, Captain," she heard her own voice say. "You'll forgive me if I point out that I have only your word for your remarkable acceleration rate and the amazing capabilities and supernatural stealthiness of those recon drones of yours. Personally, I find things like the Tooth Fairy a bit difficult to believe in."

"So should I assume from your skepticism that you think you've managed to track my actual recon platforms? You know exactly where each of them is?"

"Probably not *all* of them," Dubroskaya admitted. In fact, they'd managed to localize no more than a dozen of them, and all of those had remained beyond effective engagement range from her battlecruisers. She'd used up twenty or thirty missiles before she'd accepted that, but they were devilishly elusive targets and they kept disappearing back into stealth and zipping away from their plotted positions before her missiles could get there. She felt confident the Manties would have deployed more than that, and her sensor sections had been picking up backscatter from grav pulses which might represent additional platforms or have something to do with the Manties' obvious ability to transmit broadband data at faster-than-light speeds. Still, there couldn't be a *lot* more of them without her people having picked them up.

"Your stealth systems obviously are better than we'd expected, but I imagine we've located the majority of them at least approximately," she continued, her tone only slightly more confident than she actually felt.

"Then watch your plot, Admiral," Zavala invited in that same, cold voice, and Dubroskaya heard Diadoro inhale sharply. Her eyes darted to the main plot as CIC updated it...and an entire globe of icons—thirty of them, at least—appeared around her battlecruisers, keeping pace with them effortlessly at ranges as low as a light-second and a half, as they dropped their stealth. They glittered there, taunting her with their proximity, for at least ten seconds. Then, before her startled fire control officers could lock them up, they vanished mockingly once more. She had no doubt they were all busily streaking away to completely different positions from which to keep her under observation from within their protective cloak of invisibility.

"Admiral Dubroskaya, I can read the names on your ships' hulls from here," Zavala told her as the dusting of icons disappeared from her plot once again, "and I still haven't shown you *all* of my platforms. I warn you once again that I knew exactly what your battlecruisers were before I contacted Dueñas and I have real-time data on every move you make. You can abandon ship now and save a lot of lives, or what's left of your people can abandon what's left of your ships when I'm done with them. And if you think for one moment that I'll hesitate to pull the trigger, Admiral, you just reflect that the ships Josef Byng slaughtered at New Tuscany came from *this* destroyer squadron. I'm giving you a chance to save your people's lives, which is a hell of a lot more than he gave Commodore Chatterjee or any of our other shipmates. But that's as far as the ship goes, Admiral, and you now have seventy-five seconds to tell me you're going to abandon."

They locked eyes, and despite her best effort, Dubroskaya couldn't convince herself he was bluffing. He might be wrong—in fact, he probably *was*—but he wasn't bluffing. If she didn't accept his terms, he *would* open fire as soon as he was in range.

But she couldn't. She simply couldn't surrender four battlecruisers to only five *light* cruisers. She *couldn't* . . . and not just because of Dueñas' orders. Maybe the stories about New Tuscany, even the wild rumors coming out of Spindle, were true after all. But if they were, that only made it even more imperative that the Navy draw a line somewhere, stop the chain of humiliations and reclaim its honor.

And I will be damned *before I let this arrogant little prick of a captain dictate terms to* me, *by God*, she thought harshly. *No. Not* this *time, Captain Zavala!*

"Captain Diadoro." She never took her eyes from Zavala's face and raised her voice enough to be sure the Manticoran could hear her.

"Yes, Ma'am?"

"We will maintain this course and acceleration. Prepare to engage the enemy," Vice Admiral Oxana Dubroskaya said, and cut the com connection.

❖   ❖   ❖

"Well, so much for that," Jacob Zavala said, turning away as Dubroskaya's image disappeared from his own com.

"Hard to blame her in some ways, I suppose, Sir," Auerbach said. Zavala arched an eyebrow at him, and the chief of staff smiled crookedly. "All she can have at this point about Spindle are rumors, if that. And it'd take somebody with a lot more imagination than we've seen out of any of the Sollies yet to really believe five tincans could take out four battlecruisers on the basis of rumors. For that matter, most of *our* officers would refuse to believe it if we were looking at it from the Sollies' perspective. I mean, on the face of it, it's ridiculous."

"I'll grant you it would take at least a soupçon of imagination," Zavala acknowledged. "On the other hand, Dubroskaya sure as hell knows about New Tuscany, and she ought to be asking herself just how it was we came out on top there. And she *damned* sure ought to be asking herself why I'd have kept right on coming if *I* had any doubt of my ability to take her out."

"Can't argue with that, Sir. I'll bet you it's going to take all the Sollies a while to figure it out, though."

"Well, *this* bunch of Sollies had better start figuring it out in a hurry," Zavala said grimly.

❖   ❖   ❖

"Point Alpha in fifteen seconds, Ma'am," Abigail Hearns said quietly, looking into her plot and remembering another force of Solarian battlecruisers and the massacre of *Tristram's* division mates in New Tuscany. The range had dropped to thirty-eight million kilometers, and the closing velocity was down to 23,819 KPS.

Vengeance belongs to Me; I will repay, a voice said quietly in the back of her mind. *In time their foot will slip, for their day of disaster is near and their doom is coming quickly.*

Abigail Hearns had always preferred the love and gentleness of the New Testament, but this was an *Old*

Testament moment, and her eyes were intent and her hands steady on her tactical console.

"Stand by to engage," Naomi Kaplan replied.

❖   ❖   ❖

The *Roland* was the first destroyer class ever built to fire the Mark 16 dual-drive missile. That was the reason it was bigger than many navies' light cruisers. And it was also the reason for some of the peculiarities of its design. Like the reason it had "only" twelve missile tubes, and all of them were arranged as chase armament, mounted in the hammerheads of its hull. And the reason it had so much more fire control than any other destroyer in space. It was designed to fire "off bore," spitting missiles out of its "chase armament" to permit all its tubes to engage targets in both of a traditional ship's broadside arcs. And its fire control redundancy was designed to let it "stack" salvos with staggered drive activations, the same way the much larger and more powerful *Saganami-C*-class heavy cruisers did. The *Roland* couldn't control as many missiles as the *Saganami-C*; it was less than half the heavy cruiser's size, and there were limits in everything. But it *could* stack a double salvo of twenty-four missiles, which was better than twice Captain Kelvin Diadoro's worst-case estimate . . . and each of those missiles was just as deadly as anything a *Saganami-C* could have fired.

❖   ❖   ❖

"Missile launch!" one of Diadoro's tactical techs announced suddenly. "Multiple missile launches at three-six-point-seven million kilometers! CIC confirms one hundred and twenty—repeat, one two zero—missiles inbound. Acceleration forty-six thousand gravities! Time of flight at constant acceleration five-point-niner minutes!"

Oxana Dubroskaya stiffened in disbelief at CIC's shocking acceleration numbers. That was sixteen hundred gravities lower than a Javelin, but a Javelin's maximum powered endurance at that rate was only three minutes, with a terminal velocity of 84,000 KPS from rest and a powered envelope of only 7,575,930 kilometers. If the Manties could maintain that accel for *six* minutes, they really could engage her ships at this preposterous range!

That was her first thought, but an instant later the number of *missiles* registered, and she paled. *A hundred and twenty?* That was ridiculous! No light cruiser could fire that many missiles in a single broadside! There wasn't enough hull length to *mount* the damned tubes!

"Check those numbers!" she heard Diadoro snap.

"CIC confirms, Sir." The tech's voice was hoarse but steady. "Tracking's confidence is high."

"My God," someone murmured very quietly.

"Missile Defense Bravo!" Diadoro ordered.

"Missile Defense Bravo, aye, Sir!"

BatCruRon 491's ships altered course, turning their broadsides to face the incoming missiles to clear their missile defense systems' fields of fire.

❖　　❖　　❖

Oxana Dubroskaya's and Kelvin Diadoro's calculations had been based on six erroneous estimates. They'd gotten one thing right when they assumed, correctly, that the missiles the Royal Manticoran Navy had used at New Tuscany had been fired from pods, but they'd been wrong when they assumed that *only* pod-launched missiles could have such extended range. And to compound that initial error, they'd assumed their countermissiles, point defense, and electronic warfare systems were as capable as those of Manticore. Just as they'd assumed Manticore's penetration aids would be no *more* capable than their own, a Manticoran launch cycle of thirty seconds, and that *Rolands* could fire broadsides of no more than ten missiles per ship. And, finally, they'd assumed their laser heads were heavier than anything a "light cruiser" could launch.

It wasn't really their fault, given the inevitable slowness of interstellar communication. They had no official reports about the Battle of Spindle. They hadn't heard anything from the scattered Solarian forces which had already encountered Manticoran war-fighting technology during the course of the Star Empire's Operation Lacoön. It might not have mattered if they had. The almost inevitable reaction of the Solarian League Navy in general to the sudden revelation that it was technologically inferior to any opponent had been a state of denial, and after so many centuries of unquestioned supremacy, it was going to take time for even the most flexible of its officers to realize just how inferior their hardware truly was. Yet without those reports, without word of what was happening in places like Nolan and Zunker, BatCruRon 491's errors had been almost unavoidable.

Which didn't make them one bit less deadly.

In fact, their launch cycle estimates had been six seconds *low*, but that was only because Zavala's destroyers were launching stacked broadsides. The cycle time on his launchers was only eighteen seconds, but sequencing doubled broadsides put thirty-six seconds between each incoming flight of missiles. Unfortunately for BatCruRon 491, it also meant each of those salvos was better than twice as large as Kelvin Diadoro's worst-case estimate.

The Mark 16s streaked through space, accelerating by over four hundred and fifty kilometers per second every second, building on their motherships' base velocity as they roared towards Vice Admiral Dubroskaya's battlecruisers. At that range, with that much time to build velocity, they would be closing at better than 180,500 KPS—just over sixty percent of the speed of light—when they entered the Solarians' missile defense envelope, and the *Indefatigable* class' software had never been intended to deal with incoming, *evading* targets closing at such ridiculous velocities.

Of course, that was only part of Battlecruiser Squadron 491's problems.

❖   ❖   ❖

"Their Halo systems are active, Ma'am," Abigail Hearns announced, monitoring her displays closely. "CIC doesn't see any upgrades from what we observed at Spindle. The software tweaks seem to be handling it."

"Good," Naomi Kaplan replied, watching her own plot as a second wave of missile icons followed the first, thirty-six seconds and thirty thousand kilometers behind it, and a third followed. Then a fourth. In one minute and forty-eight seconds, DesRon 301 launched four hundred and eighty Mark 16s.

Given the differential in powered envelope, Zavala's DDs could have fired twenty-six stacked broadsides (assuming they'd had anywhere near that much ammunition) before the Solarians had the range to engage it in turn, but he'd decided four—one for each of

Dubroskaya's ships—should be enough to show her the error of her ways. And if it wasn't, there'd be plenty of time for additional launches to convince the surviving Solarians to see reason.

Assuming there are *any surviving Solarians, of course*, Kaplan thought with grim, vengeful satisfaction.

❖ ❖ ❖

BatCruRon 491's missile defense officers watched those impossible salvos stream towards them. Deep inside, every one of them hoped—prayed—the Manticoran missiles would go ballistic at any moment. That they'd been launched from so far out because the Manties had panicked, or because the enemy still thought he could bluff them. But even deeper inside, they knew that hadn't happened.

The only good thing about the extended range was that it gave them plenty of time to track the incoming shipkillers. A missile's impeller wedge was hard to miss and impossible to disguise, and that was good, because the Manty missiles' sheer closing velocity was going to make them copper-plated bitches to stop. There wasn't going to be time for more than a single counter-missile launch against each shipkiller, and anything the CMs missed was going to streak clear across the defensive basket and actually *pass* its target in only eight seconds. That meant their counter-missiles needed the best targeting and tracking data they could possibly provide, because each laser cluster was going to have a maximum of one shot before the shipkillers overflew the squadron . . . and each battlecruiser could bring only sixteen clusters to bear.

"At least they're going to be generating a lower Delta Vee for evasions than a Javelin could, Ma'am," Tucker

Kiernan murmured just loud enough for Dubroskaya to hear him. "That should help a little."

"*Something* better," Dubroskaya replied harshly, never looking away from the plot.

✧　　✧　　✧

"Coming up on initial EW activation...*now*," Abigail announced.

✧　　✧　　✧

Three hundred and forty-five seconds after launch, thirty-five million kilometers downrange from HMS *Tristram*, the electronic warfare platforms seeded throughout DesRon 301's lead missile salvo came to sudden life. They were carefully sequenced, the Dazzlers blowing holes in the Solarians' tracking systems, blinding them with furious strobes of interference, one thin sliver of an instant *before* the Dragon's Teeth spawned sudden shoals of false targets.

It came at the worst possible moment—just as they crossed the perimeter of Vice Admiral Dubroskaya's counter-missile envelope and half a heartbeat *after* the battlecruisers fired.

Fire control lost lock, throwing the CMs back onto their rudimentary seeking systems, but those onboard seekers had lost lock, as well. And when the Dazzlers faded, instead of a hundred and twenty incoming missiles, there were over *five* hundred. BatCruRon 491's pathetic total of thirty-two counter-missiles managed to reacquire and kill exactly one actual shipkiller... and its point defense clusters had barely seven seconds in which to try to find the one hundred real laser heads buried in that blinding confusion before they reached their standoff detonation range of thirty thousand kilometers.

The lasers failed. The computers and human beings behind them were still fighting desperately to find their targets when a tsunami of thermonuclear explosions sent a hurricane of bomb-pumped lasers into SLNS *Paladin*.

❖   ❖   ❖

Missile fire had always become progressively less accurate as the target got farther away from the firing ship and lightspeed lag began degrading the quality of the fire control information feeding the missiles' onboard computers. That creeping arthritis had thrown an ever greater load onto the missiles' more limited sensors and less capable computers as the range was extended, and the question of exactly when to cut the telemetry links and let the missiles look after themselves had been more of an art than a science, in many ways. That was the very reason the Royal Manticoran Navy had created Apollo, and the ability to control missiles—and EW platforms—in real time even when they were literally light-minutes downrange explained the deadly lethality of Manticoran multidrive missiles.

Under normal circumstances, DesRon 301 could have anticipated that a significant percentage of its missiles would have lost lock, been lured aside by decoys, fooled by jamming. But the circumstances weren't normal. First, the Ghost Rider platforms virtually on top of the Solarian battlecruisers *did* have FTL capability, which cut the effective communications lag between the squadron and its sensors in half. Second, Zavala had known his Dazzlers and Dragons Teeth were going to hammer Dubroskaya's missile defenses into ineffectuality, so his missiles hadn't been forced to engage in the last-minute evasion maneuvers normally required to squirm through the close-in fire of their targets' laser clusters. They'd been able to steady down sooner, maintain lock without losing sensor contact at a critical moment, and deploy their lasing rods farther out, with more time to align themselves and stabilize before detonation.

But perhaps even more importantly, the Royal Manticoran Navy had captured well over half of Sandra Crandall's fleet intact at the Battle of Spindle. They'd examined the Solarian League Navy's latest electronic warfare systems in detail. They'd analyzed their capabilities, noted their parameters and their weaknesses. Manticoran tactical officers like Abigail Hearns and Alice Gabrowski had pored over copies of the SLN's technical and tactical manuals like misers gloating over the Philosopher's Stone. They'd even been able to run captured Solarian simulations from *inside* the Sollies' systems, doctrine, and hardware during the two-week voyage from Montana to Saltash.

BatCruRon 491 might as well not have had any ECM. In fact, it would have fared better if it hadn't, because its EW systems didn't fool a single incoming missile. Instead, the defenses which were supposed to protect those ships actually became homing beacons, helping their executioners find them, and the effectiveness of his squadron's fire astounded even Jacob Zavala.

❖   ❖   ❖

Shock bleached Oxana Dubroskaya's face bone-white as hundreds of lasers ripped into Captain Borden McGillicuddy's ship.

The number of missiles, alone, had already made a mockery of her pre-engagement calculations. Their blinding speed, and the incredible power and effectiveness of the electronic warfare systems the Mark 16's onboard fusion plant made possible were even worse. She had no way of knowing her entire squadron's total defensive fire had destroyed only one shipkiller, but she knew it hadn't stopped many, and the survivors completely ignored the decoys of her deployed Halo platforms. They scorched in on *Paladin*, and her stomach clenched in horrified disbelief as CIC's estimate of the laser heads' throughput appeared on her tactical plot's sidebar.

The Mark 16's original fifteen-megaton warhead had been more destructive than any destroyer or light cruiser missile ever previously deployed, although dealing with battlecruiser armor—as Abigail Hearns had learned aboard HMS *Hexapuma* in the Monica System—had pushed it to its limits. But *Tristram* and her sisters were equipped with the Mod G version, with a *forty*-megaton warhead and improved gravity generators. That increased its effectiveness by a factor of over five... which made it more powerful than the brand-new Trebuchet *capital* ship missile the Solarian League Navy had just begun to deploy.

Paladin's armor had never been designed to face that sort of holocaust, and each of the ninety-nine Mark 16s which reached attack range carried six lasing rods. Five hundred and ninety-four x-ray lasers, each more destructive than anything a Solarian ship-of-the-wall could have thrown, stabbed out at McGillicuddy's ship. Perhaps a third of them wasted their fury on the impenetrable roof and floor of *Paladin*'s impeller wedge, but the others didn't. They punched through the battlecruiser's sidewalls with contemptuous ease, and armor shattered as the transfer energy blew into the ship's hull. The sidewalls and the radiation shielding inside them attenuated the lasers...slightly. Nothing could have *stopped* them, though, and eight hundred and fifty thousand tons of battlecruiser disintegrated in an incandescent flash like the heart of a star.

The entire attack, from the detonation of the first laser head to the last, took less than a second and a half. It was one terrible, blinding eruption of fury, crashing down upon its target like the fist of God. There was no time for life pods to launch. No time for small craft to escape the catastrophe. SLNS *Vanquisher*'s CIC couldn't even differentiate between the individual lasers that ripped the life out of her consort and took *Paladin*'s entire ship's company with them.

❖   ❖   ❖

"Tango One destroyed," Abigail Hearns heard her own voice report as the FTL Ghost Rider platforms updated her plot. "Tracking on Tango Two. Second salvo EW activation in...twenty-one seconds."

❖   ❖   ❖

"Raise Zavala!" Oxana Dubroskaya barked. "Tell him we surrender!"

❖   ❖   ❖

"Sir!" Lieutenant Wilson said suddenly. "They want to surrender!"

Jacob Zavala looked at Auerbach, and his nostrils flared.

"Put them on my display!" he snapped. An instant later, Vice Admiral Dubroskaya's face appeared before him. It was no longer the confident, angry face of a Solarian flag officer. It was ashen, the eyes huge.

"Captain—" she began over the Hermes buoy's faster-than-light channel, but a wave of his hand chopped her off.

"You're two light-minutes downrange, this link can't interface with my telemetry channels, and my birds don't have FTL links," he said sharply. "My next salvo's coming in in less than ten seconds. It's already committed, and there are two more right behind it that I can't abort before they get there. *Abandon immediately!*"

Dubroskaya stared at him for one more moment, then wheeled from her own pickup.

"Abandon ship!" she shouted. "All units, abandon ship—*now!*"

❖   ❖   ❖

SLNS *Inexorable* was Tango Four, the last ship on DesRon 301's targeting queue. She got three quarters of her personnel into life pods before she was destroyed, and SLNS *Success* managed to get almost half of her people out . . . but only one hundred and eleven of *Vanquisher's* two thousand crewmen escaped.

Vice Admiral Oxana Dubroskaya and her staff were not among them.

✦ Chapter Thirteen

"YOU HAVE ANOTHER COM request from Captain Zavala, Sir."

Maxence Kodou's voice was hushed, his expression stunned, and Damián Dueñas knew his own expression was as shocked as his assistant's. The governor looked across his office at Cicely Tiilikainen. She stood turned away from the window now, looking back at him, brown eyes wide. Then she gave herself a shake, like a cat emerging from water.

"My God, Damián," she said softly. "*Now* what do we do?"

Dueñas fought down a sudden mad urge to scream at her. How the hell did *he* know what they did now? This couldn't be happening. Dubroskaya had been confident—she'd *promised* him!—that she could easily defeat less than half a dozen Manty light cruisers! Of course he'd taken his senior naval officer's estimate at face value! This wasn't *his* fault!

His parents had grown up on a farm planet. He'd always been faintly embarrassed among his more sophisticated colleagues by his "sod-buster" origins and his parents' parochial turns of speech, yet he understood one of his mother's favorite clichés at last, because there was no other way to describe it as his mind skittered around like Elizabetta Dueñas' cow on ice, trying to grasp the immensity of the disaster which had just overwhelmed his career. There had to be some way to salvage the situation—there always *was*—but how?

"I—" he began, then realized he was just sitting there behind his desk with his mouth hanging open, waiting for words which refused to come.

"We're going to have to release their freighters," Tiilikainen said.

"No!" The single word jerked out of him without conscious thought, and Tiilikainen's lips tightened.

"We don't have a choice," she said harshly. "The man's a lunatic! We can't take a chance on what he'll do next if we *don't* let them go!"

"*No!*" Dueñas repeated, and his palm smacked down on his desk. "I'm not going to let some neobarb prick push the Solarian League around! I don't give a *damn* who he thinks he is!"

"Damián, he just took out four *battlecruisers*! You think the destroyers we've got left are going to faze him?"

"He wouldn't dare!"

"Damn it, what universe are you *living* in?" Tiilikainen stared at him. "There were eight thousand spacers on those battlecruisers, and he just blew them the hell away. He may be *crazy*, but based on his actions to date, don't you think we'd better assume he's willing to go right on doing exactly what he's *said* he'll do?"

"He won't." Dueñas shook his head stubbornly. "It's one thing to attack warships, Cicely, but there's no way he'd dare to attack the civilian infrastructure of a star system under the League's protection. He knows what we'd do to his pissant 'Star Empire' if he did anything like that!"

"You're delusional," Tiilikainen said flatly.

"You watch your tongue, *Lieutenant* Governor Tiilikainen!" Dueñas snapped.

"All right." Her voice was tight, but she nodded choppily. "You're the Governor, *Sir*, and this is your plan. So you tell me why you think he won't escalate this to whatever level he thinks he has to to get what he wants?"

"I already did," he grated. "The Manties are trying to sell themselves to the rest of the galaxy as the innocent victims of the piece, the plucky little guy willing to stand up against the big bad bully of the Solarian League. God knows they've been telling anyone who'd listen how all of those poor, oppressed citizens of the Talbott Cluster *begged* for admission into the Star Empire and whining about the way they've been 'forced' to defend themselves to protect *their* citizens! They may think they'll be able to sell that load of bullshit as far as confrontations with the Navy are concerned, but as soon as *they* start inflicting civilian casualties all their noble innocence goes right out the damn window, and they know it."

"I think you're wrong." Tiilikainen's tone was flatter than ever and she locked gazes with him. "I think this Zavala's not going to take any crap, Damián. And I think he just showed us exactly why we better not try to hand him any more of it. You know as well as I do that he's got you dead to rights on the provisions of the Treaty of Beowulf. We're in the *wrong* under interstellar law—you know that as well as I do—and he's going to push it however far and hard he has to to get what he was sent here to get. And after he does, the Manties are going to tell the entire galaxy that whoever got hurt along the way, it was *our* fault."

"No!"

She maintained lock with his eyes, both of them ignoring Kodou as he watched them from Dueñas' com. Silence hovered for several seconds, and then, finally, Tiilikainen drew a deep breath.

"You're going to insist on turning this into a *complete* disaster, aren't you?" she said almost conversationally.

His jaw muscles tightened, but she went on in that same, calm tone before he could respond.

"Well, I can't stop you. As you just pointed out, I'm only the *Lieutenant* Governor, and you've got the authority to do whatever you want to do. But I'm going on record now, officially, as recommending we give the Manties what they want and *don't* provoke them into killing anyone else. I won't be a party to any more insanity."

"You'll follow my instructions!" Dueñas snapped.

"Oh no, I won't." She shook her head. "You've gotten enough people killed for one day—you and Dubroskaya between you. I'm not going to help kill any more of them. And before you go charging off to make things even worse, I recommend you think about what Zavala told you in the beginning. MacArtney's going to want your head for a paperweight already. You really want to make him *more* pissed off at you?"

Under the surface of Dueñas' rage—and panic—a little voice whispered that Tiilikainen was right. It would be insane of Zavala to push the League even harder, but he'd already demonstrated the extent of his craziness. And the rest of the frigging Manties were just as crazy as *he* was.

This was all because of his sister's letter, he thought now. Given the system's isolation and the slowness with which interstellar news moved, Saltash was almost completely out of the loop. But Dueñas' sister had married a senior assistant undersecretary of the interior, and her last, gossipy letter (outpacing official correspondence, as private mail had a tendency to do) had mentioned rumors the Star Empire might recall its merchant fleet from Solarian shipping lanes. That would have been a blatantly hostile act—an economic act of war, really—against the entire League, and he'd found it difficult to believe even the Manties might do something like that. But then he'd realized they really might . . . and that because of Manuela's letter, he probably knew something the Manties out here didn't know yet themselves.

That was the starting point of his entire strategy: to act boldly on the information fortune had given him and preempt the Manties' plans. By moving quickly, proactively, he'd managed to stop the *Carolyn* and *Argonaut* before their ships' companies had a clue what was happening, and then Dubroskaya's battlecruisers had turned up, like a gift from God Himself, to supplement the miserable trio of destroyers he'd expected to have on hand. He'd been perfectly positioned to demonstrate that the League wasn't going to stand for such blatant economic aggression without retaliating . . . and to draw the Manties into showing their true colors and then forcing them to back down in the face of Solarian resolution and strength.

Which would just happen to make the career of one Damián Dueñas in the process.

And he'd been *right*, he told himself. He'd been right all along about what the Manties were really like, and Zavala's actions here in Saltash proved it! He just hadn't realized how insanely far they were prepared to go, and Dubroskaya's clumsy and complete incompetence had let the Manties get in another lucky—and treacherous—blow. But that wasn't how it was going to look back in Old Chicago. No, what Old Chicago was going to see was the destruction of four battlecruisers and whatever ass-covering version of events Tiilikainen turned in. She'd lay it all off on *him* in her report—he could see that already!—and MacArtney would throw him out of the air car at five thousand meters to keep any of this from spattering Frontier Security's upper echelons.

Give it up, that little voice said. *Give it up before it gets even worse.*

He wavered, but then he clenched his jaw and stiffened his spine. That was the kind of voice losers listened to. The kind of voice that ended with a man's career shuffled off forever into meaningless, dead-end assignments. What he needed was to demonstrate resolve. To show that no matter what the odds, *he* recognized the need to uphold the Solarian League's authority! Dubroskaya might have let herself be defeated by five stinking little light cruisers, and Tiilikainen might let herself be panicked into forgetting her responsibilities, forgetting that OFS' ability to do its job depended on facing down upstarts like the Star Empire of Manticore when they got above themselves. But *Damián Dueñas* wasn't going to forget!

"It may be that this Manticoran butcher *is* a big enough lunatic to attack civilians under the Office of Frontier Security's protection," he said coldly. "The Solarian League's made its position on this sort of action very plain, however, Lieutenant Governor Tiilikainen. We do *not* bargain with, and we do not make concessions *to*, neobarbs who threaten or even commit acts of terroristic violence against us or against the civilians we're charged to protect. You know as well as I do that that's been League policy for over two T-centuries!"

"You're even crazier than Zavala." Tiilikainen shook her head. "Look around you, Damián! What the hell are you going to use to *stop* him from doing whatever he wants?!"

"Maybe I *won't* be able to stop him," Dueñas said, settling back in the comfortable chair behind his huge desk and squaring his shoulders resolutely. "But unlike some people, I'm going to do my job. If he chooses to push this still further, then any additional consequences will be *his* responsibility, not anyone else's! I'll go far enough to agree to ask for instructions from higher authority, but that's as far as I'll bend. Anything else would be a violation of standing policy, as well as an act of abject cowardice."

Tiilikainen looked at him for a long moment. Then she shook her head again. There was something almost like pity under the anger in her eyes...and a lot more of something that looked a great deal like contempt to keep it company.

"You may think you'll be able to sell that to the

Ministry," she said finally. "You may even think you'll be able to sell it to the newsies as a way to keep MacArtney from hammering you for this. But you're wrong. You won't be able to, and it won't save you. The only thing you're going to manage is to get still more people killed." The last four words came out with a slow, measured emphasis, and her eyes were deadly. "You may be going to take my career down the toilet with you, and I can't stop you from doing that. But I, for one, refuse to be responsible for still more death and destruction. You do whatever you want to, *Governor*. I'm out of here."

She turned on her heel and stalked out, slamming the old-fashioned door behind her, and a scalding tide of fury darkened Dueñas' face. He came halfway to his feet, mouth opening to order her back into his office, but he stopped himself in time. She obviously wouldn't obey him, and there was no point letting her make her defiance even clearer. Besides, he could use this when it was time for him to write *his* report. Evidence of still more disloyalty, cowardice, and incompetence from his subordinates would only underscore his own determination and refusal to yield to a homicidal maniac's demands.

He settled back into his chair and inhaled deeply. Then he closed his eyes for a moment, willing his temper back under control, commanding himself to focus. When he was confident he had himself back in hand, he opened his eyes once more and looked at Kodou's holographic image.

"Put Captain Zavala through, Maxence," he said coldly.

❖   ❖   ❖

The official wallpaper of the Saltash System's governor's office disappeared—finally—from Jacob Zavala's display, replaced by the same fair-haired, hazel-eyed Solarian to whom he'd already spoken. There was something different about that face this time, though, and there damned well should be. The idiot had taken over ten minutes to respond, and it wasn't as if he had time to burn. DesRon 301 was only thirty-two minutes from Cinnamon orbit now, its velocity down to 10,568 KPS, and the range to Cinnamon was barely more than thirty-three light-seconds. Zavala would have thought that someone who'd just gotten the better part of six thousand of his own men and women killed might have felt a little urgency about keeping any *more* of them from dying, and he felt anger seething up inside him as he glared at the other man.

Just sit on that, Jacob, he told himself harshly. *Yes, he fucked up and got a lot of people killed, but so did* you. *You didn't have to sequence those launches that closely together. You could've put a couple of minutes between the first one and the second one— given Dubroskaya more time to react. But you didn't, did you?*

No, he hadn't, and he doubted anyone would ever fault him for it...except himself. Any board of inquiry would consider his actions and decisions fully justified by the disparity between his squadron's ability to absorb punishment and its adversary's potential firepower. And the accuracy of his own fire—and the sheer destructiveness of the Mod G laser heads—had taken him by surprise. He'd anticipated that it would take at least two salvos to completely cripple or destroy one of his adversaries. That was why he'd targeted one salvo on each battlecruiser, expecting to hammer it with enough damage even a Solly had to take note of it and consider that it might be wise to surrender quickly. He'd certainly never expected to *blow up* battlecruisers with a single launch each!

All of that was true, but he'd still had time. Perhaps he hadn't had the ammunition to justify going for Fire Plan Zephyr and simply wasting an entire double broadside that didn't inflict any damage at all. But he could have stretched Sledgehammer out, launched the first salvo with exactly the same targeting but waited a full minute, or even two, before launching the follow on salvos. If he'd done that, that first launch would have turned into a far more emphatic sort of Zephyr and given Dubroskaya one last chance to recognize the truth...and the time to save more of her people's lives.

He hadn't, and he knew that was one reason he felt such stark, murderous fury when he looked at Damián Dueñas.

"I trust you realize you've just murdered several thousand Solarian military personnel," Dueñas said without preamble. "I assure you the *Solarian League* isn't going to forget it!"

"Vice Admiral Dubroskaya—and *you*, Governor—were given ample opportunity to stand down and avoid any casualties," Zavala replied flatly, stepping on his own anger yet again. "And speaking of avoiding casualties, there's the small matter of those destroyers you've got hiding behind Cinnamon's moon."

"What about them?" Dueñas sounded like a man biting pieces out of a sheet of copper, and Zavala's eyes hardened.

"Governor, if I was prepared to engage your battlecruisers, what makes you think I won't engage your destroyers, as well? At my present deceleration, I'll enter their powered envelope in four minutes, and I'm no more prepared to allow them to shoot at my vessels than I was to permit Vice Admiral Dubroskaya to do the same thing. Given the piss-poor performance of your missiles and the obvious inadequacy of your antimissile defenses—not to mention your delay in bothering to reply to me—I will give your crews *five* minutes to begin abandoning ship. I don't intend to go any deeper into their engagement basket than that, however, no matter how crappy their weapon systems are. If they haven't begun evacuating their ships within that time limit, they'll receive the same treatment Vice Admiral Dubroskaya's battlecruisers received."

"Captain Zavala, the Solarian League doesn't respond well to threats, and even less well to the unprovoked massacre of its military personnel! You and you alone bear full responsibility for everything that's happened since you intruded into the sovereign territory of an independent star system under the protection of the Office of Frontier Security. Don't think for one moment that the League is going to overlook what you've done here today! Your actions have just enormously decreased any possibility of a peaceful resolution of the tensions between your star nation and mine. I have no doubt whatsoever that one of the Solarian League's demands if Manticore wishes to avoid the devastating war it's invited will be *your* surrender to face trial as a war criminal!"

"You've just used up forty-five seconds your destroyers don't have," Zavala replied in a voice of iron. "They now have four minutes and ten seconds."

"Are you *totally* insane?" Dueñas demanded. "Aren't you listening to a thing I'm saying?"

"Four minutes, Governor. And you might want to ask Vice Admiral Dubroskaya—or her ghost—if I abide by my time limits."

Their eyes locked, and Zavala found himself wondering just how pigheaded a single human being could be.

"Sir, I have another com request!" Lieutenant Wilson said quickly over his earbug. "It's a Captain Myau of the destroyer *Avenger*."

"Put it through—now!" Zavala said, and Dueñas' face vanished from his display, replaced by that of a tall, thin woman in the uniform of the Solarian League Navy. Her expression was hard, stony with hate as her eyes burned out of the com at him, but she had herself under better control than he would have expected.

"Captain Zavala?" she said flatly.

"Speaking."

"I am Captain Myau Ping-wa," she said in that same iron voice. "I feel certain the consequences of your actions are going to be profound, far-reaching, and ultimately disastrous for your star nation and your navy. Unfortunately, at this moment I'm forced to concede my tactical inferiority. It's obvious your weapons far outrange my own, and it's equally obvious you're prepared to use that advantage. I have to assume you're *not* prepared to enter my missile envelope before you do so, either. In your position, *I* certainly wouldn't be." Her lips might have twitched with the faintest shadow of a bitter smile. "That suggests you intend to destroy my destroyers as you did Vice Admiral Dubroskaya's battlecruisers unless

I accept your previous terms and stand down before you *do* enter my range. In light of how little time that leaves, as the senior officer—the senior *surviving* officer, at any rate—present, and absent instructions from the civilian authority in this star system," this time the flicker in her eyes was unmistakable, Zavala thought, "I'm ordering my personnel to abandon ship."

A diamond-dust glitter of life pods began to spill away from the destroyers' larger icons on Zavala's plot, and he felt a tremendous sense of relief.

"Be advised," Myau continued, "that my engineering officers have programmed remote self-destruct commands into my destroyers' fusion plants. Should any of your small craft approach within five thousand kilometers of any of my units, the enabling code will be sent and the ship—and any of your personnel who may happen to be aboard it—will be destroyed." She bared her teeth. "You won't be capturing any classified data in this star system."

"First, Captain Myau," Zavala told her, "I'm relieved to discover that *someone* in this star system has the mother wit to step away from avoidable bloodshed. I'm sure you don't want to hear this, but I respect how difficult your decision was, and I commend you for having the moral courage to ignore that idiot in the governor's office and save your people's lives. I take no more pleasure in killing people than the next man.

"Second, I have no intention of interfering with your destroyers in any way so long as they pose no threat to my own vessels or personnel. Had Governor Dueñas been willing to approach this situation with a modicum of rationality, I wouldn't find myself forced to require you to abandon ship in the first place . . .

and Vice Admiral Dubroskaya and several thousand of your fellow spacers would still be alive."

He held her eyes for another moment, letting her see the truth—and the flinty determination—in his own. He chose not to mention the fact that the Royal Manticoran Navy already had more captured information and hardware to play with than it could possibly use. Three obsolescent destroyers in a nowhere star system like Saltash wouldn't be worth the trouble to board. Nonetheless, he had to respect Myau's determination to see to it that they *wouldn't* be boarded.

"And now, Captain," Zavala resumed, "without any desire to appear disrespectful, I think I'd better return to my conversation with Governor Dueñas. I'm assuming you'll be in charge of search and rescue operations here in Saltash. While I can't allow your destroyers to participate, for obvious reasons, I give you my word that any civilian vessels you may dispatch for that purpose will be unmolested. And if you require any sensor assistance to locate survivors, I'll gladly provide it. In fact, we've dropped remote platforms at the site of the engagement and we're running a plot on all your pods, small craft, skinsuit transponder beacons, and debris. If you'll hold this circuit for a moment, I'll have my ops officer arrange a direct feed from our CIC to provide you with that information and keep it updated."

"Thank you," Myau said stiffly.

"You're welcome. As I said, I truly would prefer for no search and rescue operations to have become necessary." He looked over his shoulder at Lieutenant Commander Gabrowski. "Arrange it, please, Alice."

"Of course, Sir." Gabrowski nodded from her position

outside his com pickup's field of view. She also raised one hand and pressed the palm lightly across her eyes for a moment, then grinned, and Zavala nodded back. He'd known Gabrowski would make certain the sensor feed provided nothing but the most basic, essential information to the Sollies. It would never do to give Myau a look inside the RMN's actual capabilities.

"Good day, Captain Myau," Zavala said, and his mouth tightened as the Solarian officer's image disappeared.

"I suppose we'd better get the asshole back, Abhijat," he told Lieutenant Wilson.

❖   ❖   ❖

Fresh fury throbbed somewhere deep down inside Damián Dueñas as he stared at the wallpaper on his com. How *dared* Zavala simply put him on hold in the middle of a conversation?

He sat in his comfortable chair, fists clenched on the blotter in front of him, and the anger within was welcome. It fired his determination and buttressed him against fear, and however little he wanted to admit it, he needed that buttressing. He had to be strong, show his determination, if he wanted to spin this situation into something besides a disaster when the smoke cleared. The back of his brain was already busy with ways he could demonstrate that it was actually Tiilikainen's lack of support and Vice Admiral Dubroskaya's wildly inaccurate assessment of the military situation and her poor and aggressive advice as his senior military officer and expert which had created this disastrous situation. Bad as it was, it still wasn't something a skilled operator couldn't recover from, and whatever happened, Zavala's actions made it obvious he'd been right all along about the need to demonstrate the Manties' rogue behavior. So—

A symbol flickered in the corner of his display, and he scowled as he recognized Kodou's personal attention icon. He growled in irritation, but Kodou had been with him long enough to know how he'd react to any intrusion that wasn't amply justified, and he punched to accept the call.

"What?" he snapped, not trying to hide his anger at the interruption.

"Governor," his assistant said, "I've just received a report that Captain Myau's personnel have abandoned ship."

"*What?*" Dueñas barked with a very different emphasis.

"The report came in from system traffic control," Kodou's struggle to keep his own voice calm was evident. "They're arranging atmospheric clearance for the pods to planet here at Kernuish Spaceport."

"That *bitch!*" Dueñas snarled, betrayed by the Navy yet again. Myau had no business—no authority!—abandoning her command! *He* represented the Solarian League's authority in Saltash, not her! But what else should he have expected? Dubroskaya had been a fool, promising him victory over the Manties, so why shouldn't Myau turn out to be a coward too terrified even to *face* them?!

He closed his eyes once more, nostrils flaring, and made himself suck in a deep lungful of oxygen. He stayed that way for a handful of seconds, then reopened his eyes and forced his hands to relax before his fingernails dug bleeding gouges in his palms.

Actually, this could work in his favor, he realized

as the automatic spike of fury subsided. *He* hadn't ordered her to stand down; she'd done it unilaterally, without so much as consulting him, far less any *order* to do so! It was a clear case of cowardice in the face of the enemy, one which couldn't possibly be charged to him, since she hadn't even warned him of her intentions...and it could only emphasize how poorly he'd been served from the very beginning by the naval forces assigned to support him here in Saltash. It was scarcely his fault the Navy had first misled and misadvised and then betrayed him.

His mind flickered through the best ways to make the Navy's culpability clear without looking as if he were trying to alibi his own actions. Fortunately, he and Dubroskaya had discussed his original plans privately, face-to-face, here in his office. He'd have to review the records of their later com conversations, verify exactly what had been said so he could be certain his account of those initial conversations jibed with it, but he was an old hand at crafting properly phrased memoranda, and—

The wallpaper in his display—and Kodou's image—disappeared, replaced by Jacob Zavala's face.

"I apologize for the delay, Governor," the Manticoran said without any discernible sincerity, "but I had to take another call. Something about saving lives, I'm afraid."

"Should I assume you're referring to Captain Myau's cowardly decision to surrender to your threats?"

"No. You should assume I'm referring to Captain Myau's sanity and moral courage in refusing to see her personnel killed because of your pigheaded, fatuous arrogance."

Dueñas felt his face darken again, and his jaw clenched.

He's trying to make you lose your temper, he told himself. *Trying to rattle you, make you look like some out-of-control hothead.*

"Personal insults to the official representative of another star nation may be typical of the 'Star Empire of Manticore's' approach to interstellar relations, Captain," he said coldly. "And I'm sure the Solarian League's government is going to be deeply impressed by your bizarre version of diplomacy. No doubt the Solarian electorate will be equally impressed when the record of this conversation is released. Unfortunately, your insults are no more likely than your murderous actions have already been to cause me to comply with your outrageous and flagrantly illegal demands."

Zavala cocked his head, eyes narrowed as he considered Dueñas from the com, and the governor looked back with a hard, steady gaze. They stayed that way for several seconds, and then Zavala shook his head.

"Governor, I'm at a loss to understand why you're so determined to turn a disaster into a complete debacle. You've already gotten thousands of Solarian naval personnel killed. Now you're proposing to get still more people killed in pursuit of an action you know perfectly well was illegal from the outset? Have you considered psychological counseling?"

"More insults, Captain?" Dueñas smiled thinly. "They seem to be getting a little less trenchant—are you running low on inspiration? Or perhaps you're beginning to realize how the blood of the men and women you've murdered today is going to spatter your precious Star Empire once word of it gets back to the Sol System?"

"I'm not taking anyone's blood lightly, Governor." Zavala's tone could have frozen helium. "I would very much prefer for no one to have been killed. Unfortunately, you and Vice Admiral Dubroskaya took that decision out of my hands. And I don't think you quite appreciate the actual state of affairs between the Star Empire of Manticore and the Solarian League at this moment. The deaths of Vice Admiral Dubroskaya and so many of her personnel are a tragedy, and one which I deeply regret, but I doubt very much that they're going to have any significant impact on Manticore's relations with the League. Your career, yes; interstellar relations, no."

"I assure you, you're mistaken about that."

"Governor Dueñas," there was something like a note of pity in the Manticoran's icy voice, "you're clearly even more poorly informed about current events than I'd thought you could be. Just under three T-months ago, Fleet Admiral Crandall invaded the Spindle System. Twenty-three of her superdreadnoughts were effectively destroyed; another forty-eight surrendered, along with every screening and support unit. Over a *hundred thousand* of her personnel were killed, just about as quickly as Vice Admiral Dubroskaya's people were killed here, and all of the rest—*all* of them, Governor; every single man and woman—are now POWs of the Star Empire of Manticore. As deeply as I regret the lives which have been lost today, they're barely even a footnote to what's already happened. The only questions you should be thinking about right now are how to keep anyone else who doesn't have to die from being killed and how your own superiors are going to react to the consequences of your arrogant, high-handed, illegal, boneheaded actions in first seizing Manticoran merchant vessels, secondly refusing to release them, and thirdly provoking the engagement which ended so disastrously for Vice Admiral Dubroskaya's squadron."

Dueñas' eyes widened, despite himself. There hadn't been time for details of what had happened in Spindle to reach Saltash. All they'd had had been third-hand rumors and fragments carried by a single ship—a *merchant* ship, not a naval vessel or an official courier—which everyone had realized must be wildly exaggerated. Yet even those obviously inflated loss figures had fallen far short of what Zavala had just said.

You don't have any corroboration of his story, the governor reminded himself, *and he's got every reason to lie to convince you to back down. Besides, that's ridiculous! Almost* eighty *Solarian superdreadnoughts taken out by a neobarb navy with delusions of grandeur? Preposterous!*

"I trust you'll understand why I have to take that assertion with a grain of salt, Captain Zavala," he heard himself say.

"You can take it with whatever you like, but that won't change what actually happened. And in regard to that—and because this entire conversation is being recorded from my side and I intend to demonstrate that I did everything in my power to convince you to show a gram of rationality—I'm prepared to transmit to you copies of *Solarian* reporters' accounts of the Battle of Spindle from League news services with correspondents in Spindle. You may not wish to take my word for it, and I'm sure you could convince yourself any Manticoran records I showed you had been falsified, but perhaps you'd be impressed by Solarian reportage of events there."

Dueñas felt himself waver and stiffened his nerve.

"If you could falsify one set of records, you could falsify as many as you like," he replied harshly. "And whatever may have or may not have happened in Spindle, you're in Saltash now. The policies of the Solarian League and the Office of Frontier Security when confronted with acts of terrorism against star systems under Solarian protection are known to the entire galaxy. I can't prevent you from murdering still more Solarian personnel and endangering the lives, property, and livelihoods of the citizens of Saltash, but I can—and will—refuse to condone your actions or lend them any tincture of legality. If you persist in this blatant aggression, the consequences will be your responsibility, and the ultimate repercussions for your star nation will be far worse than you seem able to grasp."

"So you're categorically refusing to release the Manticoran personnel and civilian vessels you've illegally imprisoned and seized in this star system?"

"I'm categorically refusing to allow you to violate a legally declared medical quarantine, and I'm categorically refusing to kowtow to the irresponsible and illegal use of naked force against the Solarian League Navy."

"In that case, and since we seem to be making certain this is all part of the official record, be advised, Governor, that I intend to have those personnel and those vessels back." Zavala's eyes bored into Dueñas. "I'm informing you now that I intend to put a boarding party aboard Shona Station. If every Manticoran interned in this system is surrendered—*unharmed*—when my personnel board the station, and if the Manticoran freighters held in this system are allowed to depart, no one else needs to be injured or killed. If, however, our people are not surrendered, or if they are harmed in any way, or if those freighters are not allowed to depart unhindered, I will take whatever military action seems appropriate, up to and including the use—the *additional* use—of deadly force. And if any of our people are harmed or treated as hostages threatened with harm, I will regard the personnel responsible for those actions as pirates liable to summary execution. Since it's evident that attempting to convince you to see reason is about as effective as arguing with a rock, I see no point in further discussion. I've informed you of my intentions and of the consequences of continued intransigence on your part. So far as I'm concerned, this conversation is over. I advise you to inform whoever's in charge of Shona Station that my pinnaces will be docking with the station within fifteen minutes of my destroyers' arrival in Cinnamon orbit, however." He showed his teeth. "I wouldn't want anyone else to get hurt just because they didn't know we were coming."

He gazed at Dueñas for another heartbeat, and the governor stared back, trying to find a response. None had come to him before Zavala nodded coldly.

"Good day, Governor Dueñas."

✦ Chapter Fourteen

CAPTAIN VALENTINE MACNAUGHTAN OF the Saltash Space Service scowled in irritation as the distinctive signal of a private com request chimed in his earbug. In Captain MacNaughtan's opinion, this wasn't the best imaginable time for a friend to be comming him. Not with the entire star system going rapidly to hell and five Manticoran light cruisers decelerating steadily towards the space station for which he was ostensibly responsible.

He kept his eyes on the display in front of him, ignoring the signal while he wondered what the hell Governor Dueñas thought he was doing. MacNaughtan had been as stunned as anyone by the almost casual obliteration of Vice Admiral Dubroskaya's battlecruisers, but that lent a certain emphasis—a *lot* of emphasis, actually—to his present concerns. Although Shona Station's megaton mass dwarfed any battlecruiser ever built, it was also far more fragile...and stuffed full of *civilians*, not just people in uniform. It seemed self-evident to that station's CO that keeping ships which could shred battlecruisers from doing the same thing to Shona would be a good idea, yet he was beginning to think he was the only person in the entire star system that thought had occurred to.

Dueñas, you miserable asshole, he thought scathingly. *You don't have a frigging clue, do you? I really don't want to see what you screw up for an encore, but I've got a nasty feeling I'm going to. Jesus, Mary, and Joseph, Grandpa, what did you think you were doing?*

The question had all sorts of jagged personal edges at the moment, since Captain MacNaughtan's grandfather had been the President of MacPhee whose brainstorm had led to the Office of Frontier Security's being invited into Saltash in the first place. The old man had lived to regret it, but by and large, MacNaughtan didn't see where he'd had a lot of choice. Saltashans prided themselves on their stubbornness, and they'd been all set to reprise Old Earth's Final War on Cinnamon, even though the stubbornest had to admit their original quarrel had arisen out of an almost trivial dispute over *fishing* rights, of all damned things! Well, MacNaughtan's grandmother had always claimed that no one else in the entire Ante Diaspora history of the human race had been able to hold a grudge, cherish a feud, or cling to a lost cause like the Scots. Except, perhaps, she'd added thoughtfully, the Irish. Apparently some things changed even less than others.

MacNaughtan didn't know about that. He wasn't a student of history, and he'd had other things to concern himself with here in Saltash. Like dealing with the consequences of Frontier Security's arrival. While he was willing to concede even OFS was preferable to a sterilized planet, there were times he wasn't certain just *how* preferable it might be. His was one of the families which had managed to cling to a position of at least some power and privilege even under the new management, which was how he'd come to command Shona Station in the first place. But that also meant his family was in a better position than most to realize just how cynical the Sollies' exploitation of his home system actually was.

It wasn't that systems like Saltash provided enormous amounts of cash to the League compared to even the smallest Core system. Not individually, at any rate. Yet there were so *many* of them, each of them one more revenue-producing node in Frontier Security's "benevolent" little empire, that the aggregate cash flow was stupendous. And the amounts the League extracted from Saltash in the form of "service fees" and "licensing fees" were more than enough to choke off any domestic economic growth. MacNaughtan knew Saltash was better off than many—probably the majority—of the protectorate systems, and Cinnamon had escaped the kind of grinding poverty that was the fate of all too many other worlds in the Verge. But he wasn't certain stagnation was a lot better than penury, and he *was* certain that Frontier Security apparatchiks like Damián Dueñas had absolutely no interest in changing the situation. It was working just fine for *them* the way it was.

Or it had been until today, at any rate. Unfortunately, Dueñas wasn't the one who was going to pay the heaviest price. Or who'd already paid it, for that matter. MacNaughtan hadn't known Dubroskaya well— she hadn't been in-system long enough—but she'd sure as hell deserved better than she'd gotten! And the MacNaughtan clan had been around long enough for him to know that with Dubroskaya dead, Dueñas was going to heap all the responsibility for what had happened here on her, if he could. It was amazing how convenient dead scapegoats who weren't around to dispute what had happened could be.

And if anything else goes wrong, he's going to hang the responsibility for that *on anyone he can, too. Which puts* me *right in the line of fire, and—*

His earbug chimed again, louder, and he growled a silent mental curse as it added a priority sequence to the signal.

He looked around for a moment, then crooked a finger at Commander Tad Rankeillor, his executive officer.

"Take the throne for a minute, Tad," he said, jerking his thumb over his shoulder at the command chair where he should technically have parked his posterior. "Apparently I have to take a call."

"Hell of a time for it," Rankeillor grunted. The SSS wasn't all that big on spit and polish, and MacNaughtan and Rankeillor had known one another since boyhood. "Tell Maura I said hi."

"It's not Maura," MacNaughtan said, hovering on the edge of a grin despite the catastrophe looming its way towards them. He and Maura had been married for less than six local months, and Rankeillor had been his best man.

"Sure it isn't." Rankeillor rolled his eyes.

"Not her combination," MacNaughtan said, and Rankeillor's eyes stopped rolling and narrowed.

"Who the hell else would com you at a moment like this?"

"If you'll take the damned deck, I'll find out!" MacNaughtan said tartly, and Rankeillor nodded.

"Sorry," he said. "You're relieved."

"I stand relieved," MacNaughtan replied. Spit and polish or not, there were some formalities and procedures which simply had to be observed.

Rankeillor moved closer to the master plot, and MacNaughtan stepped back a few paces, far enough to stay out of everyone else's way, and punched to accept the audio-only call.

"MacNaughtan," he said tersely.

"Captain, it's Cicely Tiilikainen," a voice said, and he felt his shoulders stiffen.

Tiilikainen had been stationed in Saltash longer than any of its previous governors or lieutenant governors. If Valentine MacNaughtan had been inclined trust any OFS bureaucrat, it would probably have been Tiilikainen. As it was, he at least *mistrusted* her less than any of her predecessors. To be honest, however, that wasn't saying a great deal, and his eyes narrowed as he wondered why she was on his private circuit rather than one of the official com channels.

"Yes?" he responded after a moment, some instinct prompting him to use no names or official titles any of his watch standers might overhear.

"I'm on your private combination because I'm pretty sure this is a conversation neither of us would want to make part of the official record," Tiilikainen said, as if she'd read his mind. "The governor and I just had a . . . disagreement."

"And?" MacNaughtan said warily. Getting into the crossfire between Frontier Security bureaucrats was *not* something a prudent Saltashan did.

"And I told him where he could put any further cooperation from me," Tiilikainen told him flatly. "I never did like this brainstorm of his, and I wish to hell I'd argued harder when he first came up with it. But I didn't, and now it's come home to roost with a vengeance. You know what happened to Dubroskaya."

"Yes," he said, although it hadn't been a question.

"Well, Dueñas still refuses to back down. He even refused to authorize Myau to evacuate her ships."

"What?" MacNaughtan's brows knit, and he glanced at the plot showing the thick shower of life pods descending towards Cinnamon atmosphere. "But—"

"Myau did that on her own . . . after I gave her a heads-up." MacNaughtan could almost see Tiilikainen's tart, sharp edged grimace even over the audio-only link. "I suggested to her that it would probably be best to initiate direct contact with this Zavala before our esteemed Governor got around to complicating things for her. She still may take it in the ear, but at least she didn't have any orders *not* to abandon—yet—and she can make a pretty damned good case for having to make a quick decision without any guidance from her civilian superiors. Officially, at least."

"I see. And you're comming me to do the same thing?"

"More or less." He heard the sound of an exasperated exhalation. "You're not in the same position Myau was. You can't just evacuate the station, and I'm damned sure he's going to be ordering you and MacWilliams—and that jackass Pole—*not* to release the Manties. He's got this notion Zavala won't push it, won't dare to take any action that could get civilians hurt."

"Which you think he will?" MacNaughtan kept his voice down, but his expression tightened.

"My honest impression? I don't think he *wants* to, but this is one genuine hard-ass, Val. I don't know how typical he is of Manties in general, but this guy isn't going to take any crap from anybody, and the fact is that we're legally in the wrong on this one. Worse, Zavala *knows* we are, and I think he's just demonstrated he isn't likely to spend a lot of time dithering about his next move. I don't know what he may have said to Dueñas after I left, but if I had to guess, it would be something along the lines of give me back my nationals, and nobody else needs to get hurt. Get in my way, and a *lot* of people will get hurt. And since the nationals in question happen to be aboard *your* space station..."

Her voice trailed off in the verbal equivalent of a shrug, and MacNaughtan closed his eyes. Wonderful. This day just kept getting better and better.

"Well, I appreciate the information, Sir," he said briskly, raising his voice just enough for anyone standing close enough to him to hear the honorific's gender. "Unfortunately, I've got to get back to work now. Things are a little lively here, you know, and I probably need to keep the link open for official calls."

"I do know, and...I'm sorry. Luck."

Tiilikainen disconnected, and MacNaughtan drew a deep breath, then strode back over to Rankeillor.

"Get hold of Bridie," he said softly. "I need her and MacGeechan in my briefing room ten minutes ago. And for God's sake *don't* put it on the PA!"

"I'll do that thing," Rankeillor agreed, looking less surprised than he might have, and MacNaughtan

u've pointed out, your people are much more
ly equipped than Major Pole's gendarmes. Under
circumstances, I feel you and Lieutenant Mac-
echan would be best employed using your per-
nel for crowd control, public safety, and to back
Commander MacVey's damage control crews, in
ase they should be needed. My feeling is that we
lso ought to immediately begin evacuating civilian
personnel from Victor Seven in order to facilitate
any movements Major Pole may feel it's appropriate
for him to make."

"Yes, Sir." MacWilliams nodded.

Victor Seven was the station habitat module which
had been assigned to the gendarmes ever since their
original dispatch to Saltash. Actually, they'd assigned it
to themselves, since it had originally been intended as
the station's VIP habitat and was still the largest, most
luxuriously appointed module Shona Station boasted.
It had also been refitted to contain the Gendarmerie's
brig facilities, which were separate from those of the
Saltash Space Service's police forces. No one had
been especially happy about the notion of confining
the Manticoran merchant spacers in Victor Seven; the
general feeling had been that Saltash was already on
thin ice, and the Gendarmerie was not famous for
the consideration with which it treated individuals
in its custody. Under the circumstances, however,
MacNaughtan couldn't pretend he was unhappy to
have them in Victor Seven, because aside from a
few dozen service personnel with duty stations in the
area, the only people in Victor Seven were going to
be gendarmes and the Manties.

"It's a pity," MacNaughtan continued, "that our own

nodded and headed for the briefing room just off
Shona Station's command deck.

Lieutenant Commander Bridie MacWilliams, the
commander of the SSS police forces aboard the station,
and Lieutenant Eardsidh MacGeechan, her second-
in-command, arrived in MacNaughtan's briefing room
in under three minutes. He wasn't really surprised.
MacWilliams was young, but he'd always known she
was quick. She was also the sort who thought ahead,
and she'd probably been waiting by her com with
her track shoes already sealed, anticipating his call.

"You called, Skipper?" she said as she and Mac-
Geechan stepped through the door and it closed
behind them.

"I did indeed." He smiled bleakly. "I think it's
entirely possible things are about to get really ugly."

"Ugly as in right here aboard the Station? Or as in
getting even uglier in general?" MacWilliams asked.

"Maybe both, but I'm more concerned about Shona
than anything else. I've just been informed by a reliable source that Governor Dueñas has no intention
of meeting the Manties' demand that their personnel
be released to them."

"Jesus," MacGeechan muttered, then blushed and
shook himself. "Sorry, Sir."

"You're not thinking anything I'm not, Lieutenant,"
MacNaughtan assured him.

"Should I take it, Sir, that 'a reliable source' *wasn't*
Governor Dueñas?" MacWilliams asked, her eyes
shrewd.

"I think we should just move along quickly without
getting into that particular point," MacNaughtan told

her with a tight smile. "What matters right this minute is that the Manties are going to insist we hand their people over and Dueñas is going to order us *not* to hand their people over. Under the circumstances, I could live with telling our esteemed Governor to suck vacuum, but I strongly suspect Major Pole would be disinclined to support us in that."

MacWilliams' blue eyes hardened. She and Major John Pole, the CO of the Solarian Gendarmerie intervention battalion OFS had stationed here aboard Shona Station, loathed one another. Pole's people hadn't enforced the kind of brutal reign of terror Frontier Security had imposed—or supported, at any rate—in all too many protectorate systems, but that didn't make him a knight in shining armor. MacWilliams and her predecessor had been forced to deal with several complaints about Pole, most from women who hadn't responded favorably enough to his advances. Any Saltashan would have been hammered hard over the same sort of accusations. At the very least, he would have been dragged in while they were thoroughly investigated. But local police forces didn't go around investigating the commanders of intervention battalions. That was one of the facts of life in the Verge, and it stuck in Bridie MacWilliams' craw sideways.

Worse, as the Gendarmes' CO, Pole set the standard. Two or three of his troopers had gotten far enough out of line that the previous OFS governor had actually authorized their prosecution, and one of them had even been broken out of the Gendarmerie and sent away for ten T-years of hard time on the gas-extraction platforms orbiting Himalaya. Dueñas had promptly turned the clock back, however ...

which was how MacWilliams came to [...] ent position, since one of the governor's [...] had been to sack her predecessor precis[...] of those prosecutions.

"Skipper," she said now, "I think we hav[...] options here. I've got around five hundred [...] the entire Station, most with nothing heavie[...] side arms, and even after detachments, Pole's g[...] better part of two *companies* of gendarmes on-sta[...] I don't have an up-to-the-minute count, but he's [...] to have close to three hundred people up here, an[...] they've got a lot heavier equipment than mine do."

"Two hundred and seventy-three as of this morning, Ma'am," MacGeechan put in. "Not counting three on sick call in the infirmary." MacNaughtan and MacWilliams both looked at him with raised eyebrows, and he shrugged. "I just thought it was something I should be checking on, given the situation. Just so we could have a better feel for how we might ... integrate our own people with his if we had to, you understand."

"I believe I do, Eardsidh," MacWilliams told him with an off-center smile. "I believe I do."

Then her smile faded and she turned back to MacNaughtan.

"Sir, I think Major Pole will obey his orders—his *legal* orders, of course—from Governor Dueñas. And I can't see anything aboard Shona Station which could reasonably be expected to prevent him from doing so."

She'd chosen her words carefully, MacNaughtan noted. All of them could honestly testify that no one had even so much as suggested that they might attempt to resist the governor's instructions.

"I don't either," he told her. "On the other hand,

lack of personnel and equipment means your available manpower's going to be fully employed maintaining security throughout the rest of the station. But while we won't be able to reinforce or support the Major, I want every effort made to at least guarantee the integrity of the station in general and to ensure that he and *his* people are relieved of any responsibility which might distract them from Governor Dueñas' orders. I trust that's clear, Commander MacWilliams."

"Yes, Sir." MacWilliams smiled thinly at him. "Lieutenant MacGeechan and I will get right on that."

⬦   ⬦   ⬦

"Let's raise the station, Abhijat."

"Yes, Sir," Lieutenant Wilson replied, and Jacob Zavala sat back, watching the tactical plot while he waited.

DesRon 301 had settled into orbit around the planet Cinnamon. Traffic control hadn't assigned them a parking orbit, for some reason, but HMS *Kay*'s astrogator had managed to find one. It wasn't as if there was an enormous amount of orbital traffic to pick a way around, after all.

Captain Myau's destroyers remained in orbit around Cinnamon's moon, and Zavala was perfectly content to leave them there. A handful of civilian vessels had moved nervously away from the planet as the squadron entered orbit, but aside from that things seemed reasonably calm. Maybe that was because the majority of the star system's shipping was out rescuing the survivors of Oxana Dubroskaya's squadron.

Zavala's lips tightened again at that thought, but it wasn't one he was prepared to dwell upon. Right now, he had to concentrate on other things, and he couldn't pretend he wasn't grateful for the distraction. On the other hand, the "other things" had the potential to turn into an even more horrendous mess than the massacre of Dubroskaya's battlecruisers. After all, there'd been only eight thousand or so human beings on those warships; there were a *quarter million* human beings on Shona Station.

Which is the reason—as that pain in the ass Dueñas clearly understands—we can't use Mark 16s as door knockers this time around, he thought grimly. *And if there really is an intervention battalion in there, it's going to be one hell of a trick to pry our people loose without getting a lot of other people a lot more personally killed. Unless the station CO's another Myau, at any rate. And what're the odds of that if he's got a stack of gendarmes breathing down his neck?*

"I've got the station commander for you, Sir," Lieutenant Wilson said, and Zavala looked up from the plot.

"Thanks," he said, and turned to his com.

◆   ◆   ◆

"I'm Captain Jacob Zavala, Royal Manticoran Navy," the smallish, dark-skinned man on the com display said. He was quite unlike the dominant genotype here in Saltash, but despite his diminutive stature and polite tone, no one was likely to take any liberties with him once they got a good look at his eyes, MacNaughtan thought.

"Am I addressing the commanding officer of Shona Station?" the Manticoran continued in that same courteous yet unyielding voice.

"I'm Captain Valentine MacNaughtan," MacNaughtan replied. "I'm the senior Saltash Space Service officer aboard."

That weasel-worded evasion of responsibility shamed him, but there was no point pretending otherwise, and this Zavala no doubt understood that. For purposes of shifting blame, Governor Dueñas would be delighted to embrace the legal fiction that MacNaughtan genuinely commanded Shona Station. If MacNaughtan had ever been foolish enough to forget he simply reigned over the station administratively while OFS actually *ruled* everything in the star system, he would have been replaced with dizzying speed.

Zavala's eyes flickered, and MacNaughtan felt his face try to heat at the other man's obvious awareness of that reality. But the Manticoran simply nodded.

"I believe I understand your position, Captain MacNaughtan," he said. "Unfortunately, you and I are in something of a difficult situation at the moment. There are illegally detained Manticoran nationals aboard your station. I fully realize they were detained—I'm sorry, '*quarantined*'—on the orders of Governor Dueñas, not those of the Saltash Space Service. The problem is that I've been ordered to retrieve them, and Governor Dueñas has been . . . less than cooperative, shall we say? In fact, he's flatly refused to release them. And the reason this is unfortunate is that I'm going to have to insist on recovering them. In fact, my orders are to do precisely that . . . by whatever means may be necessary. I'm afraid Vice Admiral Dubroskaya's squadron has already discovered what that means."

If those blue eyes had flickered before, they were rock-steady and laser-sharp now, MacNaughtan observed with a sinking sensation.

"I informed Governor Dueñas I would be sending a boarding party aboard your station within fifteen minutes of making Cinnamon orbit," Zavala continued. "My pinnaces are en route now. I have no desire to inflict additional casualties—especially not *civilian* casualties—but my orders are clear and I intend to follow them. That means my personnel will be coming aboard Shona Station very shortly. I don't suppose Governor Dueñas has instructed you to release the people I've come to reclaim into my custody?"

"I'm afraid he hasn't," MacNaughtan replied.

"May I ask what instructions, if any, he has given you?"

"I've been informed that he declines to release your people from quarantine," MacNaughtan responded in a very careful tone. "Aside from that I have no specific instructions in regard to this matter."

"Should I assume that means you intend to refuse to cooperate with my boarding party?" Zavala's voice was noticeably colder, and MacNaughtan drew a deep breath.

"Your personnel aren't in the Saltash Space Service's custody," he said. "Their security and medical treatment are an Office of Frontier Security responsibility under the terms of OFS' management of traffic here in Saltash. Governor Dueñas made that point to me rather firmly when his medical staff determined that a quarantine was appropriate. As a consequence, I can't release them to you, however cooperative I might otherwise wish to be."

Zavala gazed at him for a moment, lips pursed thoughtfully. Then the Manticoran tipped back in his command chair and cocked his head to one side.

"May I assume, then, that you're as desirous as I am to avoid any unfortunate incidents aboard your station, Captain?"

"I'm administratively responsible for the safety and well-being of the better part of a quarter million civilians, not to mention a major portion of my star system's industrial infrastructure, Captain Zavala," MacNaughtan said flatly. "I think you can assume no one in the entire galaxy could be more desirous of avoiding 'unfortunate incidents' than I am."

"I can appreciate that. I trust *you* can appreciate that my people *are* coming aboard, one way or another. I would vastly prefer for my pinnaces to dock with Shona Station like any other small craft and for my personnel to come and go with the minimum disturbance of your routine, your civilians' well-being, or the operation of your industrial nodes. Since both of us would obviously prefer that outcome, will you be good enough to issue docking clearance?"

"I suspect Governor Dueñas would prefer for me to refuse you clearance, Captain Zavala. Unfortunately, he hasn't specifically told me that, and it seems evident you have more than sufficient firepower available to compel me to at least allow you access to the station. That being the case, yes, your pinnaces are cleared to dock, although I feel constrained to point out that it's only under official protest. Understand, however," he looked very steadily into Zavala's eyes, "that I *am* responsible for those civilians' safety. Should they be endangered, it will be my duty to intervene."

He spoke firmly, crisply, and Zavala nodded.

"I understand, Captain MacNaughtan, and I assure you my people will have no intention of endangering your civilians. Of course, once they board, they *will* have to make contact with the Frontier Security personnel responsible for maintaining the medical quarantine aboard your station. Would it be possible for you to provide them with a guide or a map board to direct them to the quarantine facilities when they come aboard?"

"I can certainly see to it that they have directions," MacNaughtan replied. "And in order to minimize the possibility of any of those incidents you and I both want to avoid, I've taken the precaution of evacuating both civilian and Saltash Space Service personnel from the module supporting the quarantine facilities."

"I appreciate that," Zavala said with a thin smile. "Hopefully this will be a relatively painless visit, Captain. We'll certainly try to keep it that way, at least."

❖ ❖ ❖

"All right, people," Lieutenant Abigail Hearns said, standing at the head of the pinnace passenger compartment. Her image appeared simultaneously on the main bulkhead viewscreens in each of the other three pinnaces, and she hoped she looked calmer than she actually felt.

"According to our last update, the locals don't want any part of this. They haven't come right out and said so, but we have docking clearance and their CO's withdrawn his personnel from the portion of the station between our docking bay and our people. That's the good news. The bad news is that we still don't know how many of the gendarmes stationed here are currently on board and how many may be deployed elsewhere in the system, but we do know our people are in their custody and they don't have orders to give them back."

She saw the tension in the faces actually looking back at her aboard her own pinnace and she knew the faces aboard the other small craft of her flight were just as tense. And well they should be, since only one member of her entire boarding party had ever been a Marine. Gendarmerie intervention battalions had a well-earned reputation as thugs and enforcers, rather than soldiers, but they were at least nominally trained with infantry and support weapons, and there were almost certainly more of them aboard Shona Station than there were Manticorans and Graysons aboard her pinnaces.

"Obviously, we all hoped these people would be smart enough to recognize reality when it smacked them in the face," she continued. "What happened to their battlecruisers should have convinced them it would be a really, really bad idea to make Commodore Zavala unhappy with them. They seem to be a little slow, however...even for Sollies."

Her timing on the last three words was perfect, and several people laughed out loud despite the tension curdling the pinnace's atmosphere.

"I have no intention of getting any of you killed," she told them when the laughter had faded. "A lot of you were with me and Mateo pulling SAR in Spindle, and that's why you lucky souls get to take point with the two of us. The rest of you know the plan, and I expect you to stick to it. We don't want any shooting if it can possibly be avoided. We don't want to escalate any confrontations that don't have to be escalated. Having said that, your own safety is paramount. I don't want *anyone* killed if we can avoid it, but I'd a lot rather have some Solly gendarme killed than one of you. Is that clear?"

Heads nodded, and she nodded back.

"Once we've boarded, the pinnaces will undock under Lieutenant Xamar's command. Thanks to Captain Zavala's discussions with the station's personnel, we know which module our people are in, and we already know roughly what route we're going to have to take to reach them. While we're doing that, Lieutenant Xamar will take up station on the module. Hopefully, we won't need fire support from the pinnaces, but if we need it, it'll be there."

Heads nodded again, far more grimly.

"All right. Remember your briefings, watch your backs, and come home safe. If any of you *don't* come back in one piece, I'm going to be really upset with you, and you won't *like* me when I'm upset. Understood?"

❖   ❖   ❖

Eardsidh MacGeechan was acutely conscious of how alone he was as the Manticoran pinnaces mated with Shona Station's personnel tubes and the Manty boarding party swam quickly and efficiently aboard.

All of them wore skinsuits, not powered armor, he observed, but they seemed to be frighteningly well equipped with pulse rifles, side arms, flechette guns, tribarrels, and grenade launchers. He even saw a few anti-armor launchers he hoped to hell were armed with chemical or kinetic warheads and not impeller heads. They moved with grim, disciplined competence, and he reminded himself he was effectively a neutral.

The question, of course, was whether or not *they* knew that.

A slender (and preposterously young looking) brunette with gray-blue eyes and a skinsuit showing the rank markings of a senior lieutenant crossed the bay gallery to him. A massively built fellow who would have made at least two and probably three of her followed at her heels in an armored skinsuit, carrying a flechette gun casually at port arms while a slung rifle hung over his shoulder. He also carried a pulser in a belt holster and another one in a shoulder holster, and all of his weapons had an ominously well-used look. So did his dark eyes, for that matter. He should have looked ridiculous festooned with so much firepower; instead, he looked like a man accompanied by several old friends who were ready to help out if he needed them. MacGeechan didn't recognize the insignia on his skinsuit, but he was pretty sure it wasn't Manticoran.

"Lieutenant Abigail Hearns, Grayson Space Navy," the brunette said in a pleasantly throaty contralto. MacGeechan's eyebrows rose, and she smiled. "We're Manticoran allies. Don't worry about it," she advised him.

"Whatever you say, Lieutenant," MacGeechan said. "Lieutenant Eardsidh MacGeechan, Saltash Space Service."

"Pleased to meet you." Hearns extended her hand and gripped his firmly. "This is Lieutenant Gutierrez, Owens Steadholder's Guard." MacGeechan felt his eyebrows twitch again, and she shook her head. "Don't worry about it," she repeated.

"Uh, yes, Ma'am." MacGeechan wasn't certain she was senior to him, but he suspected she was, despite her apparent youth. It was always a bit difficult to estimate someone's calendar age without knowing which generation of prolong he'd received, but this Lieutenant Hearns exuded a quiet aura of competence that spoke of a lot more experience than someone as youthful looking as her ought to have.

"I suppose we should go ahead and get ourselves organized, don't you think, Mateo?" she said, smiling up at the towering lieutenant, and he nodded.

"I'll get right on that...My Lady."

Hearns' eyes flickered as if in amusement at some private joke, but she only nodded, and MacGeechan watched her watching Gutierrez as he began briskly and competently sorting out the rest of her boarding party. Then the Saltashan frowned as the pinnaces quietly unlocked from the buffers on the far side of the bay's armorplast. He started to say something about it, then changed his mind as he saw them back out of the bay on reaction thrusters, alter heading, and drift off in the direction of Victor Seven. Surely they weren't going to—?

His thought trailed away as he remembered what had happened to Vice Admiral Dubroskaya. Under the circumstances, it was probably just as well not to invest too much confidence in what these people weren't going to do.

He considered that for a moment or two, and then, ever so slightly, he began to smile. If they hadn't been gendarme pricks, he might almost have felt sorry for Major Pole's troopers, and in the meantime...

Chapter Fifteen

"EXCUSE ME, LIEUTENANT HEARNS."

Abigail turned and raised an eyebrow at Lieutenant MacGeechan. The Saltash Space Service officer gave her an apologetic look that seemed to have an odd, almost gleeful edge to it, and extended a tablet display.

"I'm afraid it turns out we're even more short-handed than we thought we were, given the nature of the current situation," MacGeechan continued, "and Commander MacWilliams needs me back in her command center. Since that means I won't be able to personally guide you to Major Pole after all, Captain MacNaughtan asked me to give you this. I know it's not as good as having an actual guide, but I hope it'll be good enough."

Abigail started a sharp retort but stopped herself. If MacGeechan really did have orders to stay out from between the gendarmes and her people, her yelling at him wasn't going to change anything. Besides, she couldn't blame him—or any of the other Saltashans—for wanting to keep as much distance as possible between themselves and anything Frontier Security could construe as collaboration with Manticore.

She took the tablet, but MacGeechan didn't let go of it immediately. Instead, he hung on and looked across it at her.

"As I say, Ma'am, it's not as good as having an actual guide, but Captain MacNaughtan said to tell you he hoped it would help."

There was a strange emphasis on the last few words, and Abigail's eyes narrowed. Then they dropped to the tablet and widened, instead.

"I can appreciate your manpower difficulties, Lieutenant MacGeechan," she said after a moment. "And under the circumstances, we won't detain you any longer. Please pass my compliments to Captain MacNaughtan."

"Of course, Ma'am."

McGeechan released his grip, came briefly to attention, and saluted. Abigail returned the courtesy and watched the Saltashan officer step back a half-pace, turn, and stride briskly away without so much as a backward glance.

"Excuse me, My Lady, but wasn't that supposed to be our guide?" a deep voice rumbled behind her, and she turned.

"That *was* what I expected, yes, Mateo," she agreed calmly. "It seems there's been a change in plans, however. Captain MacNaughtan and Commander MacWilliams need Lieutenant MacGeechan elsewhere."

"And we're just supposed to go waltzing through this space station all on our own, are we?" Lieutenant Gutierrez sounded a tad skeptical, and the look he bestowed upon Lieutenant Hearns was remarkably similar to the looks certain of her tutors had given her back on Grayson. Usually immediately after something expensive had gotten mysteriously broken.

"I'm afraid so," she sighed. "The best they could do for us was this."

She held up the tablet, and Gutierrez's eyebrows rose.

"Is that really—?" he began, then shut his mouth tightly. He hated people who asked obvious questions.

"Yes, it is." Abigail smiled thinly. "Changes things just a little, doesn't it?"

"That's one way to put it, Ma'am," Gutierrez acknowledged, still gazing at the tablet.

Its display showed a position icon to indicate their own location here in the docking bay, but that was about its only resemblance to the standard electronic deck guide he'd expected to see. A standard guide would have shown them where they were and highlighted a route to their intended destination. The purely schematic layout would have told them when and where to turn, what lifts they needed to take, and what decks they needed to cross to get to Victor Seven. Of course, Lieutenant MacGeechan would have been a better—and, under the circumstances, a more reassuring guide—and it wouldn't have shown any details *aside* from their direct route, but it would have sufficed.

What Abigail Hearns actually held, however, was a *damage control* guide from Shona Station's engineering department. True, it would guide them to Victor Seven. But it was intended to get emergency repair crews anywhere they had to go under any conditions. Instead of showing a simple, highlighted route to Victor

Seven, it showed engineering access ways, ventilation conduits, plumbing, blast doors, emergency bypass routes, circuitry runs...and the exact location of the Gendarmerie brig in which the Manticoran spacers were confined.

"Pity there wasn't time for them to get you a standard deck guide, My Lady," Abigail's personal armsman continued. "I guess we'll just have to make do with what we've got."

❖   ❖   ❖

"Well, what do you think of Abigail's brainstorm?" Naomi Kaplan asked Alvin Tallman, and her XO laughed. There wasn't a lot of humor in that laugh. In fact, Kaplan could hear the echo of her own bared fangs.

"I like it, Skipper," Tallman replied over her earbug from his station in AuxCon. "There's a reason she decided to strike for the tactical track."

"Agreed." Kaplan nodded, but then her expression turned serious. "On the other hand, I think she's right about us owing MacNaughtan a little cover."

"I agree. Not that I think he's doing it just out of the goodness of his heart, you understand, Ma'am. Looks to me like these Saltashans have a few bones of their own to pick with the Sollies."

"Who doesn't?" Kaplan asked bleakly.

"Only people who've never met them," Tallam replied. "Returning to the matter in hand, though, how's O'Reilly doing on providing that cover?"

"Well," Kaplan's lips quirked as she glanced across at her com officer, "I think she's a little pissed the suggestion came from Abigail, but she grabbed it and ran with it, anyway. Interesting how those damage control guides tie into the emergency communication nets, isn't it? And how easy it is to invade the system when you're already inside it?" Her smile grew much nastier. "Trust me, Wanda's making sure her tracks are going to be easy to find. By the time anyone starts looking, it's going to be obvious we managed to hack their info systems from the outside—more of that 'preposterous' Manty hardware for them to worry about, I suppose—to get our hands on those schematics."

❖   ❖   ❖

Captain Jørn Kristoffersen, CO, Able Company, 10347th Independent Battalion, Solarian Gendarmerie, was an unhappy man.

As a general rule, he enjoyed his slot as the 10347th senior company commander. True, Saltash was on the backside of nowhere, and it was somewhat lacking in the more sophisticated forms of entertainment he preferred. It was still immensely better off than some of the Verge hellholes he'd been assigned to in the past, however, and as long as a man was careful, there were plenty of opportunities for him to enjoy himself. Better still, Major Pole understood the traditional Verge fringe benefits when it came to R&R, and things had improved noticeably since Dueñas had replaced the previous governor and reminded the locals who was really in charge. Kristoffersen wasn't about to go wandering around in uniform without three or four other gendarmes to watch his back, of course—no telling what some of the local yokels might do if they caught a gendarme all on his own—but that was par for the course anywhere in the Verge.

The present situation, however, was *not* par for the course, and even as he stepped on his anger, he tried to convince himself that something besides fear gave that anger so much strength.

Fucking bastards, he thought resentfully, glowering at the lift shafts and acutely conscious of the long, empty corridor stretching away behind him. *Too damned uppity, that's what they are! We need to be smacking them down, showing them why they don't want to try to pull this kind of shit with us!*

Unfortunately, Vice Admiral Dubroskaya's effort in that direction seemed not to have worked out very well. So now *he* was the one left holding the shit-end of the stick, although why it had to be a *commissioned* officer out here wasn't quite clear to him. If he'd had the option, he would have delegated it right on down the chain of command, but the order had been too specific to work around and pass it on to someone else. Besides, if these fanatics were really likely to push it, his neck probably wouldn't be any safer elsewhere, in the end.

Maybe the Major's right, though. I sure hope to hell he is, anyway! And—

His thoughts broke off as the lift shaft door opened and an extraordinarily broad lieutenant in an armored skinsuit stepped out of it. A flechette gun which looked almost like a toy in his massive grip pointed unthreateningly at the deck, but the dark eyes behind his helmet's armorplast bubble didn't look especially friendly.

Another Manticoran followed him, and Kristoffersen was careful to keep his hand away from the holstered pulser at his side as another dozen Manties spread out from the lift, behind the first two. No one blustered or threatened, but they were all well armed, and they spread out smoothly to establish a perimeter around the lift banks. One of them said something into his helmet microphone, and a moment later the second set of lift doors opened to admit another dozen Manties who fanned out just as quickly and efficiently as they had. In less than three minutes, the boarders had set up an all-round defensive position, and no one seemed to have the least interest in Kristoffersen. They were too busy keeping their eyes—and attention—on their zones of responsibility, and his heart sank at the evidence of their obviously well-trained competence.

"I'm Lieutenant Abigail Hearns," the second Manty out of the first lift car said over her skinsuit's external speaker. "And you are?"

Her brisk voice wasn't overtly threatening, but it *was* that of someone who clearly had better things to waste time on than deference to Solarian self-importance. Kristoffersen felt a quick, fresh flash of anger at that almost unconscious dismissal, but he warned himself to tamp it down.

"Captain Jørn Kristoffersen, Solarian Gendarmerie," he replied curtly.

"Well, Captain Kristoffersen, I assume you're aware of the reason for our visit. Captain Zavala's instructed me to present his compliments to the senior Gendarmerie officer and request the immediate repatriation of the Manticoran civilians illegally detained here aboard Shona Station."

"I'm afraid the personnel to whom you refer are in a legally declared state of medical quarantine, ordered by System Governor Dueñas on the advice of his medical staff," Kristoffersen replied. "Major Pole regrets to inform Captain Zavala that without specific instructions from the Governor terminating the quarantine, it's impossible for him to release any of the personnel covered by it."

He knew the response had come out sounding stilted and rehearsed, but he didn't really care. Which wasn't to say he felt especially cheerful about finding himself all alone in a compartment with the better part of two dozen armed Manties while he delivered it.

Make that three *dozen,* he amended sourly as the first lift car opened again with a second load of boarders.

"That's unacceptable, Captain." For someone with such a naturally pleasant contralto voice, Lieutenant Hearns could sound remarkably icy, Kristoffersen noted. "I think Major Pole had better reconsider his position."

"Major Pole will take your advice under consideration, Lieutenant. I'm sure he'll give it all the weight to which it's entitled."

Kristoffersen smiled unpleasantly as he delivered that sentence. Despite the anxiety percolating through his system it felt good to put this neobarb in her place, but—

"That wasn't 'advice,' Captain," Hearns replied. "It was a warning."

"A warning, Lieutenant?" A sharper edge of anger crackled in Kristoffersen's tone as the Manty's insolence registered.

"Neither Captain Zavala nor I are prepared to put up with any more Solarian obstruction, Captain Kristoffersen." Blue-gray eyes bored into him from the other side of her helmet's armorplast. "Personally, I think Governor Dueñas has already managed to get enough people killed for one day. I'd hope Major Pole isn't prepared to add to the total."

"Are you threatening the Solarian Gendarmerie?" Kristoffersen demanded, and his face darkened with anger as Hearns rolled her eyes in exasperation.

"Captain, we just blew four Solarian Navy *battlecruisers* out of space," she said with the patience of someone addressing a particularly slow-witted child. "In case you can't do the math, there were over two thousand SLN personnel with several hundred real honest-to-gosh Marines aboard each of them, and I'll be surprised if half of them survived. Precisely what part of that suggests that we should be frightened of *gendarmes*?"

Kristoffersen's face went from dark with anger to pale with fury under the lash of her scathing contempt and his hand twitched towards his pulser. It was only a tiny movement—an instinctive twitch, no more—but the muzzle of the flechette gun which had led the way out of the lift rose from the deck to about knee level, and he froze instantly. The thought of having both legs amputated by a single squeeze of the flechette gun's trigger was not an appealing one.

"I'd advise you to *start* being afraid of the Gendarmerie, Lieutenant," he bit out instead, trying to keep his eyes on her face and away from that muzzle. "However full of yourselves you may feel right this instant, the League's not going to be amused by what you people have already done here. Compounding it by threatening or attacking Solarian Gendarmes is only going to make things worse."

"You need to work up a better grade of threat, Captain Kristoffersen," Hearns replied. "Get a little more sneer into your delivery...maybe grow a mustache so you can twirl it properly...I don't know, *something*. In the meantime, however, I think you should understand that we're not especially impressed by the Gendarmerie, or the Solarian League, or Major Pole—or *you*—and save us all some trouble. We're here for our nationals who have been illegally detained in this star system; we're going to take them with us when we leave; and we're going to do whatever it takes to accomplish that objective. I'd advise you to inform Major Pole that we don't care about his 'medical quarantine' any more than we care about Governor Dueñas' threats. If he isn't prepared to release our people to us immediately, we can—and will—reclaim them by force. And just to be perfectly clear for the official record, 'by force' most definitely does include the use of *lethal* force."

"You think you can just come aboard this station and *threaten* Solarians? Just who the hell do you people think you *are*?"

"People who're sick and tired of Solarians who think they can do anything they want to anyone they want to do it to and never get called to account," Hearns replied coldly. "Of course, that's only my personal view. I think it'll probably do to be going on with, though. Now, are you going to pass my message to Major Pole? Or should I assume the time to begin reclaiming our people by force has already arrived?"

Kristoffersen was rigid with rage, but he was also acutely aware of his isolation. He wished now that he'd argued in favor of bringing at least a squad of his own people along, yet underneath the surface of that wish he suspected it was just as well he hadn't.

By now, this lunatic's attitude would have pushed at least one of his troopers into a violent response and they'd already be knee-deep in bodies...including, quite probably, his own.

"I'll pass your 'message' along, Lieutenant," he grated. "I can already tell you what the answer will be, though."

"Really?" Hearns said, regarding him coldly.

"Oh, yes." He showed her his teeth. "'Fuck off' probably sums it up pretty well. In more official language, you understand."

The Manty with the flechette gun tilted his head. His expression never even flickered, but Kristoffersen felt a sudden cold stab of terror as something stirred like Leviathan down in the hearts of those dark eyes. Hearns only reached out and touched her subordinate on the shoulder.

"Solarian command of Standard English never ceases to amaze and impress me," she said, never looking away from Kristoffersen. "All of you bring such eloquence and poetry to our common tongue. Assuming, however, that you've captured the gist of Major Pole's response accurately, I suppose we'll simply have to come and get our people."

"And just how do you propose to do that?" Kristoffersen snapped. "You may have a damned *fleet* sitting out there, for all I know. But *you* aren't out there, and neither are the assholes sitting in the brig. You're inside, with *us*, Lieutenant, and you really don't want to fuck with the Gendarmerie on our own ground. Not unless you've got a hell of a lot more powered armor and heavy weapons than *I* see! You want to try fighting your way into this section, you go right ahead, because there're going to be a hell of a lot of dead Manties before you get into it! And it sure would be a pity if the brig should be accidentally depressurized as a consequence of *your* decision to attack the Gendarmerie for refusing to release legally quarantined personnel."

His eyes glittered as he delivered the none-too-veiled threat, and Hearns' expression turned colder than ever.

"Why am I not surprised?" She shook her head. "Let me explain something to you, Captain. It already occurred to us that you noble and courageous gendarmes might threaten to kill our civilians. I mean, we *are* talking about the Solarian Gendarmerie, those champions of truth, justice, and the Solarian way. Tester knows you've shown the rest of us poor, benighted neobarbs the high road to civilization often enough! Trust me, we've all been deeply impressed by your intervention battalions' willingness to terrorize anyone who gets in your way . . . as long as they're not in a position to shoot back." Her cold contempt sent a boil of pure fury sweeping through Kristoffersen, but she only continued in that same scornful tone. "We, however, *are* in a position to shoot back, and if any of the civilian spacers in your custody are harmed in any way, we will hold you—meaning, in case you were wondering, you personally, Major Pole, and all of your personnel collectively—responsible for it. And for your information, the illegal detention of our civilians constitutes kidnapping and unlawful constraint under interstellar law. Which can be—and will be—construed as an act of piracy. And pirates, as you may be aware, are liable to summary execution."

Kristoffersen stared at her in sheer disbelief.

"So now you're threatening to try us as *pirates*?" he demanded.

"No, Captain. We're warning you that if any of our people are harmed, we'll *execute* you as pirates," she said flatly.

Despite himself, her level tone sent an icicle through Jorn Kristoffersen. No one had ever threatened to *execute* Solarian Gendarmes! But as he looked into those cold, blue eyes and heard the unflinching certitude in that voice, he felt a terrifying suspicion that she meant it.

"Captain, I think you'd better go tell Major Pole what the situation is before you dig this hole any deeper for all of you," Hearns told him with a curled lip. "Inform him that he has fifteen minutes to agree to release our personnel. After that time, we'll come get them. And be sure you tell him what will happen if any of our people are hurt along the way. I wouldn't want him to wonder why he's being kicked out an airlock without a skinsuit."

She turned her back without another word, and the Manty with the flechette gun twitched his head in the direction of the corridor to Victor Seven. Kristoffersen felt himself hovering on the brink of saying something else—or possibly of physically attacking Hearns, as suicidal as that would undoubtedly be. But sanity overpowered fury, and he turned and stalked down the corridor.

❖   ❖   ❖

"Tell me, My Lady," Mateo Gutierrez said over his private link as the Solarian stormed away, "do you think there was anything *less* diplomatic you could've said to him?"

"I certainly hope not," Abigail replied. She turned her head, glancing back over her shoulder as Kristoffersen disappeared down the corridor, then returned her attention to Gutierrez. "I tried not to miss any of his buttons, anyway."

"Oh, I'd say you got most of them," Gutierrez said judiciously. "I thought twice he was going to go ahead and go for his gun, anyway."

"In which case he'd be dead...and the universe would be a better place."

Gutierrez twitched as he heard the cold, bitter, genuine loathing in her voice. Hatred was alien to Abigail Hearns, as he knew far better than most, but she *was* a Grayson. Graysons met the Test in their own lives. They did their jobs, and they honored their responsibilities, and a thousand years surviving on a planet which tried to kill them every single day gave them a sort of implacability which could be frightening to behold. It wasn't like the fanaticism of the Faithful on their more hospitable and welcoming planet of exile, but it was something a San Martino like Gutierrez—or perhaps a Gryphon Highlander—could understand. Whether even they could have *matched* it was another question, of course, but Mateo Gutierrez had realized long ago why the mountain clansman in his own genes had responded so powerfully to the Grayson granite inside Abigail Hearns and her people.

"Well," he went on in that same judicious tone, letting none of that moment of awareness show in voice or expression, "I'd say that if the object was to piss them off, you've probably succeeded."

"Good," Abigail said coldly. But then she gave herself a little shake and smiled at him.

"Good," she repeated more naturally. "Because that means they'll be looking *our* way, doesn't it? And that being the case, perhaps you'd be good enough to organize the troops, Lieutenant Gutierrez?"

"Of course, My Lady."

Chapter Sixteen

"—WANT HIM TO WONDER why he's being kicked out an airlock without a skinsuit."

Anger smoked through Major John Pole like sea smoke as he listened to the playback of Kristoffersen's conversation with the Manty lieutenant. Through an oversight (which Pole planned to correct as soon as this current business was resolved), he had no access to the surveillance systems outside Victor Seven when the Shona Station went to emergency com conditions, which meant he'd been unable to watch or listen to Kristoffersen's conversation with the Manties until the captain had returned with his recording of the entire incident.

"Oversight" my ass! Pole thought furiously now, remembering that bitch MacWilliams' expression as she "apologized" so profusely for her "inability" to tap him into her systems. It was a purely technical problem, she'd assured him, and one Commander MacVey's tech people would rectify the instant the current emergency let them stand down from their damage control duties.

Pole felt his teeth grate together in memory, yet there was nothing he could do about it at the moment. Besides, he had other things to be worrying about.

"She's fucking crazy, Sir!" Kristoffersen said harshly. "She *wanted* me to go for my pulser and give that big son-of-a-bitch an excuse to blow me away!"

Pole's grunt of agreement might have contained a modicum of sympathy for his subordinate's frayed nerves, although, if pressed, he would have had to admit the universe would have survived quite handily if the Manties *had* taken Kristoffersen out. Unfortunately, that didn't mean the captain's estimate of this Hearns' sanity was in error.

"Excuse me, Sir," Captain Leonie Ascher, Charlie Company's CO said respectfully, "but shouldn't we consider the possibility that these people mean what they're saying?"

"What? That they'll come in here after us? Actually launch some kind of *assault* on a facility whose security is guaranteed by the Solarian Gendarmerie?"

Pole glared at her, and she shrugged ever so slightly.

"Sir, don't get me wrong. I'm not saying we should simply roll over for the first neobarb to start throwing his or her weight around. But she had a point; this Zavala *has* already taken out four battlecruisers. It may be that he's out of control, as well as out of his mind—that he's way outside what his superiors expected when they gave him his orders. All that could be true. Hell, it probably *is* true! But he's still committed an outright act of war already, and I think we have to seriously consider the possibility that he'll keep right on going. Let's face it, Sir—at this point he's *got* to get his spacers back."

"You're saying he's painted himself so far into a corner he doesn't have any choice but to keep going? He's got to get what he came for if he's going to have a prayer of covering his ass when his superiors find out he's created this kind of incident with the League?"

"Something like that, Sir." Ascher nodded.

Pole considered what she'd said. With Captain Myers and Captain Truchinski off commanding detachments elsewhere, she and Kristoffersen were the only company commanders currently aboard Shona Station. Although Ascher was junior to Kristoffersen and two of her company's platoons were off-station at the moment, she was far and away the more valuable asset. She'd always been smarter—a *lot* smarter, actually—than the other captain, which was why Pole had sent Kristoffersen out to meet the Manties. If they really were as out of control as the destruction of Dubroskaya's warships suggested, and if something went wrong and he had to lose one of them, he'd preferred for it to be Kristoffersen. All of which suggested he really should consider the possibility that Ascher had a point...and probably a damned good one.

Unfortunately, there wasn't much he could do about it. Governor Dueñas had given him his orders in person in a com conversation he'd carefully recorded as part of the official record, and that left Pole very little wiggle room. If he surrendered the interned Manties, he'd be disobeying a direct order from his legal superior. The Gendarmerie would be furious enough with him for yielding to some neobarb navy's threats, however hopeless his situation, given the disastrous precedent that would set. If he not only rolled over but did so in defiance of direct orders *not* to, he'd simply hand the inevitable board of inquiry—and the court-martial which would no doubt follow—an even bigger hammer with which to reduce him and his career to very tiny, well pulverized pieces. And he could be damned sure Dueñas would do his level best (and use every favor he was owed) to blame the disaster here in Saltash on anyone except himself.

Major Pole didn't doubt the governor was already scheming to come up with an official explanation which would make the destruction of Vice Admiral Dubroskaya's squadron entirely her fault. The idea was ridiculous, but in the competition between a dead Frontier Fleet admiral and a live Frontier Security governor, the one who was still breathing was almost certain to come out on top, regardless of any inconvenient little things like facts. Under the circumstances, the last thing Pole could afford would be to simultaneously disappoint Dueñas and give the governor an excuse to hang the League's humiliating surrender on *him*. In the end, *someone* was going to be scapegoated for what had happened here, and whoever it was would be fortunate if all that happened was that his career came to an abrupt and ignominious end. More likely, the powers that were would decide an example had to be made, and John Pole had no intention of providing the example. The survival rate for ex-gendarmes who found themselves guests of the penal system was far too low for that.

The problem was that Ascher might well be right about whether or not Zavala was willing to push things. He truly might send in those boarders to reclaim the Manties by force. For that matter, he truly might be so crazy he really would treat Solarian gendarmes as common pirates if they fell into his hands!

"We can't just play dead for him," he said finally. "That's completely unacceptable."

Kristoffersen and Ascher glanced at each other, then back at him, and he bared his teeth.

"They may think it's going to be easy to get into this module," he said. "If they do, it's up to us to demonstrate their error. We've probably got more troopers in here than they have boarders out there, there are only so many ways they can come at us, we know the station a hell of a lot better than they do, and we've also got the advantage of the defensive position. We've got a lot more heavy weapons than we saw in this, too." He jabbed an angry finger at the recording they'd all just viewed. "If they try to fight their way in, we'll massacre them!"

"And if they use their cruisers' point defense to blow a way in from the outside, Sir?" Ascher asked.

"There's no way even a maniac would do that." Pole waved his hand dismissively. "You think they're going to risk explosively depressurizing the entire module when they're so anxious to get their people back unharmed?" He shook his head. "No, if they try to fight their way in here, they're going to have to come to us on our terms. And when they do, we'll *bleed* them."

Ascher's eyes looked doubtful, and the major glared at her.

"I'm not going to just hand over their spacers against direct orders without at least trying to hang onto them," he said flatly. "And I think they may be more amenable to reason once they figure out how much trying to take them back by force is going to cost."

Ascher still looked unconvinced, but Pole didn't really care. He didn't believe for a moment that he could hang onto the interned Manties indefinitely, but he *was* confident he could inflict heavy casualties on any Manty attempt to fight their way into Victor Seven, and when he did, they'd pull back to rethink. At that point, if *he* were this Zavala, he'd find a way to tighten the screws on Dueñas. There was no doubt in Pole's mind that anyone with the only operable warships in a star system could find a way to convince that system's governor to see reason sooner or later, especially when the governor in question was stuck out in the open where the Manties could get at him without killing the people they wanted to rescue themselves. And if Zavala convinced Dueñas to *order* Pole to hand the internees over, even it was obviously only under duress, the monkey was off the major's back.

And if he can't convince Dueñas to play ball, I'm no worse off than I was before, he thought. *In fact, if I lose a couple of dozen gendarmes and then hand over the Manties "to prevent further bloodshed," I may even be able to make a case for its being Dueñas' fault for ordering me not to cough them up in the first place. If I phrase my report right, make it clear I was prepared to go all the way and only backed down to save Solarian lives from a homicidal neobarb once it became obvious my civilian superior had misread the situation disastrously, the Gendarmerie will be in a hell of a lot better position to hammer Frontier Security over this instead of our carrying the can.*

❖   ❖   ❖

"Well, time's up, My Lady," Gutierrez said.

"Indeed it is," Abigail agreed. "So I suppose we should go ahead and get this ship off the field. If you'd be so good, Mateo?"

"Of course, My Lady."

Gutierrez nodded and glanced around to be sure all his people were where he'd told them to be before he stepped cautiously to the edge of the corridor down which Kristoffersen had departed in such high dudgeon. He extended a sensor wand into the corridor's mouth, and the multi-spectrum pickup projected a detailed heads-up view of the passageway onto the inside of his skinsuit helmet. He cycled through the visible spectrum into infrared and then into ultraviolet and grunted in unsurprised satisfaction as he spotted the web of tripwire lasers covering the last third or so of the forty-meter corridor. The blast doors at the far end, where the spokelike axial passage actually entered Victor Seven, were closed, but someone had cut what looked suspiciously like firing loopholes through the heavy-duty panels.

A little closer inspection showed that the tripwires he'd picked up were connected to antipersonnel mines which had been attached to the bulkheads and deckhead. The mines were covered with nanotech chameleon skin designed to blend into the alloy to which they'd been affixed, but the people who'd emplaced them were gendarmes, more skilled in thuggery than any sort of actual military training. They hadn't even bothered to detach the laser sensors from the mines; they'd left them mounted on the mine housings, and with that for a starting point, it wasn't hard for his sensor wand to locate the mines by their internal powerpacks.

"You know, My Lady," he said absently, still cataloging threats, "if we were willing to get in line and march straight down the middle of the passageway here—and maybe go ahead and paint big bulls-eyes on our chests, too—they probably *could* get a lot of us."

"I know how good you are, Mateo," Abigail replied soothingly. "There's no need to be nasty to them just because they aren't. I'm sure they're doing the very best they can."

"The scary thing is you're probably right about that."

He studied his HUD for a few more moments, then nodded.

"'Bout what we expected, My Lady. Not much finesse, but let's be fair. It's a straight corridor into the first blast door. How much room for finesse *is* there?"

"I suppose that depends on a lot of factors," she said with a crooked smile. "Go ahead and get their attention, Mateo."

"Aye, aye, My Lady."

❖   ❖   ❖

The gendarmerie squad on the far side of those blast doors had failed to notice Gutierrez's sensor wand, but Sergeant Clinton Abernathy, the squad's leader, had grown increasingly nervous as the minutes ticked by. This wasn't the kind of crap he'd signed up for, and the rumors about what this particular batch of neobarbs had already done only made bad a lot worse.

He didn't like any part of this, and he failed to share Major Pole's confidence that these people would back down in the face of a demonstration of manly determination. Perhaps that was because he and his squad had been chosen to do the initial demonstrating.

There were three access routes to Victor Seven from the rest of Shona Station. This one, following the main axial from the lift shafts, was the most direct and the broadest, which made it the logical path for a full-fledged assault. The second route ran through the materials-handling conduit, through which consumables and refuse were transported into and out of the habitat module. It hadn't been planned for humans to use, however, and it would have been a cramped and tortuous way to get at the module's garrison. At the moment, all of its blast doors had been closed and remote sensors had been set to alert the defenders if those doors were disturbed. It seemed unlikely anyone would try coming that way, but if they did, there'd be plenty of warning in time to get blocking forces into position.

The third possible way in was really designed as an emergency evacuation route, and it was less liberally supplied with blast doors, since it was supposed to stay open and accessible for people trying to get out of Victor Seven in the face of disaster. The good news was that it had a lot more bends and was rather narrower than the axial passageway, even if it was more accessible than the materials tube. They'd had to position more people to cover it, but they had good fields of fire and the Manties would have to come out in the open around the turns in the corridor wall to get at them.

But still—

"Movement!" Corporal Marjorie Pareja snapped suddenly.

"What? Where?!" Abernathy demanded, peering at the handheld display feeding from the fixed pickup on the far side of the blast doors.

"Zebra-Tango!" Pareja replied.

❖   ❖   ❖

Gutierrez watched as the sensor remote he'd bounced up the passageway rolled to a stop just short of the first line of mines. He didn't really need it, but seeing how quickly the other side reacted to it should be informative.

"One . . . two . . . three . . . four . . ."

He'd just reached "seven" when a burst of pulser darts from one of the loopholes destroyed the remote.

"Lord," he muttered. "These clowns are as pathetic as those bas—I mean, as those jackasses on Tiberian, My Lady."

He shook his head. Seven seconds to react at all, and then instead of a single shot the morons had fired an entire burst? The ricocheting pulser darts had taken out three of their own mines, and it wasn't even as if the remote had been telling him anything he hadn't already known in the first place!

"Don't complain, Mateo," Abigail said sternly.

"I'm not. It's just—"

He shrugged irritably, a master craftsman frustrated by the slovenly workmanship of a would-be competitor, and glanced at Senior Chief Petty Officer Franklin Musgrave, *Tristram's* boatswain.

"Ready, Frank?"

"Ready," Musgrave confirmed.

"Then punch it."

"Fire in the hole!"

Musgrave slid just the muzzle of his weapon around the edge of the corridor and squeezed the firing stud. It was an awkward angle, and despite the stabilizing pressor beam projected against one of the lift shafts from the launcher's other end, the recoil was significant. Musgrave had expected that, however. He kept control of the bucking launcher without much difficulty, and the projectile's flight path had been programmed to allow for the muzzle rise as it departed downrange.

Because of the short range—the other end of the passage was actually inside the launcher's danger zone—and the fact that no one in his right mind wanted to be within forty or fifty meters of a kinetic strike from a weapon that powerful, they'd had to step down its normal acceleration rate considerably and go with the chemical shaped-charge warhead, instead of its usual dartlike penetrator. Even that was bad enough, since it was designed to take out light armored vehicles, but at least the vast majority of the blast would expend itself on the other side of the blast doors.

Sergeant Clinton Abernathy had a single, fleeting instant to realize what the launcher was before it fired, but that was all the warning he had before he, the blast doors, and his entire squad ceased to exist.

❖ ❖ ❖

"Jesus Christ!"

Surprise jerked the blasphemy out of Kristoffersen as Abernathy's squad was wiped from existence.

"That was a *tank-killer!*" his company first sergeant blurted.

"No! You think?!" Kristoffersen snarled with a baleful glare that closed the first sergeant's mouth with a snap. "Tell Lieutenant Boudreaux to reinforce Axial One and Axial Three. And tell his people to keep their heads frigging down! These bastards've got heavier weapons than we thought."

❖ ❖ ❖

"*That* was noisy," Gutierrez observed. He tossed another remote down the corridor and grimaced. "Messy, too."

"They had their chance to do it the easy way, Mateo," Abigail replied harshly. "Like you say, even those bastards on Tiberian were smarter than this! Let's keep the pressure on them."

"Aye, aye, My Lady."

❖   ❖   ❖

"Well, at least they're not shy," Major Pole growled, studying his tactical display. None of the Manties Kristoffersen had seen before he withdrew to deliver Lieutenant Hearns' ultimatum had been armed with anything like that tank-killer. That was going to make things messier, but weapons that heavy were going to be less useful to the attackers as they moved into Victor Seven proper. They weren't going to have any more firing lines as long as that first one, and without powered armor of their own, no one was going to want to be anywhere near the back blast from something like that when it was confined and channeled by one of the station's passageways.

That was the good news. The bad news was that now that they'd blown their way past the late Sergeant Abernathy's squad, their menu of approach routes got a lot broader. Pole's people knew the internal geography of their habitat far better than the Manties possibly could, but covering all the possible approaches with enough forward-deployed firepower to stop people equipped with such heavy weapons was going to take a lot of manpower.

He considered offering to hand over the internees now that the Manties had demonstrated they were serious, but he couldn't do that . . . yet. If he didn't want to be the one who ended up carrying the can for this entire debacle, he had to be able to argue that he'd genuinely tried to obey the ridiculous, unreasonable orders he'd been given, and that meant he was going to have to accept heavier casualties before he recognized the inevitable and gave in. It was unfortunate, of course, but at least his command post was well back from the point of contact. He was pretty sure he'd have time to accrue sufficient casualties to cover his ass before the actual fighting got anywhere near him.

✦   ✦   ✦

"Okay, things are about to get tricky, My Lady," Gutierrez said.

He was two blast doors deeper into Victor Seven, and Abigail had downloaded the damage control guide's memory to his skinsuit as well as her own. More copies had been uploaded to Nicasio Xamar, *Tristram's* assistant tactical officer, as well as to Senior Chief Musgrave and all the other senior noncoms attached to the boarding party. Now Abigail and Gutierrez studied the imagery together, even though they were the better part of fifty meters apart.

"We could cut through this engineering crawlway," Gutierrez pointed out, highlighting the crawlway in question on both HUDs. "That'd get us around behind them right here."

He highlighted the closed, loopholed blast doors just ahead of his current position, where the gendarmes had set up another strongpoint.

"If we were actually trying to fight our way through them, that would probably be a good idea," Abigail replied. "Since we're not . . . ?"

"Since we're not, I guess we need to knock on the door again," Gutierrez replied.

He sat back, thinking for a moment. As he'd said, things were about to get tricky. To get at the strongpoint, the Manticorans would have to make their way around a relatively sharp bend in the passageway. The problem was that they'd be exposed to fire from the gendarmes the instant they poked their heads around the turn. There wasn't room for them to use Musgrave's launcher here, either. With a Marine fire team in proper powered armor, a heavy tribarrel, and a plasma rifle, it would have been a straightforward tactical problem. Without any of those, he was just going to have to adapt, improvise, and overcome.

"MacFarlane!"

"Yes, LT?" PO 1/c William MacFarlane replied.

"Bring your little friend up here."

"On my way, LT."

MacFarlane, one of *Tristram*'s damage control specialists, crawled up behind Gutierrez less than a minute later. The Marine-turned-armsman slithered back a little so that he and MacFarlane could both look at a hand display.

"We need to make that door go away," Gutierrez said, tapping the display. "Think your pet's up to it?"

"Oh, yeah," MacFarlane replied. "Course, the people on the other side're going to be trying to stop him."

"I think we can probably do a little something about that," Gutierrez told him. "Mind you, it would work better with a Bravo Charlie, but I guess we'll just have to make do."

"Don't you be hurting Denny's feelings, LT!" Mac-Farlane retorted with a grin. "He'll do just fine."

"So let me get the cheering section organized and then you can show me."

❖   ❖   ❖

Sergeant Norman Dreyfus wished his skinsuit allowed for old-fashioned brow wiping. It wouldn't have changed anything, but at least he might have *felt* better.

He also wished to hell he knew exactly what the advancing Manties were up to at the moment. Unfortunately, they'd been systematically taking out the sensors the gendarmes had emplaced. In fact, they'd been swatting sensors with ridiculous ease as they advanced—obviously the people responsible for planting those sensors hadn't concealed them anywhere nearly as well as they'd thought—which meant the best he could do was guess about what they were doing. That didn't make him happy...and the fact that their current location appeared to be just on the other side of *his* current location didn't make him any happier.

The intruders were working their way inward along two separate routes, moving with a certain degree of caution but without any particular effort to disguise their intentions. Not that there would have been much point in subtlety, since there weren't all that many possible approaches.

"Still nothing, Altabani?" he asked his sensor tech.

"No," she replied. "You think I wouldn't've *mentioned* it if I'd seen anything? Shit, Norm! I know they're on the other side of that corner, but—"

Something rattled and rolled on the far side of the hatch, caroming along the bulkheads.

"Grenade!" Altabani shouted as it spun its way up to the far side of the blast door and stopped abruptly when the Manticoran who'd thrown it activated the tiny tractor unit.

The Manticoran in question was nowhere near anything Mateo Gutierrez would have called adequately trained, but she did pretty well for a Navy puke.

She'd watched the icon on her HUD as it bounded down the line of approach to the closed blast doors, then hit its anchoring tractor. She'd jumped the gun slightly, locking the grenade to the deck a dozen centimeters in front of the doors instead of to one of the actual panels, but that was close enough, and she hit the detonation key.

Dreyfus bounced back and sat down—hard—as the concussion came at him, transmitted through the sealed door. Altabani swore as the sensor she'd poked through one of the loopholes was destroyed, and another of Dreyfus' troopers said something in a high, falsetto tone as blast came through his own loophole and blew him back the better part of a meter. His skinsuit and body armor were more than enough to deal with it; his cry was born of shock and surprise—and fear—more than injury.

But that was all that happened, and Dreyfus felt a surge of relief as he climbed back up onto one knee.

Altabani was already shoving another sensor into place, and Dreyfus bared his teeth at the rest of his squad.

"If that's the best they've got, they're screwed!" he announced.

❖　　❖　　❖

"Very nice," Gutierrez approved. "Let's get the others in there now."

A dozen Manticorans and Graysons sent grenades rolling around the corner, bouncing them off the bulkheads towards the blast doors.

❖　　❖　　❖

The blast door rattled and banged and vibrated as grenades went off on the other side, but none of the new blasts were anywhere near as powerful as that first one had been, and all of them seemed to be going off at greater distances.

"Central, this is Dreyfus," the sergeant announced over his com. "They're making a lot of noise, but I don't think they're getting any farther in than they are now."

"Good!" Captain Kristoffersen replied. "Keep us informed and—"

Sergeant Norman Dreyfus' world ended in fire and blast.

❖ ❖ ❖

"*Told* you not to hurt Denny's feelings," MacFarlane told Gutierrez.

"I stand corrected," Gutierrez replied, studying the wreckage with his sensor wand.

He really would have preferred a Bravo Charlie—one of the Royal Manticoran Marine Corps' armored, counter-grav-equipped, robotic breaching charges. Of course, that would have constituted a pretty severe case of overkill against a mere civilian-grade blast door. And even though MacFarlane's DNI-1 damage control remote hadn't been designed for the task, it had attached its beehive shaped charge with neatness and precision under cover of the flashbangs and smoke grenades. It didn't have the armored protection of a Bravo Charlie, but it was designed to operate in an environment which would very quickly have incinerated or demolished a standard robotic unit. If the gendarmes had noticed it coming and targeted it, they could undoubtedly have destroyed it, yet the covering flashbangs had been far too light to hurt it.

Now Gutierrez surveyed the wreckage of what had been a set of blast doors.

"Frank, Wilkie, let's get up there and secure the doors," he said, starting up the passageway himself. "Looks like it's going to take a few minutes to clear the wreckage enough to move on."

◆   ◆   ◆

Major Pole swore as his tactical display updated itself.

The Manties weren't actually moving all that rapidly, yet it was painfully obvious that wasn't because his people were stopping them. He'd expected to start inflicting casualties quickly when they had to clear their way through strongpoints, but they weren't cooperating. Instead, they were taking their time, and they appeared to have an inexhaustible supply of grenades and demolition charges. All he was really accomplishing with his "strongpoints" was to compel them to use up a few more explosives blowing their way through them.

All right. They were clearly concentrating their efforts along Axial Three, and if they kept coming through another couple of sets of blast doors, that was going to lead them into one of the commons areas Victor Seven's designers had laid out for the habitat's anticipated VIP inhabitants: a spacious, landscaped compartment sixty meters across, fitted with picnic tables, scattered conversational groups of chairs, and a small ornamental pool with a fountain.

His eyes narrowed. He'd wanted short, restricted firing lines on the theory that they would favor the defender over the attacker, but this Lieutenant Hearns was obviously more experienced in boarding combat than any of his people. She was making those restricted fields of fire work for *her*, not the defenders, so maybe what he needed was a more *extended* firing range.

He considered his options. Virtually all of Kristoffersen's troopers were already parceled out across the approaches, and he didn't dare thin out his forward defenses. The last thing he needed was to open up a second invasion route! That left him only the two platoons of Captain Ascher's understrength company. He needed to maintain at least some reserve, but if he pulled up one of her platoons to reinforce the squad Kristoffersen already had covering the compartment, then ordered the other squad which was covering the blast doors between it and the Manties to fall back...

❖   ❖   ❖

"If this brainstorm of yours is actually working, My Lady, we're probably getting close," Gutierrez said over his private link to Abigail. "If I were in charge on the other side, this is where I'd be stacking my fire. Nice extended sightlines, and plenty of opportunity for converging fire on the only door the other guys could come through."

"It does look like the best opportunity for them, doesn't it?" Abigail agreed, studying the detailed imagery from the damage control guide. "I guess the only question's whether or not this Major Pole's going to pull enough strength from his reserve."

"Only one way to find out about that," Gutierrez said.

"I know." Abigail smiled fleetingly. "That doesn't mean I have to like it, though. I really don't want to be wrong about this one, Mateo."

"'Course you don't," he replied in a gentler tone. "But when you come down to it, you've got to drop the penny. I don't know if it'll work, either, but I think it's our best shot."

Abigail nodded. Her greatest fear, really, had been

that the gendarmes would drag one of their Manticoran prisoners into the middle of the firefight and threaten to kill him if she and her boarders refused to back off. Given the gendarmerie's normal disregard for civilian life—if it belonged to "neobarbs," at least—she'd anticipated from the beginning that the Sollies would eventually call her bluff, find out if she truly was willing to continue attacking in the face of a direct threat to the prisoners. What she hadn't been able to estimate with any confidence was how *soon* they might do that. It seemed unlikely they'd risk that sort of escalation until they were convinced they wouldn't be able to stop her any other way, however, which was the entire basis of the strategy she'd adopted.

Hopefully, Major Pole was bright enough to recognize the defensive possibilities Gutierrez had just described. If he was, and if he'd committed enough of his reserve . . .

"All right, everybody," she announced over the tactical net. "It's just about time to dance. Report readiness."

A chorus of responses came back to her, and she nodded.

"Mateo, start the music. Nicasio, let's be about it."

❖   ❖   ❖

"Get ready!" Captain Ascher snapped as "Denny" blew another set of blast doors into wreckage.

❖   ❖   ❖

"Now!" Lieutenant Nicasio Xamar said crisply, and the Royal Manticoran Navy personnel standing on the surface of habitat module Victor Seven moved forward.

Just finding the emergency personnel locks should have been a nontrivial challenge, and even after the

Manties had found them, they should have had to burn or blast their way inside. They certainly shouldn't have been able to override the entry codes and cycle their personnel through them without anyone noticing! But that, of course, assumed they didn't have access to Shona Station's classified damage control files.

❖   ❖   ❖

"They're behind us! *They're behind us!*"

"What the hell?!"

John Pole's head flew up as his tactical display changed abruptly. Half a dozen of his single reserve platoon's icons went crimson in the same instant, and three more blinked from green to amber—or red—even as he watched. That *couldn't* be right! The Manties couldn't—!

"Central, they're hitting us from—!"

The voice chopped off in mid-sentence, and Pole's face went white as even more icons went down. Others were falling back desperately, abandoning their positions, and he heard heavy firing and explosions over the open circuit. But that wasn't possible. There was no *way* the Manties could have—

"Sir, the Manties want to talk to you," a pale-faced communications tech said. Pole stared at him, and the tech pointed at a display. Somehow the Manties had patched into the station's "secure" communications net.

Pole stood for a moment, frozen while his brain tried to process the information coming at him. *None* of this could be happening, but—

"Sir?" the com tech said almost plaintively, and the major shook himself viciously back to life and turned to the indicated display.

"*What?*" he got out. His voice sounded strangled,

even to himself, and the young woman on the display smiled coldly.

"I'm in contact with my people who have just taken control of your brig, Major," she said flatly. "I understand at least twenty-five of your gendarmes have surrendered to them. At the moment, your people are being locked into the cells and *my* people are evacuating the way they came. I very much doubt you have anyone in a position to intervene...and if you do, I'd strongly recommend you don't try it. So far, whether you believe it or not, I've been trying to *avoid* killing any more of your people than I have to. I'm perfectly prepared to abandon that approach if you insist, however."

Her smile was icy, but her eyes were colder still, and something inside Major John Pole shriveled under their weight.

"So tell me, Major," she invited, "which way would *you* like me to handle it?"

MAY 1922 POST DIASPORA

"Oh, you ain't *seen* bad yet, but don't you go away, now. It'll be along in a minute."

—attributed to Simon Allenby
of the Cripple Mountain
Allenbys, Swallow System

Chapter Seventeen

"Look out!"

The screamed warning came a lifetime too late as the first obsolescent but still deadly Solarian-built Scorpion light armored fighting vehicle rounded the corner of the pastel-colored ceramacrete tower. It moved down the center of the broad boulevard, and two more AFVs followed it. Still others were visible beyond the initial trio, all wearing the presidential seal and crossed thunderbolts of the Presidential Guard.

Any doubt as to the Scorpions' purpose was dispelled quickly, clearly, and not with anything so potentially ambiguous as words.

The Scorpion's main weapon—a 35-millimeter grav gun—didn't fire, but its secondary, turret-mounted tribarrel spewed out thousands of rounds of solid five-millimeter darts per minute. They struck like some terrible, solid tornado of destruction, and the front of the crowd of demonstrators disintegrated in a hideous spray of crimson and shredded flesh. Pieces of bodies flew or flopped to the pavement, and shrieks of terror replaced the furious, chanted slogans of moments before.

The stink of blood and riven human bodies buried the warm summer scent of flowers from the capital's green belts, and the huge demonstration began to shed a torrent of panicked fugitives.

None of those fleeing people were armed. They'd come to express their opposition to President Lombroso's régime, not to engage in pitched warfare with the black-uniformed Presidential Guard, the most feared of the Mobius System's many security services. The current demonstration had been a long time brewing, and over half of its members belonged to Lombroso's own System Unity and Progress Party. That didn't mean as much as it might have, since the SUPP was the only legal political party in the entire Mobius System and party membership was a requirement for anybody who ever hoped for anything better than purely menial employment, but it probably said something that so many of System Unity's rank and file had been willing to come out in protest of their own founder's policies. Yet while there'd been no lack of anger in their chants' furious denunciations of Lombroso's tyranny and corruption, very few of those running for their lives had ever imagined a response like this one!

Not all the demonstrators were fleeing, however. Nor had all of them come unarmed. Less idealistic (or naïve, perhaps) than their fellows, those others had anticipated the Guard's appearance and come prepared. Or they'd thought they had, anyway; the appearance of AFVs in the heart of the planetary capital when there'd been zero violence from the demonstrators surprised even them.

Despite that, weapons began to fire back from here and there in the screaming crowd. Pulsers were few and far between, since (as Lombroso and his OFS-trained Presidential Guard had explained when confiscating all modern weapons over twenty T-years earlier) the security of Mobius' citizens was the responsibility of their government. There's no room for vigilantism on Mobius, Citizens, thank you very much! Now move along. Nothing to see here!

Less sophisticated firearms had tended to evade the government ban on personal weapons, however, and if they were less "advanced" than pulsers, they were no less deadly if they managed to hit their targets.

The Guard infantry following the Scorpions with their body armor, shields, and high-voltage stun batons found that out the hard way. Their riot gear had served them well in confrontations with outraged college students, fired more by intellectual outrage than organized hatred. It had served well enough breaking heads to discourage the occasional general strike, or moving "squatters" out of housing they happened to own but which had been condemned under eminent domain for transfer to Lombroso's corporate patrons. And the swaggering, self-proclaimed "elite" troopers who wore it were backed by heavier infantry and armored vehicles, even sting ships. They'd been confident no one could possibly be stupid enough to offer them actual *armed* resistance with all that firepower on tap to support them.

Unfortunately, this time they were wrong, and the riot gear which had always stopped improvised truncheons or thrown rocks turned out to be far less effective against bullets.

The Guard's ranks shuddered as the return fire slammed into it. For a second or two, the troopers simply froze, unable to believe such a thing could possibly happen to *them*, and over forty were killed or wounded in that handful of moments. For the first time in its history, the Guard heard its own members screaming in agony as *their* bodies were broken and rent, as *their* blood soaked the pavement. Then, as if it were a single organism, the "elite" infantry turned and fled in howling panic.

The Scorpion crews were just as astonished by the ferocity of the response. Like their infantry compatriots, they'd grown accustomed to being the ones who did the killing and maiming. The notion that someone could offer them organized violence in return had never crossed their minds, and they snarled in fury as their anticipated afternoon's amusement of slaughtering enemies of the state turned into something else.

Yet there were still plenty of those "enemies of the state" out there, and the Scorpions still had their weapons . . . and their armor. They swept forward on their counter-grav, tribarrels raving. Dozens of demonstrators—most of whom hadn't had a thing to do with the fire coming back at the Guard—were killed for every security trooper who'd gone down. Bodies (or parts of them, at least) piled in rows as hyper-velocity darts tore them apart, and scores of other people were trampled, many to death, in frantic efforts to escape the Scorpions' wrath.

Unfortunately for the Guard, however, President Lombroso's security forces hadn't managed to confiscate *all* of his citizens' modern weapons after all, and the antitank launcher on the thirtieth floor of the

O'Sullivan Tower was a very modern weapon, indeed. Its kinetic projectile weighed over five kilos, despite its slender dimensions. Accelerated to thirty KPS by the man-portable gravitic launcher, it was effectively an energy weapon. The super-dense projectile struck with the equivalent energy of well over half a ton of pre-space high explosive, concentrated into a penetrator barely one and a half centimeters in diameter, and the lead Scorpion erupted in a blue-white blaze of burning hydrogen as its fuel tanks ruptured.

A second launcher took out another light tank in equally spectacular fashion, and the Scorpion crews turned their attention from the diversion of butchering demonstrators to the desperate business of self-preservation. Their weapons tracked around, trailing swaths of destruction, hammering the faces of the towers from which the fire was coming. Display windows and businesses exploded. Flames gushed through shattered ceramacrete walls. Fire alarms wailed, smoke streamed up in dense, choking columns, and another Scorpion exploded.

The others redoubled their efforts, and main gun fire joined the tornado of tribarrel darts. The 35-millimeter projectiles were substantially heavier than, and at least as fast as, the antitank penetrators, and explosions pocked the towers, blasting deep into their internal structure.

"Intolerable! *Unacceptable!*" President Svein Lombroso shouted, pounding on his desk blotter. "Did you *see* that? *Do* you see that?"

He stopped pounding long enough to jab one hand at his office windows, which overlooked the columns of inky-black smoke rising from the heart of the of the city of Landing's financial district. The firing had finally stopped an hour ago, but the lower stories of three major towers were roaring infernos, and God only knew how much damage those fires were going to do before they were extinguished. And not just to locally owned property, either. Two satellite offices of Lombroso's major transstellar sponsor were part of the bonfire, as well.

"I've been telling you for *months* something like this was coming!" the president continued. "For months! I've been warning you about the rumors, the malcontents my security people have found! But did you *believe* me? Hell, no, you didn't!"

"Mr. President, please, calm yourself," Angelika Xydis said in her most soothing tones. Her raised hands made stroking motions in midair. "I agree this is terrible, Sir. But the situation's a long way from out of control!"

"A long way from out of control?!" Lombroso stared at her incredulously. "I lost over a hundred men. *A hundred men!* That's more Guard troopers killed in one afternoon than in the last fifty *T-years*. D'you think those malcontent anarchists don't *realize* that? Aren't going to be emboldened by their success?"

Xydis bit her tongue.

Officially, she was a State Department employee, the Solarian League's trade attaché on Mobius. Actually, as everyone realized perfectly well, the trade mission was where the local Office of Frontier Security's representative (one Angelika Xydis, as it happened) hung her hat. As a mid-level OFS bureaucrat, Xydis had seen more strongmen like Lombroso than she cared to recall. More than one had gotten his ass in a crack through sheer, stupid incompetence, too. And it was amazing how many of them would have fixated—just like Lombroso—on the losses their security troops had taken as something likely to embolden their local opposition instead of reflecting on the fury the two or three thousand *civilian* casualties were going to engender!

Because, of course, they are *civilians. They don't matter,* Xydis thought grimly. *Why, oh why, have all these back-planet jackasses heard all about the stick but don't even have a clue about the* carrot? *Who do they think supports the lifestyles to which they've become accustomed? Their* security goons, *or the workers they kill off in job lots at moments like this?*

Not that Lombroso had a corner on the unthinking brutality market, she reflected, glancing at the two Mobians standing attentively behind the president.

General Olivia Yardley, CO of the Presidential Guard, was a fairly typical blunt object in Xydis' opinion. A bit more imagination than many a uniformed enforcer, perhaps, but not a lot, and the Guard reflected its commander's personality, which explained a great deal about its reactions this morning.

Whereas Yardley wore the Guard's black uniform—and why did *all* of these back-planet thugs think black was the only possible color for their uniforms?—the man standing next to her was in civilian dress with a SUPP lapel pin in the red, gold, and black which indicated he'd been one of the Party's original cadre. He was also a general, however: General Friedemann Mátyás, the commander of the Mobius Secret Police, an organization that didn't officially exist ... which had always struck Xydis as a silly thing to pretend. Everyone knew about the MSP. It would have been pretty stupid to rely on the terror of a secret police no one knew existed, after all! But Lombroso and Mátyás seemed not to understand that "secret police" was supposed to mean that nobody knew who was *in* it, not whether or not it existed in the first place.

Still, Mátyás was at least smarter than Lombroso, and his MSP was the System Unity and Progress Party's primary counterintelligence service. Over the five decades of Lombroso's régime, Yardley and Mátyás had done a fairly impressive job of crushing all effective opposition. They hadn't managed to make him any less hated along the way, though. And while Mátyás seemed at least marginally aware of the potential downside of slaughtering his own planetary workforce in job lots, Yardley—like Lombroso—was clearly more focused on the casualties her guardsmen had taken.

Xydis considered the refreshing frankness of pointing out that she and Lombroso could always get more security troopers where the last batch had come from. Or, if not there, they could import them from off-world prisons or lunatic asylums! In fact, she considered—briefly, of course—reminding the system president who truly propped up his régime.

Appearances have to be maintained, she told herself instead. *Besides, if I really want to jerk his leash, I need to take it up with Guernicke. Not that she's any prize.*

The "attaché" suppressed a headshake of pure disgust at the thought. Georgina Guernicke was the Trifecta Corporation's chief executive in Mobius. As such, she ought to have at least some vague notion about conserving her captive labor and customer base. But Trifecta was perfectly comfortable with the slash-and-burn style of exploitation Frontier Security's sweetheart deals made practical out here in the Verge. She didn't give a *damn* what Lombroso or his cronies did as long as they didn't get any uppity ideas about who actually owned their star system.

"I realize the troublemakers are likely to be even more exercised than they already were, Mr. President," Xydis said out loud, once she was sure she had control of her tone and expression again. "And I assure you, I've forwarded all your security people's warnings to Commissioner Verrochio's office. I'm sure his people have reviewed them carefully."

Or not, she thought. *After all, you've been whining about the threats to your régime for the next best thing to four T-decades. Ever hear the story about the little boy and the wolf? Whatever the hell a "wolf" is.*

"And how much good is that going to do?" Lombroso demanded. "Meyers is over twelve days from here even for a dispatch boat! And it's not like they've paid any attention *before* this!"

"Mr. President," Xydis allowed a cold edge to creep into her voice, "you're perfectly well aware of how the Manty provocations in Talbott and Monica have threatened not just this entire region but especially the Madras sector for the last T-year. Obviously, the Commissioner's attention has been focused on that threat. I realize it may feel as if he's been ignoring your situation or the severity of the threat. I assure you that has *not* been the case, however."

"That's easy enough to *say*," Lombroso muttered. But he also sat back down, Xydis noted with satisfaction.

She'd thought reminding him who really ran the Verge might recall him to semi-rationality.

"I understand your concerns, Sir," she said in a milder tone. "And I assure you I'll send an immediate report to Commissioner Verrochio, and request an OFS intervention battalion or two. I'm sure Brigadier Yucel will send her very best troops and advisers to assist the Guard. It's hardly a situation the Gendarmerie hasn't faced before, I'm afraid."

"Good," Lombroso said. "But I hope you've also passed on my reports of Manticoran provocateurs. There's no telling what kind of assistance they're prepared to offer their proxies here in Mobius! For that matter, that's probably where those antitank weapons came from this afternoon!"

"I'll be certain to remind Commissioner Verrochio—and Brigadier Yucel—of those reports, Mr. President," she assured him.

Even if I don't think there's a chance in hell the Manties are actually trying to provoke trouble here in the armpit of the galaxy, she thought bitingly. *Not that I wouldn't be doing my best to kick Frontier Security in the most sensitive spot I could reach if I were them. But this little tempest started brewing well before that jackass Byng sailed off to New Tuscany, and whatever anyone else thinks, I don't see them deliberately courting a confrontation with the League. Even if they were, why in Mobius, of all places? I'm sure they could find a better, more effective spot to make trouble. I'll admit we're a little behind the news out here, but still . . .*

"Good," Lombroso repeated. "Good."

"Well, Xydis has promised him intervention battalions," Michael Breitbach said bitterly.

The chairman of the Mobius Liberation Front stood on the balcony of what had been the flagship tower of an early Lombroso Administration public housing project which—like all Lombroso projects—had foundered in a sea of graft, kickbacks, bribery, and bareknuckle extortion. Only one of the projected towers had ever been constructed, and even it hadn't been *finished*. The ten uppermost of its seventy floors were inhabitable only by the Mobius equivalent of rats, bats, and cockroaches.

Not that the public housing which had been completed was all that much better, when it came down to it.

Now Breitbach leaned on the balcony's rickety railing (rather recklessly, in Kayleigh Blanchard's opinion) and glared out across the darkened city. The fires still hadn't been completely extinguished, and the pall of smoke was underlit by lingering flames. Rather more attention had been given to putting out the fires than to removing the bodies, of course. It wasn't as if the dead were in any hurry, was it?

"That's confirmed?" Blanchard asked, and Breitbach turned to face her, propping his elbows on the railing and leaning back against it.

"Yes," he said, and she nodded slowly.

Although Blanchard was one of his most senior lieutenants and generally considered his heir apparent, not even she knew all (or even most) of his sources. Unlike most of the liberation movements which had come and perished in the half T-century since Lombroso won the presidency (in a "free, fair, and transparent election" overseen by no less an authority than that paragon of justice and fair play, the Office of Frontier Security), Breitbach had never cherished any illusions about the sheer scale of his task. Before he ever formed the first MLF cell, he'd spent literally years researching everything he could find about successful revolutionary movements. As a result, unlike any of the earlier movements the Presidential Guard had crushed, the MLF was a tightly compartmentalized organization which had been known to ruthlessly eliminate security threats. There were far better ways to die than to be identified by the MLF as a government informer, but there was no better way to guarantee one *would* die. Or that one's body would end up deposited in some prominent location as a message to the Guard...and any other potential traitors.

"Do you think Verrochio will send them?" she asked after a moment.

"I think it's a toss-up," Breitbach said frankly. "If—"

He broke off, then smiled a bit crookedly as Blanchard gently but firmly pulled him away from the deathtrap railing. He gave her a quizzical look, but he also followed the pressure of her tugging hand obediently.

"Better?" he asked.

"Yep." She nodded. "I'd just as soon you don't do Lombroso a favor by plummeting to your doom." She regarded him sternly until he shrugged and leaned against the frame of the door giving access to the balcony from the vermin-ridden tower, instead of the railing. Then she nodded in satisfaction. "Now, you were saying about the intervention battalions?"

"I was saying that if it's left up to Yucel, and if they're available, they'll be here on the fastest transport she's got," Breitbach said, his brief amusement fading. "Verrochio would be more likely to vacillate, judging from his record, but Yucel's like our own *dear* General Yardley, although from what I've heard, Yucel's probably at least a little smarter than Yardley. Then again, I suppose it would be hard to be *stupider* than she is!"

His face twisted in familiar disgust, and Blanchard snorted harshly. It had taken Lombroso a decade or two to find someone as willing to kill everyone and let God sort them out as *he* was, but Olivia Yardley had been the PG's commander for over twenty-five T-years ... mostly because her personal security, unfortunately, was too tight for the MLF to get an assassin into position to let God sort *her* out. On the other hand, that could be just as well. As Breitbach had just pointed out, she was scarcely a mental giant, and killing her off might simply have made room for somebody less compulsively brutal but ultimately more dangerous. Now, if they could only get someone inside *Mátyás'* security ... especially if they could convince him that *Yardley* had been behind it ...

"Hongbo's more of a wildcard," Breitbach continued, pulling her back up out of her thoughts. "I think he's smarter—or more likely to think things through, at least—than Verrochio, but that doesn't mean a lot."

Blanchard nodded again. That was another thing about Breitbach; he'd done his homework on his adversaries, and his estimates of their actions and reactions had proven accurate again and again.

"On balance," he continued, "I think it's more likely they *will* send the battalions than that they won't, especially if Guernicke signs onto the request, too. After what happened in the Talbott Sector, they've got to be feeling nervous about the possibility of any of us getting uppity. I think Verrochio's probably running scared, if only because of how he expects his bosses to react. And if he *is* frightened, he's going to be even less inclined to irritate—or disappoint—someone like Trifecta, which is only going to make him more likely to embrace the iron fist approach."

"Wonderful," she muttered.

"Actually, it's not the intervention battalions I'm most worried about," Breitbach said, and Blanchard's eyes widened in surprise. "I'm more concerned about the possibility of his sending along a couple of Navy destroyers to ride herd on their transport and possibly provide a little orbital fire support."

"You think they'd use *starship* weapons on planetary targets?" Blanchard couldn't hide her alarm, but Breitbach shook his head.

"I doubt they'd use them on any target in an urban area, if only because of how that would piss off the Lombroso toadies the city in question belongs to. And we're not going to give them any nice, isolated targets out in the countryside where they could make big craters *without* pissing off Lombroso's supporters. No, I'm more worried about their managing to effectively interdict any additional arms shipments."

Blanchard cocked her head, frowning in thought for a moment or two, then nodded slowly. The Guard's brutal reaction to the peaceful demonstrations had surprised the MLF. Despite the general effectiveness of its penetration of the régime's middle echelons, no one in the movement had had a clue what was coming in time to even contemplate doing anything about it. In this instance, despite what had happened, that was probably a good thing, Blanchard thought. If they *had* known, they might have been drawn into the open, into a standup fight with the Guard, too early. Their stockpile of modern weapons, like the antitank launchers which had taken out a total of five Scorpions before they themselves were destroyed, was growing steadily, but it was nowhere near large enough yet.

And if they wound up with a couple of Frontier Fleet destroyers in orbit around Mobius Beta, the system's capital planet, the chance of getting any additional arms shipments delivered would become virtually nil.

"So what do we do?" she asked.

"For the moment, we use what happened today." Breitbach bared his teeth. "One of the things you can always count on a thug for is plenty of martyrs. God knows I never would've supported anything like the demonstrations if I'd expected Yardley would react this way, but now that she has—now that she's managed to kill that many people—I think she's going to *hate* what Thomas and his people do with that death toll. The hard part's going to be convincing people that this time we aren't inflating the body count, really."

Blanchard nodded. Thomas Marrone headed the MLF's agitprop section. There were undoubtedly many better and more stylistically refined writers in the universe, but Marrone had a gift for putting the people of Mobius' hatred and fury into words at any time. Probably that was because that hatred and that fury were so deeply *his*, as well. There was no cynicism, no ideology, in his hard-hitting anonymous posts or the graffiti slogans and cartoons with which he'd decorated more than one wall even in downtown Landing. There was only outrage, wrath, and passion, and the people who saw and read his messages knew it.

"I just hope Thomas doesn't take any chances along the way...again," she said.

"I do, too."

Breitbach's expression tightened for just a moment, for Marrone's one weakness as a revolutionary was the very passion which made him so effective in his role of spokesman and propagandist. He wanted—*needed*—to be hands-on, and the Guard had damned nearly caught him putting up one of his own graffiti less than three months ago. Breitbach had read him the riot act over that episode, ending by pointing out how disastrous it would have been for the Liberation Front if Lombroso's thugs had gotten their hands on a member of their central committee. Marrone had argued that they probably would have figured he was only one more rank-and-file member of the movement, or even no more than a sympathizer, but his heart hadn't really been in it.

"I hope he doesn't, and I don't think he will," Breitbach said now. "I think I scared the crap out of him by pointing out what Mátyás could get out of him in the end if anyone did figure out who he really is. Of course, I also think I'll have another little conversation with him about it before we turn him loose on this one, just to be on the safe side.

"In addition to anything we do here locally, though, I think it's time we sent off our own dispatch boat. If Lombroso and Xydis are running to Verrochio, we need to do some running of our own."

"Dispatch boat?" Blanchard didn't even try to conceal her surprise at that one. "You've got access to a *dispatch* boat, Michael?"

"In a manner of speaking," he said with his customary

evasiveness. Then he shrugged. "What the hell, if anything happens to me you need to know about this anyway. We have a...call him a friend on the crew of one of the local transstellars' dispatch boats. I'm not going to tell you which, even now, although I will tell you Landrum knows how to get in touch with him."

Blanchard nodded again. Joseph Landrum was one of Breitbach's senior cell leaders. In fact, Landrum had been with the movement longer than Blanchard herself. He was one of the MLF's smoother operators, too, and she wasn't surprised Breitbach had chosen him to manage whatever interstellar communications link they'd been able to establish.

"Anyway, the dispatch boat in question will be leaving Mobius in the next couple of days," Breitbach continued. "Doesn't have anything to do with us, but that doesn't mean we can't make use of it. Especially when, despite the current unpleasantness between the League and the Manties, it's headed into the Talbott Sector. In fact, it's heading to Spindle by way of Montana, which is certainly in the right direction, don't you think?"

"Spindle?" Blanchard repeated, then smiled. "Oh, yes," she agreed. "Spindle would be just *fine* with me, Michael!"

JUNE 1922 POST DIASPORA

"By this time, even that moron Gold Peak has to realize how badly she fucked up at New Tuscany and Spindle! Their government has to be shitting bricks thinking about the mess she's dragged them all into. If the order relieving her ass and hauling her home hasn't gotten to Spindle yet, it's damned well on its way, Commissioner!"

—Brigadier Francisca Yucel,
Solarian Gendarmerie,
To Sector Governor
Lorcan Verrochio,
Office of Frontier Security

✧ Chapter Eighteen

"THAT WENT MORE SMOOTHLY than I expected," Mackenzie Graham said, standing by the apartment window and gazing out at Cherubim's snow-covered streets. Then she turned away from the window... just in time to catch her brother raising his eyebrows in her direction.

"Don't look so complacent at *me*, Indiana Graham! And don't try to pretend *you* weren't nervous about all these new arrangements, too!"

"Never had a moment's doubt," he told her virtuously.

"Bullshit," she said tartly, and he chuckled.

"Well, if you're going to be *that* way about it, I guess I admit I felt a little bit nervous. A *little* bit." He raised a thumb and index finger, perhaps a centimeter apart, and grinned at her.

"Yeah. Sure!"

She shook her head, and the look she gave him was that of a long-suffering sister, not the co-leader of a revolutionary movement.

He only grinned even more broadly (and unrepentantly), but she had a point. The three T-months since their first meeting with Firebrand might have seemed like plenty of time, but given the slow speed with which ships moved between stars, it really wasn't. In fact, the first shipment of weaponry had arrived over a T-month sooner than they'd expected it could. When the routine notification of waiting cargo containers hit the message account Firebrand had set up, it had come as a total surprise.

Fortunately, as Firebrand had suggested, the cargo agents responsible for sneaking those containers into the smuggling queue really didn't want to know anything about their contents. That wasn't how it worked, and if it turned out they contained something with negative consequences, deniability—the ability to say, honestly, "*We* didn't know what it was!"—was actually a fairly acceptable defense in what passed for the Solarian legal system. Or, at least, in what passed for the Solarian legal system where little things like smuggling were concerned.

Bruce Graham had been a student of history, and Indiana had become one himself, especially since his father's imprisonment. He wasn't in his dad's league yet, but he also wasn't confined in Terrabore Prison, which left him free to pursue his self-education wherever it led, as long as he exercised a modicum of caution. He was pretty sure President McCready and General O'Sullivan had no idea how much "subversive" knowledge was tucked away in the Seraphim libraries' files. Some of it was even in old-fashioned hardcopy *books* gathering dust in the physical stacks. And from his reading, Indiana had come to realize there'd actually been periods in human history when the courts would never have tolerated the omnipresent corruption of OFS and its sweetheart deals.

Well, they probably had problems of their own, even then. On the other hand, I think I'd trade my problems for theirs, if I had the option. Which I don't.

"All right," Mackenzie said, shifting from put-upon sibling back to co-conspirator, "now that we've got them, what do we do with them?"

"Now *that*," Indiana conceded, "is a pretty good question, Max."

For the moment, the containers were sitting in a warehouse he and Mackenzie were pretty sure was off the scags' grid. It was located in the heart of the Rust Belt, and while it was in better physical shape than their meeting place with Firebrand, that wasn't saying a lot. But it was mostly weathertight, at least, and the containers themselves were hermetically sealed and virtually indestructible. Of course, getting them there had been a not-so-minor challenge. The Krestor Interstellar shipping barcodes which had ensured their passage through customs without inspection would have stood out like sore thumbs in the Rust Belt, and so would any of the spaceport's more modern cargo vehicles.

But Firebrand's colleagues had anticipated that. The containers were sized to fit inside standard cargo trailers of the sort Seraphim had built for its own use before Krestor and Mendoza of Córdoba arrived to "rescue" its economy. Even better, they were equipped with built-in counter-grav units, so the trailers hadn't ridden suspiciously low on their suspensions. It also made the containers much easier to manhandle with strictly limited manpower once they reached their destination.

"I'm still not happy about the transport arrangements," Indiana went on. "Oh, they worked this time, but we had to put the whole thing together on the fly. Now that we've got them under cover, I want to take a little longer to think before we start moving them around."

"Works for me," Mackenzie said fervently. But then she cocked her head, looking up at her taller brother. "It works for me, but at the same time, I don't want to leave them sitting in one big, undigested lump where we could lose all of them in a single disaster if the scags get lucky!"

"Me either. But the more we spread them around in smaller caches, the more likely one of O'Sullivan's informers'll stumble across one of them. Or, for that matter, that the recon platforms'll spot something."

"Not if we get them out into the country," Mackenzie argued. "I'm thinking about handing them over to Saratoga."

Indiana started to reply, then stopped, thinking about it. "Saratoga" was Leonard Silvowitz, a Seraphim Independence Movement area leader. He didn't know he was taking instructions from Indiana and Mackenzie, both of whom he'd known for years, since he'd been a silent partner in the business effort which had led to Bruce Graham's arrest. As far as their SIM roles were concerned, he knew them only as "Talisman" and "Magpie," and his communications with them were indirect and circuitous.

"You know," Indiana said slowly, "that might not be a bad idea at all. I'm not crazy about putting him at risk this early, but the Farm *would* be a good place to stash them, wouldn't it?"

"The Farm," fifty kilometers north of Cherubim, had been a part of Leonard Silvowitz's modest business empire: a commercial farming operation which had employed several dozen people and shown a tidy profit supplying fresh vegetables and dairy products to Seraphim's more urbanized areas. Unfortunately, that very profitability had drawn the attention of Krestor Interstellar's local manager, and the Macready Administration had "suggested" Silvowitz lease the operation to Krestor at about twenty percent of what it was actually worth. Krestor had then proceeded to fire virtually all of Silvowitz's employees, some of whom had been with him for as much as twenty or thirty T-years, and replace them with automated equipment.

Technically, Silvowitz still owned the Farm, although he had no control over its operation, and Krestor hadn't been interested in his employees' housing (since there were no longer any employees to be housed). Those once sturdy, reasonably comfortable units were slowly decaying into ruin, like most of Seraphim, but they were still there, and Indiana and Mackenzie had planned on using them as a training site when the time came. They were far enough out to be beyond the scags' normal zone of interest, and there was enough traffic transporting the Farm's produce to the city and the necessary supplies back to its fields to cover quite a lot of movement on the SIM's part.

"I think it would be a good place, or I wouldn't have suggested it," Mackenzie pointed out. "At the same time, there's always the chance some service tech out there to work on a broken down cultivator or harvester might spot something."

"That was always going to be the case when we

started training out there, anyway," Indiana replied. "And these containers are a lot sturdier and more weathertight than I expected, so he could hide them out in the woods instead of one of the barns where your service tech might be poking around. Or someplace even better than that."

He smiled at her, and she frowned back for a couple of seconds. Then her expression cleared.

"You're thinking of Culver Hill, aren't you?"

"That's exactly where I'm thinking about." Indiana nodded. He and his sister had spent a lot of childhood summer nights camping out by the small lake just east of Culver Hill. Which was how they happened to know about the cave system that ran for kilometers under the hill itself. The caves were on the damp side, but with the containers' hermetic seals . . .

"That's not a bad idea at all," Mackenzie said approvingly. Then she grinned. "How did *you* happen to have it?"

"Very funny." Indiana scowled at her. "But since I seem to be doing the intellectual heavy lifting today, I hereby nominate you to figure out exactly how we're going to get them to the Farm in the first place."

"Well, the first stage is to let Saratoga know they're coming," Mackenzie pointed out. "We're going to need him to take a look at the caves and be sure he can get them in. Even with the counter-grav, moving them's going to be a pain, especially without a lot of warm bodies to help, and there are some pretty narrow spots just inside the caves' entrance."

"Agreed. But let's not tell him what we're planning to send him." Indiana's expression was considerably more serious than it had been. "There's no point telling him the guns have arrived if it turns out he can't handle them."

Mackenzie nodded soberly. One of their guiding principles was that what someone didn't know, someone couldn't spill accidentally . . . or under the sort of the duress Tillman O'Sullivan's scags were expert at applying.

"All right." Indiana gave a brisk nod of his own. "I'll put the message together and get it into the secure drop for Osiris." "Osiris" was Janice Karpov, Indiana and Mackenzie's contact with Silowitz. "If I get my butt in motion, I can probably make the drop this evening still."

"Just don't take any stupid chances, Indy," Mackenzie said a bit sharply. He looked at her, and she scowled again, more darkly than before. "You've always just had to run right out and start playing with your toys, ever since you were a kid, and some things really don't change, do they? I swear, I've known *five*-year-olds with more patience than you have! Well, *discretion*, anyway." She snorted. "Those weapons aren't going to get all old and worn out sitting there for an extra day or two."

"I know they aren't, Max." Indiana's tone was more soothing than agreeing, but Mackenzie was willing to settle for that. Getting him to admit she had a point would probably have been expecting too much, but that wasn't the same thing as his not *knowing* she had one.

"If I can make the drop without pushing too hard, I'd still prefer to get it done tonight," he continued. "All the same, we didn't set up secure communications routes just so I could blow things when a really important message comes along, did we?"

"That wasn't why *I* thought we were doing it, no," she agreed.

"Point taken," he capitulated. Then he grinned. "You know, I know all about secure communications and how important they are, but still, I'd really *love* to see Uncle Leonard's face when he finds out he's about to receive an entire battalion's worth of small arms and support weapons!"

Chapter Nineteen

"—HAVEN'T HEARD ANYTHING NEW out of Gold Peak or Medusa, anyway," Captain Sadako Merriman said, looking up from the notes on her minicomp's display. "That doesn't mean they aren't up to something, of course, Commissioner." She grimaced. "The truth is, we're pretty sure they *are* up to something. We just don't have a clue what."

The slender, fine-boned Frontier Fleet officer wasn't one of Lorcan Verrochio's favorite people for several reasons. Among other things, she had an annoying habit of seeming unimpressed by his own august presence, but she also had an equally annoying habit of telling him the truth. He supposed that counted for something, even if "don't have a clue" wasn't exactly what he wanted to hear out of his senior naval intelligence specialist.

"We're trying to get better information, of course, Commissioner," Commodore Francis Thurgood (who had the distinction of being someone Verrochio liked even less than Merriman) put in. "In the wake of what happened to Admiral Crandall, though, we're not in a position to push as hard for it as I'm sure we'd all like to. I don't think the Manties would be very receptive to any 'port visits' on our part, for example."

"I'm aware of that, thank you, Commodore," Verrochio said as pleasantly as he could.

The stocky commodore had a weathered-looking appearance which Verrochio found strange in someone who spent his entire working life in artificial environments. And, although Thurgood was reasonably careful to avoid emphasizing it, he'd also tried to warn Sandra Crandall about what she was walking into. Of course, even his gloomy projections had fallen well short of the reality; they'd just been closer than anyone else's.

"The Manticorans' decision to recall their merchant shipping from Solarian space isn't helping, Governor," Merriman added. "I realize we didn't have much of their shipping here in-Sector to begin with, but there was always at least some . . . cross-pollination, let's say. Merchant spacers talk to each other wherever their paths happen to cross. They always seem to know a lot more than you think they should about what's going on, and you can usually pick up a lot listening to them. In this case, though, there's no one to do the talking."

Verrochio nodded, not that he needed reminders about how painfully the Manties had wounded the League's interstellar commerce. He'd managed to sidestep any responsibility for Sandra Crandall's decision to attack Spindle, but its disastrous consequences had created enough crap to splash everyone in the sector, especially its commissioner. Official news of the Manty merchies' recall had reached Meyers less than two weeks earlier, and the ruinous consequences of the withdrawal of Manticoran vessels from the League's shipping lanes had been none too gently pointed out to him by higher authority. Some of those higher authorities hadn't been shy about suggesting that it was the direct result of events in *his* sector, either.

"With all due respect, Commissioner, it's also possible we're not hearing anything because there's nothing to hear *about*," Brigadier Francisca Yucel put in.

The Madras Sector's senior Gendarmerie officer had blonde hair, gray eyes, and the short, square muscularity of a heavy-worlder. She also had an unhappy expression, and Verrochio scowled mentally as he looked at her. She'd never liked Thurgood (whom she referred to as "that old woman") or Merriman (whom she regarded as an interloper into internal security matters which were none of her affair), and she disagreed strenuously with their analysis of the Manticorans' probable intentions. She was also a bigger pain in his posterior than Merriman and Thurgood combined, but that didn't necessarily mean she was wrong.

"I realize you have a different perspective from the Navy's, Francisca," the commissioner said. "But it's Commodore Thurgood's and Captain Merriman's responsibility to look at the worst case from a naval perspective."

"I agree." Yucel didn't try very hard to sound as if she meant it, Verrochio observed. "I'm simply saying we shouldn't scare ourselves into hiding in a corner on the basis of what happened at Spindle. By this time, even that moron Gold Peak has to realize how badly she fucked up at New Tuscany and Spindle! Their government has to be shitting bricks thinking about the mess she's dragged them all into. If the order relieving her ass and hauling her home hasn't gotten to Spindle yet, it's damned well on its way, Commissioner!"

Verrochio nodded in acknowledgement, although he was a far cry from agreeing with her. Nothing he'd seen out of the Manties suggested any inclination on their part to give ground, and he very much doubted Elizabeth Winton was going to recall her cousin from Talbott anytime soon. He did have to agree with at least one of Yucel's underlying premises—that no one except a maniac would willingly contemplate an all out war with the Solarian League, no matter how good his weapons technology was. Unfortunately, every indication *he'd* seen said the Manties *were* maniacs. That was why he rejected her opposition of anything that smacked of "appeasement." It was her view that giving ground to Manticore would only increase the Star Empire's arrogance and ambition, whereas refusing to be bullied and panicked into giving it whatever it wanted would cause it to pull in its horns. She might actually be right about that. In fact, he hoped she was. But after the string of disasters which had landed on his doorstep, he had no intention of being the one who refused to be "bullied" and found out the Manties weren't bluffing after all.

"It's possible Brigadier Yucel is right about that, Commissioner," Thurgood said. Without, Verrochio noticed, sounding any more sincere than Yucel had. "For the moment, however, Gold Peak's still in command—according to our most recent information, at any rate—and I think we can safely assume she's going to at least redeploy her forces. She may be more . . . confrontational than her government would like, but in a tactical sense, at least, she's demonstrated she's nobody's fool. And, as she demonstrated for better or worse at New Tuscany, she's not afraid to act on her own authority, either." He smiled thinly; he'd tried to warn Josef Byng, too. "I anticipate encountering a heavier Manty naval presence along our frontier very soon now. I'll agree that I don't think she's going to push any confrontations with the League if she can help it, but she's not going to be backing down, either."

"Are you suggesting she's likely to begin offensive operations into the Madras Sector, Commodore?" Vice Commissioner Junyan Hongbo asked.

"To be honest, Mr. Vice Commissioner, I don't see any reason she should, if not for exactly the same reasons as Brigadier Yucel. The truth is, though, that it's not like we've got the firepower to threaten the Talbott Quadrant. I'm sorry, the Talbott *Sector*." The commodore grimaced slightly as he corrected himself. Obviously he found Frontier Security's continued insistence that the Talbott Quadrant's incorporation into the Star Empire of Manticore was legally suspect more than a bit silly. "I don't see Manticore wanting to push any sort of conquest in our direction, for a lot of reasons, including the desire—as the Brigadier's suggested—to keep some kind of lid on this whole confrontation. I don't expect her to back off if push comes to shove, but I also don't see her going looking for unnecessary fights or dissipating her resources against anything she doesn't consider is a genuine, immediate, and pressing threat. So, since we don't have any naval bases that *could* threaten them, I'd expect her to look elsewhere in an operational sense. Frankly, little though I'm sure any of us would like to admit it, we're just not important enough for her to be worrying about at the moment."

Oh, thank *you, Commodore,* Verrochio thought sourly. *"Not important enough"* to *worry about. Doesn't that just underscore the hit Frontier Security's prestige has already taken!*

That thought wouldn't have bothered him so much if he hadn't suspected Thurgood took a certain satisfaction in pointing it out. The commodore would have been more than human if he hadn't felt gratified—or *justified,* at least—at having been right when everyone else (especially Sandra Crandall) had all but accused him of cowardice for warning them the Manties might just conceivably be serious when they said they were.

"So your recommendation would be that we should basically stay home and avoid provoking her," Hongbo said, and Thurgood shrugged.

"I wouldn't put it quite that way myself, Mr. Vice Commissioner. We don't have the *capability* to 'provoke' her. What I'm saying is that unless we're significantly reinforced, about the best we can realistically expect to do is to police our own merchant traffic—such as it is, and what there is of it—and provide reaction forces if any of the sector's planets should get . . . restive. Obviously, that constitutes 'staying home,' but that's another way of saying it constitutes doing our job, too." He regarded Hongbo levelly across the conference table. "If anyone wants us to do something more proactive, they're damned well going to have to send us the means to do it. And given the weapons capability the Manties have demonstrated, I don't know that anyone has the means *to* send."

Hongbo looked back at him for a moment, then nodded.

"Point taken, Commodore," he said in an almost

conciliatory tone. "I didn't mean to sound as if I were suggesting you intended to shirk your responsibilities. I guess I'm just not any more immune to frustration and, well, *nervousness* than anyone else."

Thurgood's fleeting smile acknowledged the vice commissioner's semi-apology, and Merriman cleared her throat.

"At any rate, Commissioner," she said to Verrochio, "I'm afraid that really does constitute all the Navy can contribute to the intelligence picture at this point. I wish we could tell you more, but we can't."

"In that case, if you don't mind, Commissioner, *I've* got a couple of points I'd like us to consider," Yucel said harshly.

"Oh?" Verrochio looked at her. "What would those be, Brigadier?"

"Ms. Xydis' dispatches from Mobius." Yucel's voice was flat, and Verrochio was conscious of a distinct sinking sensation.

"I realize President Lombroso's concerned about the situation," he said, "but, let's be honest, Francisca, he's *always* concerned about the situation."

"I'm aware of that, Sir." Yucel's tone carried a hint of frost. "But 'the situation's' changed significantly, given the sophistication of the weapons used against the Presidential Guard this time around. Nobody cooked those up in some backwoods workshop, Sir, and nobody bought them for hunting or even self-defense, either. Someone damned well sent them in from the outside specifically to be used exactly the way they *were* used."

"I think we want to be a little careful about leaping to conclusions about those weapons reports, Brigadier," Junyan Hongbo said coolly. He and Yucel saw eye-to-eye on very few subjects, and especially not on her theory that there was no such thing as "excessive force." In her view, there was no problem she couldn't solve by killing enough people, and the two of them seldom found themselves on the same side of any policy debate.

"Lombroso, Yardley, and Mátyás are scarcely disinterested observers," the vice commissioner added, "and they've been trying for years to get an official OFS presence to back up the local régime."

Verrochio felt himself nodding slowly in agreement. Given the way Svein Lombroso had become steadily more hated by the Mobius System's citizens, virtually from the first day he'd taken power, it wasn't surprising he saw clearly visible OFS backing for his régime as the only way to stave off disaster. A smarter (and less brutal) president might have reflected that inviting Frontier Security in was like a farmer inviting a fox to a slumber party in his henhouse, but Lombroso was obviously feeling the strain.

"Yes, I'm aware of that, too, Mr. Vice Commissioner," Yucel said. "I'd just like to point out, though, that according to Xydis' messages, President Lombroso definitely isn't fabricating this. It really happened, he's got a lot of civilian casualties, and the terrorists opposed to his administration are clearly better organized—and one hell of a lot better armed—than they've ever been before. There are signs Mobius isn't the only place this is happening, too. In fact, he's scarcely the only local reporting evidence of Manty involvement in providing both weapons and financial support."

Verrocchio managed not to roll his eyes. It wasn't easy, given how persistently Yucel, despite her firm belief that Manticore wouldn't dare confront the League openly, seemed to be finding Manty plots under her bed every night. Apparently she had no problem at all with believing Manticore would resort to any *clandestine* means of opposing OFS it could come up with, regardless of the risk of Solarian retaliation, which struck him as more than a bit inconsistent. Maybe she'd spent so long arranging "deniable" operations of her own that she was simply programmed to assume everyone else thought the same way she did? Now *that* was a frightening concept. At the same time, however, she had a point about Lombroso's reports.

"I realize we're all under a lot of strain," Hongbo said, "and I fully agree that we need to be more safe than sorry about the Manties, but I also think it would be a mistake to rely too heavily on those reports, Brigadier." Yucel glowered at him, and he shrugged. "The unrest in Mobius started well before Admiral Byng's deployment, and I fail to see any reason for the Star Empire to have invested in the considerable effort and expense to foment general unrest in our vicinity before they even knew he was coming!"

"*Someone's* providing modern weapons, and not just to Lombroso," Yucel said stubbornly. "If it's happening on anything like the scale our reports indicate, that same someone is obviously willing to invest the effort and expense you've just mentioned. And at the moment, I don't see anyone with a *better* reason than the Manties to be doing that."

Her gray eyes challenged him coldly across the conference table, but he didn't back down.

"Neither do I," he said. "Which, I'm afraid, suggests to me that the reports you're referring to are exaggerated. Understandably, I'm sure," he added, not trying to sound any more sincere than she or Thurgood had, "given all the unrest that's been swirling around since the Battle of Monica, but nonetheless exaggerated. And while I've just agreed it's better to be safe than sorry, our resources—as Commodore Thurgood has just pointed out—are limited. I don't think it would be wise to waste them responding to threats which may not even be real."

"I'm inclined to agree, Junyan," Verrochio said quickly, before Yucel could fire back. "I'd like to stay focused on the specific case of Mobius at this point, though. Brigadier?"

Yucel sat in brief, fulminating silence, then inhaled deeply.

"It's possible President Lombroso *is* seeing Manticoran involvement when there isn't any," she conceded, although her tone made it obvious she thought nothing of the sort. "Nonetheless, it's clear his problems are much more serious than our earlier assessments suggested. And I think it's equally clear he's losing whatever nerve he may once have had. That's not a recipe for success, so I think we have to decide whether we're going to support him or the time's come to go ahead and supplant him. And the Vice Commissioner—and the Commodore—are right that we have limited resources. We can't afford to waste them, and, frankly, providing a garrison to maintain direct control on a long-term basis would cut deeply into my available strength."

Verrochio winced. One thing of which no one could ever accuse Francisca Yucel was subtlety. Still, she had a point. Lombroso was a lot less valuable to Frontier Security than he might think he was. In fact, under normal circumstances, as Yucel had just implied,

Verrochio would have been simply biding his time until things got bad enough to provide OFS with an unassailable case for—regretfully, of course—moving in to restore public order and safety. In the process of which, Mobius would just happen to find itself an official protectorate and President Lombroso would just happen to find himself unemployed.

Circumstances weren't normal, however, and the last thing he needed was to have Mobius melt down right on his doorstep. Manty meddling in the Mobius System or not, the restiveness of Lombroso's opposition undoubtedly owed a lot to what had already happened in Talbott. The example of a whole cluster of worlds seeking and receiving admission into the Star Empire hadn't been lost on any of the nominally independent planets in the vicinity. They were bound to see that as a better deal than being systematically sucked dry by one transtellar or another or engulfed by Frontier Security, at any rate, and he never doubted that his ultimate superiors back in Old Chicago would recognize that as well as he did. And they wouldn't thank him for allowing the dike of OFS' prestige and power to spring any fresh leaks, either.

Which didn't even consider the way Trifecta Corporation and its economic allies would react if he let anything like a genuine Mobian régime topple Lombroso. It might take years for Trifecta to get its hooks properly into Lombroso's successor, and they'd undoubtedly raise hell about it the entire time.

"Should I take it you concur with Brigadier Yucel's reading of the situation, Colonel?" the commissioner inquired, looking at Colonel Armand Wang, Yucel's equivalent of Captain Merriman.

Wang was a good forty centimeters taller than Yucel, with dark hair, dark eyes, and a high-arched nose. He was also, in Verrochio's opinion, rather less of a blunt object. Now he glanced at Yucel from the corner of one eye, then shrugged.

"It's possible"—he stressed the adverb ever so slightly—"President Lombroso and General Yardley are overreacting. As you say, Sir, they've insisted the sky was falling in the past. But we've looked at their reports, especially the most recent ones from General Mátyás, and at Ms. Xydis' messages carefully. We've also sent back a request for additional information from Trifecta Corporation's sources in the system, although it's going to be a while before we hear from them in reply." He shrugged. "On the basis of all information currently available to us, there's no question but that at least some modern weapons have found their way to President Lombroso's opposition. That's obvious, however they got there, and even if the local authorities *are* overreacting, this isn't the time to let something like this get out of hand."

Well, Verrochio really hadn't expected him to contradict Yucel. The commissioner looked at Hongbo, who also shrugged. Which was a lot of help, Verrochio reflected sourly.

The commissioner suppressed a temptation to gnaw on a fingernail. Anything he dispatched to Mobius would be unavailable if something decided to blow up on one of the Madras Sector's planets, and the excuse that he'd been trying to prevent a Mobius meltdown was unlikely to appease critics in Old Chicago if the troops he needed to prevent his own sector from burning to the ground were elsewhere at the critical moment. But if he let Mobius turn into another Talbott Quadrant . . .

"All right," he sighed. "I see your point, Francisca. And yours, Colonel Wang. And, all things considered, I don't think this is the time for us to be supplanting any more local régimes. So, having said that, what would you recommend?"

"I think we don't have any choice but to meet Xydis' request for boots on the ground." Yucel smiled unpleasantly. "The locals may be willing to come out into the open against Lombroso's Presidential Guard, but I doubt they'll be so eager against an intervention battalion or two."

"Is that strong a response really necessary, Brigadier?" Hongbo asked distastefully.

"We don't have a lot of options here, Mr. Vice Commissioner." Yucel pointed out testily. "Anybody I send to Mobius will be out of my order of battle insector for months, so if we're going to send troops at all, we have to send enough of them—and with clear enough rules of engagement—to break these terrorists' backs quickly. Get in, kick the shit out of them, turn the situation back over to Lombroso—maybe with a Gendarmerie adviser or two and a company or so of troops for support—and then get the rest of our people back here. Do it hard and fast and we may just be able to complete the entire operation before anyone here in the Madras Sector even realizes we've diverted any of our strength elsewhere."

"Something to be said for that, Mr. Commissioner." Thurgood clearly didn't enjoy saying that, but his expression was unflinching when Verrochio looked at him.

"Whether it's a good idea to intervene at all is outside my area of competence, Sir," the Frontier Fleet officer said. "I'm no expert at controlling insurrections on the ground. But if the decision's that we ought to intervene in Mobius, I'm in favor of getting in and getting out as quickly as possible." His lips tightened in distaste. "If we're sending in troops on the ground, I'll need to come up with at least a couple of destroyers to control space around the planet. If for no other reason than to make sure no more shipments of modern weapons get through to the other side while we've got troops down there. That means that in addition to any troop strength Brigadier Yucel has to divert, I'm going to have to divert *naval* strength, as well. And, frankly, the longer any of my ships are away, the more likely it is that something's going to get past us here at home."

It was obvious that, outside his area of competence or not, Thurgood was opposed to the entire notion. That didn't invalidate his points, unfortunately.

Verrochio closed his eyes for a moment, thinking, then sighed.

"I want an estimate of the troop strength you're proposing to commit, Francisca," he said. "And I want to see your operations plan before I make any hard decisions. Having said that, I think you're probably right and we need to get support in there for Lombroso before bad turns to worse. Commodore," he turned back to Thurgood, "as soon as the Brigadier and I have determined exactly how many troops we're committing, I'm going to need your best numbers on transport requirements and what kind of warship support you expect to be necessary." He smiled bleakly. "If we're going to do this, let's at least try to get it right."

✦ Chapter Twenty

"*What* DID YOU SAY?"

Albrecht Detweiler stared at his oldest son, and the consternation in his expression would have shocked any of the relatively small number of people who'd ever met him.

"I said our analysis of what happened at Green Pines seems to have been a little in error," Benjamin Detweiler said flatly. "That bastard McBryde wasn't the only one trying to defect." Benjamin had had at least a little time to digest the information during his flight from the planetary capital of Mendel, and if there was less consternation in his expression, it was also grimmer and far more frightening than his father's. "And the way the Manties are telling it, the son-of-a-bitch sure as hell wasn't trying to *stop* Cachat and Zilwicki. They haven't said so, but he must've deliberately suicided to cover up what he'd done!"

Albrecht stared at him for several more seconds. Then he shook himself and inhaled deeply.

"Go on," he grated. "I'm sure there's more and better yet to come."

"Zilwicki and Cachat are still alive," Benjamin told him. "I'm not sure where the hell they've been. We don't have anything like the whole story yet, but apparently they spent most of the last few months getting home. The bastards aren't letting out any more operational details than they have to, but I wouldn't be surprised if McBryde's cyber attack is the only reason they managed to get out in the first place.

"According to the best info we've got, though, they headed toward Haven, not Manticore, when they left, which probably helps explain why they were off the grid so long. I'm not sure about the reasoning behind that, either. But whatever they were thinking, what they accomplished was to get Eloise Pritchart—in person!—to Manticore, and she's apparently negotiated some kind of damned *peace treaty* with Elizabeth."

"With *Elizabeth*?"

"We've always known she's not really a lunatic, whatever we may've sold the Sollies," Benjamin pointed out. "Inflexible as hell sometimes, sure, but she's way too pragmatic to turn down something like that. For that matter, she'd sent Harrington to Haven to do exactly the same thing before Oyster Bay! And Pritchart brought along an argument to sweeten the deal, too, in the form of one Herlander Simões. *Doctor* Herlander Simões...who once upon a time worked in the Gamma Center on the streak drive."

"Oh, *shit*," Albrecht said with quiet, heartfelt intensity.

"Oh, it gets better, Father," Benjamin said harshly. "I don't know how much information McBryde actually handed Zilwicki and Cachat, or how much substantiation they've got for it, but they got one hell of a lot more than *we'd* want them to have! They're talking about virus-based nanotech assassinations, the streak drive, *and* the spider drive, and they're naming names about something called 'the Mesan Alignment.' They're also busy telling the Manty Parliament—and, I'm sure, the Havenite Congress and all the *rest* of the fucking galaxy!—all about the Mesan plan to conquer the known universe. In fact, you'll be astonished to know that Secretary of State Arnold Giancola was in the nefarious Alignment's pay when he deliberately maneuvered Haven back into shooting at the Manties!"

"What?" Albrecht blinked in surprise. "We didn't have anything to do with that!"

"Of course not. But fair's fair; we did know he was fiddling the correspondence. Only after the fact, maybe, when he enlisted Nesbitt to help cover his tracks, but we did know. And apparently giving Nesbitt the nanotech to get rid of Grosclaude was a tactical error. It sounds like Usher got at least a sniff of it, and even if he hadn't, the similarities between Grosclaude's suicide and the Webster assassination—and the attempt on Harrington—are pretty obvious once someone starts looking. So the theory is that if we're the only ones with the nanotech, and if Giancola used nanotech to get rid of Grosclaude, he must've been working for us all along. At least they don't seem to have put Nesbitt into the middle of it all—yet, anyway—but their reconstruction actually makes a lot of sense, given what they think they know at this point."

"Wonderful," Albrecht said bitterly.

"Well, it isn't going to get any better, Father, and that's a fact. Apparently, it's all over the Manties' news services and sites, and even some of the Solly newsies are starting to pick up on it. It hasn't had time to actually hit Old Terra yet, but it's going to be there in the next day or so. There's no telling what's going to happen when it does, either, but it's already all over *Beowulf*, and I'll just let you imagine for yourself how *they're* responding to it."

Albrecht's mouth tightened as he contemplated the full, horrendous extent of the security breach. Just discovering Zilwicki and Cachat were still alive to dispute the Alignment's version of Green Pines would have been bad enough. The rest . . . !

"Thank you," he said after a moment, his tone poison-dry. "I think my imagination's up to the task of visualizing how *those* bastards will eat this up." He twitched a savage smile. "I suppose the best we can hope for is that finding out how completely we've played their so-called intelligence agencies for the last several centuries will shake their confidence. I'd *love* to see that bastard Benton-Ramirez y Chou's reaction, for instance. Unfortunately, whatever we may hope for, what we can *count* on is for them to line up behind the Manties. For that matter, I wouldn't be surprised to see them actively sign up with the Manticoran Alliance . . . especially if Haven's already on board with it."

"Despite the Manties' confrontation with the League?" The words were a question, but Benjamin's tone made it clear he was following his father's logic only too well.

"Hell, we're the ones who've been setting things up so the League came unglued in the first place, Ben! You really think someone like *Beowulf* gives a single good goddamn about those fucking apparatchiks in Old Chicago?" Albrecht snorted contemptuously. "I may hate the bastards, and I'll do my damnedest to cut their throats, but whatever else they may be, they're not stupid or gutless enough to let Kolokoltsov and his miserable crew browbeat them into doing one damned thing they don't *want* to do."

"You're probably right about that," Benjamin agreed glumly, then shook his head. "No, you *are* right about that."

"Unfortunately, it's not going to stop there," Albrecht went on. "Just having Haven stop shooting at Manticore's going to be bad enough, but Gold Peak is entirely too close to us for my peace of mind. She thinks too much, and she's too damned good at her job . . . and too damned willing to draw lines in the sand. That business at Saltash comes to mind, for instance."

Father and son looked at one another with sour expressions. Word of Gold Peak's actions in Saltash had reached the Mesa System two and a half T-weeks earlier. They weren't supposed to know about it, since the Frontier Security courier passing through on his way to Visigoth and Sol had been sworn to silence. Frontier Security couriers weren't particularly well-paid, however, and Benjamin had been viewing a copy of Governor Dueñas' dispatches even before the dispatch boat had disappeared into the Mesa Terminus.

"She probably hasn't heard about any of this yet, given transit times," Albrecht continued, "but she's going to soon enough. And if she's feeling adventurous—or if Elizabeth is—we could have a frigging Manty fleet right here in Mesa in a handful of T-weeks. One that'll run over anything Mesa has without even noticing. And then there's the delightful possibility that Haven could come after us right along with Gold Peak, if they end up signing on as active military allies!"

"The same thought had occurred to me," Benjamin said grimly. As the commander of the Alignment's navy, he was only too well aware of what the only navies with operational pod-laying ships-of-the-wall and multidrive missiles could do if they were *allied* instead of shooting at one another.

"What do you think the Andies are going to do?" he asked after a moment, and his father grated a laugh.

"Isabel was always against using that nanotech anywhere we didn't have to. It looks like I should've listened." He shook his head. "I still think all the arguments for getting rid of Huang were valid, even if we didn't get him in the end, but if the Manties know about the nanotech and share that with Gustav, I think his usual 'realpolitik' will go right out the airlock. We didn't just go after his family, Benjamin—we went after the *succession*, too, and the Anderman dynasty hasn't lasted this long putting up with that kind of crap. Trust me. If he thinks the Manties are telling the truth, he's likely to come after us himself! For that matter, the Manties might deliberately strip him off from their Alliance. In fact, if they're smart, that's what they ought to do. Get Gustav out of the Sollies' line of fire and let him take care of us. It's not like they're going to need his pod-layers to kick the SLN's ass! And we just happen to have left the Andies' support structure completely intact, haven't we? That mean's they've got plenty of MDMs, and if Gustav comes after us while staying out of the confrontation with the League, do you really think any of our 'friends' in Old Chicago'll do one damned thing to stop him? Especially when they finally figure out what the Manties are really in a position to do to *them*?"

"No," Benjamin agreed bitterly. "Not in a million years."

There was silence for several seconds as father and son contemplated the shattering upheaval in the Mesan Alignment's carefully laid plans.

"All right," Albrecht said finally. "None of this is anyone's fault. Or, at least, if it *is* anyone's fault, it's mine and not anyone else's. You and Collin gave me your best estimate of what really went down at Green Pines, and I agreed with your assessment. For that matter, the fact that Cachat and Zilwicki didn't surface before this pretty damned much seemed to confirm it. And given the fact that none of our internal reports mentioned this 'Simões' by name—or if they did, I certainly don't remember it, anyway—I imagine I should take it all our investigators assumed he was one of the people killed by the Green Pines bombs?"

"Yes." Benjamin's mouth twisted disgustedly. "As a matter of fact, the Gamma Center records which 'mysteriously' survived McBryde's cyberbomb showed Simões as on-site when the suicide charge went off." He sighed. "I should've wondered why those records managed to survive when so much of the rest of our secure files got wiped."

"You weren't the only one who didn't think about that," his father pointed out harshly. "It did disappear him pretty neatly, though, didn't it? And no wonder we were willing to assume he'd just been vaporized! God knows enough other people were." He shook his head. "And I still think we did the right thing to use the whole mess to undercut Manticore with the League, given what we knew. But that's sort of the point, I suppose. What's that old saying? 'It's not what you don't know that hurts you; it's what you *think* you know that isn't so.' It's sure as hell true in *this* case, anyway!"

"I think we could safely agree on that, Father."

The two of them sat silent once more for several moments, then Albrecht shrugged.

"Well, it's not the end of the universe. And at least we've had time to get Houdini up and running."

"But we're not far enough along with it," Benjamin pointed out. "Not if the Manties—or the Andies—move as quickly as they could. And if the *Sollies* believe this, the time window's going to get even tighter."

"Tell me something I don't know." His father's tone was decidedly testy this time, but then he shook his head and raised one hand in an apologetic gesture. "Sorry, Ben. No point taking out my pissed-offedness on you. And you're right, of course. But it's not as if we never had a plan in place to deal with something like this." He paused and barked a harsh laugh. "Well, not something like *this*, so much, since we never saw this coming in our worst nightmares, but you know what I mean."

Benjamin nodded, and Albrecht tipped back in his chair, fingers drumming on its arms.

"I think we have to assume McBryde and this Simões between them have managed to compromise us almost completely, insofar as anything either of them had access to is concerned," he said after a moment. "Frankly, I doubt they have, but I'm not about to make any optimistic—any *more* optimistic—assumptions at this point. On the other hand, we're too heavily compartmentalized for even someone like McBryde to've known about anything close to *all* the irons we

have in the fire. And if Simões was in the Gamma
Center, he doesn't know crap about the operational
side. You and Collin—and Isabel—saw to that. In
particular, nobody in the Gamma Center, including
McBryde, had been briefed about Houdini before
Oyster Bay. So unless we want to assume Zilwicki and
Cachat have added mindreading to their repertoire,
that's still secure."

"Probably," Benjamin agreed.

"Even so, we're going to have to accelerate the
process. Worse, we never figured we'd have to execute
Houdini under this kind of time pressure. We're going
to have to figure out how to hide a hell of a lot of
disappearances in a really tight time window, and
that's going to be a pain in the ass." Albrecht frowned,
his expression thoughtful as he regained his mental
balance. "There's a limit to how many convenient air
car accidents we can arrange. On the other hand,
we can probably bury a good many of them in the
Green Pines casualty total. Not the really visible ones,
of course, but a good percentage of the second tier
live in Green Pines. We can probably get away with
adding a lot of them to the casualty lists, at least as
long as we're not leaving any immediate family or
close friends behind."

"Collin and I will get on that as soon as he gets
here," Benjamin agreed. "You've probably just put
your finger on why we won't be able to hide as many
of them that way as we'd like, though. A lot of those
family and friends *are* going to be left behind under
Houdini, and if we start expanding the Houdini lists
all of a sudden..."

"Point taken." Albrecht nodded. "Look into it,

though. Anyone we can hide that way will help. For the rest, we're just going to have to be more inventive."

He rocked his chair from side to side, thinking hard. Then he smiled suddenly, and there was actually some genuine amusement in the expression. Bitter, biting amusement, perhaps, but amusement.

"What?" Benjamin asked.

"I think it's time to make use of the Ballroom again."

"I'm not sure I'm following you."

"I don't care who the Manties are able to trot out to the newsies," Albrecht replied. "Unless they physically invade Mesa and get their hands on a solid chunk of the onion core, a bunch of Sollies—most of them, maybe—are still going to think they're lying. Especially where the Ballroom's concerned. God knows we've spent enough time, effort, and money convincing the League at large that the entire Ballroom consists of nothing but homicidal maniacs! For that matter, they've done a lot of the convincing for us, because they *are* homicidal maniacs! So I think it's time, now that these preposterous rumors about some deeply hidden, centuries-long Mesan conspiracy have been aired, for the Ballroom to decide to take vengeance. The reports are a complete fabrication, of course. At best, they're a gross, self-serving misrepresentation, anyway, so any murderous response they provoke out of the Ballroom will be entirely the Manties' fault, not that they'll ever admit their culpability. And, alas, our security here is going to turn out to be more porous than we thought it was."

Benjamin looked at him for another moment, then began to smile himself.

"Do you think we can get away with its having

been 'porous' enough for them to have gotten their hands on additional nukes?"

"Well, we know from our own interrogation of that seccy bastard who was working with Zilwicki and Cachat that it was the *seccies* who brought them the nuke that went off in the park," Albrecht pointed out. "Assuming anyone on their side's concerned with telling the truth—which, admittedly, *I* wouldn't be in their place—that little fact may just become public knowledge. In fact, now that I think about it, if Cachat and Zilwicki are telling their side of what happened, they'll probably want to stress that they certainly didn't bring any nukes to Mesa with them. So, yes, I think it's possible some of those deeply embittered fanatics, driven to new heights of violence by the Manties' vicious lies, will inflict yet more terroristic nuclear attacks upon us. And if they're going to do that, it's only reasonable—if I can apply that term to such sociopathic butchers—that they'd be going after the upper echelons of Mesan society."

"That could very well work," Benjamin said, eyes distant as he nodded thoughtfully. Then those eyes refocused on his father, and his own smile disappeared. "If we go that way, though, it's going to push the collateral damage way up. Houdini never visualized *that*, Father."

"I know it didn't." Albrecht's expression matched his son's. "And I don't like it, either. For that matter, a lot of the people on the Houdini list aren't going to like it. But messy as it's going to be, I don't think we have any choice but to look at this option closely, Ben. We can't afford to leave any kind of breadcrumb trail.

"McBryde had to know a lot about our military R &

D, given his position, but he was never briefed in on Darius, and he was at least officially outside any of the compartments that knew anything about Mannerheim or the other members of the Factor. It's possible he'd gotten some hint about the Factor, though, and he was obviously smart enough to've figured out we had to have something like Darius. For that matter, there are a hell of a lot of Manties who're smart enough to figure out that we'd never have been able to build the units for Oyster Bay without it. So it's going to be painfully evident to anyone inclined to believe the Manties' claims that the Mesan Alignment *they're* talking about would have to have a bolthole hidden away somewhere." He shook his head. "We can't afford to leave any evidence that might corroborate the notion that we simply dived down a convenient rabbit hole. If we have to inflict some 'collateral damage' to avoid that, then I'm afraid we're just going to have to inflict the damage."

Benjamin looked at him for several seconds, then nodded unhappily.

"All right," Albrecht said again. "Obviously, we're both responding off the cuff at the moment. Frankly, it's going to take a while for me, at least, to get past the simple shock quotient and be sure my mind's really working, and the last thing we need is to commit ourselves to anything we haven't thought through as carefully as possible. We need to assume time's limited, but I'm not about to start making panicked decisions that only make the situation worse. So we're not making *any* decisions until we've had a chance to actually look at this. You say Collin's on his way?"

"Yes, Sir."

"Then as soon as he gets here, the three of us need to go through everything we've got at this stage on a point by point basis. Should I assume that, with your usual efficiency, you've brought the actual dispatches about all of this with you?"

"I figured you'd want to see them yourself," Benjamin said with a nod, and reached into his tunic to extract a chip folio.

"One of the joys of having competent subordinates," Albrecht said in something closer to a normal tone. "In that case," he went on, holding out one hand for the folio while his other hand activated his terminal, "let's get started reviewing the damage now."

Chapter Twenty-One

"WELL, *this* IS AN interestin' development," Rear Admiral Michael Oversteegen drawled.

Michelle Henke restrained an urge to hit him over the head. It was difficult.

"I realize we aristocrats have a certain image to uphold, Michael, but is this *really* the best time to be displaying the depth of your sang-froid?"

"Um?" Oversteegen blinked, then gave himself a shake and actually smiled apologetically at her. "Sorry about that, M'Lady. Didn't even realize I was doin' it. This time, anyway."

He smiled again, more like his old self, and Michelle shook her own head.

Glory be, something's finally knocked Michael's aristocratic, nothing-surprises-me superiority on its ass! Too bad it took something like this to do it.

"To be fair, Milady, I don't think Admiral Oversteegen's the only person this has...taken by surprise, let's say," Cynthia Lecter observed. "It's going to take some getting used to."

"Really?" Michelle cocked her head and pursed her lips judiciously. "Let's see. President Pritchart just decided to turn up in Manticore last month and offer a peace treaty. Followed by the offer of a military alliance. And it turns out the reason for this is that according to Anton Zilwicki and the notorious Victor Cachat something called the 'Mesan Alignment' has been plotting against both the Star Kingdom and Haven—among other people—for the last five or six T-centuries. You think we're not going to be able to take those minor changes in stride, Cindy?"

"Excuse me, Milady, but what was that you were just sayin' about aristocratic sang-froid?" Oversteegen inquired.

"Point," Michelle admitted. "On the other hand, I'm the admiral, and you're the *rear* admiral. Rank hath its privileges. Or so I've heard, anyway."

"Actually, the thing I'm wondering is how accurate this intelligence really is, Ma'am," Sir Aivars Terekhov said. All eyes turned towards him, and he shrugged. "I'm not saying I don't believe it. For one thing, it makes a whole lot of things that have been happening out here suddenly fit together a lot more neatly. My only concern is that it may make them fit together *too* neatly. Well, that and the fact that we don't really *know* anything at all."

As usual, Michelle reflected, Terekhov had a damned good point.

She tipped back in her own chair, contemplating the deckhead. The fact that Tenth Fleet was only now learning about what was almost certainly the most momentous political development in the entire history of the Star Empire—*or* Star Kingdom—of Manticore was a stark comment on the information lags built into interstellar distances. And that was with the Lynx Terminus factored into the equation!

The dispatch from Baroness Medusa and Admiral Khumalo had arrived here in the Montana System less than six hours ago. The duplicate dispatch to Vice Admiral Theodore Bennington, commanding the other half of Tenth Fleet's heavy units at Tillerman, wouldn't reach its destination for another ten T-days or so. It was obvious Medusa and Khumalo had wanted to get the initial flash message to her and Bennington as quickly as possible, and she could understand that. All the same, she could also wish they'd waited long enough to get at least a few additional details before banging it off to her.

"I admit it would be nice to have at least some idea what kind of treaty proposals Pritchart has in mind," she said after a moment. "And I suppose I really would like a little more detail than 'Captain Zilwicki, Ballroom buddy and general all-round Manpower-hater extraordinaire, and his friend Victor Cachat, well known Havenite spy, assassin, godfather to Torch, and saboteur of our alliance with Erewhon, both *promise* Mesa is really at the bottom of all this.' But I think we have to take it as a given—for now, at least—that they're basically telling the truth, Aivars. Ariel and Nimitz would know if someone was lying, and I'm going to go out on a limb here and assume the Empress wouldn't be taking a Havenite's word for *anything* without one hell of a lot of corroboration from someone she totally trusts. These people may be wrong, but they're not lying."

"I didn't mean to suggest they were, Ma'am,"

Terekhov replied. "I'm just wondering how much responding to this we want to do before we get some kind of amplification?"

"That's a very sensible question, Milady," Vice Admiral Aploloniá Munming said. Like Oversteegen, the tallish, brown-haired, brown-eyed admiral was a native of the Star Empire's capital planet, but her accent was about as far removed from Oversteegen's aristocratic drawl as a Manticoran accent could be. She was not only of lower class origin, but of *immigrant* lower-class origin (her family had fled the People's Republic of Haven eighty T-years before), and as proud of her commoner birth as Klaus Hauptman himself. Despite which, she and Oversteegen got along well.

She was also the commander of Battle Squadron 16, the superdreadnought core of the force Michelle had led to Montana as part of her redeployment plan.

"This is something we're going to have to factor into all our planning," Munming went on, "but until we have more information, we're going to have to be very cautious about *how* we factor it in, I think."

"Oh, I agree entirely, Aploloniá." Michelle nodded vigorously. "Still, in a lot of ways, it only underscores a lot of our existing contingency thinking where Mesa was concerned. We've all been worried about them ever since their proxies ran into Aivars at Monica. The main change I think we need to make in our thinking is that if this dispatch is accurate—if the *Mesans* put together the Yawata Strike out of their own resources—they've got one hell of a lot more organic combat strength than we've thought. Frankly, most of my thinking where they're concerned has been concentrated on the possibility of their using more Solly proxies, and I think that's probably true for pretty much all of us. If *they're* the ones who have the 'invisible starship drives' and they're willing to come out into the open, they could be a lot more dangerous—a lot more *immediately* dangerous, I mean—than we've allowed for. I'm sure there'll be a lot of other changes once we get Sir Aivar's 'amplification,' but that's going to have to wait until additional information actually gets to us."

"Another question, if I may?" Oversteegen said.

"Go," Michelle replied, and he shrugged.

"Another thought that's occurred t' me is t' wonder just how far we might want t' disseminate this information at this point, Ma'am."

"According to the header on the dispatch, Sir," Lecter said before Michelle could reply, "this same basic message was sent to the chief executive of every system government in the Quadrant. Including President Suttles."

"Makes sense, I suppose," Oversteegen said. "Did the Governor attach a specific security level t' the information, Captain?"

"It's classified top secret, but there's nothing in the classification to preclude someone like President Suttles sharing the information with any member of his system government. Obviously Baroness Medusa and Prime Minister Alquezar expect them to show discretion, but they *are* the local civilian authorities, so I don't really see how she could have restricted it any more tightly than that, Sir."

From Oversteegen's expression, it was evident *he* could have imagined Medusa and Alquezar clamping an airtight lid on something like this quite easily. And, for once, a part of Michelle found itself in grudging agreement with him. Still . . .

"I don't think they really had a lot of choice about that," she observed. "If there's anything to this 'Mesan Alignment' business, then everyone's got to be on her guard. My feeling is that we took them so badly by surprise with our original expansion into the vicinity that they're probably still playing catch-up, at least to some extent. I mean, not even a diabolical centuries-old conspiracy could have anticipated our stumbling across the Lynx Terminus! And I don't think it could have had anything to do with Dueñas' little brainstorm in Saltash, either. You've all read Zavala's report, and I don't see how anybody could have counted on him to decide to seize our merchantships."

Several heads nodded. DesRon 301 had rejoined Tenth Fleet at Montana a month ago, and if one or two of Michelle's more senior officers could have wished for a less spectacular resolution of the problem, none of them had questioned Zavala's actions given the situation he'd discovered.

"But if Pat Givens' guess is right"—Michelle continued, one index finger tapping the message on the display in front of her—"and they not only managed to get Byng and Crandall deployed out this way more or less on the fly—and *meant* for both of them to get reamed all along, just to put us exactly where we are with the League—then they're entirely too good for my peace of mind. We need all the eyes we can get looking for what *else* they may be up to."

"As long as those eyes don't start seein' things that aren't actually there, Ma'am," Oversteegen replied with an unusual note of diffidence. He raised one hand in a pacific gesture before anyone could respond. "I'm not tryin' t' suggest that th' Quadrant's civilian leadership's a batch of alarmist paranoiacs, because I don't think it is. And if anyone *does* think he's seen anythin' that could be this Mesan Alignment's doin', then I hope t' *hell* he tells someone about it! But we've got a very finite amount of naval and military strength here in Talbott. We can't afford t' waste any of it on somethin' that turns out not t've been hostile action, after all."

"Agreed." Michelle nodded. "Trust me, Michael, as the person whose resources are 'very finite,' that's not something I'm likely to forget. All the same, I think we probably need our 'cat whiskers spread as far and as sensitively as we can get them. It's even more important to be sure we don't miss something that *does* turn out to have been hostile action, and we're just going to have to hope our filtering and evaluation are up to discriminating between real threats and false alarms."

Oversteegen nodded back soberly.

"One thing I'd like to do, Ma'am," Munming said, "is to spend some time brainstorming. I know I just said we had to be cautious about how we factor this into our planning, but I don't think it would hurt a thing for us to start considering what we might do if *we* were Mesa and it turns out this information about the 'Alignment' is accurate after all. Let's kick out some possibilities— think about worst-case scenarios they might spring on us—and start thinking of ways we might deal with them."

"I'm in favor of that, Ma'am," Oversteegen agreed, nodding vigorously. "Th' only resource that's likely t' use up is brainpower, which just happens to be one of th' few resources I'm familiar with that only reproduces itself th' more you use it!"

"Well, in that case," Michelle replied, "does anyone have any 'worst-cases' they'd care to throw out before the meeting?"

❖   ❖   ❖

"I wish I was more confident this was a good idea," Sector Governor Verrochio admitted quietly as he stood on the reviewing stand beside Junyan Hongbo.

Hongbo refrained from pointing out that he'd raised that same point when the deployment was first suggested.

It's too late to change our minds, anyway, he thought. *Besides, I'm not sure Yucel didn't actually have a point this time. It'd be a first, but even unlikely things happen . . . sometimes.*

The black-uniformed Gendarmerie battalions marched past the reviewing stand, body armor gleaming like polished ebony, shouldered flechette guns sloped at precisely the right angle, boot heels crashing on the ceramacrete pavement in perfect unison. They actually looked like soldiers, Hongbo thought. For that matter, whatever her other failings—and God knew they were legion—Francisca Yucel genuinely had instilled a level of discipline and training that was unfortunately rare among Solarian Gendarmes. He never doubted that the megalomaniac in her loved watching them train, sort of like a little girl playing with toys she knew could kill people. That didn't mean she hadn't turned them into a far more effective unit along the way, however, and this business of passing in review before the sector governor had been her idea, as well—a way to help promote and support their morale, their esprit de corps, as she put it.

Esprit de corps, right! he snorted mentally. *Bunch of thugs and leg-breakers is what they are.* This *batch just happens to be even better at it than most of the others!*

Yet that was precisely what Frontier Security had always wanted, when it came down to it. He knew that as well as Yucel did, but unlike her, he wasn't convinced it was a good idea, especially in this case. Turning them loose with what amounted to a free license to break heads—or worse—especially in a theoretically independent star system, struck him as an excellent recipe for increasing unrest and hatred in the Protectorates.

And it's not as if we don't have enough of that to go around already.

He listened to the steady beat of boot heels and cursed himself for having crawled into bed with Mesa and Manpower all those years ago. It shouldn't be this way. It was only supposed to be another of the comfortable little arrangements OFS officials formed all the time. But this arrangement was different. Unlike anyone else in the Madras Sector administration, he knew Manticore was right about the Mesans' involvement in both New Tuscany and Crandall's attack on Spindle because they'd used him to help set those events in motion, and he wondered what snake was going to crawl out from under a rock next.

As he watched the pair of intervention battalions marching past the reviewing stand, a cold, hard lump in his chest suggested he might just be looking at that next serpent.

❖   ❖   ❖

Lorcan Verrochio was unaware of what his vice commissioner was thinking, but Junyan Hongbo might have been surprised by how his nominal superior's thoughts paralleled his own. Verrochio wished passionately that he hadn't let Yucel talk him into authorizing this deployment, and he wished even more passionately that she wasn't commanding it in person. But she'd talked him into that, too, and it was too late to change his mind now.

You said you wanted this whole thing settled fast, he reminded himself, *and she's got a point. No one else in the Sector could settle something like this as quickly as she will. The only question is how many eggs she's ready to break for her omelette.*

That worried him, because he suspected the answer was "a lot," and that could be disastrous with all the attention being focused on the Madras Sector and the Manties' Talbott Quadrant. God only knew what some bleeding heart innerworld newsy might do with an "exposé" of OFS "brutality" out in the Protectorates! In fact, the mere thought of what someone like Audrey O'Hanrahan would do with Yucel's idea of the best way to deal with restive populations was enough to tie Lorcan Verrochio's stomach in knots.

But what else can I do? I need to get in and out of Mobius, and I need to do it before the situation gets any worse. So far, nobody outside the Sector even seems to've noticed—probably because they're all so busy watching to see what happens between Manticore and the Navy. But if it drags on, if it gets even worse, somebody will pick up on it. After all, this is where the entire confrontation started, isn't it? Of course the bastards in the media are keeping an eye peeled this way! So if I don't keep the lid screwed down, GHQ is going to have my ass, because another spectacular fiasco in-sector—or anywhere remotely near it, for

*that matter!—is sure to draw the newsies' attention.
That's the* last *thing the home office wants... except
some equally spectacular allegation of "excessive force"
or "Gendarme brutality"!*

He kept his shoulders back, maintaining a properly attentive, nobly determined expression for the troops' benefit, but even this review could turn out as a public relations disaster. If the men and women marching past him in their black uniforms and shiny boots turned in the sort of performance intervention battalions had turned in so often before and the newsies *did* get wind of it, the fact that he'd sent them off with such public fanfare and obvious approval was only going to make things even worse.

It's all the damned Manties' fault, he thought bitterly. *Until they shoved their noses into Talbott, who the hell cared what happened out here in the armpit of the galaxy?* Nobody, *that's who! Now anything that happens has the potential to be another interstellar incident!*

He glanced at Hongbo, standing beside him with an equally grave expression. The vice commissioner had covered his own ass quite neatly, Verrochio reflected resentfully. He was on record as opposing the deployment. Of having come around to it only reluctantly, only because all of Verrochio's security advisers had endorsed it. So if it all blew up in Verrochio's face, Hongbo could always point out that he'd been opposed to it from the beginning. And if it worked, he got credit for having been open-minded and thoughtful enough to put aside his initial opposition when those security advisers' reasoned arguments convinced him they had a point.

The universe, Lorcan Verrochio concluded resentfully, wasn't exactly brimming over with fairness.

✧ Chapter Twenty-Two

THE LEAD AIR VAN wore the colors of SINS—System Information and News Service, the Mobius System's official government news agency—as it moved sedately down the broad canyon between the business towers that dominated downtown Landing. There was no obvious connection between it and the other pair of vans or the two somewhat battered looking private air cars, and all five vehicles were careful to obey all traffic signals as they made their way towards their various destinations.

Appearances could be deceiving, however, and the eleven men and seven women in the lead van sat grim and silent, final weapons checks completed, waiting for the carnage to come.

"Three minutes," the driver said quietly over his shoulder.

None of the passengers replied. They didn't have to. Everyone knew what his or her job was, just as all of them knew that a strike like this in the middle of the day was more than merely risky. In many ways, it approached the suicidal, yet that was one of the strengths of their plan. No one—not even that kill-crazy bitch Yardley—was going to see *this* one coming.

The glittering tower of the Trifecta Corporation loomed ahead of them. Trifecta held a special place in the hearts of the Mobius Liberation Front. It was scarcely among the great transstellars of the Solarian League—barely a bit-player compared to Technodyne or Zumwalt of Old Terra, really—but it still owned something like sixty percent of the Mobius planetary economy outright. It wasn't shy about proclaiming the fact here in its private little preserve, either. The ivory-tinted Trifecta Tower—known to its owners as the "Silver Lady" and to most citizens of Mobius (privately, at least) as the "White Whore"—was the tallest structure on the entire planet. No pains had been spared to turn it into the sort of glittering showplace and monument to corporate grandeur an outfit Trifecta's size could never have afforded, for many reasons, in the Core. It was a brazen statement that Mobius was Trifecta's private preserve . . . and that everyone who lived there was effectively a Trifecta serf.

Well, the strike team's leader thought grimly, *our lords and masters are about to find out* these *serfs aren't very happy with them. And* they're *not going to be very happy with* us *in a few minutes.*

"Here we go!" the driver said.

❖   ❖   ❖

The SINS van shot forward, accelerating suddenly, turning out of its traffic lane and cutting across three others. Air cars and lorries swerved wildly as the rogue vehicle violated their airspace and the traffic control frequencies exploded with abrupt imprecations, controllers' questions, and emergency orders.

The air van didn't care about any of that. It simply altered course, climbing steeply, and arrowed straight into a restricted, high-security access point. The portal in the side of Trifecta Tower was specifically dedicated to the use of its senior executives. Entry by anyone else was strictly forbidden, and the eleven Trifecta Security personnel manning the access point had standing orders to use lethal force if anyone tried to break into it anyway. Unfortunately for Trifecta's intentions, the people who'd planned this attack had been right in at least one respect; no one in his right mind would have expected *anyone* to launch an attack like this in the middle of the business day.

The security detail's initial reaction was that they were looking at a traffic accident about to happen on a grand scale, courtesy of a drunk or somehow suddenly incapacitated driver. It was the only logical assumption, especially given the van's livery, and before they could realize how wrong they were, the accelerating vehicle was right on top of them, the side windows had slammed abruptly open, and eighteen military-grade pulse rifles opened fire.

Despite their body armor, the security men never had a chance in the face of that much concentrated firepower. Most of them were killed outright. The three survivors were all badly wounded—all of them would quietly bleed to death eventually—and the van went scorching past them.

It was moving too rapidly to stop in the available space, but the strike leader had planned on that, as well. There *was* room for the vehicle to kill a lot of speed before it crashed into the assistant planetary operations manager's parking stall, crumpling the last third of his limousine in on itself before it staggered to a halt. Specially reinforced shoulder harnesses and Solarian-manufactured combat helmets protected its passengers from the impact, and all of them bailed out instantly through the side doors.

Four of them moved quickly to the security station they'd just shot up. They ignored the dead and wounded, except to kick any personal weapons away from anyone who seemed to still be breathing, and shot open the lockers the Trifecta personnel hadn't had time to get to. They dragged out the military-grade tribarrels—heavy enough to take down an armored stingship if they hit it right—which President Lombroso had personally authorized for Trifecta's private security force and slammed them onto the swivel mounts built into the security office.

The rest of the strike force lunged for the emergency fire exits. The doors were locked, of course, but that had been anticipated, and incendiary charges turned the locks to slag. Shoulders rammed into the suddenly unlocked panels, smashing them open, and boots clattered on the risers as the attackers stormed up the old-fashioned stairs.

They burst into an expensive foyer just as the first security men came spilling out of the lift banks in response to the alarms. Security had the advantage of internal cameras and free flow communications links; the attackers had the advantage of knowing exactly what they were doing and where they were going to accomplish it. The result was that they were ready—and the security team wasn't—when the lift doors opened. Pulser darts turned the two lift cars into abattoirs, and a grenade tossed into each of them made sure all of *these* bodies were dead.

Four more team members peeled off, covering the foyer, while the ten remaining attackers burst into the inner sanctum of the Trifecta Corporation.

"Down on the floor!" the team leader bellowed. *"Down on the floor or die!"*

The highly decorative receptionist and both of his assistants dived for the floor instantly, sliding under their desks and covering their heads with their arms. Aides and secretaries who didn't have a clue what was happening poked their heads out of office doorways, gawking at the sudden eruption of roughly dressed, armed proles. Most of them got the message as quickly as the receptionist had. The faster ones popped back into their offices, like Old Terran prairie dogs. Others dropped to the floor, burying their noses in the expensive carpet. But—

"Who the *fuck* d'you think you *are*, you god—!"

Both pulser darts took the red-faced man dead center as he came storming out of his office. The expanding antipersonnel darts tore through his body in a spray-painted red cloud, and he went down, furious question chopped off in mid-word as his lungs and heart shredded and most of his right shoulder blade disintegrated into splinters of finely separated bone.

There were lots of screams now, and the leader charged down the corridor with five other men and women as a third quartet peeled off to hold the foyer. He smashed his way through the ornate, expensive door at the end of the hall, and a pulser dart whined past his ear. The head of one of his fellows exploded under its impact, and he triggered a return burst that sawed the bodyguard standing in front of the huge desk almost in half.

The bodyguard went down, and the leader vaulted the desk. A richly dressed, wild-eyed woman cowered under it, both hands pressed to her mouth, expensively coiffured hair wildly awry, and he smiled coldly.

"I think you'd better come out, Ms. Guernicke," he said.

◇　　◇　　◇

Sirens howled all across the city of Landing. Public buildings went into lockdown. Corporate structures mustered their own armies of private security goons. Presidential Guard armored vehicles thundered into ground level and subsurface roadways. Stingships streaked into the air above the city, and unmanned reconnaissance platforms went swarming through the airspace around Trifecta Tower.

The traffic in the vicinity, obedient to the strident commands of City Traffic Control, cleared the area as quickly as possible. In the case of two nondescript vans (neither of which looked the least bit like the one which had crashed into Trifecta Tower), the fastest way to do that was to land. One set down hastily and awkwardly on the surface roadway a half-block down Trifecta Boulevard from the tower; the second landed on the ground level of a public parking garage directly across the street from it. Their drivers, who obviously had no desire to find themselves in the middle of what looked like turning into a free fire zone, locked their vehicles and took to their heels.

They were hardly alone in that. After the previous month's riots, no Mobian was going to be stupid enough to hang around when the Presidential Guard could be expected momentarily. A mass exodus turned the busy downtown blocks into a ghost town in mere minutes, leaving streets, slide-walks, and aerial walkways to the security troops already storming into the area.

Six blocks from Trifecta Tower (in opposite directions), the pair of battered air cars swooped down just long enough to pick up the fleeing van drivers, then vanished into the city's anonymity.

✧　　✧　　✧

The communicator on Georgina Guernicke's desk buzzed loudly. The strike leader looked at it for a moment, then pressed the voice-only acceptance key.

"Yes?"

"This is General Yardley," a hard female voice said from the blank com. "Who am I speaking to?"

"Did you screen just to waste my time asking stupid questions?"

"You realize, of course, that none of you are getting out of this alive," Yardley replied flatly.

"That's possible," the strike leader acknowledged. "We won't go alone, though. In fact, I think the body count's already in our favor."

"The one who dies with the most kills is still dead," Yardley shot back, and the leader surprised himself with a harsh chuckle.

"That's clever, General. Cleverer than I would've expected out of a homicidal bitch like you. Do you really want to talk, or should I just hang up?"

"I presume you have some sort of demands to make. Why don't you go ahead and make them so we can get it over with?"

"My demands are pretty simple, actually. You turn loose all of the innocent men and women you've arrested over the last two or three T-weeks and provide us with an air car, and Ms. Guernicke takes a little trip with us. You fulfill your side of the bargain, and we turn her loose alive and unharmed. You screw around with us, and Lombroso gets to explain to Trifecta why it's going to need a new system operations manager here in Mobius."

"No fucking way." Yardley's voice was even flatter than before. "You harm Ms. Guernicke in any way, and I promise you'll take a long time dying."

"That would suppose you managed to take any of us alive," the leader responded. "Which isn't going to happen. Mind you, we'd rather get out of this in one piece, but we're okay with it either way. Your fucking Presidential Guard made sure of that last month. You know what I've got left to lose, *General* Yardley? Last month it would have been a wife, a teenaged daughter, and a ten-year-old son. Today? Well, I'll let you *guess*."

There was silence for a moment, and the leader heard Guernicke whimpering in terror as she crouched in a corner with a pistol barrel pressed to the side of her head. Once upon a time, his heart might have felt at least some pity for her, but that had been then, and this was now.

"Should I assume the rest of your murdering little band feels the same way?" Yardley asked finally.

"I've got you on speakerphone, General," he replied, looking up to meet the others' eyes. "You hear anybody disagreeing with me?"

"It's still not going to happen," Yardley shot back. "I let you go with Ms. Guernicke, and you're not going to turn her loose. You're going to hang onto her, and you're going to keep on making demands that get steeper and steeper until there's no way in hell you're going to get what you ask for. And then you kill her anyway, and you blame it on *us*. I don't think we're going to play that game."

"Up to you, General. But before you make up your mind—"

He beckoned to the woman holding the gun to Guernicke's head, and she jerked the Trifecta executive to her feet and half-dragged, half-led her across to the desk. The leader looked at Guernicke for a moment, then pointed at the com terminal.

"For God's sake, Yardley!" Guernicke screamed into the mike. "What the fuck are you *thinking*? Give these people whatever the hell they *want*!"

The leader nodded, and Guernicke was hauled back to her corner and shoved back onto her knees. He waited another moment, then turned back to the com himself.

"There you go—your mistress' voice has spoken, General. Now you know she's still alive, and you've got your marching orders. What're you going to do? I don't think Trifecta's going to be very happy with you and Lombroso if she ends up dead in a firefight now that she's told you what you're supposed to do."

The silence from the other end of the com link was profound.

❖   ❖   ❖

"Jesus, General!" Colonel Tyler Braddock exclaimed. Colonel Braddock, who was very fond of his self-assigned callsign "Tiger," was a good ten centimeters taller and far broader across the shoulders than Olivia Yardley. At the moment, his swarthy complexion was pale and sweat beaded his hairline. "They've really got Guernicke in there. What the *fuck* do we do now?"

"Shut up, Colonel," Yardley said in a flat, dangerous voice. Her hazel eyes were hard as she glared up at the taller Braddock. It was his Scorpions which had opened fire last month and touched off the May Riots, and she wasn't feeling particularly charitable where he was concerned at the moment.

He looked down at her, opened his mouth, then clamped it shut again and nodded, and she snorted. At least the idiot had some sense of self-preservation.

"What we're *not* going to do," she told him then, "is let these bastards panic us into promising them what they want. Not unless I can figure out a way to make it look like they're actually getting it right up to the second we shoot them all in the head. If we let them out of that tower with Guernicke, this shit is just getting started. At the moment, we've got them penned up in there, and I want to make damned sure they aren't going anywhere, so start moving your goddamned troops into position. And *try* not to kill anybody you don't have to, this time!"

Braddock flushed angrily, but he kept his mouth shut, nodded, and climbed out of Yardley's command vehicle. He stalked down the frozen slide-walk towards his own command post, and Yardley watched him go.

I suppose it's too much to hope for that the bastards on the other side will manage to kill him for me, she reflected. *I can always dream, though.*

In the meantime, she had to figure out what she was going to recommend to President Lombroso, and she grimaced at the thought. The president wasn't a lot happier with her than she was with Braddock, and this wasn't going to help. Maybe she could figure out a way to make it an intelligence failure and put it all on Friedemann Mátyás? She'd have to think about that.

❖　　❖　　❖

The parking garage on the far side of Trifecta Boulevard, the surface level street east of the corporate tower, offered an ideal staging area for Colonel Braddock's Scorpions. Each Scorpion individually exceeded the maximum vehicle weight for the garage by about twenty percent, but there were only thirty of them. Distributed across four floors, their weight was more than sufficiently spread out. Better yet, the garage had accesses on both its east and west sides, which meant the AFVs could be moved into the garage from the west without anyone in Trifecta Tower seeing them.

One might have wondered how useful armored vehicles were going to be in a situation like this one, but over the last few weeks, it had become the Presidential Guard's policy to deploy overwhelming force in order to overawe and terrify potential dissidents. Besides, it was always possible there was a ground assault element involved in this insane plan after all, and having the firepower on hand to deal with one if it came along seemed like a good thing.

Braddock personally supervised the movement of his vehicles into the garage, then moved his own command vehicle to the roof. The vehicle crew was clearly uncomfortable sitting out there in the open as they remembered the antitank launchers they'd encountered last month. Braddock didn't care about that. First, because he doubted these bastards were going to escalate the confrontation by using heavy weapons (assuming they had any) any sooner than they had to.

And, second, because *he* wasn't in the command vehicle. He'd moved to a better vantage point just inside the ground-level entrance facing the Tower, maintaining his connection to the command vehicle on a secure frequency while its position on top of the garage gave it the best transmission reach he could come up with.

Now he keyed the mike.

"Command One," he said, and waited for the earbug tone to tell him the communications computer had automatically patched him through to Yardley. "Command One, Tiger is in position," he said then.

"Good," Yardley replied.

❖   ❖   ❖

The desk com buzzed again, and the strike leader punched the key.

"What can I do for you, General?"

"You could start by cutting your throats and saving me the effort," Yardley suggested.

"Sorry to disappoint you, but we're not going anywhere without Guernicke and we're planning on killing a lot more of you bastards before you ever get into this office. So shall we move on to your second suggestion?"

"Let Ms. Guernicke leave the building unharmed, and we'll let you and the rest of your murderers withdraw unmolested."

The leader laughed out loud.

"Oh, I don't think so!" he half-chortled. "As fairy tales go, it's not bad, but we stopped believing in the tooth fairy a long time ago. Try again."

"All right, third option. You stay right where the fuck you are, we sit outside here, and we starve your asses out. How does that sound?"

"At least a little more like you're telling the truth.

On the other hand, we brought a fair amount of food with us. Of course, we won't be able to share any of it with Ms. Guernicke or the other Trifecta employees in here with us, so they'll probably get hungry—and dehydrated—a lot faster than we will. If you want to try it, though, more power to you."

"Oh, I'm just getting started," Yardley told him. "There's always the possibility of knockout gas through the environmental systems. Or we send in SWAT teams. That's a damned big tower, and you can't begin to put fire teams everywhere you'd need to be to stop us. We can work our way around you, get our own teams in position, then blow our way through walls and floors to take you out."

"Probably," the strike leader acknowledged. "I'd say the chances of your pulling that off without our killing Ms. Guernicke before you get in here are no more than forty-sixty, though, and that's if you wait a couple days, until fatigue and anxiety start dulling our alertness. Of course, that's also assuming we're willing to wait that long before we just go ahead and shoot the bitch. For that matter, we've got somewhere around fifty more Trifecta employees up here, most of them pretty damned senior, and we don't especially like any of *them*, either. You want some of them air-mailed back? They'll make an awful mess when they hit the pavement without counter-grav."

There was silence from Yardley's end, and the strike leader leaned back in Guernicke's sinfully comfortable chair.

"I've been informed by President Lombroso that you're not getting your air car, and you're not getting out of that building, without handing Ms. Guernicke over to us unharmed," Yardley said finally. "That's not negotiable."

"No, that's not negotiable *yet*," the strike leader corrected her. "And I didn't expect it to be, either. But we're not going anywhere, and you're not moving anyone else into this building, until he's had an opportunity to . . . rethink that position."

"You think not?"

"Not unless you want to start getting bits and pieces of Trifecta's senior management team back as greasy spots on the street."

"You start throwing people out of windows, and I may just decide the only chance Ms. Guernicke has is for us to get in there before you throw *her* out one."

"I'll take my chances on that. Besides, what makes you think that's the only string to our bow?"

"I know how many people got inside with you," Yardley said. "That tower is lousy with security cameras, you know. I know about the people you've got covering your entry portal—and those tribarrels of theirs won't do squat if I decide to send in the Scorpions, by the way—and I know how many people you've got covering the lift banks. I even know how many people got into Ms. Guernicke's office with you . . . and that you lost somebody on the way in."

"And are you getting very much information from them now?" the strike leader inquired in an interested tone.

He almost imagined he could hear her teeth grinding together in the silence from the other end.

"Yeah, we know about the cameras," he went on after a moment and shrugged. "There was no way to take them out before we got inside, but you're not seeing a damned thing from them now. Which means you don't know whether we've pulled SAMS out of our van—or ATWs, for that matter—or not. You don't even know if we've still got Guernicke in her office or staked out across the lift bank doors. Oh, and by the way, did you know Ms. Guernicke has the master codes to access all of the building's surveillance and environmental control systems from her desk? She was kind enough to give them to us when we insisted. So if you want to try infiltrating SWAT teams into the building, you go right ahead."

"Listen," Yardley said, "I'm not going to send people up there after you—not *yet*. But I damned well *am* going to secure the lower floors of that tower."

"You try to do that and someone's going to get hurt," the strike leader said flatly. He was watching the feed from the tower's ground level security cameras as he spoke. At least two companies of the Presidential Guard were advancing across Trifecta Boulevard from the parking garage. "Even if you manage to get troops inside the tower, it's not going to buy you any edge you don't already have. But if they keep coming, you're going to regret the attempt."

"Are you threatening the hostages again?" Yardley laughed harshly. "You're not going to kill Ms. Guernicke, or even any of the other management personnel with her, until you feel a hell of a lot more threatened than that! And if you do, you lose your bargaining chips, and we come straight in however hard and fast we have to."

"Last warning," the strike leader told her, still watching the advancing troops. "Call them off now."

❖   ❖   ❖

Yardley's eyes narrowed. His voice was flat, unwavering. In fact, there was something almost like . . . satisfaction in it, and alarm bells sounded in the back of her brain. But she couldn't back off. She had to shake his nerve, destroy his confidence that he was in control of the situation, calling the tune while she had no option but to dance to it. She had to assert *her* ability to control the situation, and so she simply sat back, folded her arms, and watched her command vehicle's visual displays.

"Have it your way, General," the strike leader said, and pressed a button.

The van which had parked so quickly at street level when Air Traffic Control ordered the local airspace cleared had been abandoned with unseemly haste. The driver hadn't even wasted any time trying to straighten it out; she'd simply left it there, dumped across three parking slots with its nose pointing out across the street at a sharp angle. It was sloppy of her, no doubt, but other vehicles had been abandoned with equal haste.

There was, however, one difference between her van and any of those other vehicles, as the Presidential Guard discovered when it disappeared in a horrendous fireball.

The weapon was technically an "improvised explosive device," since it had been manufactured for the purpose out of readily available components by largely amateur hands. There was nothing haphazard or slipshod about it, though. A solid partition, both sides concave in shape, had been run lengthwise along the van's generous cargo space. The outer surfaces of the partition had been coated in explosives—civilian explosive compounds stolen from construction crews, not military-grade, but amply powerful for the task in hand—and the explosives, in turn, had been coated with a thick layer of screws, old-fashioned nails, bits and pieces of scrap metal, broken glass, and chunks of ceramacrete. The van had been transformed into a huge directional mine which sent a lethal sheet of shrapnel sweeping out in both directions simultaneously.

The driver hadn't achieved a perfect angle, but she'd come close, and the strike leader had judged his moment carefully. He caught at least ninety percent of the advancing Presidential Guard infantry in the IED's blast area, and destruction crashed over them like a thunderbolt. The blast front swept up weapons, helmets, equipment, and body parts on its fiery breath. It shredded its victims like toys . . . and painted the pavement and slide-walks in ghastly sprays of blood decorated with bits and pieces of mangled flesh.

"I told you to call them off," the voice on Yardley's com was cold and precise. "You should've listened. But since you didn't—"

He pressed a second button.

"Tiger" Braddock was astonished he was still alive. His position had been just deep enough inside the parking garage for its sturdy walls to intercept the shrapnel which had butchered his infantry. One moment, the next best thing to three hundred of his elite troops had been sweeping across Trifecta Boulevard towards their objective. The next moment, at least two hundred of them were dead and a lot more were dying. He stumbled to the garage entrance, head ringing from the force of the explosion, and peered out in horror at hell's own landscape as men and women with no legs tried to drag themselves out of the charnel house of the boulevard on their elbows and forearms. He saw another rocking on his knees while he tried to stuff his own intestines back inside his ruptured body. Another stumbled helplessly about, hands clasped over the blind, red ruin of what had been a human face only moments before. Still others only lay there, unable to drag their mangled bodies anywhere, shrieking amid the motionless dead.

He was still trying to comprehend the enormity of what had just happened when the third van—the one parked in the garage which the strike leader had recognized just as clearly as Braddock was the perfect place to stash the Guard's armored vehicles—exploded.

It was a much larger bomb this time, and the driver had carefully parked it directly beside the central support pillar of the garage's entire structure.

A huge sheet of flame shot out both open sides of the garage. Fresh flame billowed as the fuel tanks of parked vehicles fireballed, joining the fury of the original explosion. Braddock flung himself down on his belly, covering his helmeted head with his arms in instinctive self-preservation. For an instant all he was aware of was the terrible, concussive force of the explosion. Then his stunned ears heard another sound—a grating, grinding rumble—and he had one more second to realize his instincts had played him false.

If he'd run out into the body-strewn nightmare of Trifecta Boulevard, he might have survived after all.

The entire parking garage came down, puffing out concentric rings of smoke and dust as its floors collapsed, one by one, into the roaring inferno which had engulfed "Tiger" Braddock's entire regiment.

❖　　❖　　❖

"Looks like you need another regiment, General," the icy voice on Olivia Yardley's com observed.

"Pity about that."

✧ Chapter Twenty-Three

"I DON'T NEED THIS kind of shit, General," Svein Lombroso said unpleasantly. "I could go out and fuck everything up by the numbers myself without paying you and the rest of the Guard such obscene amounts of money! Hell, I could probably even have gotten Guernicke killed without you, if I'd really tried!"

"Would you rather I'd let the bastards walk away after taking out Braddock's entire regiment?" General Yardley's tone was rather pointed, Lombroso thought. Which probably had something to do with the fact that she knew she was irreplaceable . . . at least for now. "It was a no-win situation from the outset, Mr. President. Once they got in and had Guernicke in their possession, we either gave them what they wanted, or we lost her. And you told me *not* to give them what they wanted." She shrugged. "So I didn't."

"Goddamn it!" Lombroso snarled. "This makes what happened last month look like a frigging *picnic*! And when Trifecta's home office hears about this . . . !"

"We didn't move in until Frolov personally okayed

it," Yardley pointed out, and Lombroso's jaw muscles clenched.

He started to tell her exactly what he thought of that threadbare excuse, then stopped. First, because it wouldn't do any good. He could chew her ass out all he wanted, and it wouldn't pour the blood back into Tyler Braddock's slaughtered men or put Georgina Guernicke's shattered head back together again. And, second, because she had a point. The standoff had lasted for over three T-days before Christianos Frolov, the *assistant* planetary operations manager for Mobius, had—as Yardley put it—"okayed" the assault. In fact, he'd effectively *ordered* the assault in a demonstration of manly determination that would probably go down well with his corporate superiors after he got done spinning his report properly.

And which just happened to put his ass in Guernicke's chair, the president thought grimly. *Well, she always was a pain in my ass, anyway. And we've got Frolov on chip telling us the standoff was costing Trifecta millions of credits every day and that it was time we got in there and took the Tower back. If somebody back on Old Terra wants to chew me out over that one, I'll just dump it on their own golden boy.*

Who knew, it might even do some good. And it might not, either.

"All right," he grated in a marginally calmer voice. "I'll give you that one. But I still want to know how the *hell* this happened in the first place. You and Braddock got fucking reamed. How?"

"Because no one saw it coming," Yardley told him frankly. She glanced at Friedemann Mátyás. "*We* didn't, and neither did the MSP."

"Friedemann?" Lombroso gave the commander of his secret police a rather harder glance than Yardley had, and Mátyás frowned.

"Olivia's right; we *didn't* see it coming," he confessed. "We're still trying to get someone inside the MLF. So far we've *almost* pulled it off three times, and I'm running short of volunteers, given what happened each of those times." He showed his teeth briefly. "The problem, Mr. President, is that this is the best organized opposition group we've faced yet. They're good." He shrugged. "I don't like admitting it, but they are. And so far they've always been smart enough to avoid high-profile challenges like this one. Our estimate at MSP—and I think from Olivia's people, as well—is that they're really still in the infrastructure building stages. They're building membership, laying in caches of weapons, and setting up their communication chains."

He raised his eyebrows at Yardley, who—despite their long-standing rivalry—nodded sharply.

"That's been our impression in the Guard," she agreed. "It's one of the reasons we've both been arguing that we needed to nip these people in the bud, before they get themselves fully organized, Mr. President."

"Well, if they're so damned smart and if they're still so unprepared for major operations, what the hell was this all about?" Lombroso demanded. "I can't think of a more 'high-profile challenge' than murdering Guernicke in her own office! And how the hell did they get inside in the first place?"

"We've identified what was left of the body of the guy we're pretty sure was the mastermind," Yardley told him. "His name was Kazuyoshi Brewster, and he was telling the truth. He lost his entire family in the May Riots." She shrugged again. "We've only been able to identify six other members of his team. Five of them lost their entire families or at least their closest family members the same time he did. Obviously, Brewster was a damned good planner, but what really made the difference was that all of them had apparently decided they had nothing left to lose. They just wanted to do as much damage as they could before they went down, and I have to admit they did a damned good job."

"'A damned good job,'" Lombroso repeated, glaring at her.

"Well, they did," she responded. "And the fact that they didn't care whether they got out or not meant they were prepared to take chances nobody except a bunch of suicidal nut cases would've considered for a moment. That's why we never saw it coming—this time, at least. We've beefed up security across the board on off-world corporate offices."

Lombroso glared at her for a moment, remembering an ancient cliché about locked barn doors and missing horses. Or was it cows?

He brushed off the irrelevant thought and inhaled deeply.

"So tell me how this changes our situation," he commanded. "You first, Olivia."

"Well, after examining Brewster's equipment, it's obvious someone's managed to stockpile even more off-world weapons than we thought. Given all of the deep cover informants we've got out there, that says more than I want to hear about how good the MLF's security is. I know Friedemann's just pointed out that we haven't managed to get anyone inside the MLF itself, but we damned well ought to have enough surveillance systems and human intelligence sources out there to at least be able to spot modern weapons moving in quantities like this." She shrugged. "We didn't."

Lombroso suppressed a desire to throttle her. Strong as the temptation was, he knew it wouldn't do any good. Besides, what she'd just said was self-evidently true, and at least she'd had the nerve to say it.

"Friedemann?" he said, looking at Mátyás.

"Olivia's right. We've always known they were better than anyone else who's come along, but I'm beginning to think we've underestimated them for some time, anyway."

Lombroso's jaw muscles clenched as he glared at the two of them. They were his senior security officers. It wasn't a case of "we've underestimated" the MLF; it was a case of the two of *them* underestimating the terrorist bastards, and he considered pointing that out. Unfortunately, it would have accomplished exactly nothing.

"All right," he said once he was certain he had his voice under control. "So you've underestimated them." He emphasized the personal pronoun only very slightly, but Yardley's hazel eyes glinted with anger anyway. Mátyás had better control than that, probably because he wasn't the one in the primary line of fire at the moment. "Obviously, it's time you stopped doing that. So how bad does the situation look *now*?"

Yardley's eyes didn't soften. For a moment, she seemed to hover on the brink of something rash, but apparently she realized no one was genuinely irreplaceable when it came down to it.

"I'm not really certain," she admitted levelly. "Things are clearly escalating since the riots last month. My best estimate is that the MLF leadership doesn't *want* to escalate, though."

"What?" Lombroso interrupted. He stared at her in disbelief. "They just fucking wrecked Trifecta Tower and killed Guernicke! Nobody's *ever* done that kind of damage to us before!"

"Brewster and his team did," Yardley acknowledged. "But there was no MLF statement about the attack until it was all over. And even then, their 'Commandant Alpha,' whoever the hell he is, didn't claim direct credit for it." She shook her head. "I think Brewster and the others put this together on their own. They were obviously MLF, because nobody else's that good, and as far as we know, nobody else has the kind of off-world weapons support they seem to have. But I don't think Commandant Alpha or the rest of his cadre knew anything about it before *we* did. And I don't think they'd have okayed Brewster's plan if he'd asked them to authorize it, either."

Lombroso shook his head.

"I'd think those bastards would be getting behind and pushing for all they're worth!" he said. "What the hell makes you think they aren't?"

"Because they're not ready," Yardley said flatly. "That's what Friedemann and I have been talking about. They've got *some* modern weapons on-planet, yes, but not anywhere near as many as they want. We've confiscated around a hundred pulsers—total—so far. Most of them aren't new, but they're all in first-class condition; it looks like they've been refurbished as needed by some very competent armorers. But we've been picking them up in ones and twos. Frankly, most of them got grabbed because someone just pretty much stumbled over them, and Brewster's team is the first one we've seen armed entirely with military-grade pulse rifles. I think they've got more of them than we thought they had, but we're still picking up substantially greater quantities of old-fashioned chemical-powered firearms. So they've made an off-world connection somewhere, but they still don't have enough modern weapons to go around. And without more modern firepower, they're going to be at a significant tactical disadvantage in any confrontation with us, much less any Solly intervention battalions. They know that." She shrugged again. "That being the case, my analysts say the leadership cadre can't be in favor of opening the dance this early."

"Then what the fuck is going on?" Lombroso demanded. "We've got transit bombings, ambushes of isolated security forces, and more acts of minor sabotage and cyber attacks than I even want to think about. All in addition to what happened to Guernicke, of course!"

"I think Olivia's right, Mr. President," Mátyás said unexpectedly, and Lombroso looked at him sharply. "I think what we're seeing here is primarily a more or less spontaneous reaction to the May Riots, not a planned campaign by the MLF," the secret policeman continued. "It certainly was in Brewster's case, and I don't see any reason to assume it's not for the rest of these people, either. And it would explain why we're seeing this now, when all indications are that the MLF is still in the building stage."

"The short version is that they feel provoked,"

Yardley said in a flat voice, meeting Lombroso's eyes levelly. She'd recommended relying solely on infantry for crowd control during the protests, but the president, irked by the challenge coming at him from some of the senior ranks of his own political party, had wanted a more visible and more intimidating deterrent. Well, he'd gotten *that*, hadn't he?

He looked back at her for several seconds, then he grimaced angrily and strode across his office to look out the window at downtown Landing.

All right, he admitted to himself. *So maybe the Guard overreacted when it started taking fire. Hell, no 'maybe' about it, Svein, and you damned well know it! They got out of hand, but it's hard to blame them for wanting to make an example out of the bastards who'd opened fire on them. Not the kind of behavior you want to encourage, is it?*

Maybe not, yet the better part of three thousand casualties, two thirds of them fatal, hadn't gone down well with the régime's opponents. And the Trifecta Tower attack had obviously enheartened the people already furious over the "May Day Massacre." It might be unlikely that there were any more Brewsters out there, prepared to make what amounted to suicide runs against high visibility targets, but that wasn't keeping a hell of a lot of other people from striking back in less spectacular fashion wherever and whenever they could, and their efforts were gaining momentum.

He glowered down from the window at the boulevard where the Scorpions had gone on their May rampage. Physical damage from that little episode was still easy enough to see, and the rebuilding efforts were one of the favored targets for the saboteurs who seemed to increase in numbers every day. He'd been hearing about *that* from his transstellar sponsors, too. They wanted their buildings back up and running, and they weren't especially shy about pointing out how much the May Riots had cost them in damages and lost profits.

He thought about leaning closer to the window, looking up Trifecta Boulevard towards the emergency vehicles and construction equipment clustered around the ruins of the parking garage where an entire regiment of his elite troopers had been entombed. He didn't think about it very hard, though.

"So you saying this is mostly freelance?" he asked, never turning away from the window. "That it isn't the MLF, just some of its members who're too pissed off for the leadership to control?"

"That's my analysts' read," Yardley agreed, and Mátyás nodded in agreement.

"So what do we do about it?" Lombroso wheeled to face them once more, clasping his hands behind him. "Do we back the pressure off in hopes things will quiet down again, at least some, until Verrochio's intervention battalions get here? Or do we try to bring the hammer down harder?"

"I think that depends in part on whether or not the battalions are really on their way," Yardley replied. "Is it your impression they are, Mr. President?"

"I think they almost certainly are," he said after a brief hesitation. "Xydis wouldn't have gone as far out on a limb promising she'd ask for them if she didn't expect to get them. And let's face it, we've always known that if she'd really asked for them before, they'd have been here a long time ago. Besides, she attached her endorsement to my messages to Commissioner Verrochio. I don't think she would've done that if her own messages weren't urging Verrochio to do the same thing. For that matter, even if she wasn't then, she damned well is now that we've lost Braddock's regiment! As for how long it's going to take them to get here"—he shrugged—"your guess is as good as mine."

"If that's the case, then I think we should hammer them now—*hard*," Yardley said. "I think failing to hit them whenever and however we can, especially after Brewster's escapade, is only going to further embolden them, and I don't think 'restraint' is going to cool any tempers on the other side. The best we might accomplish would be to get them to back off enough to let the MLF leadership reassert control, and, frankly, if there really are Solly Gendarmerie intervention battalions on the way, backing off is the last thing we want them to do."

"Excuse me?" Lombroso's expression was perplexed, and she shrugged.

"Mr. President, the MLF is the best organized batch of malcontents we've ever faced. They're tightly compartmentalized and—usually—highly disciplined. That's one reason we've had so much trouble penetrating them. But if the present provocations are spontaneous, not ordered from above, then they're probably going to be less meticulously planned and executed than the MLF operations we've seen in the past. That increases our chances of catching them at it and maybe scoring a few successes of our own. Taking some live prisoners we can . . . talk to at our leisure, let's say. Pushing them into hasty, ill-conceived, wildcat attacks—and, no, I'm not putting *Brewster* into that category, but it's the best way to describe this other, smaller crap—can only increase their vulnerability. It's bound to generate confusion, and Friedemann's people are a lot more likely to be able to get someone inside or crack one of their communications lines open if they're trying to control their people on the fly. For that matter, even if we don't manage to break a single cell, any operations they mount are going to pull them further out into the open, at the very least. If we can suck them off balance, get them to expose themselves where we can get at them—especially if they don't know the intervention battalions are on their way—they'll be a much softer target for whoever Brigadier Yucel sends to kick their asses for us."

Lombroso frowned thoughtfully. He'd never considered the problem in those terms, yet now that he thought about it, Yardley's recommendations actually made sense. In fact, they were more imaginative than he was accustomed to hearing out of her.

"If that's the case, should we expand our own offensive operations?" he asked after a moment. "Turn the heat up even further?"

"I don't see where it could hurt," Yardley said. "And, to be honest, there are some agitators and so-called 'newsies' out there who've been giving the MLF one hell of a lot of aid and comfort, especially since the May Riots. I'd like to have the opportunity to entertain some of them, too. And whether we go after them now or later, we're still going to have to break a few necks in the end. Might as well make a start on it now."

Lombroso nodded, then turned back to the window once again, lips pursed. He thought about it for perhaps a minute, then shrugged.

"All right," he said grimly, "go do it."

✦ Chapter Twenty-Four

"EXCUSE ME?"

Stephen Westman, of the Montana Westmans, tipped back his spotless white Stetson the better to raise both eyebrows at the rather unassuming looking man who'd just been shown into his office.

"I don't suppose you've got any kind of documentation to support this tale of yours?" he went on.

"No, Mr. Westman," his visitor admitted. "Not that you'd recognize, anyway."

"Ah, I see. You have some kind of code word or secret handshake Admiral Gold Peak will recognize, but for some reason you need me to introduce you to her." He shook his head, blue eyes hard. "Mister, I realize it wasn't so very long ago I got played like a fiddle, but you know, even a Montanan can learn. Hell, even a *Westman* can learn if you use a big 'nough cluestick!"

"I'm not sure what you're talking about," the visitor said with a puzzled expression. "I was just given your name as a person to contact here on Montana who might have the connections—and be willing—to put me in touch with the senior Manticoran naval officer in the system. All I need is the opportunity to speak to whoever that is. If that's this 'Admiral Gold Peak,' then that's who I need to talk to."

Westman frowned. He'd never seen this stranger before, and he couldn't place the man's accent. The fellow had just turned up in the office he maintained here in the Montana capital of Brewster, shown credentials identifying him as a purchasing agent for the Trifecta Corporation, and announced his interest in acquiring Montanan beef for export to the Mobius System. Given that Mobius was little more than a hundred and ninety light-years from Montana—about two T-months for a normal bulk hauler, but barely three T-weeks for the faster ships that served the passenger and perishable goods trades—the idea actually made quite a lot of sense. According to the purchasing agent, the cost of beef in Mobius, where livestock producers were few and far between and even genetically engineered cattle had adapted only poorly to the local environment, was about ninety Manticoran dollars a kilo, as opposed to considerably less than *three* dollars a kilo here on Montana. Mobian beef wasn't especially good, either, whereas Montana's beef had a galaxy-wide five-star quality rating (and quite a few gourmands would have given it six stars, if they'd been allowed to), and interstellar freight rates were ridiculously cheap. He could easily afford to pay Westman five or six times the spaceport delivery price on Montana and still show a five or six hundred percent profit.

From what little Westman knew about Mobius, it

seemed unlikely the typical Mobian was going to be able to afford prices like that. There were probably enough transstellar employees and their flunkies to make it a viable long-term proposition, though. And that wasn't really his problem, either way, so he'd flown into Brewster to meet with the man. At which point the "purchasing agent" had sprung his surprise.

Question is, is he really as pig ignorant about my little dustup here on Montana as he's pretending? Seems unlikely, if I'm s'posed to be willing to act as his introduction, but let's be fair, Stevie. Montana's not exactly the center of the known universe as far as people living somewhere else are concerned. Things might'a got just a little garbled in transmission.

The real problem, he admitted to himself, was that he *had* been played like a fiddle by "Firebrand," the Mesan agent provocateur who'd offered to provide his own resistance effort with weapons for his campaign to prevent Montana from becoming part of the Star Empire of Manticore. He'd done some stupid things in his life, but right off hand, he couldn't think of any which had been stupider than that one. For one thing, he'd been wrong about the Manties. For that matter, he'd even been wrong about Bernardus Van Dort, and that had been a really unpleasant pill to swallow. But what he found even harder to forgive himself for was accepting Firebrand at face value. When he'd discovered he'd actually been working with something as foul as Manpower, Incorporated...

Come on, Steve, he told himself. *Even if this fella knows all about your bout of temporary insanity, nobody'd be stupid enough to try and suck you in the same way twice. Well, maybe they would if they really knew you, but assuming they'd figure you actually have a working brain, they wouldn't try to set you up the same way all over again. But still, this whole thing sounds loonier than a tenderfoot trying to cross the Missouri Gorge on foot.*

"'Scuse me for asking this, Mr. Ankenbrandt, but you said somebody gave you my name because I might 'be willing' to sort of introduce you around. Exactly why did whoever it was seem to think *I* might be willing to do any such thing? And what made 'em choose me over all the other lunatics on this planet?"

"I'm afraid I don't know the answer to either of those questions," the purchasing agent replied. "Except for the obvious, that is."

"Obvious?" Westman chuckled sourly. "Pardon me for saying this, but nothing about this strikes me as 'obvious.'"

"Sorry." Ankenbrandt smiled briefly. "What I meant was that Trifecta really is interested in exploring the market in Mobius for Montana beef. That means nobody's going to ask any questions about my happening to meet with somebody who exports beef from Montana. Aside from that, I really don't know why they put your name on my list of contacts."

"And who might this 'they' be?"

"I'm afraid I'm not at liberty to disclose that to anyone except the senior Manticoran officer in-system." Ankenbrandt's tone sounded genuinely apologetic.

"I see." Westman studied the Solarian narrowly. "And if I should happen to turn all suspicious and hand your out-world ass—if you'll pardon my language—over to the Marshal Service with the recommendation that they just purely investigate the hell out of you?"

"I really wish you wouldn't do that," Ankenbrandt said. "It wouldn't be a pleasant experience, and they wouldn't find anything anyway. On the other hand, it could get me, and a lot of other people, into a lot of trouble if the wrong people back in Mobius were to hear about it. And to be honest, I don't think the Manties would be very happy with *you* if that happened."

Damned if he doesn't sound like the real deal, Westman reflected. *And from his expression, I think he's telling the truth about how much trouble he could get into back home. He's mighty insistent on how bad the Manties're going to want to talk to him, too. Even if they don't know he's coming!*

"Well," he said out loud after a moment, "I'm afraid if you want me to introduce you to Admiral Gold Peak, you're out of luck. I've met the lady, but she and I don't frequent the same circles." Ankenbrandt's expression fell, but Westman continued unhurriedly. "Just happens, though, that I do know at least one Manty officer who'd be able to get you in to see her. Assuming, of course, you can convince *him* that'd be a good idea." The Montanan smiled slowly. "Mind you, he doesn't convince real easy, and he's just a mite on the stubborn side himself. 'Fraid that's about the best I can do for you, though. Interested?"

Ankenbrandt was obviously torn. He turned and looked out the office windows for a good fifteen seconds, clearly thinking hard, then turned back to Westman.

"If that's the best you can do—and if you're willing to go that far for me—I'll take your offer and be grateful," he said.

"Fine."

Westman tapped his personal com awake, entered a combination from memory, and turned to look out the windows himself, waiting. It took a little longer than usual for the connection to go through, then he smiled out at the passing air cars of downtown Brewster.

"Howdy, Helen," he said, and his voice had grown much warmer. "Tell me, would it happen the Commodore—and you, of course—would be able to join me at The Rare Sirloin for dinner in a couple of hours, say?" He listened for a moment, still looking out the window, and snorted. "No, I haven't gone back to my wicked ways, young lady! But"—his expression sobered—"it 'pears somebody else may have something along those lines he wants to talk about." He listened again. "I don't mind holding," he said then.

He stood at the windows, whistling softly, for several seconds. Then—

"Yes?" He listened again, then nodded in satisfaction. "Fine! Tell the Commodore I appreciate it, and I'll see both of you then. Clear."

He deactivated the com again and turned to the Solarian.

"Well, there you go, Mr. Ankenbrandt. You've got your meeting. Just bear in mind that neither the Commodore nor I are real fond of people who try to play us for fools."

     ❖   ❖   ❖

"Yes, Aivars? What can I do for you?" Michelle Henke asked.

"This is going to sound a little strange, Ma'am," Sir Aivars Terekhov said from her com display.

"There's a lot of that going around lately," she replied dryly.

"I meant, it's going to sound even stranger than most of what's been happening," he explained with a slight smile, and she raised her eyebrows.

"You fill me with dread. Go ahead."

"Well, Ensign Zilwicki and I had dinner down on Montana with an old . . . acquaintance of ours an hour or so ago. And that acquaintance had brought along a guest with an odd request. It seems—"

❖   ❖   ❖

The admittance signal chimed, and Michelle Henke glanced over her shoulder at Master Sergeant Massimiliano Cognasso. Master Sergeant Cognasso—Miliano to his friends—was scarcely accustomed to hobnobbing with flag officers who also happened to be fourth in line for the imperial throne. He was, however, a twenty-T-year veteran of the Royal Manticoran Marines, and while he might not have been precisely comfortable, he didn't seem all that distressed, either.

Nor did the real reason for his presence seem especially flustered. The treecat on Cognasso's shoulder had his head up and his ears pricked as he turned to look at the inner side of the cabin hatch, but although the very tip of his fluffy tail was kinked up in a question mark, it was also still and alert. There were exactly two treecats in Tenth Fleet, as Michelle had made it Gervais Archer's business to discover. That was actually an amazingly high number, given how few treecats adopted humans, but only Cognasso and Alfredo had been close enough for Gervais to get them aboard HMS *Artemis* in time for this meeting.

"Are you two ready, Master Sergeant?" Michelle asked, and Cognasso nodded.

"Yes, Ma'am," he replied.

"Good." Michelle smiled, then looked at the treecat. "And remember, Alfredo. We don't want him to know if you catch him in a lie."

The 'cat raised his right hand, signing the letter "Y" and "nodding" it up and down, and Michelle nodded back. Then she pressed the admittance stud on her desk and sat back as Chris Billingsley led Sir Aivars Terekhov and a civilian stranger into her day cabin.

"Commodore Terekhov and . . . guest, Milady," Billingsley announced formally, and Michelle rose behind the desk and extended her hand.

"Sir Aivars," she said, speaking a bit more formally than usual herself.

"Admiral Gold Peak," he replied, shaking her hand firmly. "Thank you for agreeing to see us so promptly, especially under such unusual circumstances."

"Ah, yes. '*Unusual*,'" she repeated. "That does seem an appropriate adjective. And this"—she transferred her gaze to the civilian at Terekhov's side without extending her hand—"must be the mysterious Mr. Ankenbrandt."

"Yes, Admiral." Ankenbrandt gave her a small bow.

He was one of the most unmemorable people Michelle had ever seen: well dressed and well groomed, but with an almost mousy look. The sort who was obviously a numbers kind of person, a master of the internal dynamics of a corporate office, perhaps, but not the kind who got out much.

That was her first thought, but then her eyes narrowed slightly. According to Terekhov's briefing, Michael

Ankenbrandt hadn't known a thing about her before the commodore agreed to get him in to see her. He hadn't even known the Manticoran fleet commander's *name*, much less who she was related to. Yet even though he was obviously more than a little nervous, he was also composed. There was *anxiety* in his eyes, perhaps, but not a trace of panic.

"So what can I do for you, Mr. Ankenbrandt?" she inquired, pointing at the pair of chairs arranged to face her desk.

She glanced up at Billingsley and nodded in dismissal while her guests sat. The steward gave her a grumpy look—obviously, he didn't much care for the thought of leaving her with a stranger in an age of nanotech assassinations—but he didn't argue. He did exchange a speaking look with Master Sergeant Cognasso before he withdrew with what he probably thought was reasonable gracefulness, however.

Michelle did her best to ignore the exchange, although her lips twitched ever so slightly as she gazed at Ankenbrandt attentively.

"The situation's a bit . . . awkward, Countess Gold Peak," the civilian said after a moment. "To be frank, when I left Mobius, no one had any idea there might be a fleet presence this powerful at Montana. This was supposed to be just an intermediate stop on my way to Spindle and Baroness Medusa."

Despite herself, Michelle's eyebrows rose, and he shook his head.

"As I said, it's awkward. Under the circumstances, though, I felt I had no choice but to dust off one of the optional plans I was given when I left."

"Optional plans?" Michelle repeated.

"The people I represent have been in communication with the Star Empire for some time now, Admiral," Ankenbrandt said levelly. "It's been an indirect communication, through some fairly roundabout conduits, and I don't know whether or not you've been briefed on it from Manticore's end."

His rising tone made the last statement a question, and Michelle shook her head.

"To be honest, Mr. Ankenbrandt, what I know about the Mobius System is minute, to say the very least. And nobody in Spindle—or anywhere else—has briefed me on anything where the system's concerned."

"I was afraid that would be the case." Ankenbrandt sighed. "I hoped I might be wrong, though."

"Why?" Michelle asked bluntly.

"Because I'm afraid time is running out for Mobius," Ankenbrandt replied flatly. "If you'd been briefed, you might be prepared to do something about that. Since you haven't been . . ."

His voice trailed off, and he shrugged heavily.

Michelle looked at him for a moment, then glanced at her desktop display. It was set to mirror mode, showing the reflections of Master Sergeant Cognasso and Alfredo, and she reached out to fiddle with a crystal paperweight engraved with the hull number of her first hyper-capable command. An instant later, Alfredo casually laid his left true-hand on Cognasso's head.

So whatever else is going on, this fellow at least thinks he's telling us the truth, she thought. *Which is all just as mysterious as hell, isn't it, Mike? Oh, the joys of senior flag rank!*

"No, I haven't been briefed," she said calmly, tipping her chair back and resting her elbows on its arms so she could steeple her fingers under her chin. "If you'd care to tell me what's going on, though, I'm more than willing to listen. Whether I'll be prepared to *believe* you, or to act on whatever you have to say, is another matter, of course. So, on that basis, is there something you'd care to tell me about?"

◇   ◇   ◇

"I'm sorry, Milady, but that's got to be the most ridiculous thing I've ever heard of," Aploloniá Munming said some hours later. Then she seemed to realize what she'd just said and shook her head. "Scratch that. We've been hearing some pretty damned ridiculous things generally over the last few months, and it seems an appalling number of them are more accurate than we'd like. So let's just say I find this Ankenbrandt's story a bit difficult to accept."

"I'd put it a bit more strongly than that, myself, Admiral Gold Peak," Rear Admiral Mickaël Ruddock said.

The red-haired, blue-eyed Ruddock commanded the second division of Munming's superdreadnought squadron, and he was even more bluntly spoken (if possible) than Munming, Michelle reflected. That could be because he was on the smallish side and felt a little defensive about his lack of centimeters. Or, even more likely, it could be because he was a Gryphon highlander...*and* on the smallish side.

"I'd be inclined t' go along with Admiral Munming and Admiral Ruddock," Michael Oversteegen mused out loud, "if Alfredo and Master Sergeant Cognasso hadn't vouched for him."

"I thought the same thing," Michelle admitted, sipping from the steaming mug of coffee Billingsley had deposited on the briefing room table at her elbow.

"But Alfredo *does* vouch for him. Whatever else he may have been doing, he wasn't lying. And Alfredo also confirms that his anxiety over what's going on in Mobius is genuine." She shrugged. "However bizarre it sounds, Ankenbrandt really is playing messenger for a bunch of people who've been—or who *think* they've been, anyway—in contact with and receiving clandestine support from the Star Empire."

"Forgive me, Ma'am," Cynthia Lecter said, "but that's crazy. I mean, from the timetable he's described, they've been in contact with us since before Commodore Terekhov even sailed for Monica." She nodded respectfully in Terekhov's direction without ever looking away from Michelle. "We had absolutely no interest in this region at that point. Why in God's name would we have been making clandestine contacts with a resistance movement directed at *Frontier Security*?"

"Now, now, Cindy," Michelle corrected, waving an index finger gently. "It's not a resistance movement against OFS. It's a resistance movement against this President Lombroso. He's just an OFS *lackey*, not the real thing, like they have in Madras."

"That doesn't change my point, Ma'am," Lecter replied with a certain respectful asperity. "It would still have been an incredibly foolish, risky, ultimately pointless thing for us to have done. And if we *had* been doing anything of the sort, and if Baroness Medusa really knew about it, do you think she would've sent us out here without at least *mentioning* it to you?"

"No, Cindy, I don't," Michelle said calmly. "That doesn't mean they haven't been in contact with *somebody*, though. And it doesn't mean they don't *believe* it's Manticore they've been talking to."

"But...what would be the *point*?" Lecter asked almost plaintively.

"Aivars?" Michelle invited, looking at the tall, blond commodore.

"The same points you're raising occurred to me when I first heard Ankenbrandt's story, Captain Lecter," Terekhov said, looking down the table at Michelle's chief of staff. "In fact, I was inclined—especially in the absence of a treecat lie detector of my own—to write him off as either a complete crackpot or a Frontier Security plant trying to suck us into a misstep. Frankly, I'm still not completely ready to dismiss the second possibility. Even if he believes he's telling us the truth, he and all of his friends in Mobius could've been set up by OFS for that very purpose. On the other hand, as you pointed out yourself, there's the timetable. I can't see why Frontier Security would have been worrying about setting anything like this up before we ever crossed swords with Monica.

"As I say, I was about to write him off when Ensign Zilwicki suggested a third possibility to me. I realize some people"—he carefully refrained from looking in Admiral Munming's direction—"may be inclined to wonder if her father's...radicalism, let's say, might affect her judgment. I don't happen to think that's very likely in her case, but even if it were, her suggestion still made a lot of sense to me."

"And that suggestion was, Sir Aivars?" Munming asked, but she was eyeing him intently, and her tone suggested she'd already figured out where he was headed.

"Ensign Zilwicki suggested that it's possible we—and, for that matter, the resistance people in Mobius—*are* being set up, but not by Frontier Security. As she pointed out, it's obvious from Crandall's movements that Mesa must have put her into play at the same time they started providing battlecruisers to Monica. Which, just coincidentally, would have been about the same time Ankenbrandt says his resistance organization was initially contacted by 'Manticore.' Or, for that matter, the time somebody began talking to Mr. Westman here on Montana and Nordbrandt in Kornati."

"You're suggesting it's actually this Mesan Alignment, Commodore?" Roddick said slowly.

"The original notion wasn't mine, Admiral, but I think it makes a lot of sense. Especially if the rather sketchy information we have so far from home is accurate and Mesa's been maneuvering us into a shooting confrontation with the League all along. If one of the local régimes or OFS itself were to break a resistance movement, all of whose leaders genuinely believed they'd been instigated, coordinated, and supplied by the Star Empire, how do you think the League would have reacted even before our current confrontations?"

There was silence for several seconds. Then Oversteegen nodded.

"Always did think Helen had a pretty good head on her shoulders," he drawled. "An' sometimes a little paranoia's a useful thing. And speakin' about bein' paranoid, does anyone think—assumin' this little scenario holds atmosphere—that the bastards would've stopped with settin' up *one* resistance movement?"

"I don't know about 'anyone,'" Michelle said, "but *I* don't. Assuming, as you say, Ensign Zilwicki's hypothesis holds atmosphere. And I'm very much afraid it could. For that matter, I'm afraid there's still worse to come." She cocked her head at the commodore. "Would you care to go ahead and share the rest of your unpleasant ruminations with everyone else, as well, Aivars?"

"I wouldn't like to take complete credit for them, Ma'am," Terekhov pointed out. "In fact, once Helen— Ensign Zilwicki, I mean—had gone that far, another rather nasty thought occurred to her. If this really is Mesa, and if they've contacted not just Mobius but other independent or protectorate star systems out this way, what happens when the balloons start going up? When OFS and Frontier Fleet move in to put down the 'rebellions' and the blood starts to flow? It wouldn't just be a matter of the PR damage we'd take in the League. Bad enough hundreds or thousands of people would be killed, but if dozens of resistance movements start sending us messengers like Mr. Ankenbrandt, expecting the open assistance and support they've been promised, and we don't deliver, what happens to the tendency for independent star systems to trust us more than the Sollies?"

"Those fucking bastards," Ruddock said softly, then shook himself. "Sorry about that, Milady," he said apologetically, "but I believe Commodore Terekhov and—Ensign Zilwicki—have just converted my skepticism into something else." His eyes hardened dangerously. "You've almost got to admire them. Aside from the time they've invested in it, look how little it's cost them to set all this up!"

"That thought occurred to me, too, when Commodore Terekhov first shared this whole fascinating train of thought with me," Michelle said sourly. "And it leads to an interesting quandary, doesn't it?"

Heads nodded all around the table, and she inhaled sharply.

"All right." She sat up straighter, tapping an index finger on the table for emphasis as she continued. "All of this is hypothetical, of course. I'm not going to pretend I don't think there's something to it, though. And, to be honest, there are some potential upsides to the situation. For one thing, although I don't think the strategy ever actually occurred to anyone on our side, it really is a damned good way to force the League to disperse its efforts. That's one of the things that's going to make our supposed complicity so convincing to the Sollies when the shit finally gets around to hitting the fan. At the same time, we don't have any way to know how many other Mobiuses may be ticking away out there. And the truth is that Ensign Zilwicki's final hypothesis is downright scary. The damage this could do to the Star Empire's reputation *outside* the League doesn't bear thinking about."

She looked around the table again.

"So we're going to begin contingency planning now. Especially after how effectively Captain Zavala's squadron performed in Saltash, I don't think it's going to take wallers to support something like Mobius. A destroyer division or a couple of cruisers should be able to handle anything Frontier Fleet's likely to be able to spare for rebel-thumping. I'm not going to disperse my main combat strength, but I want plans to peel off light forces to respond to any of these 'Manticore-supported rebellions' we hear about. We can't do anything about the ones we *don't* know about, and I sure as hell don't want to encourage even more 'spontaneous uprisings.' For that matter, what I'd really prefer would be to turn up in the role of peacemaker before things get too far out of hand. In the real world, that's not going to happen, though, and we all know it. So the way I see it, in this respect at least, we have no choice but to dance to the Alignment's music . . . assuming Mesa really is behind it, of course. I've already sent a dispatch boat on to Spindle with my conclusions, and to be frank, I'd be delighted to have guidance from Baroness Medusa and Prime Minister Alquezar before things get even more lively out here. In the meantime, though, I'm not going to let Mesa get away with branding us not just as instigators of rebellion but as the sort of people who abandon our catspaws when the blood actually begins to flow."

✧ Chapter Twenty-Five

"**WHAT THE HELL WAS** Kazuyoshi *thinking?*" Kayleigh Blanchard demanded.

Almost a week had passed since the apocalyptic conclusion of Kazuyoshi Brewster's attack, and she and Michael Breitbach sat at a picnic table in Landing's Central Park. A checkered cloth covered the table between them, and their plates were piled with potato salad, baked beans, and hot dogs. Sitting out in the open was enough to make Blanchard nervous, but she knew Breitbach was right. Security forces paid less attention to people eating picnic lunches out in the sunlight where everyone could see them than they did to people who seemed concerned with hiding in the shadows. Their current table was on a little point of land, pushing out into the lake. Directional microphones could undoubtedly hear every word they said, if anyone were suspicious enough to point one of them in their direction, but there weren't going to be any other diners near enough to overhear casual conversation.

Breitbach took another bite of his hot dog, chewed with every evidence of enjoyment, swallowed, and took a swig of beer. Then he shrugged.

"We'll never know, for sure," he said. "Personally, though, I think it was just as straightforward as it looks." He shook his head. "Kaz and his entire cell just plain lost too many people they cared about. He didn't kick an authorization request up the ladder because he knew damned well he wouldn't get it, and he didn't care."

"But—" Blanchard began.

"Eat your hot dog," Breitbach interrupted, and waited until she'd obediently taken another bite.

"I don't say it doesn't piss me off, because it does," he said then, putting ketchup on his own hot dog as he spoke. "And it's going to play hell with all our plans. At the same time, I can't be too mad at him. I knew his family, you know. I wasn't supposed to, but I did. So, yeah, I understand exactly what was pushing him. I didn't know the others, but from what we've seen, they were cut from the same cloth. And don't forget—four members of his cell walked away clean. We haven't tried to contact them yet, and they're keeping their heads down just the way they ought to, but it looks to me like they're probably the ones who *didn't* lose family in the May Riots. They helped Kaz and the others get in, set up the van bombs, then got the hell out of the way."

He put down the ketchup and bit into the hot dog again.

"You're probably right," Blanchard said after a moment. "And I'm like you; I can't really *blame* them either, however much I wish they hadn't done it.

But what do we do now? Whether we like it or not, they were effective—and visible—as hell. Now that they've hammered Yardley's bastards so hard, some of the other cells are going to want to hit back, too. For that matter, I'm thinking a lot of this 'freelance' stuff we're seeing is probably our people."

"Probably," Breitbach agreed. "And it's going to get even harder to hold them now that Yardley's started arresting 'dangerous dissidents.'" He grimaced. "Once people in general figure out how many people she and Lombroso are 'disappearing' it's going to get really ugly. And once the Gendarmes get here, it's going to get even worse."

He seemed remarkably calm about the prospect he'd just described, Blanchard thought.

"So you're sure now that Verrochio's going to send them?" she asked, and he snorted.

"After Kazuyoshi's operation?" He shook his head. "I think they were probably going to send them in the first place; after Kaz and his people took out a whole fucking regiment of the Guard—*and* a Solly operations manager—our Ms. Xydis for damned sure started screaming for everything she could get! If they weren't already in the pipeline, I guarantee Verrocchio's going to cough them up now, damn it. That's why I sent off another message to the Manties three days ago."

"You did?" She blinked at him in surprise, and he shrugged.

"Yardley'd already begun her crackdown, Kayleigh," he pointed out. "It was obvious things were only going to get worse, and I had to make a quick call. There was a fast Trifecta freighter heading for Montana to follow up on the contract our first contact was sent to negotiate. Of course, that whole deal was one of Guernicke's brainstorms, so it's possible Frolov will scrub it now that she's so fortuitously retired. But in the meantime, the first freighter was off to pick up whatever their agents had been able to purchase, and we had another 'secret friend' in her crew." He shrugged again. "The opportunity wasn't likely to present itself again anytime soon, so I decided to take it."

"I see." She regarded him steadily for several seconds. "Do you think the Manties are actually going to respond?"

"I wish I were as confident that they're going to as I am that Verrocchio's going to," Breitbach admitted. "Having said that, though, I do think it's more likely they will than that they won't." He shrugged slightly. "They committed themselves to, and they have to figure that if we go down, Yardley and Lombroso are almost certain to find evidence of that in the wreckage. Having the rest of the galaxy find out they encouraged us and promised us support and then pulled the plug on us when we needed them most would hurt them badly with the independents out here in the Verge. And not coming through for us *wouldn't* do them any good with the Sollies, either. The League's going to be almost equally pissed off even if we do go down, especially because they'll blame the Manties for encouraging us in the first place."

"Cynical . . . but probably accurate," Blanchard conceded after a moment, taking another bite of her own hot dog.

"Don't get me wrong," Breitbach replied. "I don't think it was all cynical calculation on the Manties' part in the first place. I think they really do hate the Solarian League and OFS, and I think they find people like Lombroso and Yardley almost as morally reprehensible as we do. But let's be realistic, Kayleigh. All the moral revulsion in the universe isn't going to bring somebody into conflict with something the size of the Solarian League unless there are good, solid and pragmatic reasons to go with it. From everything I've seen, it looks like Manticore realizes it's fighting for its life, and if it's going to win, it's going to have to fight smart. That means not throwing away its claim to the moral high ground by encouraging people to revolt against régimes like Lombroso's and then just walking away. And to be honest, I don't care whether or not they're saints as long as it's in their own best interests to help us take down him and that butcher Yardley."

"I can get behind that," Blanchard agreed with feeling.

"I figured you probably could." Breitbach smiled at her, but the smile faded, and he shook his head.

"I figured you probably could," he repeated, "but that doesn't make me any happier about this mess. Yardley *is* going on the offensive, and I think she's doing it deliberately, trying to force our hand."

"Push the entire Resistance out into the open where she can get at it?" Blanchard looked unhappy at her own suggestion, and Breitbach nodded.

"That or *pull* it out into the open," he agreed. "I'm not sure she realizes just how well organized we actually are, but even if she does, she probably figures that if she hits us hard enough—especially after Kazuyoshi hit *them* as hard as he did—she can goad our people into coming out where she can get at them. She's got to be pretty damn confident she's still got a lot more heavy weapons than we do, not to mention the Guard's air assets, satellites, surveillance systems, and spies. I'm pretty sure her thinking's going to be that if she can only get us out in the open she'll be able to smash us once and for all, or at least prune us back pretty damned drastically."

"And if she's wrong about that little calculation?" Blanchard asked with an unpleasant smile.

"And if she's wrong, she figures she's got Yucel coming in right behind her," Breitbach said, and Blanchard's smile disappeared.

"So what do we do?" she said after a moment.

"For right now, we go ahead and try to keep a lid on things until we hear back from the Manties." Breitbach finished his hot dog and picked up his beer in both hands, propping his elbows on the picnic table so he could nurse the stein properly. "I'd say the odds are at least sixty-forty against our being able to do that, but we've still got to try. We just plain aren't *ready* yet, Kayleigh."

"And if it turns out we *can't* keep a lid on?" Blanchard's eyes were troubled, and she shook her head. "I've got to tell you, Michael—I don't think we *are* going to be able to."

"To be honest, neither do I," he said heavily. He sipped beer, his own eyes hooded, then shrugged.

"Neither do I, and the hell of it is that I don't really want to. I wouldn't have approved Kaz's operation if he'd asked me to, but I would have *wanted* to. There's nothing I want more than to see Lombroso and Yardley hanging at the ends of ropes the way they damned well deserve. So the whole time I'm standing there waving my hands and screaming 'Stop! We're not ready yet!' what I really want to be shouting is 'Kill the bastards!'"

He managed to keep his picnicker's expression in place, yet his voice was harsh and ugly and his hands tightened convulsively on the stein.

"But my brain knows better than that," he continued in a voice which sounded more like his own. "So before we do anything else, I'm going to do my damnedest to sit on the other hotheads—the hotheads just like *me*—until I hear something back from the Manties. Which doesn't change the fact that I agree with you that I'm not going to be able to in the end."

He swallowed a little more beer, then set the stein down very neatly and precisely in front of him.

"If we're both right and it looks like we're going to lose control, I really only see one thing we can do. What we *can't* do is allow everything we've managed to build to just come apart, and that's what's going to happen if more of our cells start doing what Kazuyoshi did. So however unready I may think we are, we'll just have to go for it. Now."

"'Go for it'?" Blanchard repeated carefully, and he gave her a thin smile.

"The only reason we've gotten as far as we already have—further than anyone else's ever gotten against Lombroso—is that we've been organized and disciplined, Kayleigh. If we lose that, Yardley breaks us even without the Gendarmerie's support. And one of the most important principles of successful command I came across in all my research is that you don't give an order you *know* won't be obeyed. If we're going to maintain our discipline, we'll have to get out in front of our people's anger. We'll have to demonstrate to all those other Kazuyoshis that we're committed to move and that we *are* moving. If we do that, and do it effectively, they'll get behind us and push instead of dragging us all out into Yardley's sights behind *them*. And whether I think we're ready or not, we're a hell of a lot *closer* to ready than anyone else's ever been. I think we've got a shot—probably a pretty good one, and sure as hell a better one than Yardley *thinks* we do—against the Guard and Lombroso. Which really leaves only three things to worry about."

"Only *three*?" Blanchard looked at him with what might have been an edge of incredulity, and he smiled.

"Sure. First, whether or not I'm right that we do have a shot at winning. Second, whether or not we can pull it off before the first intervention battalions get here. And, third, whether or not Verrocchio and Yucel will back off and throw in their hand if we do pull it off before the gendarmes get here."

"And just what do you think the odds of *that* are?" she demanded, and his smile grew thinner than a razor.

"Just about zero," he said softly. "Which is why I really, really hope the Manties get here before the Sollies do."

Chapter Twenty-Six

"WELL, IT JUST KEEPS getting better and better, doesn't it?" Albrecht Detweiler observed sourly. He tossed the document reader onto the small table beside his armchair and reached for his beer stein. He took a hefty swallow and shook his head. "I suppose we should at least be grateful we found out about it before that loose warhead Gold Peak!"

"It could be a lot worse, dear," his wife, Evelina, pointed out, looking up from her own viewer and the analysis of the pros and cons of the weaponization of mutagenic nanotech she'd been studying. Her busy crocheting hook went right on working, and her expression was calm. She always had been more philosophical about bumps in the plan than he'd been, he reflected. "At least the battle itself worked out the way you had in mind."

There was a certain satisfaction in her tone, Albrecht noted. Evelina had always personally despised Massimo Filareta. She'd been willing to admit the man's competence, but she'd never been able to detach herself properly from the less savory ways in which Manpower's endless supply of disposable slaves could be used to manipulate individuals like him. Despite which, she had a point. Filareta's defeat had been as complete, total, and humiliating as Albrecht could have desired. Unfortunately...

"You're right, of course," he replied. "The problem is it could have been a lot better, too. We always counted on Beowulf supporting Manticore—as long as the Manties lasted, anyway—and that was part of our calculus for the League's disintegration. But we'd hoped the Sollies would be able to at least give the Manties a run for their money. In fact, they were supposed to weaken Manticore to a point that let the Havenites plow it under at last. Nouveau Paris certainly wasn't supposed to end up deciding to help the Manties kick the crap out of the *League*, instead! And by the time Beowulf started to figure out what was going on and began actively looking for military allies against us, Manticore wasn't supposed to be around for them to ally *with*, much less the damned Havenites! Which doesn't even consider the fact that no one was supposed to know about the Alignment's existence until we were well into Phase Three, and we're not even out of Phase *One* yet."

"I know." She nodded. "But like you've always said, we've known from the beginning that we were going to have to adapt and improvise, and you and the boys are pretty good at that." She smiled reflectively. "They were always good at improvising to get out of trouble as kids, anyway!"

"Yes they were," he agreed fervently, smiling himself. But then his smile faded. "They were, and they still are. But I can't say I'm happy about accelerating Houdini as much as we're going to have to." He shook his head. "Ben and Collin and I have looked at this from every angle we could come up with, and we really don't see any alternative to the Ballroom Option."

Evelina's face tightened unhappily. She started to say something, then paused and looked back down at her crocheting, visibly rethinking before she opened her mouth again.

"That's...likely to cause problems," she said.

"Oh, don't I just know it!" His own expression was grim. "And I don't blame the people who're going to have problems with it. I just don't see another way to go, now that those bastards Simões and McBryde have blown the secret."

"They still don't have any *proof*," Evelina pointed out. "If they did have any, I'm sure they'd have trotted it out by now."

"In a way, that only restricts our options further," Albrecht said gently. "If they don't *have* proof, then they're going to be under a lot more pressure to *find* proof. And there aren't a lot of places they can go looking for evidence...except right here. Which is the reason I'm glad Gold Peak doesn't know about *this* yet."

He tapped the document reader, and Evelina nodded unhappily.

"I suppose you're right," she sighed. "I can't help thinking it's likely to cost us some...collateral damage, though. Besides the obvious, I mean."

"I know what you meant," Albrecht agreed. "And that's why Ben, Collin, and I have scheduled a meeting with all of the inner onion section heads tomorrow.

Well, everyone but Daniel's section, since he's still stuck out at Darius. We're going to tell them what we have in mind—and why we don't have a choice—and ask them to be thinking about any weak spots we need to look at. I'm going to have Psych start a prescreen for potential trouble spots, too." He shrugged. "Frankly, I think those sorts of problems will be handleable. I don't expect to like it very much, but I think we can get through it. What worries me more from a pragmatic perspective is that the more we have to rush Houdini, the more likely our cleanup teams are to miss something. Which, when you come down to it, is another reason to consider the Ballroom Option. Nobody's going to vacuum anything out of a computer that doesn't *exist* anymore."

Evelina nodded again, thoughtfully.

"All right, dear. I can see you've thought it through. And however little I may like the conclusion you've reached, I can't really argue with it. Sometimes, though, I wish your father hadn't put all of his eggs in one basket the way he did."

"Oh?" Albrecht straightened in his chair and lowered his brows ferociously. "I happen to think he came up with a pretty damned good basket, myself!"

"Stop fishing for compliments!" she scolded. "I think he did, too." She smiled warmly at him. "But your decision to . . . diversify with the boys—and go ahead and bring them all in at the highest level early—was a good one. All of them know exactly what's going on, and they're not afraid to argue with you. But despite that, you're still all alone in a lot of ways." Her smile faded into a look of sadness. "I wish you'd had some-one else to help carry the full responsibility when you were the boys' age. In fact, I wish you had someone else to carry it with you *now*. Because I think you're right about the need to push Houdini harder, and I think the decision is going to haunt you."

Albrecht reached across from his chair to touch her hand gently.

"It is," he agreed with a crooked smile. "Of course, that's true of a lot of decisions I've had to make, and it's going to be true of a lot more before this is over. But you're wrong in one respect. I may not have anyone else to carry the *ultimate* responsibility, but as you say, at least I've got you—and the boys—to help me deal with the hard jobs . . . and the ghosts. And that helps, Evie. It helps a lot."

❖　　❖　　❖

Michelle Henke scowled at her display, then flipped her chair to a semi-reclining position and transferred her scowl to the inoffensive, indirectly lit deckhead of her sleeping cabin.

She wore her favorite set of academy sweats and her fuzzy purple treecat slippers, and Billingsley had left her an entire extra doughnut. She appreciated his solicitude, his effort to pamper her while she dealt with this particular can of snakes, but she made a mental memo to remind him she didn't have Honor Alexander-Harrington's metabolism and ask him to find something with a few less calories. Carrot sticks perhaps, or maybe celery, even if she wasn't a treecat. Dietitians had been producing calorie-neutral "foods" for centuries now, but Michelle was old-fashioned. If she was going to eat food, she wanted it to be *food*, not just a space filler. At least she wasn't one of those people who used nanotech to scavenge calories, sugars, and fats out of her digestive system so she could gorge on whatever she wanted, although there *were* times . . .

No, she told herself firmly. Carrot sticks. It was definitely going to be carrot sticks. She felt quite virtuous and ever so decisive, and she made a firm resolution to start her new regimen the very next day. In the meantime, however, being a person of deplorably weak will, she was already halfway through doughnut number two.

Thought being mother to the deed, she reached for the doughnut again, only to pause as a pair of soup spoon-sized paws reached up to knead her thigh gently. She looked down into the desperately appealing eyes of an obviously starving waif of a Maine Coon cat who looked like he could take out a Pekingese with one whack of a paw . . . and then eat it in fifteen seconds flat, hair and all.

"No," she told Dicey firmly. "If you want a doughnut, go catch your own, you rotten feline! Or at least go pester Chris for one. This one's mine, calories and all!"

Dicey only kneaded her thigh harder, purring insistently. It sounded like a shuttle turbine that needed alignment, she thought, wondering how even a cat his size could produce such a volume.

"No!" she said even more firmly, shaking the doughnut at him for emphasis. "*Mine*, not yours!"

Dicey's eyes followed the doughnut as millions of years of his ancestors' eyes had followed small prey animals and birds, and the tip of his tail lashed. Then his purr stopped. That was all the warning Michelle had, and it wasn't enough. With an agility that ought to have been impossible for a creature of his bulk, Dicey launched himself vertically. The paws which had been patting her thigh pleadingly struck with unerring accuracy, and he thumped back to the deck with a third of her remaining doughnut firmly in his possession.

"Come back here!" she said, starting to jump out of her chair. "I swear, I'm going to turn you into a *vest*, no matter what Chris says!"

Dicey paid her command no attention. He was too busy emulating a streak of light as he shot triumphantly out of her sleeping cabin and disappeared under one of her day cabin armchairs with his prize.

Michelle stopped halfway out of the chair and regarded the shard of doughnut she still retained. Then she shook her head, settled back, replaced the surviving fragment on its plate, and reached for her coffee instead.

Somehow it doesn't strike me as a good omen when a damned cat's tactics are better than the fleet CO's, she thought. *Probably something I should keep to myself. Wouldn't want the troops to come to the same conclusion. Or for Beth to decide Dicey'd make a better admiral than I do!*

She smiled slightly at the thought, but then the smile faded as she contemplated the report she'd just finished viewing.

The dispatch had been forwarded to her by Augustus Khumalo the same day it reached Spindle from Manticore. That made it the very latest news . . . and seventeen days out of date from the moment it arrived. By now Massimo Filareta had certainly reached the Manticore Binary System, and while Michelle had no doubt the defenders had handled the threat, especially with Honor Alexander-Harrington in tactical command, she really would have liked to know just how bad things had gotten first.

Well, that information's in the pipeline on its way to you by now, too, girl. And it's not like they didn't send along enough other things for you to be worrying about in the meantime!

The good news was that she now had a much more complete explanation of just what Anton Zilwicki and Victor Cachat had brought home from Mesa. She also had a personal message from Honor, confirming her and Nimitz's confidence that Simões was telling them the truth. The bad news was that it was easy enough to understand why a hell of a lot of Sollies were going to demand ironclad proof of such "preposterous" Manticoran claims, and there was still no way to independently confirm a single thing he'd said. And the *worse* news, as far as Michelle was concerned, was that all anyone could tell her about the "Mesan Alignment's" possible intentions in her own command area was "We don't have a clue in hell what they're going to do next, but we don't expect you to like it."

Very useful that was.

She grimaced. Her first inclination was to start kicking in doors on Mesa and drag the Alignment out into the open by the scruff of its misbegotten neck. Unfortunately, she still didn't have enough information to know whether or not that was justified or even where to look for the Alignment after she *got* to Mesa. And while her opinion had been steadily hardening towards the desirability of taking the war to the League, whether she was in a position to go after Mesa or not, she needed to know what had happened to Filareta, first. If he'd been smart enough to surrender the way Honor wanted him to, this whole war might be in a way towards being settled. In that case, invading and conquering a half dozen or so Solarian-claimed star systems might not be the very best way to help the peace process along.

Maybe not, but the chance of the League actually backing down, whatever happened to Filareta, is—what? Maybe one in a thousand? And even that's assuming somebody shoots Kolokoltsov and puts someone remotely rational into his place!

She grimaced some more, remembering that old aphorism about asking for anything but time. In her own mind, she was certain the confrontation with the League was far from over. It was possible her own experiences with people like Josef Byng, Sandra Crandall, and Damián Dueñas were prejudicing her thinking. She admitted that, but the admission didn't change her analysis. And if she was right, if more and worse hostilities were still to come, she hated the thought of not moving as quickly and decisively as possible while she had the opportunity to do so effectively unopposed.

Calm down, she told herself yet again. *Unless something changes radically, you're going to be* effectively unopposed *for a long time to come, given the tech imbalance. Hell, just look what Zavala did in Saltash!*

Which was probably true, but—

But it doesn't mean they're not going to try to oppose you—just like they did in Saltash, damn it—and if they do, you're going to have to kill a hell of a lot more Sollies to take your objectives. And that's what sticks in your craw, isn't it?

She sighed, took another sip of coffee, and commanded herself to stop fretting over things she couldn't change.

Besides, you may not have heard anything about

what happened to Filareta yet, but you are going to hear about it a hell of a lot more quickly than any of the Sollies in the vicinity! You'll still have the advantage of a shorter communication loop, better intel, and the strategic initiative when the time comes, unless those bastards in Mesa figure out some way to bollix everything up again.

For that matter—

The soft buzz of her terminal interrupted her thought, and she brought the chair upright and reached for the accept key.

"Yes? What is it, Gwen?" she asked as Gervais Archer's image appeared on the display.

"Sorry to disturb you this late, Milady," Archer said, "but something's come up that I think you may need to deal with."

"What?" she asked, eyes narrowing.

"Another ship's just arrived in-system from Mobius, Ma'am. It's a Trifecta freighter. According to what her master told the port authorities, he's here to see whether or not Mr. Ankenbrandt was able to find a supplier for that meat-buying contract."

"But—?" she prompted when he paused.

"But her purser's transmitted one of the code words Ankenbrandt supplied, Ma'am. I think she wants to talk to you."

❖   ❖   ❖

"You know," Michelle said three hours later as she regarded the com images of her senior officers, "when we were discussing the situation in Mobius, I'd really hoped we'd have a little more time—like, say, maybe even a whole *week*—before we actually had to decide what we're going to do about it. Silly of me, I suppose."

"It does bring to mind the old cliché about raining and pouring, Ma'am," Munming agreed.

"I suppose it could be argued you still don't *have* t' rush t' a decision, Ma'am," Oversteegen pointed out. "I mean, even if we'd really been the ones they were talkin' to all along, this is still a good two or three months sooner than Ankenbrandt told us they were supposed t' be callin' us in."

"I realize that, Michael. But this"—she tapped a hardcopy summary of her Alfredo-verified interview with Yolanda Summers, the new messenger from the Mobius Liberation Front—"puts a different complexion on things. It's pretty clear the situation's gone to crap faster than Ankenbrandt ever expected when he was sent out. In fact, that's the entire reason this Summers turned up so soon, and I don't blame the MLF leadership one bit for sending her out so quickly after Ankenbrandt. If even half of what's in here is accurate, things are getting ready to drop straight into the crapper in that star system, and it's going to be ugly when they do. Especially given this information that Lombroso's expecting intervention battalions to arrive shortly. I'm going to assume that if he thinks they're coming, the odds are they're already in the pipeline, which means that even if we send someone immediately, Frontier Security's likely to be in-system and boots-on-the-ground by the time anything of *ours* can get there."

"With all due respect, Ma'am, that might be an argument *against* reacting quickly," Rear Admiral Ruddick suggested. She looked at him, and he shrugged. "Assuming you're right about that, we probably can't get there in time to prevent a bloodbath in the first place. If that's the case, all our 'intrusion into the star system'—and that's how we all know the League is going to describe it—will achieve is to pump extra hydrogen into our face-off with the Sollies without preventing whatever's already happened to Ankenbrandt's resistance movement by the time we do get there."

"I understand your argument, Mickaël, but I'm not going to pussyfoot around the League in the name of expediency. People've been doing that for centuries, and look how well *that's* worked out!" She shook her head. "No. If they want to go on playing this kind of game, this time they're going to have to show me their cards or fold, because I am *damned* well going to call them on it! Having said that, though, I'm not just shooting from the hip, either. There's a genuine method to my madness on this one.

"First, Mobius isn't a member of the Solarian League, and it's not an official protectorate, either. It doesn't even have an officially sanctioned OFS presence like Saltash. Technically and legally, it's an independent star nation, even if the Lombroso Administration *is* as corrupt and tyrannical as they come, not to mention being in Frontier Security's hip pocket. So it'll be a bit difficult for the Sollies to call us on intruding into *their* space. They'll do it anyway, of course, but we'll have plenty of opportunities to attack their claims.

"Second, even if their arrangement was really with someone else, the people in Mobius think it was with us, and that's what everyone else is going to think. That hasn't changed; the timetable's simply been moved up a bit. And if we were going to respond by supporting them when they rebelled 'on schedule,' all the same arguments for doing that apply to getting in there *now*.

"And, third, I'm sick and fucking tired of watching Frontier Security and its bastard friends grind their heels into people's faces. According to this"—she never raised her voice, but her expression could have been carved out of battle steel as the tapped the report again—"Lombroso's resorted to mass arrests, 'stringent interrogations,' and shutting down all nongovernment channels of public communication. Not to mention the fact that a lot of his opponents have started mysteriously disappearing." She shook her head, brown eyes grim. "I'm not going to find any more of those people in unmarked graves than I can help, Mickaël. Not when they went there thinking *my* Star Empire got them into Lombroso's line of fire in the first place."

There was silence for a moment. Then Aivars Terekhov cleared his throat.

"I think you have a point, Ma'am," he said.

"Only *a* point?" Michelle smiled humorlessly.

"What I meant, Ma'am, is that whatever we do or don't do, the *perception* is still going to be that we fomented the situation in Mobius. I happen to agree with you that keeping people from being killed by a corrupt government is worthwhile in its own right, but even from a purely pragmatic political viewpoint, I don't see that we have any choice. If we *had* engineered it, we'd have a moral responsibility to the people who're being arrested and 'disappeared,' and that's the standard we're going to be held to, whoever actually set this in motion. For that matter, even if it later comes out—even if we're later able to prove—that we *weren't* the ones stirring the pot, intervention on the resistance's side is still going to work out in our favor with everyone except the Sollies." He shrugged. "I'm not trying to be cold-blooded or calculating about it, but if the independent star systems out this way realize we're willing to stand by them when they think they have our word, even when that means facing the Solarian League and even when we weren't actually involved from the beginning, it can only improve their perception of us."

"Somethin' to that, Ma'am," Oversteegen remarked. "Quite a lot, really."

"I agree," Munming said firmly.

"Good." Michelle smiled a bit more naturally. "It's always nice to know my loyal subordinates approve of what I'm going to do anyway."

One or two of the others smiled back, and she returned her attention to Terekhov.

"I'm especially glad to hear *you* feel that way, Aivars. For a lot of reasons, I don't want to look like I'm . . . overreacting, let's say. At the same time, I think a big enough force to make a firm statement—and hopefully to provide any Solly Frontier Fleet commander with a sufficiently overpowering threat that he can back down without losing face and touching off another Saltash—is in order. And, given the delicate questions of interstellar policy and diplomacy involved, I think it would be as well for us to send along a senior officer with Foreign Office experience. Someone like *you*."

"Yes, Ma'am." If Terekhov was dismayed—or surprised—he showed no sign of it.

"I'm thinking that I'm going to send one division of your cruiser squadron, a destroyer squadron, and one of Admiral Culbertson's CLACs. The carrier'll have plenty of life-support to carry a battalion or so of Marines, as well. That should give you a ground combat component if you need one. I'm hoping you won't, but better safe than sorry."

"Yes, Ma'am."

"I'll want you underway within twelve hours," she continued. "In the meantime, I'll be leaving your other division and Scotty Tremaine's division here in Montana, along with the rest of Culbertson's CLACs, and the rest of our destroyers, all under Culbertson. I'll leave him detailed instructions about what to do if any interesting little messages should happen to arrive from other resistance movements we didn't realize we were supporting."

"Pardon me, Ma'am," Munming said, "but that seems to suggest you don't plan on staying here yourself?"

"No, I don't plan on that. And you won't be staying either, Aploloniá. I'm taking your squadron, Michael's battlecruisers, and Admiral Menadue's carriers to join Admiral Bennington at Tillerman."

More than one set of eyebrows rose this time, and she shrugged.

"By this time, Filareta's either been blown to dustbunnies, surrendered, or run like hell," she said. "When Admiral Khumalo and Baroness Medusa find out which it was, they'll be sending dispatches both here and to Tillerman. I'd find out about it a bit sooner if I stayed here, but I'd still have to move to Tillerman—or waste time ordering Bennington to join us here—to concentrate our wall before we make any moves of our own. And I've come to the conclusion that if things have fallen still further into the crapper, we *are* going to be making some moves. Specifically, as I see it, our first step has to be to cover our backs before we do anything else. Which means taking out the Madras Sector."

The assembled officers sat very still.

"If we're going to find ourselves in a genuine war with the League, I'm not going to sit here and let them bring it to us," she said flatly. "We know, because we've demonstrated it against the Havenites and they've demonstrated it against us, that the deep strike can be decisive . . . and that standing on the defensive surrenders the initiative to the other side. From everything we've seen out of the Sollies so far, they *haven't* figured that out. Oh," she waved one hand impatiently, "they went straight for Spindle and straight for the home system, but both of those moves were completely in line with their step-by-step approach; it just happened that we didn't have a lot of depth. But I don't think there's much doubt that they'll be thinking about staging any additional operations against the Quadrant out of Madras or one of the other sectors out this way. They almost have to, in a lot of ways, because their logistics are so short-legged. They don't have a fleet train organization with the kind of strategic mobility and flexibility we and the Havenites have developed, and I doubt there's a single Battle Fleet admiral who has the *mental* flexibility to work around that. Given time, they'll develop it or find someone—probably from Frontier Fleet—who *does* have it, but it's going to *take* time for that to happen. And that's why we're not going to stand on the defensive. If these idiots persist in dancing to Mesa's piping, then we're going to take the war to them. I want to eliminate their basing infrastructure out here. I want them fully on the defensive—psychologically, as well as strategically—from the get-go. That means punching out every sector capital behind us as we advance, so if we do end up pulling the trigger, we're going into the Meyers System hard and fast and in sufficient strength that nobody's going to even *think* about shooting back. I want that system taken with as close to zero bloodshed as humanly possible, and after that, we're going to punch out the *rest* of the sector."

Chapter Twenty-Seven

CAPTAIN PETER CLAVELL FROWNED grumpily as he checked his chrono for the third time in the last fifteen minutes. His relief was late—again—and Clavell didn't like the rumors he'd been hearing. All very well for General Yardley to announce a general offensive against the rabble-rousers and malcontents, but she wasn't the one out here in command of a checkpoint whose relief was dragging in late . . . again. And she wasn't the one wondering if maybe *this* time his relief was late for a reason nobody would like. Or if some terrorist son-of-a-bitch was going to come along and ruin his entire night when he should have been safely back in his quarters while some other poor bastard took over the checkpoint in question. God knew it had happened to enough other Guardsmen in the last two or three weeks!

He scowled at the thought and reminded himself that it would be a very bad idea to say anything like that out loud where it might get back to Internal Affairs. "Defeatism" was well on its way to becoming a capital offense, and at least one other field grade officer Clavell knew had been posted to one of the penal battalions for "sedition" when she'd questioned an intelligence appreciation of the general public's support for the terrorists who'd taken down the White Whore. Against that sort of backdrop, suggesting General Yardley didn't care diddley about how many Guardsmen she might have to sacrifice to make this particular omelette probably came under the heading of something other than career enhancement.

And given the sort of welcome a member of the Presidential Guard was likely to receive from the citizens of Mobius this day, it wasn't as if Captain Clavell could expect much of a career in the civilian sector. Most jobs tended to go to people who were still breathing, after all. Not that he wouldn't have been simply delighted to embrace some other form of employment if he *had* been able to find it.

Clavell sighed heavily, tipped back in the Scorpion's command chair, and yawned and stretched—hard—before he crossed his ankles and clasped his hands behind his helmeted head.

It wasn't that he had any qualms about breaking heads if the president told him to, he reflected. That was his job, after all, and Svein Lombroso understood that men and women of proven loyalty deserved to be rewarded. The perks that went with Clavell's career choice were fairly awesome, when he came down to it, and it wasn't as if the work had ever been especially difficult. Break the occasional head, send a few unionists or protesters to the hospital, pull the occasional stint guarding one of the concentration camps, make your own quota on arrested malcontents . . . all fairly straightforward and routine. If there weren't enough protesters or genuine malcontents around when you needed them to look good on your annual efficiency reports, it wasn't too hard to find someone to stand in for them, and it wasn't as if the courts were going to waste time listening to protestations of innocence, anyway.

There'd been the occasional—*very* occasional—moment when Cadet Clavell or even Lieutenant Clavell had questioned the system and his own participation in it. But *Captain* Clavell, older and wiser than those younger personae, knew someone had to maintain order and public discipline, and if the someone in question was rewarded for his efforts with special privileges, better pay, and the respect which the authority he represented properly deserved, that was no more than he merited for all the sacrifices he'd made. And he'd never much worried himself about the Intelligence pukes' claims that hundreds of plots against the presidency simmered perpetually away. *He'd* never seen any sign of it, at any rate—not on any organized basis. The people who might have made real trouble knew better than to cross swords with the Guard or poke their heads up to be broken.

Until the May Riots, at least.

But the Riots—and the White Whore attack—had changed all that. Now, every time he looked around someone was painting antigovernment graffiti, or vandalizing a government office or a System Unity office, or sabotaging public transportation. The police were everywhere, backed up by the Guard's ominous presence more and more openly. Arrest totals were soaring (and executions were climbing), and System Information and News made sure the proles knew about it. Commentators and government spokesmen underscored the many ways in which a tiny handful of malcontents, rabble-rousers, radicals, and anarchists like the so-called "freedom fighters" of the thoroughly misnamed Mobius Liberation Front poisoned the society around them. Presidential news secretaries bemoaned the imposition of the ever sterner security measures which a handful of violent extremists had made necessary and the way in which those measures intruded into the lives and personal affairs of the huge majority of citizens who wanted only to obey the laws and get on with their own lives. Stern penalties, however reluctantly enforced, were the only argument vicious criminals like the "Liberation Front" seemed able to understand, however, and so the president had found himself with no option but to seek the death penalty for crimes against the state in hopes that imposing that punishment upon those whose guilt had been proven might deter others from their predatory actions against a law-abiding society.

And beneath the surface, behind the newsies and uniformed law enforcement personnel, underscoring the drama of public trials, convictions, and sentences, were General Mátyás' *secret* police. No one spoke about *them*—not openly, anyway. Everyone knew they were there, but no one knew who they were. They did their work in the shadows, without fanfare or glory, accountable only to their own superiors, General Mátyás himself, and the Presidential Special Courts whose task it was to deal with the most hardened enemies of the state. It was their invisibility that made them most intimidating, the knowledge that they were perpetually on guard, unseen and ready to pounce. And it was the silence which enveloped and erased the enemies of the state with whom they dealt which deterred the troublemakers who might otherwise have dared to defy the forces of public order.

Yet now the system which had worked so well for so long found itself confronted by a level of unrest, verging on outright insurrection in some areas, such as it had never before experienced. Despite the newscasts, despite the spokesmen, despite the public arrests and the rumors of *secret* arrests, despite the publicly announced executions and the unexplained disappearances of agitators and protesters, anonymous posters became daily more aggressive, more vituperative, on the public boards. The graffiti multiplied, the vandalism spread, and government employees had been assaulted. Over three dozen of them had been hospitalized, and one of them had actually died! And just trying to keep *count* of the ever mounting avalanche of threats against *Trifecta* employees was using up more and more police resources. Not to mention *Guard* resources, like Clavell's own Scorpion platoon and the infantry platoon attached to it while they sat here guarding the approaches to Summerhill Tower. He understood the need to reassure Trifecta's personnel of their own and their families' safety, but parking this much firepower in the middle of a residential district in the middle of the night seemed a little excessive.

But perhaps it wasn't, he thought. After all, things had gotten even uglier over the last week or so. They'd been fairly quiet here in Landing itself—since the Trifecta Tower attack, anyway—but just the day before yesterday a mob had gathered outside a regional police station in the city of Granger, pelting it with stones and improvised incendiary devices in a protest over the hanging of three convicted seditionist agitators. Eleven officers had been injured, two of them seriously, before the mob had finally been dispersed, and there were conflicting reports about the anarchists' casualties, although SINS was flatly denying the ridiculous claims that over sixty of them had been killed.

Clavell didn't know about that, although he rather hoped the newsies were wrong about how low the anarchist casualties had been. The more he heard about the way things were going out in the boonies, the more in favor he was of showing the yokels the error of their way before things got completely out of hand. Or even spread to Landing, for that matter!

Some of his fellow Guardsmen scoffed at his worries, and he was careful not to be too vocal about them. But he heard things, even when he wasn't supposed to. Like that shootout in Brazelton, for instance. SINS hadn't so much as mentioned it, and even the Guard's daily intelligence reports had treated it as only one more minor incident in a sleepy little town of no more than a hundred and twenty thousand or so. Clavell wasn't so certain, though. True, Brazelton wasn't Landing, and the security assets concentrated here in the capital were a lot better than anything a provincial town boasted. And, true again, they were talking about small town cops who probably hadn't had a clue what real security measures were all about. But even having said all of that, he personally might have argued that the assassination of a city police chief—and the successful ambush of his entire six-man security detail—came under the heading of a fairly *major* incident, no matter where it happened. Of course, everybody from General Yardley on down was denying Chief Brinkman was dead, and confidence that the perpetrators would soon be run to earth was high, but Clavell figured he could believe as much of *that* as he wanted to.

Stupid, he thought, checking the time again and then scanning the Scorpion's displays. *What? They think scuttlebutt isn't going to pass the word around anyway? And given the fact that at least half—probably a hell of a lot more than half, since the* official *report says 'less than half'—of the bastards got away, the* other side *sure as hell knows how much damage it did. I mean, go ahead and put a lid on it for the proles. Fine. I'm all in favor of that. But don't hand a line of obvious bullshit to the* Guard, *for God's sake!*

He shook his head. The brass had better get a clue pretty damned quick, in his humble opinion. So far, things hadn't been that bad here in Landing—since the Trifecta Tower attack, at least—but if the sort of crap happening in Granger and Brazelton ever did spread to the capital, it was going to get ugly. He didn't doubt the Guard could deal with these MLF bastards if they'd only come out into the open and stop skulking around in the shadows like the cowards they were, but that didn't mean they weren't going to do a lot of damage first. And the sooner General Yardley and the rest of President Lombroso's advisers figured that out and turned the Guard loose on the "resistance's" sympathizers with open hunting licenses and no bag limit the better it was going to be for all concerned. The last thing they needed was to let the MLF build up some kind of effective support structure in Landing! In fact—

A shrill, high-pitched buzz interrupted Captain Clavell's reflections. He jerked upright in his chair, reaching for his console, and his blood ran cold as the bright red icon flashed in his helmet visor's HUD.

Laser! his brain screamed. *We're being* lased, *but*—

The five-kilo kinetic penetrator struck the Scorpion's thinner, vulnerable rear armor at thirty kilometers per second, within less than a centimeter of the target designation laser's aiming point. Not that it really mattered where it had hit, of course; no light AFV had the protection to resist that kind of attack, and Captain Peter Clavell, late of the Presidential Guard, united with the alloy and fuel of his light tank—and the other two members of its crew—in a fireball that towered against the night.

Three more penetrators struck within half a second of the first one, killing the remaining Scorpions of Clavell's platoon. More fireballs billowed, painting the faces of surrounding towers and buildings in bloody crimson light, and then the tribarrels opened up, scything down the Guard infantry troopers lounging in their unarmored personnel transports while they waited for their relief.

One of the infantry noncoms, protected in the heavily sandbagged CP, had time to scream for support, but she never got through to HQ. She was still trying to get a com response when one of the antitank launchers retargeted on the command post and turned it into an expanding cloud of dust, debris, and human remains.

It wouldn't have mattered if she had gotten through, really. No one could possibly have gotten there in time to do any good. Besides, the elimination of Captain Clavell's security detail was only one of dozens of simultaneous attacks spread across the city of Landing.

❖   ❖   ❖

"Where the hell are they all *coming* from?" Svein Lombroso demanded, his expression haggard as he stared at the map displays in the command center under Presidential Palace. Leprous scarlet splotches glared across them, marking the death and destruction which had exploded out of the night all across the capital city. "My God, there must be *thousands* of them!"

"I doubt it, Mr. President," Olivia Yardley replied. She wore two separate earbugs, and her own attention was focused on a much larger scale holographic display of the residential area around Summerhill Tower. "Not here in Landing, anyway."

"Oh, really? Well just why in hell should I listen to what *you* doubt?" Lombroso snarled. "You were the one who thought it was such a wonderful idea to turn the screws on the MLF! Get them to come out into the *open*, you said. Force their hands. Suck them out where we could get at them!" He glared at her. "Well *that's* working out just goddamned fine, isn't it?!"

Yardley swallowed an almost overwhelming impulse to snarl right back at him. He'd seen the same analyses she had, and it was clear she'd been right about the dangerous escalation in the Mobius Liberation Front's organization and equipment. In fact, she'd obviously *under*estimated both of them! And it was just like him to vent his frustration and his fear by blaming the situation on everyone—*anyone!*—other than himself.

Yet tempting though it was to point that out to him, actually yielding to the temptation would all too probably have been a fatal mistake. He was perfectly capable of ordering her shot, and she could think of at least three of her own subordinates who'd pull the trigger themselves if it let them step into her shoes.

That would have been uncommonly stupid of them under the current circumstances, but that minor fact wouldn't have prevented any of them from doing it.

"Mr. President," she said instead, interrupting the reports she should have been listening to and the orders she should have been giving, "this is exactly what the analysts and I warned might happen." She met his fiery eyes levelly. "It's happening on a lot wider scale than we ever anticipated, and I have to admit the MLF's degree of organization outside Landing's taken us by surprise, but it was the influx of modern weapons and the MLF's increasing militancy that had all of us concerned in the first place! God only knows what would've happened if we'd sat back and let them choose the moment to kick off their offensive!"

"Well, I don't see how it *could* be a whole hell of a lot worse," Lombroso shot back. He jabbed an index finger at the maps. "Brazelton, Granger, Lewisville— how many more towns are we planning to *give* them?"

"I said their organization and strength outside Landing came as a surprise, Sir," Yardley replied coldly. "Apparently, our intelligence assets let us down pretty badly in that respect. I'm sure General Mátyás shared all of his information with the rest of us, but you saw the analyses." She saw the president's eyes flicker at the mention of Mátyás' name. "I'm not trying to pass the blame," she continued with consummate insincerity, "because all of us screwed up in that regard. But the truth is that we can lose all of those towns, and half a dozen more, if we have to. As long as we hold the capital, we can always take them back again, especially after the gendarme battalions get here. And with all due respect, Sir, they *have* come out into the open. I think it's obvious we're going to get hurt more badly than any of us wanted or expected, but they're going to get hurt even worse because now we know where to *find* them."

Some of the steam seemed to go out of Lombroso's glower. He remained anything but happy, yet Yardley's firm tone and projection of confidence were having their effect.

At least until the next time Frolov gets on the com to rattle his cage, the general thought sourly.

She'd heard quite enough from the Trifecta manager herself, and she wished to hell that he'd just leave her alone. And that Lombroso would, too, for that matter. She had more important things to do than sit around holding frightened politicos' hands! Still, it would have been foolish to expect anything else. The attack on the Summerhill security point had penetrated into one of the Trifecta uppercrust's more palatial residential districts before Guard quick response teams could reinforce the Trifecta Security detachments. The security personnel had taken heavy casualties. Worse, over a dozen Trifecta bureaucrats had been hurt or killed before the attackers withdrew, and Frolov had made it abundantly clear that lapses like that were unacceptable.

And considering how much Trifecta's invested in Lombroso, Frolov obviously thinks he's entitled to a better return. I'll bet he hasn't been shy about making that point, either. Funny how much more enthusiastic about "taking the fight to the terrorists" he was when all it was likely to do was get Guernicke killed, isn't it?

"All we have to do is hold them until the gendarmes get here," she said out loud. "I'm going to hit them as hard as I can anywhere I can in the meantime, and I think there's a damned good chance we'll be able to handle this on our own," she added with rather less than total truthfulness, "but in the final analysis, all we *really* have to do is hold them. If the first batch of gendarmes doesn't do the trick, Governor Verrocchio and Brigadier Yucel will send in however many reinforcements they have to. Do you really think either of them wants Trifecta screaming for their blood to OFS headquarters, Mr. President?" She smiled unpleasantly. "This is going to turn into the best chance we've ever had to burn out the infection once and for all, Sir, and all *we* have to do is hold them."

"What's the latest from Lewiston?"

Michael Breitbach looked exhausted and his shoulders sagged with fatigue. His voice was pretty much gone, too, but his eyes were still focused and intent as he asked the question, and Kayleigh Blanchard checked her notepad display.

"Segovia says his people are making good progress now," she replied. "They've got over half the city and they're moving in on Beaver Run Heights. He says that once they take out the satellite police station there, they should be able to start sending additional manpower to us here in Landing. He—"

She broke off as her com beeped at her. She listened intently for several seconds, then nodded with a grunt of satisfaction and looked back at Breitbach.

"That was Leamington. She says her people have hacked the Guard's satellite feeds. She doesn't know how long she'll be able to stay in the system, but for right now we've got access to their recon birds right along with them."

"Good, Kayleigh. Good!" Breitbach managed a weary smile, but there was worry—a lot of worry—in those focused eyes, and Blanchard looked a question at him.

"All of that sounds good," he told her after a moment, "but I'm not sure it's good enough." He shook his head, looking down at the map displayed on the terminal in front of him. "We needed to get deeper quicker here in Landing. Even with Leamington getting into their recon, we just aren't deep enough, and I'm not sure we're going to get there, either."

"But we're winning in almost all of the outer cities," she pointed out. "And practically the entire farm belt's come in on our side."

"I know." He nodded. "And I know they're going to be a hell of a lot more cautious before they try any more of those air assaults." He showed his teeth in a vicious smile. The Presidential Guard had lost twenty-three sting ships and nineteen counter-grav transports trying to reinforce Brazelton. Now that they'd discovered that the MLF had modern impeller wedge SAMs, they were unlikely to try that again—not without far better EW capabilities than any of their antiquated equipment boasted, anyway! He savored the memory of that moment, but then his smile faded and he shook his head once more.

"I know," he repeated more softly, "but even Lombroso's always recognized that Landing's the real key. There are eight and a half *million* people in Landing and the suburbs, not to mention the main planetary spaceport, the Guard's central barracks, Trifecta's entire planetary headquarters complex—and staff—and most of the SUPP's core membership and *all* of its leadership. If we're going to claim that we control the planet, which makes us the legitimate—or at least the de facto—system government, we've got to hold Landing. And you can bet your ass that as long as Lombroso and Trifecta hold it, *they're* going to claim to be the legitimate government. And, frankly, we need it for its hostage value."

"*Hostage* value?" Blanchard looked at him in shock.

One thing he'd always insisted upon was that the MLF had to target legitimate objectives and do its level best to hold collateral civilian casualties to an absolute minimum. He'd even successfully opposed the demands of some of his rank and file that the Liberation Front go after anyone who did business with Trifecta. She knew part of that was a cold calculation that the MLF had to avoid providing any grist for SINS' "independent newsies'" efforts to label it a terrorist organization. But she also knew that another part of it—probably the *greater* part of it—was his personal hatred for the Lombroso régime's policy of ruling by terror and atrocity.

"I'm not planning on shooting people in the street, Kayleigh," he said wearily. "But there's a quantitative difference between Landing and any of the other cities, even Laurent." Laurent, Mobius' second-largest city, had a population of almost two and a half million. None of the planet's other cities topped three hundred thousand. "Lombroso—or the frigging gendarmes, when they get here—could take out twenty or thirty cities the size of Brazelton and Lewiston combined without killing as many people as live in Landing all by itself. And don't think for a moment that Frolov doesn't recognize that, too. I want us holding Landing when the gendarmes get here because I doubt even

OFS is going to be willing to take out eight and a half million revenue-producing Trifecta helots with an orbital strike. Not when they know how all the other transstellars are going to react to that kind of threat to *their* bottom lines. And the longer they hesitate to take us out from orbit, the longer we've got for the Manties to come riding over the hyper limit in the proverbial nick of time."

Blanchard looked at him for several more moments, and then she nodded slowly.

"I guess there's hostage value and then there's *hostage* value," she said.

"Exactly." Breitbach turned his attention back to the map display and squared his sagging shoulders. "And maybe I'm wrong." He sounded as if he were willing confidence and fresh determination back into his voice. "Maybe we can get deep enough quick enough, especially with Leamington getting us inside their recon. And if Segovia really can free up some additional manpower soon enough." He smiled grimly. "And even if we can't take the entire city, I damn well *guarantee* we'll manage to kill enough more of the bastards to make sure any of them who are still alive remember us for a long, long time."

Chapter Twenty-Eight

"YES, AUGUSTUS? What can I do for you this morning?" Dame Estelle Matsuko, Baroness Medusa, asked with a smile.

The expression felt a bit strange, but not because she wasn't happy to see the face on her com. Although there'd been a time when Augustus Khumalo hadn't been her favorite person, those days were gone. It was just a bit hard to find a lot of things to smile about in the wake of the dispatches which had finally reached Spindle two T-days ago. Close to two million dead—two million *more* dead—even if most of them were from the other side, and confirmation that the Star Empire truly was at war with the Solarian League, wasn't the sort of news that made someone want to turn handsprings of delight.

Still, it's better than having the two million dead on our side, which is what those Solly bastards had in mind, she reminded herself grimly. *And at least the Solarian League's present management obviously can't find its own backside with both hands. That's a two-edged*

444

sword, since it means they're unlikely as hell to realize the smart move would be to rethink their policies and let both of us back away from a war that's going to get God only knows how many more people killed. But if they're bullheaded and arrogant enough to keep right on pushing harder, instead—and it looks an awful lot like they are—then thank God they're at least incompetent about it! And having Haven—Haven!—on our side for a change is a lot better than a kick in the head, too.

"Good morning, Milady," Admiral Khumalo responded. "Sorry to disturb you this early, but I've just received dispatches from Admiral Gold Peak." There was something a little peculiar about his tone, Medusa thought. "Under the circumstances, I thought I should probably share them with you as soon as possible."

"Is there a problem?" she asked, her smile fading.

"Not any immediate problem, no," he replied. "But it's definitely something we're going to have to deal with, probably in the not too distant future. And I guarantee you you're going to think it was as . . . unexpected as I did."

"I'd feel a lot better without that qualifier, 'immediate.' And I'm not all that fond of 'unexpected,' now that I think about it," she said sourly. He nodded, and she sighed. "Should I roust out Joachim or Henri for this?"

"At the moment, I think this is more of a matter for your Imperial Governor persona than for anybody in the Talbott Quadrant," Khumalo said after a moment's thought. "It may be appropriate for you to bring them in later—in fact, I think it probably will be—but for right now I think you should hear about this yourself before you decide what else to do."

"You're not making me feel any happier here, Augustus," she said dryly as she tapped a command to open her daily calendar in a window in the corner of the com display. "I've got just under an hour and a half clear, starting now," she told him. "Can you get here in that window? And if you can, should I see about clearing the rest of the morning?"

"I can be there in thirty minutes," he replied. "As to how long this is going to take, in some ways your guess is as good as mine. It *could* take a while, though."

"Wonderful. Should I ask Gregor to sit in?"

"Actually, I think that would be a very good idea. As a matter of fact, with your permission, I think it might be a good idea for me to bring along Loretta and Ambrose, as well."

"Fine. In that case I'll see you here in Government House in half an hour."

✧   ✧   ✧

Admiral Khumalo, his chief of staff, and his senior intelligence officer actually arrived in barely twenty minutes. In fact, Gregor O'Shaughnessy had reached Medusa's office less than five minutes before the three naval officers were ushered through its door. He and Medusa stood to greet the newcomers, and the baroness' eyes narrowed in speculation as she spotted the fourth member of Khumalo's party. The one the admiral had somehow forgotten to mention to her might be coming.

The stranger was a civilian, and a supremely unre-markable looking one. His sandalwood complexion was perhaps a shade darker than Medusa's own, his hair and his eyes were brown, and he was of average height. A Solarian by his dress, but not a Core Worlder; his standard upper-mid-level bureaucrat's outfit was at least six or seven T-years out of date by Core World standards. Probably a fairly senior local employed in a managerial role by one of the transstellars doing business in the Shell, she thought.

And just what exactly does Augustus think he's doing bringing a Solarian civilian into my office?

The thought was not a happy one, but she donned her politician's face and smiled in welcome.

"Augustus. Captain Shoupe, Commander Chandler. Good to see you. And this would be—?"

She let the question hover and cocked her head at the Solarian.

"This is Mr. Ankenbrandt, Madame Governor," Khumalo supplied. "And to be honest, he's the reason for this meeting."

"I beg your pardon?" Despite herself, Medusa's response carried a sharp edge of surprise, and Khumalo gave her a slightly apologetic smile.

"Mr. Ankenbrandt arrived with a coded dispatch from Admiral Gold Peak, Milady," he explained. "I've had my crypto section verify it, and it's definitely from the Admiral. It explains why she sent Mr. Ankenbrandt on to speak to us, but she suggested—and I think it was a good suggestion—that you should talk to him yourself before reading her own report. I think she'd like you to form your own first impressions without any prior influence from her."

"Well, that all sounds suitably mysterious," Medusa said a bit tartly, then gazed at Ankenbrandt for several seconds. Despite his somewhat mouselike initial impression, he looked back without flinching. Not that he wasn't nervous; she could see that. But he concealed well.

"Very well, Mr. Ankenbrandt, I'll listen to what you have to say. Why don't we all be seated first though?"

Everyone found a chair, and the baroness sat back comfortably behind her desk.

"One thing I should add before we begin, Madame Governor," Khumalo said. She looked at him, and he shrugged. "Admiral Gold Peak personally interviewed Mr. Ankenbrandt before sending him on to us. I thought you should know she did so with a treecat present."

Medusa's almond eyes narrowed for a moment, then she nodded.

"Very well," she said again, then turned her attention back to Ankenbrandt. "Why don't you start, Mr. Ankenbrandt?"

✦   ✦   ✦

"My God, Admiral. Couldn't you give us just a *little* warning before dropping something like that on us again?" O'Shaughnessy demanded acidly the better part of two hours later.

Medusa's senior intelligence analyst was a lifelong civilian who had never been a huge fan of military intelligence before joining her staff. Over the last few years he'd learned to get along better than he ever had before with his uniformed colleagues, but there were moments when he backslid. And it was seldom helpful when he did, the baroness thought acerbically, since he tended to engage his mouth before his brain when that happened. Which was a pity, since he really did have a very *good* brain when he remembered to use it.

"If I may remind you, Gregor," she said, intervening before Khumalo could respond, "the Admiral

specifically told us when he introduced Mr. Ankenbrandt that *Admiral Gold Peak* wanted us to form
our own initial impressions cold. I happen to think
that was a good idea on her part, but whether it
was or not, he'd made it very clear before we ever
began why he hadn't pre-briefed either of us on it."

O'Shaughnessy colored at the unmistakable frost
in the governor's tone. He started to say something,
then made himself stop, and his nostrils flared as he
drew a deep breath.

"Yes, Milady." He looked Khumalo in the eye. "My
apologies, Admiral."

"Don't worry about it." Khumalo's tone might have
been just a little short, but he didn't let irritation
distract him. Instead, he turned back to Medusa.

"Milady, I very much doubt that you and Mr.
O'Shaughnessy could have been any more surprised
than I was when Ankenbrandt screened me and introduced himself with one of Admiral Gold Peak's authen-
ticator code words. And I *know* you couldn't have been
any more surprised than I was when he arrived aboard
Hercules and handed over a secure Navy message chip
from her. Having read her message—I've brought a
copy of it along for you and Mr. O'Shaughnessy—and
heard Ankenbrandt's story, though, I think we've got
a hexapuma by the tail in this one. And it's not even
really *our* hexapuma!"

"Assuming Ankenbrandt really is telling us the truth
and not a plant who's somehow found a way to fool
even a treecat when he lies, I'm afraid it *is* our hexapuma, Admiral," O'Shaughnessy said thoughtfully. He'd
obviously gotten over his initial pique and reengaged
his brain, Medusa noted. "This is incredibly clever on

someone's part. The potential consequences if dozens of planetary resistance movements get slaughtered when they believe—completely accurately, as far as they know—the Star Empire's promised to support them..."

He shook his head, his expression grim, and Khumalo nodded.

"That's approximately the analysis Admiral Gold Peak's sent along." The tall, heavily built admiral chuckled suddenly. "The analysis, I might add, which was initially proposed by Ensign Zilwicki."

"No, really?" Medusa smiled. "The acorn doesn't fall far from the tree, does it?"

"I don't believe she has any inclination to become a 'spook,' Madame Governor," Khumalo said. "Doesn't mean she doesn't have the instincts, though. And personally, I'm pretty sure she's onto something here. This has this Mesan Alignment's fingerprints all over it."

"Maximum return for minimum investment," O'Shaughnessy agreed, nodding firmly. "And misdirection, and directed at at least three targets I can see already. God only knows how many *secondary* targets this thing is aimed at!"

"The question is how we respond to it," Medusa pointed out. "I think you were right that this was something I had to hear first while wearing my Imperial Governor's hat, Augustus, but I'm going to have to go ahead and brief Joachim and his cabinet on it. Among other things, if Ankenbrandt's really a representative sample, the majority of messengers from any of these resistance movements are going to be heading right here to Spindle. The Quadrant's government needs to know they're coming."

Khumalo nodded, and Medusa pursed her lips, thinking for several moments. Then—

"Should I assume Lady Gold Peak sent a recommendation along with her report?"

"She did, Madame Governor."

"And you're not going to tell me what it was unless I pull it out of you with a pair of pliers, right?"

"A simple order to come clean will do, Madame Governor," Khumalo replied with a smile. "Still, I have to admit I'm curious to see whether your response parallels hers."

"All right, I'll give it to you." Her own smile faded, and her eyes hardened. "I think we need to send back orders to treat any messenger from a genuine resistance movement—it was as smart of her as I would have expected to use a treecat to verify Ankenbrandt's truthfulness—as if they really had been in contact with Manticore all along. I don't see how we can afford not to. At the same time, though, we have to be cautious. We don't know what kind of booby-traps the Alignment could have built into something like this. Don't forget those invisible starship of theirs. A few of them tucked away to ambush our units responding to a resistance movement's call for assistance could do a lot of damage."

She cocked an eyebrow at Khumalo, and the burly admiral nodded.

"That's almost exactly what Admiral Gold Peak recommended," he said, and reached into his breast pocket. He extracted a chip folio and laid it on Medusa's desk. "Here's her actual report, including the treecat's—Alfredo's—assessment of Ankenbrandt's truthfulness."

"Thank you." Medusa scooped up the folio. She looked at it for a moment, then tossed it to O'Shaughnessy.

"You take a run through it first, Gregor. Be thinking about it after you finish so we can exchange notes as soon as *I'm* through with it."

"Yes, Milady."

"Admiral Khumalo, unless Gregor and I come up with something that causes me to change my mind, we'll be sending a dispatch to Lady Gold Peak before the end of the day confirming her own analysis and proposed course of action. At the same time, though, we obviously need to kick this farther up the chain to Foreign Secretary Langtry, Prime Minister Grantville, and Her Majesty, as well. I'd like you, Captain Shoupe, and Commander Chandler to provide your own individual appreciations to accompany that report back to Landing."

"Yes, Milady."

"In that case, as Duchess Harrington would say," she smiled, "let's be about it."

✧ Chapter Twenty-Nine

"YOU KNOW," MICHELLE HENKE said thoughtfully, "I'm beginning to wonder exactly what qualifications the Sollies look for in candidates for their naval academy. I mean there has to be a filtering process. You couldn't just go out and pick middies at random and get such an invariably stupid crop of flag officers. There *has* to be some kind of system. If you just picked names out of a hat, for example, *somebody* would have to have a functional brain. Right?"

"You'd like to think so, anyway, Ma'am," Gervais Archer replied. He'd been working quietly on his minicomp when the dispatches couriered to Tillerman from Spindle arrived. "May I ask what prompted the observation at this particular time, though?"

"Oh, you certainly may," she said much more grimly, and entered a command. The dispatch she'd been viewing appeared on Gervais' display, and his eyes widened slightly as he saw the security header. He started to ask her if she was sure about giving him access but quickly changed his mind. Countess Gold Peak didn't make that sort of careless mistake. Besides, as her flag lieutenant, he needed access to all sorts of information that didn't generally come the way of someone as junior as he was.

The message had come directly from the Lynx Terminus, relayed to the Tillerman System and addressed to Admiral Bennington for his information, since the Lynx CO hadn't been aware the countess had moved to that system herself. The addressee list in the header showed the same message had been sent to Admiral Khumalo and Baroness Medusa in Spindle. It would have reached the Quadrant's capital star system just over two weeks ago, but the decision to copy it to Bennington in Tillerman meant Tenth Fleet's CO had gotten the information at least four or five days sooner than she would have if she'd had to wait for it to be relayed from Spindle. Now Gervais sat back, reading quickly, and his expression grew bleaker with every sentence. Then he came to the tabular data at the end.

"*Shit.*"

He blushed suddenly, that dark magenta shade only a true redhead could accomplish, and looked up.

"Sorry about that, Ma'am. But... but—"

"But shit," she said, nodding. "I've heard the term before. Even used it on occasion, Gwen. And I can't say I fault your word choice."

"What was the lunatic *thinking*?" Gervais shook his head. "I don't think even Crandall would've fired in a situation like that!"

"I'm not so sure there's *anything* Crandall wouldn't have done," Michelle. "On the other hand, you may have a point. And apparently there's been some speculation back in Manticore about just how he might have been 'helped' into doing it."

"More of that mind control stuff, Ma'am?" Gervais' tone mingled disgust, apprehension, and doubt, and Michelle shrugged.

"I don't know, Gwen. Nobody knows what the damn stuff is or exactly how it works, and we're way behind the curve out here, thanks to how slowly information from home gets to us. According to the most recent speculation Duchess Harrington's shared with me, it's not really *mind* control, though, and I have to wonder whether or not it would be capable of arranging something like this."

Michelle sat silent for a handful of seconds, eyes narrowed and lips pursed while she considered the possibilities. Then her eyes refocused and she shrugged again.

"I'm afraid the most important point isn't *why* he did it but *that* he did it," she pointed out. "The cat, as my mother was always fond of saying when someone screwed up, is definitely amongst the pigeons now. Pile this on top of what happened to Crandall, and everybody's on the back of the hexapuma. So if we don't want to end up inside—or to lose a few fingers and toes to it, at least—I think it's time we do something a bit more proactive than just waiting around for the next Solly fleet to sail obligingly into disaster."

"Yes, Ma'am." Gervais nodded in understanding. "Do you want me to set up an electronic conference, or would you prefer to have them over for supper tonight?"

"A rule I learned from Duchess Harrington a long time ago, Gwen," Michelle said with a smile. "Two rules, actually. Never discuss electronically what you have time to discuss in person, and nothing builds a sense of teamwork and mutual trust like talking things over across a meal. You might want to write that down for your own later career."

"Yes, Ma'am. I will," Gervais replied. "So who do you want invited?"

"Better make it all the task group and squadron commanders," she said after a moment. "Talk to Chris, though. If there's room in my dining cabin to fit in the divisional commanders, as well, that might not be a bad idea. And see to it that Commander Adenauer and Captain Armstrong are on the guest list. For that matter, let's get Commander Larson into the mix, too."

"Yes, Ma'am." Gervais nodded. "I'll get right on it."

❖   ❖   ❖

Chris Billingsley had done his usual efficient job of arranging the dining cabin. They'd been able to fit in more people than Michelle would have thought possible, and all of her divisional commanders were present, after all. It made for a large crowd, and she doubted they were going to accomplish a great deal of detailed planning and organization for what she had in mind, but that wasn't really why she'd called these people together. She and her staff had already completed most of that.

She waited until the excellent supper had been completed, the deserts had been consumed, the dishes had been cleared away, and her subordinates sat back with their beverages of choice. Then she tapped her crystal brandy snifter lightly with a fork. It chimed musically, and she cleared her throat as heads turned towards her all along the linen-covered horseshoe of the supper tables.

"I trust all of you enjoyed the meal?" she asked

with a smile, and a rumble of approval came back. "Good." Her smile grew broader. "I wouldn't want Master Steward Billingsley to get a swelled head or anything, but he does set a nice table, doesn't he?"

This time the rumble was one of laughter, broken here and there by a few fervent declarations of agreement. She let it subside, then sat back in her chair and surveyed the officers of her fleet.

She'd arrived at Tillerman only ten T-days ago, and she could have wished for a little longer to exercise with her complete order of battle—minus, of course, what she'd sent off to Mobius and what she'd left in Montana. Admiral Bennington had obviously kept his people on their toes, however, and the units she'd brought with her from Montana had slotted smoothly back into place with them.

No admiral's ever really satisfied with how much time she's had to work up her command, Mike, she told herself. Or at least, no admiral worth her beret is ever satisfied, because you can always tweak things somewhere. But they're good. They're really good, and there'll be time enroute for more exercises. If you screw up, it won't be because of them.

"I'm sure you've all had time to at least skim the dispatches we've received from Spindle," she continued, her expression and voice both considerably grimmer than they had been. "And I'm also sure that, like me, you find it difficult to believe even a Solly flag officer could have been stupid enough to pull the trigger when Duchess Harrington had the deck so totally stacked against him. Nonetheless, he did, and that leaves me with some decisions to make."

She paused, and the dining cabin was silent, every

set of eyes fixed upon her. Somehow the stars on her collar seemed heavier than they had when she sat down.

"The Solarian League has now deliberately violated the territory of the Star Empire of Manticore twice. Both of those violations were clearly preplanned acts of military aggression in what the perpetrators believed would be overwhelming force. In both cases, the senior Solarian officer was offered multiple opportunities to rethink his or her actions and back off. In both cases, the officer in question chose not to do so. The Star Empire's sought a diplomatic resolution to this confrontation—which, I remind all of us, began when a Solarian admiral destroyed a Manticoran destroyer division in time of peace and without warning—from the beginning. The Solarian League has declined to meet our efforts even halfway.

"I realize there's considerable evidence to support the idea that the League is being manipulated by this Mesan Alignment. In fact, I believe that to be true. But however it's happened, we've been placed on a collision course with the Solarian League and it shows absolutely no sign of being willing to turn aside. Moreover, Mesa couldn't manipulate the League into such actions if the League weren't already primed for them and corrupt enough to find them a comfortable fit."

She paused once again, briefly, letting eyes like brown flint sweep the assembled faces.

"What we face is a war against the largest, most populous, most powerful star nation in history. Not a confrontation, not a conflict, not a crisis. Not any longer. A *war*. And wars, as we've discovered against the People's Republic of Haven, aren't won by standing on the defensive. At the moment, we enjoy a crushing combat advantage. How long that advantage will last is impossible to estimate, and it seems evident to me that it's our duty to our Empire and our Empress to use that advantage as decisively as possible and as quickly as possible. And it's also this fleet's specific responsibility to safeguard the star systems and citizens of the Talbott Quadrant. The best way to do both of those things, in my opinion, is to take the war to the Sollies. We didn't start it; they did, and now they can deal with the consequences of their own actions."

Her voice was ribbed with battle steel, and her face might have been carved out of obsidian. Most of the officers listening to her knew she had been given no new orders along with the dispatches. That what she was truly proposing was to act entirely upon her own initiative. Yet they also knew the Manticoran tradition was that flag officers were *expected* to exercise their initiative. Not normally in situations with the potential consequences this one offered, perhaps, but still...

"I propose to move upon the Meyers System as soon as possible," she said flatly. "Tenth Fleet will depart Tillerman no later than thirty-six hours from now. Our mission will be to force the surrender of Commissioner Verrochio and the entire Madras Sector. My intention is to neutralize this sector as a potential base for operations against the Talbott Quadrant and to position ourselves to threaten the League's flank in order to force them to split their attention between us and any additional future operations against the Old Star Kingdom or our allies. I've already dispatched a request to Spindle to send forward additional ground forces from the Quadrant Guard's new training programs as quickly as possible to serve as garrisons. With them to provide a 'boots on the ground' occupying force and LACs and missile pods to provide a space-based deterrent to anything short of a heavy Solly battle squadron, we should be able to secure the sector and thus protect the Talbott Quadrant and cover our backs. I anticipate that once we've done that, we will move on towards additional objectives in the Verge or even into the Shell."

She paused once more and inhaled deeply. It was very quiet in the dining cabin as the weight of her measured words sank home. As her subordinates grappled with the realization that their admiral truly did intend to take the war to the Solarian League.

"In a few moments," she said finally, "we'll begin discussing the nuts and bolts of that movement. My staff has already completed the plans to get us underway and for our initial entry into the Meyers System. We've put together several possible scenarios for operations there, and we'll spend the trip gaming them out in the simulators. But before we get to that—"

She gathered up her brandy snifter and looked down the table to her flag lieutenant. He looked back at her, and she nodded slightly.

Gervais Archer rose, gathering up his own wine glass, and raised it.

"Ladies and Gentlemen," he said, "I give you the Empire, the Empress, and the Navy. *And damnation to the Sollies!*"

JULY 1922 POST DIASPORA

"Why is it that people like you always think you're more ruthless than people like me?"

—Commodore Sir Aivars Terekhov,
　　Royal Manticoran Navy

⬩ Chapter Thirty

LIEUTENANT COMMANDER HIROSHI HAMMOND, SLNS *Oceanus'* tactical officer, had the watch. At the moment, he was tipped back in the chair at the center of the light cruiser's command bridge, trying unsuccessfully to think about nothing at all as yet another late-night watch crept towards its end with all the fleetness of a crippled snail. There hadn't been anything for *Oceanus* to do over the last local week or so, thank God, but he hated nights like this. Sitting in orbit around a backwater planet like Mobius Beta with nothing to do had to be the most mind-numbingly boring duty in the entire galaxy even at the best of times, far less times like these, and he hated the way it turned his mind inward, left him no choice but to contemplate things he'd far rather not think about at all.

Still, thinking about some things damned well beat hell out of actually *doing* them. Hiroshi Hammond had been called upon to do some pretty crappy things during his career. That happened a lot in Frontier Fleet, whatever the recruiters said, and Hammond came from a well-established naval family. He couldn't pretend he hadn't known that was the case going in. But the first week or so after their arrival in-system... that had been bad.

At least it's going to be over soon, he told himself, gazing up at the deckhead, trying to close his mind to what was happening on the planet so far below his ship. *One way or the other, it's going to be over. And I'm not going to have to kill any more towns before it is.*

Now if he could only figure out some way to absolve himself of his crushing sense of guilt for what he'd already done.

God damn *Brigadier Yucel*. The thought rolled through the back of his brain with the cold, measured precision of a prayer. His had been the hand that pressed the button, but the order had come from her, and if there was any justice in the universe—

"Hyper footprint! *Multiple* hyper footprints!"

The sudden announcement from the senior tactical rating of the watch twitched Hammond up out of his bleak reverie. He snapped his chair upright and turned towards Lieutenant Gareth Garrett, *Oceanus'* junior tactical officer, who was holding down the tac section at the moment.

It was obvious Garrett had been just as surprised as Hammond, but the JTO was already leaning forward, hands moving across his console as the icons from the combat information center appeared upon his display.

"CIC makes it thirteen sources, Sir," the lieutenant reported after a moment, and Hammond felt his muscles tighten. "They're half a light-minute outside the hyper limit," Garrett continued. "That puts them at a range of two-one-five-point-nine million klicks.

Current closing velocity niner-one-three KPS. Acceleration five-point-seven KPS squared."

"Class IDs?" Hammond asked.

"We won't have anything lightspeed for another twelve minutes or so, Sir," Garrett replied in a curiously flat voice. "But from the footprints, CIC is calling it twelve cruisers...and a superdreadnought."

"A *super*—?"

Hammond cut off the automatic—and stupid—repetition and closed his mouth tightly. Garrett was young, but not young enough to make that kind of mistake. If he said CIC had identified a superdreadnought, then that was what CIC had told him.

Even if the massive ship's observed acceleration *was* a full KPS² higher than *Oceanus* could have turned out with a zero safety margin on her inertial compensator.

Manties, Hammond thought while icicles formed in his bone marrow. *With that kind of accel, it's got to be Manties. And if it is...*

He decided not to think about that as his thumb reached for the general quarters button.

❖   ❖   ❖

"Anything from them?" Commander Tremont Watson demanded as he strode explosively onto *Oceanus'* bridge.

"No, Sir." Lieutenant Branston Shang, the light cruiser's communications officer, had managed to beat the CO to the command deck. Now he looked over his shoulder at Watson and shook his head. "Given the range, there won't be for at least another three minutes, even assuming they know we're here to be transmitting to, Sir," he added respectfully.

Watson nodded curtly and crossed to the command chair Hammond had abandoned upon his arrival.

It was an indication of the CO's state of mind that he'd asked the question in the first place, Hammond thought. Or perhaps the original range figures simply hadn't registered with him. Of course, if that was true, it was a pretty significant comment on Watson's state of mind all by itself, he reflected as the CO dropped into the chair he'd just vacated.

"Any more details on them, Hiroshi?"

"Not really, Skipper." Hammond shrugged unhappily. "They only made their alpha translation nine minutes ago, so we still don't have any lightspeed confirmation, but CIC's confident about their mass estimates and wedge strengths."

"And about the acceleration numbers, I presume," Watson said grimly.

"Yes, Sir." Hammond wasn't looking—or feeling—any happier. "They're up to a closing velocity of just under four thousand KPS. GG"—he nodded at Garrett—"makes it three hours and fourteen minutes to a zero/zero intercept with the planet . . . and us, of course. Turnover in about an hour and a half. Velocity at turnover will be right on thirty-five thousand KPS."

"Wonderful."

Watson punched controls on the command chair armrest, deploying his own displays, then looked back up at Hammond.

"All right. You're relieved. Take your station and send GG off to the Exec."

"I stand relieved," Hammond said formally, and twitched his head at Garrett. "You heard the Skipper, GG. I've got it; shag your butt down to Command Bravo."

"Yes, Sir!"

Garrett popped up out of his station chair and left for the cruiser's backup command deck at a run. Hammond settled into his place, taking over the tactical console and wishing he could believe anything he might do could make any difference at all to what was about to happen.

❖   ❖   ❖

"I don't suppose anyone's tried to contact us yet, Atalante?" Sir Aivars Terekhov asked.

"No, Sir." Lieutenant Atalante Montella looked up from her console and shook her head, her expression grim. "I wish someone would," she added. "I'd a lot rather be dealing with that than listening to *this*, Sir."

She gestured at the small display in front of her, where a man in the uniform of the Mobius Presidential Guard sat at a desk in front of crossed planetary flags, reading from his prepared notes. The sound was muted, but she'd shunted the feed to her earbug. Commander Pope, Terekhov's Chief of Staff, and Lieutenant Commander Mateuz Ødegaard, his staff intelligence officer, were listening along with her over their own earbugs, and their expressions were as grim as her own.

Terekhov nodded in understanding. He'd listened to five or six minutes of the "news" transmissions from Mobius himself before he'd handed it off to Pope and Ødegaard. He'd felt guilty about doing that, but he'd also decided it would be far better to distance himself from it, at least for now. The last thing he needed was to be listening to that kind of crap when he might very well be making decisions about who lived and who died in the next few hours. He couldn't afford to open himself to that sort of rage, however deserved it might be, so he turned to Commander Stillwell Lewis, instead.

"How much longer for the platforms to give us a good look at the planetary orbitals, Stilt?" he asked.

"Not long, Sir," his operations officer replied. "They're only about ninety-six light-seconds from Mobius Beta, now. In fact, if there's anything in orbit with active impellers, it's got to be on the far side of the planet from us at the moment, or we'd already have picked it up."

"Good."

Terekhov tipped back in his command chair, gazing at the master plot. *Quentin Saint-James* had reentered normal-space twenty-six minutes earlier. During that time, she'd increased her n-space velocity to just over ninety-four hundred kilometers per second and traveled just under 7.8 million kilometers towards the planet officially designated Mobius Beta. During that same interval, the Ghost Rider recon platforms they'd deployed as soon as they'd made their alpha translation had traveled ten and a half light-minutes—almost 200 million kilometers—at their vastly higher acceleration. In fact, they were already decelerating towards a zero/zero rendezvous with the planet.

He had a pretty good idea what those platforms were going to find. The "news" transmissions to the Delta Belt habitats which *Quentin Saint-James* had intercepted since translating back into normal-space made it abundantly clear that the Solarian intervention battalions the MLF had feared were underway had beaten his own force to the Mobius System. And that meant there had to be—

"We've got them, Sir," Lewis said suddenly, and Terekhov's eyes narrowed as a quartet of impeller signatures appeared on the plot, creeping around the icon of the planet. "The platforms are still ninety-two light-seconds out, but we should be getting good visual in another minute or so," the ops officer continued. "CIC is calling them destroyers for now, but—"

He paused again for a moment, studying his displays carefully, then looked back at Terekhov.

"Correction, Sir. It looks like a *Morrigan*-class light cruiser and a trio of *War Harvest*-class destroyers. One of the tincans could be a *Rampart*, though. With all the refits Frontier Fleet's destroyer fleet's been through—"

He shrugged, and Terekhov nodded. At this range, even Ghost Rider platforms were doing well to have given them that much information.

"Nothing else with hot nodes?" he asked.

"No, Sir. But we're picking up a good-sized merchant hull on visual. If I had to guess, I'd guess it was the transport OFS used to haul in its troops, but we can't confirm that at this point. I don't see anything else they could've used, though."

"Makes sense," Terekhov agreed. He gazed at the display for another minute or so, then sat back in his chair again and looked at his chief of staff.

"If their nodes are up, I'm guessing it's because they've figured out we're coming to call, Tom," he said.

"Probably," Commander Pope agreed. "I can't think of any other reason they'd be sitting in orbit putting time on the nodes, and even Sollies should've picked up our footprints at this piddling little range. Of course," he smiled thinly, "if they've got a good read on our tonnages, they've got to be feeling mighty unhappy right now. Especially if they figure *Cloud*'s a waller!"

Terekhov snorted in agreement. Just his cruisers would have been enough to make mincemeat out of those obsolescent vessels, even without Mark 16s.

With Mark 16s, his flagship could have killed all of them all by herself. And a superdreadnought—*any* superdreadnought, far less an SD(P)—which was exactly what Captain Simone Weiss' CLAC had to look like to the Sollies' gravitic sensors, could have obliterated them with a single broadside.

Of course, if these . . . people had any idea what modern LACs were capable of, Cloud *would probably scare them even worse than an SD,* he thought. *And the acceleration numbers have to be giving them furiously to think, too.*

"Now that we've found them, do you want to talk to them, Sir?" Pope asked after a moment, and Terekhov scratched his chin thoughtfully.

"An interesting question," he decided after a moment. "In fact—"

He turned to look at his youthful flag lieutenant.

"Tutorial time, Helen," he said with a slight smile.

"Yes, Sir?" If Ensign Zilwicki felt any trepidation she hid it well, he thought.

"Opinion, Ms. Zilwicki. Do we talk to them now, or do we let them wait?"

Helen's eyes narrowed as she considered the question. She was too busy thinking to notice the way several of Terekhov's staffers looked at one another with smiles, not that it would have bothered her if she had noticed. She'd grown accustomed to Terekhov's impromptu quizzes, and she knew it was a serious question, despite his quizzical tone.

"I think not, Sir," she said after a moment.

"Why not?" he asked.

"As you and Commander Pope just said, they have to know we're here by now, Sir. And from our acceleration numbers, they've got to have a pretty good guess who we are. Under the circumstances, I think it makes more sense to let them sweat until either they break down and talk to us or *we're* good and ready to talk to *them*."

"Why?"

"Anyone with a working brain would have to realize they're toast if it comes to a fight, Sir," she said. "On the other hand, these are Sollies, and we all know how reasonable *they* are. And to be fair, they probably haven't heard anything but bits and pieces—if that—about what's been going on elsewhere. Since they came from Meyers, they have to know what happened at New Tuscany and Spindle, but they probably haven't heard anything about Saltash." She shrugged. "If they haven't, they may think the same way Dueñas did and figure we'll hesitate about pulling the trigger if it comes to it. So I think it'd be a good idea to let some of that Solly arrogance soften, and if we let them sweat, we take the psychological advantage no matter who finally winds up opening communications. If they end up driven to talk to us, they start out in a position of weakness, and Sollies just aren't used to finding themselves places like that. And the longer *we* wait to talk to *them*, the longer they have to see our 'superdreadnought' coming at them and think about all the things it can do to them." She smiled nastily. "I don't care if they *are* the Invincible Solarian League Navy, that's *gotta* make 'em nervous, Sir! And if we use a Hermes buoy when we finally do talk to them . . ."

Her voice trailed off, and her expression turned absolutely beatific.

"I see." Terekhov regarded her thoughtfully for a moment, then nodded. "Works for me," he said, and smiled at Pope. "And now that Ensign Zilwicki has so masterfully summarized her proposed approach, let's give some thought to making it work most effectively."

◇   ◇   ◇

"And I don't give a good goddamn *who* the hell it is!" Brigadier Francisca Yucel snapped.

"But, Ma'am," Commander Watson began desperately, "that's a *superdreadnought*! We can't fight a super—"

"That's enough!" Yucel barked. "You don't even know who it is yet!"

"At those acceleration rates, the only people it *can* be are the Manties," Watson replied. "And if it is—"

"And if it is, they have exactly zero right to be here," Yucel shot back. "Mobius is a sovereign star system. The Manties have no legal standing here at all!"

"Ma'am, I realize that. But given what happened at Spindle, I think we have to assume—"

"You're not going to 'assume' *anything* until I tell you to, Commander. Is that perfectly clear?" Yucel glared at him from his communications display, gray eyes flinty. He stared back at her for a handful of seconds, then nodded jerkily.

"Better," she said in a marginally less angry tone. She sat back in her chair and waved one hand in an impatient gesture. "I understand why you're anxious, Commander Watson, but let's not let panic start dictating our reactions, all right? Yes, they hammered Admiral Crandall at Spindle. And, yes, as far as I can tell the Manties don't have a single functional brain cell among them. But not even *Manties* could be stupid enough to actually open fire on a Solarian Navy squadron in the territorial space of a Solarian ally!"

"With all due respect, Ma'am, they fired on Admiral

Byng in New Tuscany," Watson responded, and her nostrils flared.

"Yes, they did, Commander," she agreed coldly. "But New Tuscany wasn't a Solarian ally at the time, either. And whoever this is, it's not that crazy bitch Gold Peak, either—not in command of a force this small. No." She shook her head. "This is some captain or commodore or junior rear admiral, and whoever it is probably doesn't even know we're here yet."

"Ma'am, you're senior to me," Watson said. "But their track record suggests to me that they might just go ahead and pull the trigger after all."

Francisca Yucel closed her eyes and counted to ten. What she really wanted to do was to rip someone's eyeballs out. Watson's preferably, but almost anyone else's would have done in her present mood.

Why? she wondered. *Why does every single idiot in a Navy uniform think the frigging Manties are ten meters tall? Why can't any of them see that it doesn't matter how good their damned missiles are? They're one little pimple of a "star nation," and Frontier Security should have squashed them years ago instead of letting them get so fucking full of themselves. Them and their precious wormhole. They think it makes them the lords of creation, that their shit doesn't stink! But they're about to find out differently, aren't they? That maniac Gold Peak's gone too far, and now her precious Star Empire knows exactly how a cockroach feels before the hammer comes down.*

Personally, Francisca Yucel couldn't wait for that moment, and she was getting sick and tired of so-called officers who couldn't get their heads out of their asses long enough to realize that any Manty with a brain bigger than a radish had to be scared shitless of pissing the League off even worse.

"Commander," she said after a long, fulminating moment, "there's no way the Manties would risk another shooting incident with the SLN, especially in a podunk little system like this one. Whatever they may have managed to do to Admiral Crandall at Spindle, I doubt they brought their damned system defense pods along with them. And even if they did, they have to know what would happen to them in a real war with the League. *Gold Peak* might be crazy enough to push it, but by this time, their government has to be trying to figure out some way—any way—to crawl out of the crack she's gotten them into. If these bastards had gotten here before us, managed to help the frigging terrorists overthrow President Lombroso and then signed some sort of treaty with the 'new government,' that might be one thing. But they don't have even *that* much of a legal fig leaf. That leaves them with no standing at all under interstellar law, and the League would have every right to assist Lombroso in resisting any demands they might make. That's a tripwire nobody in command of a force this small is going to want to cross."

Watson looked at her com image, trying to believe she might be right. Unfortunately, he didn't think she was. And even more unfortunately, she was in command.

"So what, exactly, do you want me to do, Ma'am?" he asked finally.

"I don't want you to do anything, Commander. Just sit there. They're the ones intruding into Mobian space, so let them do the talking when they finally realize we got here before them."

"And if they start making threats, Ma'am?"

"Then you tell them to go straight to hell, Commander," she said flatly.

✧   ✧   ✧

"Coming up on thirty-one million kilometers, Sir," Commander Lewis announced.

"Thank you, Stilt."

Terekhov took another sip from the cup of coffee Chief Steward Agnelli had just delivered to him, then looked at Lieutenant Montella.

"Are you ready to transmit, Atalante?"

"Yes, Sir." Montella grinned at him. She was rather looking forward to this. "Whenever you are, Sir."

"Fine. Helen?" Terekhov smiled at Helen and held out his coffee cup. "Take care of this for me for a few minutes, would you? It probably wouldn't help my hard-bitten commodore's image."

"Oh, I don't know, Sir." She smiled back as she took the cup obediently. "Personally, I think it might actually underscore your aura of confidence."

"Of course it would. Just don't go drinking it!"

"Wouldn't dream of it, Sir. Joanna would hurt me."

Terekhov chuckled with a bit more amusement than he actually felt, then turned back to face the com pickup.

"All right, Atalante. Let's do it."

✧   ✧   ✧

"Sir!" Lieutenant Shang announced. "I've got a com request from the Manties!"

Commander Watson looked up quickly. The announcement was scarcely unexpected. In fact, the tension of *not* hearing from the Manties had been twisting his nerves tighter and tighter as the silent juggernaut of those tactical icons swept steadily towards his own outnumbered and outgunned command.

They'd been in-system for almost two and a half hours now. In fact, they'd made their turnover and begun decelerating forty-eight minutes ago. The range was down to thirty-one million kilometers—under two light-minutes—and he'd started sweating the moment it dropped to forty million. If they'd brought along any of the missile pods they'd used on Admiral Crandall, he was inside their envelope, and they were still better than twenty million kilometers *outside* his.

He knew everyone else on his command deck could do the math as well as he could, and he'd seen the tension growing in his officers' faces as the minutes crawled past. Yet there was something about Shang's announcement . . .

"Calm down, Branston!" Watson said. "Let's not get too excited here."

"But, Sir . . . they're asking specifically for you. And they're transmitting from less than forty thousand kilometers out!"

"What?" Watson straightened in his command chair. "What do you mean, specifically for me? By *name*?"

"Not by *your* name, Sir, but they're requesting SLNS *Oceanus'* commanding officer."

Watson stared at the communications officer. None of his ships had activated their transponders, so how the *hell* could the Manties possibly know his flagship's name? And what was that about forty thousand kilometers? How could anybody get a communications relay that close without any of his sensors even noticing it on its way in? And why should they *bother* to, even if they could?

My God. The thought hit him like a sudden bucket of ice water. *My God, they didn't just get a* com relay *that close; they got* sensor platforms *that close—close enough to read ships' names off our goddamned hulls—and we never saw a frigging thing!*

The implications were terrifying, and he suddenly wished Francisca Yucel was up here in orbit and *he* was safely down on the planet.

"Very well, Branston," he said as calmly as he could, suppressing a sudden urge to lick his lips. "Put it on my display here."

"Yes, Sir."

The small communications screen deployed from his command chair came to life with the face of a dark-haired, olive-complexioned young woman in the black and gold uniform of the Star Empire of Manticore. For a moment, nothing about her struck him as peculiar, until he suddenly realized she was in *uniform*, not wearing a skinsuit.

"I am Lieutenant Atalante Montella, Royal Manticoran Navy," she said. "Am I addressing the commanding officer of SLNS *Oceanus*?"

"You are," he said, his mind still grappling with the absence of that skinsuit. It was like a deliberate declaration that the lieutenant on his display was beyond any range at which he could possibly have threatened her. Which was true enough, he supposed, but still...

"I'm Commander Tremont Watson, Solarian League Navy," he continued. "What can I do for you, Lieutenant?"

He sat back to wait out the two hundred-second lightspeed delay, but—

"Please stand by for Commodore Terekhov," she said, less than *two* seconds later.

He twitched, his eyes flaring wide open. That was

impossible! They were still more than thirty million kilometers away! Nobody could—

Oh, shit, a little voice said almost calmly deep down inside. *They* do *have FTL com capability! And if they've got recon platforms that close, platforms that can send back targeting data faster-than-light . . .*

He closed his eyes for a moment as the implications crashed over him.

"Good evening, Commander Watson." A blond haired, bearded Manticoran officer replaced Montella on his display. The Manty wore a commodore's insignia, and his blue eyes were remarkably cold. "I am Sir Aivars Terekhov, Royal Manticoran Navy."

Every Solarian officer in the Madras Sector knew *that* name, and Watson felt a solid lump of ice materialize in the pit of his stomach as he recognized it and remembered a star system named Monica.

We are so fucked, that same little voice whispered.

"Commodore," he replied out loud, fighting to sound normal . . . and knowing he'd failed. "May I ask what brings you to Mobius, Sir?"

"Yes, you may." Terekhov smiled thinly, and his voice was cold. "We're here in response to an urgent request for humanitarian assistance."

"Humanitarian assistance?" Watson heard the faint, sickly edge in his own voice as he repeated the words.

"I think that's a suitable way to describe it," Terekhov said. "Certainly in light of the 'news broadcasts' we've been monitoring for the past couple of hours."

Sweat beaded Watson's hairline, but this time he said nothing. There was nothing he *could* say, really.

"Let me put this as clearly as I can, Commander," Terekhov continued after a moment. "I intend to put a stop to the butchery the Solarian League has been actively abetting in this star system. I intend to put a stop to it *now*, and I intend to take whatever steps are necessary to accomplish that objective. Which brings me to you."

"In ... what way?" Watson asked, cursing the slight catch in his voice.

"As I see it, you're part of the problem," Terekhov told him flatly. "You escorted the intervention battalions currently operating on Mobius Beta from the Madras Sector, and you've been supporting them since your arrival." Those icy blue eyes turned even colder. "We've already recorded the evidence of kinetic strikes, Commander Watson, so let's not waste anyone's time pretending you don't know exactly what I'm talking about. I'm willing to assume—for the moment, at least—that you're not the senior officer of this abortion of an operation. As such, I presume you were following someone else's orders, which gives you at least some legal cover. As one serving officer to another, however, we both know exactly what you should have said when given that order, don't we? So I'm afraid the technicalities of your chain of command don't buy you a whole lot with me."

Something shriveled inside Tremont Watson—in shame, this time, not in fear—but Terekhov gave him no opportunity to defend himself.

"You have two options, Commander, but only one chance to pick between them," the Manticoran said. "You can choose to take to your escape pods and small craft and scuttle your ships. Or you can choose not to, in which case I will blow them, and you, and every other man and woman aboard them, straight to hell from a range at which you won't even be able to scratch my paint. As a general rule, I don't much like butchering people who can't fight back. Given what's been happening on this planet, I'm willing to make an exception."

Those ice-blue eyes bored into Tremont Watson's soul.

"You have ten minutes to decide whether or not I do. Terekhov, clear."

✦ Chapter Thirty-One

SIR AIVARS TEREKHOV WATCHED his tactical plot as his flagship and the other units of his small task group settled into orbit around Mobius Beta. HMS *Cloud*'s LACs spread out around the planet, and Colonel Alex Simak's Marine assault shuttles moved out of the big CLAC's boatbays behind them. The bulk of the task group's small craft were otherwise occupied, however. They were busy collecting the lifepods of the Solarian personnel whose ships had blown themselves up an hour and a half before.

"All right, Atalante," he said. "Given how well Helen's prescription worked out with Commander Watson, I think we'll just let President Lombroso and Brigadier Yucel and friends sweat for a little bit before we talk to them, too. See if you can get a response over Ms. Summers' link, instead."

"Yes, Sir." Lieutenant Montella turned to her console, and Terekhov folded his arms across his chest as he gazed into the master visual display at the blue, green, and dun colored planet so far below.

Commander Pope stepped up beside him.

"Do you really think Breitbach's going to be in a position to answer, Sir?" the chief of staff asked softly.

"I don't know, Tom," Terekhov replied. He twitched his shoulders. "Given what these people have been up to, I just don't know. If his security held, maybe. But..."

His voice trailed off, and he shook his head. The news reports had been bad enough on the way in; now that they'd entered orbit and deployed air-breathing recon platforms, it was even worse. Several square blocks of Landing lay in charred, flattened ruins. Most of the destroyed structures—which happened, just coincidentally of course, to lie in the middle of the capital city's low income housing, far away from the important corporate assets downtown—seemed to have been old-style construction, possibly left over from the city's earliest days and built out of native materials. Few of those buildings had been more than five or six stories tall, but two much more modern towers had been caught in the holocaust and towered over the ashes at their feet like burned out Sphinxian crown oaks.

And then, of course, there were the half-dozen or so craters which could only have been created by kinetic strikes. Three of them, not that far from Landing, were surrounded by the tattered ruins of fire- and blast-shredded towns. None of them liked what that suggested, and not just because of the loss of life they undoubtedly represented. Kinetic weapons were a routine method of supplying fire support for planetary forces and had been for well over a thousand T-years. Over that time, they had been refined into precision weapons, capable of pinpoint strikes and almost infinitely variable effective yields. But no one had been interested in pinpoint accuracy when it came to *those* strikes. They'd been terror attacks—exactly the sort of attack the Eridani Edict was supposed to prevent, although he was certain Yucel and Lombroso would justify them as "military necessities"—and as he thought about them, Terekhov found himself wishing Watson hadn't taken his offer to abandon ship. But those scars were at least a week old; they lacked the immediacy of what was happening in Landing even now.

As Terekhov and Pope watched, the image on one of the secondary visual displays CIC had tied into their air-breathing recon platforms changed, and Terekhov's blue eyes were colder than arctic ice as he saw the line of bodies hanging from an obviously prefabricated, mass-produced gallows. There must have been twenty-five of them, he thought as the platform zoomed in on them, and not all of those bodies had belonged to adults.

"I want this imagery absolutely nailed down, Stilt," he said without looking away. He didn't raise his voice, yet a couple of people on the flag bridge flinched when they heard it. "I don't want any doubt, any ambiguity, about what we saw or where we saw it before we ever landed."

"Yes, Sir," Commander Lewis acknowledged.

Helen sat very still at her own console. She wanted to look away from those dangling bodies. They'd obviously been there for a while, judging by the extent of decay. Even as she watched, one of Mobius Beta's avians landed on the central beam of the gallows. It was one of the local planetary ecosystem's buzzard analogues, and she felt her gorge trying to rise as it stretched down its long, sinuous neck and began ripping at what had been the face of one of the smaller bodies.

So this is the ultra-civilized, oh-so-superior Solar-ian League's view of "protecting" another planet, she thought grimly. *And they have the gall to label the* Ballroom *terrorists?*

She felt her hands clenching into fists and made herself sit back, breathe deeply, and remember what Master Tye had taught her about channeling anger. It didn't seem to help as much as usual.

"Do you think that was Yucel or Yardley, Sir?" she heard Commander Pope ask, and Commodore Terekhov snorted harshly.

"Do you think it *matters?*" he asked in reply. "If it was Yardley, she did it with Yucel's knowledge and support. And from our intelligence reports on Yucel, not to mention what we monitored on the way in, she's the kind who's going to be 'hands-on' whenever she gets the opportunity."

"Agreed, Sir." Pope nodded. "But if it was Yardley's Presidential Guard thugs who actually carried out the hanging instead of the Gendarmerie, you know Yucel's going to claim it was all the local authorities of an independent star nation. *She* sure as hell didn't have anything to do with it!"

"And?" Terekhov turned his head to look at the commander. "No matter what really happened here she'll claim that in front of any tribunal. Or she would, if the opportunity ever arose." He smiled thinly. "And no tribunal or court of inquiry we could possibly impanel is ever going to prevent Abruzzi and his E & I shills from *claiming* it was Lombroso or Yardley. Unless, of course, they decide they can actually convince the Solly public *we* did it in the process of crushing the courageous local resistance to our callous imperialistic invasion. Then, having produced all of these perfectly serviceable atrocities, we decided we'd record them all and use them so our propaganda could fasten responsibility for them onto that splendid patriot and democratically elected president, Svein Lombroso, and Mobius' stalwart ally and defender, Brigadier Yucel."

Commander Pope, Helen noticed, looked like he really wished he thought Terekhov was joking with those last two sentences. For that matter, *she* wished she thought that.

The commodore saw his chief of staff's expression and grimaced.

"The last thing anybody on the other side's going to be interested in at this point is accurate reportage," he pointed out. "They've never felt any compunction about distorting the truth to justify their peacetime policies; why in heaven's name should they hesitate for a minute to manufacture atrocities out of whole cloth in *wartime*? And they won't even have to manufacture these. We'll have provided the visuals; all they'll have to do is cut and edit and modify the audio."

"Should we be providing it at all, then, Sir?" Pope asked, his eyes troubled.

"Of course we should. Sooner or later this war's going to be over. When that happens, accurate records are going to be essential, and not just from a dry, historical perspective. Even more importantly, we need to show our people what this is really about right now, while it's happening. That's the real reason I want Stilt to make sure we have every bit of this absolutely certified and verified. I'd love to see some of the people in Old Chicago responsible for this"—he tossed his head in the direction of those pitiful, decaying bodies—"treated to the same penalty, but I don't see that happening unless we actually physically occupy Old Terra, and somehow I don't see *that* happening, either. We can always hope, though. And in the meantime," his voice dropped, turning as icy as his eyes, "I want this evidence available when we deal with the people who actually did it."

"Yes, Sir." Pope nodded firmly. "I understand. But it's—"

"Excuse me, Commander," Atalante Montella interrupted respectfully. Pope and Terekhov turned towards her, and she looked at the commodore. "I don't have Mr. Breitbach, Sir," she said, "but I do have Ms. Blanchard."

"Do we have visual, or just audio?" Terekhov asked.

"Both, Sir. The signal quality isn't very good, though."

"Put her on the main display," Terekhov directed, and turned towards the display as a woman's image appeared on it. She was dark-haired and dark-eyed, with a strained, exhausted face smudged with dirt. An ugly bruise discolored her right cheek and temple, and a Solarian built pulse rifle was slung across her shoulder as she crouched over what was obviously a handheld com.

"Ms. Blanchard, I'm Commodore Aivars Alexsovitch Terekhov, Royal Manticoran Navy," he said. "We're here in response to Ms. Summers' message."

"Summers?" Blanchard's voice was as exhausted as she looked, and she shook her head. "Was that the name?" She grimaced. "I didn't know. Operational security."

"I don't think operational security's going to be an issue very much longer," Terekhov told her grimly.

"Maybe not. It's the only reason some of us are still alive, though." She scrubbed her hand across her face, smearing the dirt.

"I can believe that. Are you ready to trust me, though?"

"You had this com combination, and we saw the explosions from down here." She shrugged. "We've been getting our asses kicked for the last week. I don't see the bastards deciding they have to get tricky at this point."

"So I'll take that as a yes?" he asked dryly.

"Exactly." She managed a quick, fleeting grimace of a smile. "Oh, and by the way, we're happy as hell to see you." She shook her head again. "I've got to say, when Michael told me you folks were backing us, it surprised the hell out of me."

"You're not the only one," he said even more dryly. Then his eyes narrowed. "On the other hand, you just mentioned 'Michael.' Am I correct in assuming that was a reference to Michael Breitbach?"

"Yeah." She made a face. "After all this time, knowing you know both of our names makes me a little nervous. Nothing personal."

"Understandable. But may I ask why we got you at this combination and not him? My understanding from Ms. Summers was that this was Mr. Breitbach's combination."

"It is." Her weary voice was suddenly leaden. "Unfortunately, he's not here to answer."

"What happened?"

"He was on his way to meet with one of our cell leaders and there was a sweep through the area. He didn't come back." She raked the fingers of her right hand through her short cut, filthy looking hair.

"Do you think Yucel and Lombroso know who they caught?"

"No way." She shook her head hard. "It would've been all over what's left of the news channels if they knew they'd gotten him. He was unarmed, and he wasn't even carrying his com...which is why I happen to have it." Her image moved dizzyingly on the display as she swept the hand holding Breitbach's com around for emphasis. "I'm guessing they figure he's just one more civilian they've swept up."

"All right." Terekhov nodded. "That makes sense." He pursed his lips for a moment. "I haven't contacted Lombroso or Yucel yet. What's your situation? The *real* situation, I mean, not what they're putting out on the information channels."

"To be honest, it's almost as bad as they're saying it is," she admitted, setting the com down on a table or desk of some sort and perching herself on an overturned trash can. "Lombroso and that bitch Yardley started the sweeps a couple of weeks before Yucel got here. Beatings, casual brutality, secret arrests, something more imaginative when they had time for it. That kind of thing. Then they started the public executions." Her jaw tightened. "Not just for people who were actually caught doing something 'criminal,' either. They were making examples, and they didn't even pretend they weren't."

She fell silent for a moment, nostrils flaring, and Terekhov waited patiently.

"We couldn't hold our people when that kind of shit started. If Michael hadn't moved—and hadn't made sure everyone *knew* he was moving—he'd have lost control and Yardley would've picked us off one at a time as each cell tried something on its own. And he had a pretty good 'nothing left to lose' plan already in place. We damned near took Yardley, the PG's HQ, and the President's Palace in the first eighteen hours. Killed a bunch of the bastards, and shot up at least two thirds of their remaining armor."

For a moment, her eyes were fierce, proud. Then her shoulders slumped.

"Damned near wasn't good enough, though. We had three quarters of the capital, five other cities completely, and most of the countryside on this continent, but we couldn't break into the final compound, and then Yucel got here. Landed her damned intervention battalions and launched orbital strikes on half a dozen smaller cities and towns that had come over to our side. That's when Michael pulled us out of the other cities. He wouldn't give them any kind of excuse to do the same thing to a major population center. But he figured they wouldn't try the same crap on Landing. Too much real estate they don't want to lose, and any strikes would be too damned close to them. He was right about that, too, so they've been coming after us house by house." She bared her teeth. "We've been costing them, but you've seen the news channels."

"Yes, I have." Terekhov's eyes were fiery blue ice. "We haven't seen any imagery about the orbital strikes, though. Do you have a casualty estimate from them?"

His tone was calm, almost conversational, but his expression wasn't.

"Best guess is somewhere around four hundred and fifty thousand," Blanchard said.

"I see." Terekhov looked at her for a moment or two, then inhaled sharply. "Our recon platforms show you holding a crescent around the southern and western edges of the capital. Is that accurate?"

She nodded.

"And Yucel and Lombroso hold the area around the Presidential Palace?"

"They hold everything we don't," she said frankly. "Everything from the sports center to the tower complex just east of where I am now." She managed a tired grin. "I'm assuming you've got my signal located?"

"We know where you are," Terekhov agreed with a brief answering smile. "What about the eastern side of town, in closer to the Presidential Palace?"

"That's mainly been cleared. I mean, they've run out all the civilians, except for a handful of residential towers dedicated to off-worlders and corporate employees."

"And I gather from the newscasts that they're holding their prisoners in the soccer stadium?"

"That's right." She nodded again. "President Lombroso Memorial Soccer Stadium. Son-of-a-bitch just loves naming things for himself."

"What can you tell us about their security situation around the stadium?"

"Not much. They've pushed us too far back. I'm guessing you can see more from orbit than we can see from down here."

"You're probably right about that." Terekhov nodded again. He stood thinking, arms still folded across his chest, then nodded slowly, more to himself than to Blanchard.

"Thank you, Ms. Blanchard," he said. "I think it's time I had a few words with President Lombroso and his associates. Perhaps I can convince them of the error of their ways."

❖　　　❖　　　❖

Brigadier Francisca Yucel took another quick, angry turn around the luxurious office she'd been assigned in the Lombroso Arms Tower. The Lombroso Arms was across President Lombroso Boulevard from the Presidential Palace, and its thick ceramacrete walls made it virtually impervious to anything the rebels had been equipped with when she first arrived. It also gave her a commanding height as an observation post and a ground-based communications station.

"Her" office was huge, lavishly decorated, with floor-to-ceiling windows that looked directly down on the roof and ornate façade of the Presidential Palace. She'd enjoyed its comfort since her arrival, and her communication section had set up along with the rest of her staff in the larger office suite next door. Her lofty perch had let her oversee the systematic destruction of the scum who'd been about to kick Lombroso's worthless ass before she arrived, and she'd felt nothing but satisfaction as the effort progressed. She probably could have finished it sooner, but she'd wanted to be sure these worthless proles never forgot. That they never again even dared to think of raising their hands to Frontier Security or its allies.

Only now the fucking Manties had turned up and that worthless asshole Watson hadn't even *tried* to stop them. He'd just rolled over and blown up his own ships so the Manties didn't even have to waste any missiles on them! One of these days she'd settle his cowardly ass the way it deserved to be settled, but for now she had to deal with the goddamned *Manties*.

You didn't believe it, did you? she asked herself viciously. *Didn't want to.* Wang *did, damn him. But not you. You knew better.*

She snarled, burying the fear she didn't want to admit under fresh anger. They hadn't had anything to go on, really. A couple of hints from interrogation. Nothing concrete, and God knew the lying bastards would say anything—invent anything—if they thought it was going to keep somebody they cared for alive.

Admit it, she told herself. *You did believe the Manties were* involved, *it just never occurred to you they might be* this *involved. You figured you had plenty of time to settle these fuckers' hash before anyone back in Spindle even knew you were here. Jerk their goddamned rebels out from under their feet, and they wouldn't have any 'spontaneous uprising' to support. But you* didn't *have time, did you?*

No, she hadn't, and she gritted her teeth as she remembered how positive she'd been that the Manties would back down. That even they had to realize taking on the Solarian League was nothing more than glorified suicide. Obviously they were even stupider than she'd thought, and even now she took a grim, vengeful satisfaction from the thought of what this was going to cost them in the end. They'd pay one day—pay in spades!—for everything they'd done, for all their treachery and deceit.

But this wasn't "one day." This was *today*, and today the Manties were sitting up there in orbit, and they hadn't even tried to talk to her or that idiot Lombroso yet. They were just sitting there, letting her sit down here and rot, but it wasn't going to work. She had their fucking number. If they thought they were going to waltz in here and—

"Excuse me, Ma'am."

"What?" she snarled, wheeling around to face the

Mobian communications tech who'd dared to enter her office.

"There's someone on the com asking for you, Ma'am," the Presidential Guard tech said nervously, sweat beading his forehead. "He says he's somebody named Terekhov. Commodore Terekhov."

"Oh, he does, does he?"

Yucel felt her lips twist in anger. Terekhov. The same son-of-a-bitch who'd shot up the Monica System and started this whole frigging nightmare. She should've guessed.

The Mobian only stood there, looking at her, obviously uncertain whether he was supposed to answer or not and terrified to make the wrong choice. Her fingers flexed with the urge to rip his head off, but she made herself draw a deep breath, instead.

"All right. Put him on my desk display."

"Yes, Ma'am!"

The tech disappeared like smoke, and Yucel turned towards the office's enormous desk just as the display lit with the face of a blond, blue-eyed officer in the black and gold of the Royal Manticoran Navy.

"What?" she snapped.

"I assume I have the dubious privilege of addressing Brigadier Yucel?" The contempt in Terekhov's tone flicked Yucel like a whip.

"I'm Yucel," she confirmed in a harsh, hard-edged voice. "What the fuck d'*you* want?"

"I thought, much as the idea disgusts me, that I might offer you a chance to get off this planet alive." Terekhov's voice was like ice, his expression one of indifference. "Personally, I'd prefer to kill you where you stand. I've had the opportunity to observe your handiwork in some detail. However, since we're all civilized people here, I decided to give you my terms, first."

"Your *terms*?" she sneered. "Who the hell do you think you are? You come waltzing into this star system, you attack Navy starships, and now you have the sheer, unmitigated gall to tell me you're going to offer me *terms*? Well fuck you! One of us is here at the invitation of the legally constituted government of this star system, *Commodore* Terekhov, and it sure as hell isn't *you!*"

"A legally constituted government that's massacred— or allowed *you* to massacre—a half million or so of its citizens with kinetic strikes? *That* legally constituted government?"

"What a sovereign star nation does to suppress criminal insurrection is none of your goddamned business," she said harshly. "And what the Solarian Gendarmerie does at the request of that sovereign star nation is none of your business, either! So get your ships the hell out of this system."

"Not going to happen." Terekhov's calm, cold precision was a sharp contrast to the seething fury of her own tone. "To put this in terms even you may be able to understand, Brigadier, you're screwed. I don't care if we have to kill every single gendarme down there, and I certainly don't care if we have to kill *you*. But I'd just as soon avoid any additional damage to the Mobians' planet if I can. So here are those terms. You lay down your weapons, you march all your personnel out of Landing to a point to be designated by me, and you wait there until my Marines take you into custody."

"And then what happens in this fantasy of yours?" she demanded. "You shoot us all on the spot?"

"I'll admit the thought has a certain appeal," he said. "But, no. We take you into custody and we keep you there until a proper court can be convened to consider the actions of your personnel on this planet. All of you will receive a fair trial, and the guilty will receive the sentence commensurate with their crimes."

"You're out of your fucking mind." Yucel's voice was almost conversational. "You really think you're going to get away with trying and *shooting* Solarian gendarmes?"

"I was thinking more in terms of hanging, actually, since that seems to be your own favored form of execution, but we'll probably leave that up to the Mobians," he told her, and she barked a scornful laugh.

"And just what the hell do you think is going to happen to your pissant little Star Empire when the League finds out about that?" she demanded.

"I'll cross that bridge when I get to it," he told her flatly. "Not that I'm particularly worried about it in the short term."

"You may have kicked Crandall's ass at Spindle, but it's going to be different when the Navy knows what you've got and comes after you!" she spat.

"You obviously haven't paid any attention to reality in some time," Terekhov said. "And you're just a bit behind the news, too. For example, on the basis of what you've just said, I don't suppose you've heard about what happened to Vice Admiral Dubroskaya at Saltash, when five of our destroyers destroyed all four of her *battlecruisers*. Or about the fact that the Star Empire is now allied to the Republic of Haven. Or that between us, we now have somewhere around five hundred ships of the wall, any two of which could have controlled every missile we fired at Crandall in Spindle. Let's do some math here, Brigadier. If two of our ships can kill seventy of yours, and we've got five hundred of them, that means we can kill every superdreadnought in Battle Fleet, including the Reserve, about three times each."

He paused, smiling coldly at her, letting her see the total confidence in his eyes, then continued.

"According to the latest dispatches before I headed out for Mobius, your Admiral Filareta was on his way to Manticore with somewhere around four hundred of the wall. By this time, I'm sure he's arrived . . . and if he was foolish enough to actually fight when he got there, I doubt any of his ships lasted long enough to surrender. *I'm* certainly not worried about the outcome, anyway. Now, do you accept my terms or not?"

Yucel stared at him, her face momentarily slack with shock. Manticore and Haven *allied*? Allied against the *Solarian League*? He was lying. He had to be lying! But even as she thought that, something with thousands of icy little feet started crawling up and down her spine. If he wasn't lying, if he was telling the truth, that would explain why he'd been willing to take out Watson's ships. And if he really was ready to do what he'd just said he'd do to her personnel, to *her* . . .

The ice moving up and down her back seemed to settle in her belly. It was odd. She'd never realized her stomach could be simultaneously nauseated and frozen into a solid lump.

Panic surged suddenly, rising into her throat like

vomit, and she swallowed hard. For a moment, she knew exactly what it had felt like for countless malcontents and troublemakers when her gendarmes' pulser butts hammered on their doors. But then she forced herself to push the panic aside and glared at Terekhov's image.

"All right," she said. "Those are your terms. Well, here are *mine*. You stay the hell off this planet. You put one shuttle down here, one frigging Marine, and I start shooting prisoners. I've got over thirty thousand of them in the stadium. You're welcome to take a look for yourself. And I've got two companies of gendarmes over there. I can kill every fucking person in that stadium in five minutes flat, and if you try any shit like landing on this planet, I swear to God I will!"

"Courageous and determined to 'serve and protect' to the last, I see," Terekhov observed contemptuously, and Yucel flushed as he tossed the Solarian Gendarmerie's official motto into her teeth.

"Just try me and see," she snarled through gritted teeth.

"One more time, Brigadier, and my patience isn't unlimited. If you choose not to accept the terms offered, the consequences will be on your own head."

"What? You think I believe you'd come down here after me? Wreck the rest of this podunk city coming after my people *and* get everybody in the frigging stadium killed?" She sneered at him. "Not you. You've got to be the goddamned white knight in shining armor. Well, you come down here and screw around with us, and you'll get plenty of blood on that armor. I guarantee it!"

"I see. Perhaps I should be having this conversation

with President Lombroso. He might be perfectly willing to hand you and your gendarmes over to me if he thought it would save his own skin."

"Lombroso couldn't hand you candy from a baby! He's hiding in the damn basement—him and Yardley both! He deputized me to 'negotiate' with you, and I'm all done, friend. Now. Are you going to accept *my* terms? Or do I need to pass the order to shoot the first hundred or so prisoners to make my point?"

"Why is it," Terekhov asked conversationally, "that people like you always think you're more ruthless than people like me?"

Something about his tone rang warning bells in the back of Yucel's brain, but she refused to look away. She held her glare locked on him, refusing to back down, and he shrugged.

"Stilt?" he said without glancing away from Yucel.

"Yes, Sir?" a voice replied from outside his com pickup's field of view.

"Pass the word to Colonel Simak. Then set Condition Zeus."

"Condition Zeus, aye, aye, Sir."

"What the hell are you talking about?" Yucel snapped.

"I can't say it's been a pleasure speaking to you, Brigadier," Terekhov replied. "Educational, yes, in a disgusting sort of way, but not a pleasure. In fact, I'm just as happy we won't be speaking again."

"Good," she said. "Now get the fuck out of here before I change my mind and decide to shoot a couple of dozen of them to hurry you on your way!"

"Oh, I'm not afraid of that," he assured her. "In fact," he raised his wrist and glanced at his personal chrono, "you should be receiving my response to your terms"—those ice-blue eyes flicked back to her face—"just about now."

She frowned, wondering what the hell he was talking about.

She was still wondering two and a half seconds later when the kinetic projectile struck Lombroso Arms Tower at approximately thirty kilometers per second.

❖   ❖   ❖

The Mark 87 "Damocles" Kinetic Strike Package was a containerized weapon system designed to fit into any standard shipboard magazine and sized to deploy through a counter-missile launch tube. The KSP could be configured with several different types of payloads, but the most common variant—like the one which had been deployed from *Quentin Saint-James'* number three CM tube shortly after she'd entered orbit— carried a rack of six of the Royal Manticoran Marine Corps' M412 kinetic penetrators. Each penetrator was a six hundred and fifty kilogram dart fitted with its own small, short-lived but powerful impeller drive, a capacitor ring for onboard power, and a guidance package. By controlling acceleration rates and times, the M412 could produce an effective yield of up to one megaton...but this particular application called for a slightly smaller sledgehammer than that.

The projectile impacted at barely one tenth of a percent of light speed. The tower was enormous, the projectile wasn't all that huge, and its velocity might seem snail-like compared to the eighty percent of light speed a Mark 23 could attain, but it was sufficient. In fact, it produced an effective yield of just over sixty-seven kilotons as it struck dead center on the tower's roof at an angle of exactly ninety degrees and punched straight down, pithing it with a spike of plasma that vaporized everything in its path.

Admittedly, the results were positively anemic compared to those of the far heavier strikes Yucel had used to obliterate "rebellious towns" as object lessons, but that suited Aivars Terekhov just fine. The structure's massive ceramacrete walls confined and channeled the blast, and the towers around the impact point acted as cofferdams, further confining the blast and restricting the damage. Yet the explosion still reached out to obliterate the Presidential Palace and everything else (including the residential towers in which the System Unity and Progress Party's leadership and the majority of the transtellars' off-world personnel had been quartered) in a three-block radius. Within the primary zone of destruction virtually nothing survived; outside it, except for shock damage, there was remarkably little devastation.

Even as the shockwave rolled outward from what had been the Lombroso Arms Tower, two dozen assault shuttles plummeted out of Landing's sky. Eight of them swooped down on the soccer stadium, heavy with wing-mounted precision guided munitions that launched and screamed in on the tribarrels Yucel's gendarmes had mounted on the stadium's uppermost row of bleachers to cover the prisoners below. Precisely calculated fireballs crushed them like some giant's brimstone boots, and the shuttles reefed back around, going into hover, dropping their noses to bring their bow-mounted heavy cannon to bear.

The rest of the shuttles streaked by overhead, and three companies of battle-armored Manticoran Marines plummeted from them on counter-grav drop harnesses.

Here and there an isolated gendarme or two had survived the PGM strike with enough courage—or stupidity—to fire on the hovering shuttles or try to nail one of the plummeting Marines. They didn't have much luck. The Marines came in far too hard and fast to be easily targeted by men and women terrified of what was happening, and the gendarmes had no antiair weapons. The Mobius Liberation Front hadn't had any aircraft for them to worry about, so none had been issued to the stadium guards, and the shuttles were too well armored for their surviving light weapons to pose any threat.

Those far enough away from any prisoner discovered that their body armor was worth precisely nothing when a thirty-millimeter round from a shuttle pulse cannon hit them at several thousand meters per second. The others lasted a little longer—until the Marines grounded and they discovered that their pulse rifles were as useless against battle armor as they'd been against the shuttles.

A handful threw their weapons to the ground and got their hands clasped behind their heads quickly enough to survive.

❖   ❖   ❖

Helen Zilwicki stood behind Commodore Terekhov, watching the recon platforms' imagery in the main visual display. The kinetic strike's towering, ugly, anvil-headed cloud of dust and smoke was still climbing when the first Marine landed. The prevailing wind had barely begun to bend it before the entire stadium had been secured.

The sheer, stunning speed of it left her feeling vaguely dazed. She'd been at Terekhov's elbow as he,

Commander Lewis, and Colonel Simak planned and organized Zeus. Yet she'd been convinced, somehow, that Yucel was at least smart enough to realize how hopeless her position was.

I guess Daddy was right when he told me to never underestimate the power of human stupidity, she thought. *God, I hope the word gets around and finally starts penetrating even Solly skulls! If we have to keep on killing every damn one of them...*

"Well," Terekhov said after a moment, blue eyes still on the visual display, "I suppose we should see if whoever's still alive in their chain of command is more willing to listen to reason."

Chapter Thirty-Two

"I WISH WE KNEW what he wants to talk about," Mackenzie Graham groused as she locked the door behind them. Then she and Indiana headed down the rickety stairs—their apartment building's elevator was on the fritz again—from the sixth floor. "I'm not crazy about unexpected emergency meetings."

"We'll find out why he's here soon enough," Indiana pointed out, keeping a cautious eye peeled.

The landings were none too well lit, and muggings weren't unheard of even inside apartment complexes. Especially not here, on the older side of town, where so many "historical" buildings from Seraphim's early days remained in use. Most of those older buildings had been constructed using natural materials and without counter-grav capability. They were smaller, built closer to the ground than the later towers, and easier to break into, and they'd never boasted the security systems that were part of the city's newer structures. They were also firetraps, but on the limited plus side, there were fewer public security cameras on this side of town, and the rundown tenements offered their inhabitants a much higher degree of anonymity. And given what had happened to Indiana and Mackenzie's father, and the complete destruction of the family's financial fortunes, not even the scags were likely to find it remarkable that they'd been reduced to such miserable quarters.

The light was out again on the second-floor landing, Indiana noticed when they reached the third floor, and he slid his right hand casually into his pants pocket as the made the turn and started on down. If anyone was going to try anything, it should happen just... about... *now.*

The two men lurking in the landing's shadows had obviously done this before. They came out of the darkness in a concerted attack, rushing the brother and sister from both sides, and he saw the dull gleam of a knife.

His right hand came out of his pocket in a practiced move. His thumb pressed a button, the collapsible baton extended instantly to its full seventy centimeters even as his left arm swept Mackenzie behind him.

"Gimme your wal—" the one with the knife snarled, only to break off with a scream as Indiana brought the weighted baton down.

It was a whipcrack strike, a quick, powerful flick of the wrist rather than a full-armed blow, and he recovered from it instantly. He stepped towards the knife-wielder, not away *from* him, as the injured mugger clutched his own shattered wrist and hunched forward. The second man had targeted Mackenzie, but she wasn't where he'd expected her to be thanks to her brother's shove, and Indiana's move took *him* just out of the mugger's reach, as well. The second attacker shouted an obscenity and turned towards Indiana, one hand going back over his shoulder. Indiana saw the blackjack against the third-floor landing light, but he had plans of his own, and the other man collapsed with a hoarse, whistling scream as the rigid baton's rounded tip slammed into his solar plexus like a rapier.

The second man went down, writhing in agony, trying desperately to breathe. It didn't look like he was going to have much luck with that, given the serious internal injuries he'd probably just suffered, a corner of Indiana's mind reflected. At the moment, he had other things to worry about, however, and he turned back to the first mugger. He stood like a swordsman, baton poised, and the broken-wristed attacker gawked at him in disbelief.

"My sister and I were just leaving." Indiana was amazed at how level his own voice sounded...and the fact that he could actually hear it through the thunder of his pulse. "I think your friend needs a doctor, and as far as we're concerned, you can find him one. But I wouldn't advise choosing this building again in the future."

The still-standing mugger's mouth dropped open, and Indiana extended his free hand to Mackenzie without ever taking his eyes from the other man. She took it and stepped across the still spasming, gagging body on the landing.

"I'll give you five minutes before I call the cops," Indiana continued, although God knew he had no intention of doing anything of the sort. "I think you should both be gone by then, don't you?"

He nodded to the other man, then followed Mackenzie down the remaining stairs without ever turning his back on the mugger until they reached the vestibule. Then he glanced at his sister and shook his head as he saw the compact automatic pistol sliding back into her pocket.

"Idiot," she said, shaking her own head. "There were *two* of them, Indy! You did notice that, didn't you? What did you think you were doing taking both of them on by yourself?!"

"It seemed like the thing to do at the time," he told her mildly, collapsing the baton and opening the apartment building's front door for her with his left hand.

"Only because you suddenly decided to go on a testosterone jag! I'm not exactly a little girl anymore, you know!"

"No, you're not. And you're a better shot than I am, too," Indiana acknowledged. "On the other hand, it occurred to me that shooting someone full of holes in our own building might not be the best way to keep a low profile. The Cherubim PD hates filling out the paperwork on dead bodies, but they do investigate them, you know, even on our side of town. When firearms are involved, at least."

Mackenzie had opened her mouth. Now she closed it again. After a moment, she even nodded in agreement.

"Point taken," she said after a moment, because Indiana was right.

The Cherubim Police didn't give a damn how many muggers managed to get themselves killed, and if the one Indiana had dropped was found dead on the landing from blunt force trauma, there probably wouldn't be any investigation at all. Those cops who weren't on the take were too overwhelmed trying to look out for law-abiding citizens to worry about what happened to the capital city's predators, and the ones who *were* on the take had more profitable things to worry about. But they stood up and took notice when firearms were used, and any case involving them was automatically flagged to Tillman O'Sullivan's Seraphim System Security Police. Not because the scags cared how many proles slaughtered each other, but because the possession of firearms by private citizens was illegal. That hadn't always been the case, but one of President McCready's first acts in office had been to amend the System Constitution to delete its guarantee of a citizen's right to be armed.

After all, they couldn't have all those weapons floating around contributing to the unacceptably high crime rate, now could they?

"I'm glad you agree," Indiana said with a grin as the two of them stepped out onto the slushy sidewalk. More snow was drifting down, and the east wind felt raw and cutting. "Mind you, I'm a little concerned. It's not like you to give up so easily, especially when I'm right."

"Don't push it, Indy," she said severely, and he chuckled.

They walked down the sidewalk to the tram station in the middle of the next block. The public transit system looked as worn out as anything else in Cherubim, and the often-vandalized tram cars' broken windows made gaping punctuation marks in the colorful, usually obscene graffiti that caparisoned their sides. Despite that, the trams were mechanically reliable and, unlike a great many other things in the Seraphim System, they actually ran on a reliable schedule. Primarily,

Indiana and Mackenzie knew, because they were the only means of transportation available to most of the capital's population, and the system's transstellar masters wanted their serfs to get to work on time.

The tram was just pulling to a stop as they arrived, and Indiana followed Mackenzie aboard. They presented their Transit Authority passes for scanning, and managed to find seats that weren't in a direct draft from one of the broken windows.

The tram moved off through the snow and slush, and the brother and sister gazed out at the crowds of poorly dressed, shivering, head-bent pedestrians. There was a lot of foot traffic in Cherubim, even this late and in weather like this. They passed an occasional ground car, but those were few and far between, and the parking spaces which had once been filled to capacity and beyond stood mostly empty. Downtown Cherubim had once been home to a bustling, thriving district composed of privately owned small businesses—restaurants, bookstores, art galleries, boutiques, jewelers, pawnshops, clothiers, and electronics stores. Their owners and operators hadn't been wealthy, perhaps, but they'd made ends meet and they'd worked for *themselves*. Now every other storefront stood empty. Most of those which remained looked rundown, worn out, tattered around the edges. Yet here and there an oasis of well-lit, clean crystoplast display windows offered gleaming goods for sale.

Indiana's eyes hardened as he saw those thriving windows, because there was a reason for their prosperity. They were the ones that belonged to the mayor's friends, or even the president's. The ones whose owners had connections, who didn't have to pay protection to corrupt cops and city councilmembers, or to one of the transstellars' local managers. Hell, two thirds of them didn't even pay city taxes!

There's always someone willing to play jackal, he thought bitterly. *Always someone willing to "go along to get along." They may not be the ones who decided to rape Seraphim in the first place, but they sure as hell don't have any problem squabbling over the scraps and grabbing whatever they can get on the side! And not one of them would dream of raising a hand to do anything about McCready and her bottom feeders.*

Mackenzie reached out and squeezed his knee with one hand. He looked at her, and some of the bitterness leached out of his eyes as she smiled sadly at him. She knew exactly what he was thinking, of course. Once upon a time Bruce Graham had been one of those shopkeepers... until his livelihood had been destroyed by others' corruption. Indiana saw the understanding in that smile, and he smiled back at his sister, patted the hand on his knee, and then turned back to the window.

❖　　❖　　❖

The tram deposited them two corners away from The Soup Spoon, a restaurant they both liked and which somehow managed to keep its doors open despite its owners' lack of connections. Probably because the place looked like a dump, Indiana reflected as he and Mackenzie slogged through the last of the slush, stamped their feet clean, and stepped out of the damp, raw cold into the warm, delicious-smelling humidity. The restaurant windows were heavily misted with condensation, and Alecta, their favorite server, greeted them as soon as she saw them.

"Indy! Max! I've got your regular table open. Come on back!"

The Grahams smiled and followed her towards the back of the restaurant. The Soup Spoon had absolutely no ambience to recommend it to the better type of customer. The silverware, plates, and bowls were thoroughly mismatched, the tables and booths were worn, and the cheap holo posters on the walls couldn't hide the fact that they were badly in need of paint and maintenance. Water stains in one corner of the ceiling indicated a leak management hadn't been able to get fixed for almost three months, and the floor really needed to be recovered.

But what it lacked in polish and upkeep was more than compensated for by the sense of welcome. It was a warm, friendly place, one whose owners knew the vast majority of their customers by first name. A place where the food might come in mismatched bowls but the kitchen was spotless, every dish was just as delicious as it smelled, and the daily special was priced to let honest people wrap themselves around a warm, sustaining meal. Indiana and Mackenzie heard other regulars greeting them by name as they passed, and they smiled and nodded and waved back while they followed Alecta to the table in a rear corner.

"He's been waiting for you," Alecta said much more quietly as they walked. She smiled as if she'd just made a joke. "Ben and Allen kept an eye out. They didn't see anyone following him."

Indiana nodded, laughing at the joke she hadn't made.

"Thanks," he said, and then nodded to the man called Firebrand as they reached the table.

"Glad you could make it," he said casually, pulling

out Mackenzie's chair and seating her before he sat down himself, facing Firebrand across the tattered looking checkered tablecloth.

"I said I'd look forward to trying the menu the next time I was in town," Damien Harahap replied, and sniffed deeply. "If it tastes as good as it smells, I'll be back, too!"

"I don't think you'll be disappointed," Alecta assured him, pulling out her order pad and looking back and forth between the three of them. "You guys ready to order yet?"

"They just got here!" Harahap protested with a laugh, and she snorted.

"Hey, it's Thursday. That means Indy here is going to have the clam chowder with a side of hush puppies and coleslaw. McKinsey's going to have the beef stew over rice, tossed salad with oil and balsamic vinegar dressing, and a side of garlic bread. Coffee for him, hot tea for her. So that only leaves you."

She gave him the challenging grin she would have given any other new customer, and he laughed again and shook his head.

"Since it's my first time here, why don't you surprise me? What do you recommend?"

"Oh, man, are you letting yourself in for it!" Indiana warned him, and Alecta whacked him on the shoulder with her order pad.

"Don't listen to him," she told Harahap. "The problem is he doesn't like coconut milk."

"Coconut milk?" Harahap repeated a bit blankly, and she nodded.

"Yep. You want my advice, you'll have the Massaman curry with duck. And maybe"—she eyed him consideringly—"in your case, we'll add a little pineapple and some peanuts. Trust me, you'll love it."

"Well, I do like curry," Harahap admitted (honestly, in this case), and nodded. "All right. Sounds good to me."

"How spicy do you want it—scale of one to ten?"

"Make it a nine."

"Brave man!" Alecta laughed. "White rice, or fried?"

"White. And bring the fish sauce, if you have any."

"All right!" Alecta beamed at him. "Coffee, tea, or water?"

"Tea. And let me have chopsticks, please."

"Gotcha."

Alecta waited long enough to top off their water glasses, then disappeared with the order, and Harahap sat back in his chair and looked at Indiana and Mackenzie.

"I like her," he said sincerely, and Mackenzie nodded.

"So do we," she replied, not mentioning that Alecta, The Soup Spoon's owners, and two other members of the wait staff were part of the SIM. There was no need for him to know that.

"Good place to meet, too," he went on, looking around the restaurant. "In most ways, anyway. Lots and lots of ambient noise, people talking loud enough no one's in a good position to hear what anyone else is saying, and a clientele of regulars who recognize a newcomer in a heartbeat. Makes it hard to plant somebody on you, but it's got its downsides, too." He shook his head wryly. "Trust me, I got quite a few second glances when *I* turned up! Enough to make any good spy nervous."

"Don't worry about it," Indiana told him. Harahap cocked an eyebrow at him, and Mackenzie leaned forward slightly in her brother's support.

"We've been regulars here since before our father was arrested, Firebrand," she told him. "People may have wondered who you were when you walked in. In fact, that's one of our better defenses. Nobody in here is real fond of the police, McCready, or the scags, trust me, but they know the two of us. The fact that you're meeting us here makes you one of them, provisionally, at least."

Harahap looked at her thoughtfully for a moment, then nodded.

"Which brings us to the reason you wanted to talk to us in the first place," Mackenzie went on. "We didn't expect to be hearing from you again quite this soon."

"And I didn't expect to be back here quite this soon," he told her, picking up his water glass. He took a sip and grimaced slightly. "On the other hand, this isn't the sort of profession where you get to count on reliable schedules."

"So why *this* schedule change?" Indiana asked.

"Things are heating up between us and the Sollies," Harahap told him. Which was true enough in its own way, assuming he was reading his tea leaves correctly, if not in the sense his listeners' might expect. "It's not general knowledge out this way yet, but the Sollies sent a fleet—over four hundred ships-of-the-wall—to take out the Manticore System."

Indiana's eyes widened in shock and the beginning of dismay, but Harahap shook his head quickly.

"Didn't work out very well for the Sollies," he said with a thin smile. "As a matter of fact, Admiral Harrington handed them their asses, if you'll pardon my language. Blew the hell out of them, and captured every surviving unit."

Indiana sat back abruptly and Mackenzie's eyes brightened.

"You kicked their asses?" Indiana asked. "Really?"

"Like they've never been kicked before," Harahap assured him with a delight which was completely unfeigned. He suspected some of his actual superiors might have preferred for the Manties' victory to have been just a tad less overwhelming, but that didn't dampen *his* enthusiasm for seeing the SLN kicked flat on its back one single bit. Even when he'd worked for the Solarian Gendarmerie, Damien Harahap had loathed the Solarian League. It had simply been the best game in town.

The brother and sister looked at one another, and he was impressed by how well they controlled their obvious glee. *He* could see it, sitting across the table from them, but he doubted anyone else could.

"It's going to be a while yet before anyone else on Seraphim knows about this," he went on, not bothering to mention that the only reason *he* knew already was that more and more Mesan Alignment dispatch boats were equipped with the streak drive no one else possessed. "When it does, though, the transstellars are going to be more than a little unhappy. Especially since we're busy closing down all the warp termini, as well." He chuckled nastily. "The bottom's about to fall out of a hell of a lot of the League's interstellar economy, and people like Krestor Interstellar and Mendoza are going to take a hammering. For that matter, the *federal government's* going to take an incredible beating when so much of its revenue stream goes belly up."

Indiana and Mackenzie nodded in understanding, and he shrugged.

"The thing is—and the reason I'm here is—that things are moving faster than we ever really anticipated." Which, he reflected, was damned well true. In fact, it was probably as true for a real Manticoran as it was for the Alignment at the moment! "That means we've got both additional opportunities and additional risks to think about."

"I can see that." Indiana's expression was thoughtful, his tone cautious. "Exactly how does that affect us here in Seraphim, though? I mean, obviously it *does*, or you wouldn't be here so far ahead of schedule."

"No, I wouldn't," Harahap acknowledged. "First though, have the weapons shipments gotten through all right?"

"Yeah." Indiana nodded. "You took us by surprise by getting the first one in here so quickly, but everything's worked like clockwork so far. We've gotten them out of the capital to a secure location, too. And we've started establishing secondary weapons caches now." He shrugged slightly. "We're still working out the best way to handle training our people, and I won't pretend we wouldn't like to have more guns to go around, but we're in a lot better shape than I would've believed we could've been a few months ago."

"Do you have an actual plan to *use* them?" Harahap asked, looking at Mackenzie this time, and she shrugged.

"We've got a long-range plan, a short-range plan, and at least a dozen contingency plans," she said.

"What kind of timetable are you looking at?"

"For the long-range plan?" She snorted. "Try two or three T-years."

"That's not so good," Harahap said.

"Depends on what you mean by 'good,'" she responded. "It would take two or three T-years, yeah, but we figure the odds of success, even without fleet support from the Star Empire, would be three or four to one."

"I can see where that would appeal to you," he conceded. "On the other hand, a lot of things can change—or go wrong—in that long, which means odds can shift a lot. So what's the time frame for your short-range plan?"

Indiana and Mackenzie looked at each other for a moment, then turned back to him.

"A minimum of ninety T-days," Mackenzie said flatly. "A hundred and twenty would be a lot better. And, frankly, our chances of success without outside support would suck."

"Um." Harahap frowned down into his water glass for several seconds before he looked back up.

"Okay, cards on the table time. I don't have complete information myself. I'm sure you both understand why that's the case. But what I've been told is that the current strategic position is very favorable for our side. The problem is that like I just said, things can change, sometimes quickly. From what they're telling me, I'm guessing—and it's only a guess, not the kind of thing anyone would be confirming to someone at my level—that the Admiralty's thinking in terms of going onto the offensive now that they've kicked the Sollies' butts in Manticore.

"The reason I say that is that they want to accelerate all of the liberation movements we've been supporting. Not just you guys—*all* of them. Now, for some of them, that would be nothing short of outright suicide at this point, and in their cases I'm recommending that they don't do anything of the sort. I'm not sure my bosses would be delighted to hear about that." He smiled tightly. "On the other hand, my bosses aren't out here, and I am. And, frankly, I don't see where sending someone off half-cocked and getting them wiped out before we can get them any support is going to help anybody very much."

He shrugged and took a sip of water, giving them time to absorb the fact that nice-guy Firebrand was looking out for them.

"At the same time, though," he continued, lowering the glass again, "I *can* see where raising all the hell we possibly can in the Sollies' backyard would work to everyone's advantage. Especially if I'm right, and the Admiralty is planning on kicking in the League's front door. In fact—"

He paused, obviously considering what he was about to say, then shrugged.

"Beowulf didn't let the Sollies through the Beowulf Terminus to support the attack on the home system," he said softly. "Instead, they've signed on with us." He smiled thinly. "That means we've got a protected avenue directly into the heart of the Core Worlds. I think the Admiralty's planning on using it, too. But when they do, they want the Sollies looking over their shoulder. Given what's already happened to Battle Fleet, the League is probably going to have to call in Frontier Fleet units to reinforce closer to home. What I think my bosses have in mind is to make such a ruckus out here in the Verge that OFS won't turn loose a damned thing without kicking and screaming the whole way."

"*Beowulf's* sided with the Star Empire?" Indiana asked half-incredulously. His knowledge of astrography outside a twenty or thirty-light-year radius of Seraphim wasn't exactly profound, but he knew Beowulf was no more than a T-week or so from the Sol System itself for a ship with a military grade hyper generator and particle screens.

"That's what the dispatches say, and, frankly, it's the only way we could know what happened in the home system this quickly," Harahap pointed out. He shrugged. "Only way the home office could've gotten a dispatch boat out here this fast would have been through the Beowulf Terminus, which suggests to me that—"

He shrugged again, holding up one hand, palm uppermost, and Indiana nodded slowly.

"So just how soon would 'your bosses' like us to start raising a 'ruckus' here in Seraphim, Firebrand?" Mackenzie asked, her eyes narrow.

"As soon as you feel you possibly could," Harahap replied. "Hopefully within the next three T-months or so."

"Ninety T-days, in other words," she said flatly.

"Yes," he said.

"And you can get us naval support in that time-frame?"

"Yes," he replied.

"How?" Her tone was a bit skeptical. "I'm as excited about the possibility as Indy is, Firebrand. But if your navy's going to be going directly after Sol, how is any of it supposed to make its way all the way out here?"

"It's not." He shook his head. "What's going to happen is that Admiral Gold Peak is about to launch an offensive out of the Talbott Cluster in the next month or so." He met Mackenzie's eyes levelly, confident in his ability to lie convincingly. "Her main objective is going to be the Madras Sector," he continued, blithely ignoring the fact that Gold Peak almost certainly wasn't going to do anything of the sort. "That's going to require most of her heavy units, but it should leave plenty of cruisers and destroyers available for . . . other duties, let's say. Like turning up here in Seraphim to provide you with some orbital support. And to make sure Frontier Fleet doesn't provide any orbital support to McCready and O'Sullivan."

Mackenzie looked at him for several moments before, finally, she nodded slowly. It actually made sense, she thought. Assuming Gold Peak managed to meet the schedule Harahap had described. And assuming there was some way to coordinate properly.

"Do you need an answer tonight?" she asked.

"To be honest, I'd prefer one as soon as possible," Harahap said, and this time he was telling the truth. "On the other hand, I know this came at you completely cold, and the last thing either of us needs is for you to rush into something that's just going to get you all killed without accomplishing anything for us. I'll be on-planet for another couple of days, so you've got that long to think about it, but then I'm going to have to move on to my next destination."

"I don't know if we can have a decision for you that quickly," Indiana put in. He looked across the table at his sister, then back at Harahap. "We'd be putting a lot of people at risk, and we're going to have to go back and evaluate the assumptions of our contingency plans."

"I can understand that. But if I head out of the Seraphim System, I take your communications link with me." He grimaced. "Once I'm out of here, I won't be able to communicate with Admiral Gold Peak to warn her you're planning to move."

"We might be able to work around that," Mackenzie said slowly, and Harahap's eyebrows rose. He hadn't expected to hear that.

"How?" he asked. He'd hoped giving them a two-day window would push them into making a decision, and he was none too delighted by the suggestion that there was a factor in the equation that he hadn't known about.

"Mendoza of Córdoba imports beef from Montana," Mackenzie said. "They make regular trips, and they maintain an irregular schedule of dispatch boats between here and Meyers. About half the time, the boat stops off in Montana to check on market conditions, see about renegotiating contracts if the market price's changed, that sort of thing." She shrugged. "We've got contacts in the crews of some of the freighters on the Montana run. For that matter, we've got contacts on at least two of the dispatch boat crews. It's about twenty-eight T-days from here to Montana by dispatch boat; more like six T-weeks for one of the high-speed freighters. If we can use the dispatch boat, we could get a message to Meyers in a couple of T-months. If we have to use the freighter and arrange a message relay from Montana, we might be looking at as much as four T-months. Maybe even longer."

"I didn't know about that," Harahap admitted truthfully.

And I wish you *didn't know about it, either,* he added silently. *On the other hand, as far as I know*

Gold Peak isn't going anywhere near Meyers without direct orders from home. So, worst-case scenario, you get a message to Montana in two months. Hmmm . . .

He thought about it. The odds were that any messenger from Seraphim would be regarded as a nutcase, if not a Solarian agent provocateur, by any Manticoran naval officer. The Manties certainly weren't going to fall all over themselves dispatching warships into Solarian territory on some wild goose chase substantiated by nothing more than somebody who claimed his revolutionary organization had been in contact with them all along! In fact, he could probably help that reaction along just a bit.

"All right," he said, nodding with an expression of profound relief. "Actually, I'm relieved to hear you have another means of communication. I'd still prefer to know what your plans are before I have to leave, for a lot of reasons, but I can understand why you're going to have to think about this, and at least you're not as dependent on us as I thought you'd be to communicate with Admiral Gold Peak. Is your contact arrangement such that you know now if you'd be able to send a message off?"

"The schedules aren't cast in ceramacrete, if that's what you mean," Mackenzie said. "They usually hit within, oh, a local week or so of their regular departure times, though." She shrugged. "That's for the freighters, of course. The dispatch boats are on a lot more irregular schedule."

"But you could count on getting one off within a one-T-month window?"

"Oh, that we could do," Indiana assured him.

"All right. I'm going to give you a code phrase for

Admiral Gold Peak. When she hears it, she'll know I sent you, and on that basis, she'll be prepared to dispatch an appropriate naval force to support you immediately." Actually, it would probably finish off any chance Gold Peak might believe them. Since there was no such code phrase, she'd have to take it as proof that their messenger was an imposter, but there was no point worrying them with that, he thought. "With that in mind, would you be prepared to go ahead and kick off your 'short-range' plan within, say, two T-months of having sent off your messenger?"

"I don't know," Mackenzie said hesitantly. "Without having coordinated directly with Gold Peak, without knowing support is on its way, we'd be asking our people to take an awful risk."

"I realize that, but this is the kind of business risks have to be taken in," Harahap pointed out. "And you'd be in complete control of whether or not you sent the messenger in the first place. It would be a case of your having looked at the situation here in Seraphim and decided you really can pull it off, assuming you get Admiral Gold Peak's naval support before anybody from OFS or Frontier Fleet could respond to McCready. If you aren't satisfied you can do that, then you never send your messenger off in the first place."

Indiana was nodding thoughtfully, and Mackenzie looked at her brother with a worried expression. He saw it and smiled at her.

"I'm not going to rush off into anything without your support, Max," he reassured her. "But Firebrand has a point. We'd be the ones calling the shots."

"Could we do that and then wait until Admiral Gold Peak actually gets here?" Mackenzie asked.

"I suppose." Harahap injected a doubtful note into his tone, and both Grahams looked at him. He shrugged. "Look, I understand your concerns. But the Star Empire's up against it, too, you know. We've supported you this far, as the weapons shipments you've already received indicate. We'd like to support you further, and as I explained to you the first time we met, it wouldn't be in our interest to encourage people to revolt and then stand back and watch them get the chop.

"All of that's true, but I also have to say that we've got to allocate our resources carefully. Not things like weapons shipments. *Those* we can arrange basically whenever and wherever we need to. But we're talking about warships, about naval support, and we're up against the Solarian League, the biggest navy in the history of the galaxy. If you can't commit to a specific date for your own organization to strike until you've actually got Manticoran warships in orbit around the planet, you're probably going to get pushed further down the priorities queue. I'm not trying to make any kind of threat here, or give you any kind of ultimatum. I'm just saying that if Admiral Gold Peak is looking at requests for support, she's probably going to give priority to the people running the greatest risks. And if she's strapped for light units, she's probably not going to give very much priority to somebody who tells her they can't take action until they have Manticoran units actually in their skies. She'll figure that if you're waiting for that kind of response, you won't be coming into the open until you get it, and if you're not out in the open, you're probably not going to take any heavy hits from the scags, so she can afford to let you wait while she deals with more pressing commitments."

"You're saying she'd refuse to send us support?" Indiana asked.

"No, I'm saying there'd be a good chance she'd move you down the list." Harahap shrugged. "She'd probably send word back by your contact telling you how soon she'd be able to free up units to send in your direction. It might not be very long. On the other hand, given how other operations go, it could be you'd be looking at your original two or three-T-year timeframe. More probably, it would fall somewhere in the middle."

The Grahams looked at each other again. Indiana raised one eyebrow, and Mackenzie shrugged. Then he turned back to Harahap.

"We understand what you're saying. We understand the logic behind it, too. And the truth is, as I'm sure you realized before you said it, that there's no way we want to leave our dad—or anyone else—rotting in Terrabore Prison one minute longer than we have to. We'll look at our options, and at our communications channels, and see what we can do. I don't think there's any way we could possibly give you an answer before you have to leave the system, but we *will* make our minds up as quickly as possible."

"That's all I can ask for." Harahap smiled. "Like I say, no one wants you running *stupid* risks, so look at those options carefully. But if you do decide to move, Admiral Gold Peak will be there for you."

"Good."

Indiana looked as if he wanted to say more, but at that moment Alecta reappeared, carrying a tray laden with steaming bowls. She set it down and began distributing food, and Harahap settled back, sniffing appreciatively. The curry smelled just as good as she'd promised, and he allowed himself to look forward to it.

He wasn't completely satisfied with the evening's work, and his bosses wouldn't be either. Fortunately, they were professionals who understood timing was always a problem in an operation like this one, and no one could ever predict how it would work out in the end. Not really. There was always some damned unknown factor waiting around to screw things up, like that idiot Zagorski in Loomis. An entire T-year of preparations and quiet contacts right down the tubes because of him and MacQuarie, and the fumblers hadn't even turned up evidence that Manticore had been involved with the LLL! Talk about wasted effort! As a general rule, incompetent opponents were a blessing, but when they were too frigging stupid to do their own jobs just when you actually *needed* them to...

He brushed that thought aside. Done was done, and Loomis hadn't been his op, anyway. This one was, and he was a craftsman who took pride in his work.

So did those superiors of his who weren't going to be happy if he couldn't talk these kids into accelerating their schedule. He didn't know exactly why that was, and those superiors weren't about to tell him, but that was fine. He understood the rules, even if they could turn around and bite someone on the ass too often for comfort, and he'd do his best to pull it off. It was obvious he wasn't going to rush these two after all, though. Indiana was clearly more inclined to act quickly, yet it was equally clear he wasn't prepared to overrule Mackenzie's more cautious, analytical approach. His employers were just going to have to settle for the best he could do, and at least they were far more pragmatic—and aware of operational realities and limitations—than some of the people he'd worked for in the past. As long as he was honest in his reports to them they were unlikely to send him a pulser dart just because he hadn't been able to accomplish the impossible.

Harahap considered the odds as he began ladling curry over a plate of rice. Fifty-fifty, he decided. Maybe as high as sixty-forty, his favor, given Indiana's aggressiveness, but not any better than that. Still, he'd won a lot of bets at worse odds than that, and if this one didn't work out, all he and his employers lost was the time and the piddling expense of the weapons they'd provided. Whereas if it *did* work…

I can live with fifty-fifty, he decided. *After all, it won't be my ass, whichever side craps out.*

AUGUST 1922 POST DIASPORA

"And best of all, if we do it right, the bastards won't even realize we're onto them until we hand them over for trial!"

—Captain Cynthia Lecter,
Royal Manticoran Navy

✧ Chapter Thirty-Three

"I SUPPOSE THAT'S JUST about it, then." Michelle Henke tipped back in her chair, rested her right ankle on her left knee, and clasped her hands behind her head. "Unless anyone else has something they think we should be looking at?"

She looked around the officers gathered at the long table in her dining cabin, most of them sipping coffee or munching their chosen form of fingerfood, and quirked an eyebrow. It was an informal looking group, which wasn't too surprising, considering the fact that their commanding admiral had chosen to hold it here, rather than in her briefing room . . . and to attend in her Academy sweats and treecat slippers. None of the others were quite that informal, of course—rank did have its privileges, which none of them were so rash as to usurp, however congenial their CO—but there was still an undeniably casual, comfortable feel to the meeting.

"It looks to me like you've covered all the points from the agenda, Ma'am," Gervais Archer said, consulting his minicomp. Then he smiled wryly. "For that matter, you've, ah, hit on at least a few *additional* points."

Several people chuckled, and Michelle grinned unrepentantly. Organization was a good thing, and she was as organized as anyone until she was certain she'd covered all the points she'd planned on covering. After that, free association was the order of the day as far as she was concerned. In fact, she encouraged it as a way to expose points she hadn't thought about ahead of time.

"Obsessive organization is the sign of a mind not prepared to thrive upon chaos," she pointed out, and the chuckles were louder.

"Actually, there is one thing it might be appropriate to bring up, Ma'am," Veronica Armstrong said after a moment. The flag captain sat at the opposite end of the table from Michelle, flanked by Commander Larson, her executive officer, and Commander Wilton Diego, her tactical officer. At the moment, Armstrong's green eyes were unwontedly serious, and Michelle frowned mentally.

"Go, Vicki," she invited.

"Well, I've actually been thinking about this for a while," Armstrong continued with a slight shrug. "The thing is that as honored and pleased as I am to be your flag captain, I have to question whether or not a battlecruiser—even a *Nike* like *Artemis*—is the best place for you to keep your flag. We've got two and a half squadrons of modern ships-of-the-wall now, and they've not only got better flag deck accommodations, but they're a hell of a lot tougher, too."

"Trying to get rid of me, Vicki?" Michelle asked quizzically, and Armstrong shook her head.

"No, Ma'am. Of course not!" She smiled. "I'm just pointing out that a superdreadnought is more traditional for a fleet commander's flagship. When it's available, of course."

"You may have noticed that I've never been exactly trammeled by the bonds of tradition," Michelle said dryly. Then she straightened in her chair, leaned forward, and folded her hands on the table in front of her.

"I appreciate the sentiment, Vicki," she said in a considerably more serious tone. "And I'll admit I considered—briefly—whether or not it would be a good idea to move to one of the SD(P)s when they became available. But I decided not to for several reasons. One is that for the immediately foreseeable future, I don't think the question of survivability really enters the equation. Unless we screw up, the Sollies aren't going to be able to threaten us significantly. For that matter, even if they manage to get into range, a *Nike* like *Artie* is a hell of a lot better protected against anything but pointblank energy fire than almost anyone else's ships-of-the-wall.

"There is a little something to be said for the superiority of a superdreadnought's—what was it you called them?—'flag deck accommodations.'" Michelle shrugged. "But that's mainly a comfort factor and a matter of having more room to pack the admiral and her staff into. The actual command facilities aren't that much superior to what we've got right here aboard *Artie*, and our CIC's receiving the input from every sensor in the entire fleet.

"The decisive factor, though, is that I'm comfortable aboard your ship, Captain Armstrong." She smiled. "You and your senior officers are an extension of my staff, and you and I have been thinking together long enough for me to be sure you understand the intent as well as the wording of any order I may give. And while I hesitate to mention it in front of all these awestruck junior officers," her smile became a grin as she glanced at the other officers seated around the table, "there have been occasions—rare, perhaps, but nonetheless real—upon which you have . . . respectfully raised considerations which have tempered my own perhaps overly enthusiastic notions. Frankly, I'd just as soon not have to break in another flag captain who's willing to do that."

Her whimsical tone became rather more serious with the last sentence, and Armstrong looked down the length of the table at her for a second or two. Then the flag captain nodded, and Michelle nodded back.

I wonder if someone else has been complaining about Vicki's relative lack of seniority? she thought. *Funny how people can piss and moan over something like that at a time like this. And it'd be like Vicki to offer me a way to make the move without looking like I'm conceding anything to the complainer. Or like a lack of confidence in her, for that matter.*

She made a mental note to have Cynthia Lecter look into the matter quietly. She didn't expect to discover anything like a serious problem, but it never hurt to be proactive about things like that. Shrinking violets, by and large, didn't make it to flag rank. Overall, that was a good thing, but ego involvement was one of the most pernicious producers of friction, and one with which Michelle had never sympathized.

And I'm not about to discombobulate my command arrangements at a time like this, especially if it's just somebody with a nose bent out of shape because she's senior to Vicki and thinks she ought to be Tenth Fleet's flag captain!

She snorted mentally at the thought. In less than one T-day, Tenth Fleet would be dropping out of hyper in the Meyers System. *Not* a good time to be tinkering with its command structure.

"All right, people," she said out loud. "Now that that particular pressing question has been dealt with, I think it's time all of us got some sleep." She smiled again, this time without any humor at all. "After all, we're likely to be just a bit *busy* tomorrow."

❖   ❖   ❖

"Oh, *shit*."

"What was that?" CPO Sylvia Chu, chief of the watch in Meyers Astro Control, looked up from the endless stream of memos and directives on her own display with a stab of irritation as she heard the soft, fervent mutter. Commodore Thurgood's upcoming exercise loomed large in Chu's thoughts at the moment, and she needed to get her paperwork at least under control (she was never going to get it *finished*; that was a given in the Navy) to clear the decks for it. As Lieutenant Bristow had pointed out to her only that morning, screwing up the exercise because they'd missed dotting some "i" or crossing some "t" would constitute a Bad Thing.

And so would a last-minute sensor snafu, which was why the comment from Petty Officer 2/C Alan Coker, who was currently manning the outer system surveillance platforms, had set off Chu's internal alarms. The outer platforms were even more urgently in need of upgrade and replacement than the *inner* platforms, and the last thing she needed with the exercise looming on the horizon was for one of her primary sensor nodes to report a malfunction. That would *not* look good on her next efficiency report... which was due in less than two T-months.

There was no immediate response to her question, and she frowned as Coker leaned closer to his own console. Coker could be a royal pain in the ass, but although she would have gone far out of her way to avoid admitting it, Chu regarded him as one of the three best sensor techs assigned to the Meyers System. His defects—and the reason someone of his ability was still only a second-class petty officer—stemmed from a certain lack of patience with officers in general coupled with what Chu thought of as the "old Frontier Fleet hand" syndrome. Coker had seen more incompetent officers with family connections than he could have counted come and go during his career, and he'd spent more than his fair share of time cleaning up after them. It gave him an edge of something entirely too much like insolence towards the commissioned nitwits who came his way, but his decades of service had also made him very good at his job. He was, quite literally, too valuable to be canned.

Which was why his present expression sent another, sharper tremor of unease through Chu's professional instincts.

Coker's hands moved across his console for several seconds, obviously double-checking and refining whatever had drawn his attention. Then he straightened and looked at Chu.

"We are *so* screwed," he said flatly.

"I realize you have a reputation to maintain as a

character," Chu replied tartly. "But unless you want to be ripped a new one, I'd appreciate a report one hell of a lot more detailed than 'We are so screwed.'"

"Sorry about that, Chief." His smile was a grimace, but there was also genuine apology in it. "It's just—" He gestured at his display. "The outer platforms are calling it twenty-eight superdreadnoughts, Chief." He shook his head. "And whoever they are, they sure as hell aren't ours!"

❖   ❖   ❖

"It's confirmed, Commodore," Captain Thora Macpherson said flatly. "Definitely twenty-eight in the superdreadnought range, judging from their impeller signatures. Not only that, but their accel inbound is over five hundred and thirty KPS squared." A smile as grim as her tone flitted across her face. "They haven't said anything to us yet, but given that number and that accel, there's not much question who they are."

Commodore Thurgood nodded, not that he'd really needed his operations officer's last sentence. For that matter, he hadn't needed the acceleration rate. There was no way in hell anybody he *wanted* to see would be sending that many ships-of-the-wall to a miserable, back-of-beyond system like Meyers, and that left only one candidate.

"Well, that's a pisser," Captain Hideoshi Wayne, Thurgood's chief of staff, observed.

"You do have a way with words, don't you, Hideoshi?"

"Sorry, Sir." Wayne grimaced.

"You didn't say anything I'm not thinking," Thurgood confessed with a sigh. He shook his head. "I've warned Verrocchio and Hongbo something like this could happen, but I have to admit I didn't really expect it. And I'd never have expected them to arrive in this kind of strength!"

He twitched his head in the direction of the master display. It was currently set to astrographic mode, showing the entire star system. The G0 star's twenty-two-light-minute hyper limit was represented by a green sphere, and a glowing rash of red icons was just about to cross into it, headed for the inner system.

There were a lot of them.

"It does seem like using a sledgehammer to swat flies," Howell Chavez, CO of SLNS *Edgehill*, Thurgood's battlecruiser flagship, agreed. Thurgood glanced at the com display which linked his flag bridge to Chavez's command deck, and the flag captain chuckled humorlessly. "I mean, I'm flattered and everything, Sir, but it *is* a little excessive, don't you think?"

"It's possible they think we've been reinforced," Wayne said, but Thurgood shook his head.

"Possible, but not too damned likely. Not way the hell and gone out here."

"Then why do you think they brought along so much heavy metal, Sir?" the chief of staff asked.

"Aside from the obvious, you mean?" Thurgood smiled thinly. "Your guess is as good as mine, Howell."

"Actually, Sir, I might have an idea," Captain Merriman said quietly, and all eyes turned to the petite, fine-boned intelligence officer. It was an open secret, at least among Thurgood's staff officers, that he and Sadako Merriman were lovers. That was too common in the Solarian League Navy to merit comment, except that in this case Merriman had become Thurgood's intelligence specialist on the basis of raw ability well before she'd become his lover.

"Fire away, Sadako," he invited now. "We've got better than three hours before they get here, after all."

"It's just a theory, of course, Sir," Merriman said, "but I've been thinking a lot about Gold Peak's character ever since Admiral Byng ran into her in New Tuscany. She's perfectly willing to kill anybody she has to—what happened in Spindle's proof enough of that, too, I suppose. But I think she'd prefer not to kill anyone she *doesn't* have to, as well. In fact, Spindle's part of the reason I think that. She could've gone right on shooting without allowing Admiral O'Cleary to surrender, just like she could have taken out Admiral Byng's entire task force. She chose not to."

She shrugged.

"And?" Wayne prompted.

"And I think she deliberately brought along enough firepower to make it obvious to *anyone* we wouldn't stand a chance against her," Merriman said.

"Her way of giving us an out, unless we're as pig-headed as Byng, you mean?" Chavez said thoughtfully.

"I doubt she thinks the Commodore'd be pigheaded enough to get all our people killed for nothing, anyway, Sir," Wayne pointed out. "We're *Frontier* Fleet, after all. That means we have *working* brains."

One or two of the officers on *Edgehill*'s flag bridge actually chuckled at the comment, despite the situation, and even Thurgood's lips twitched in an almost-smile.

"Probably not," he said after a moment. "But Sadako could have a point. With this kind of odds, it's a hell of a lot less likely some idiot—uniformed or civilian—is going to try to overrule any outbreak of sanity on my part. For that matter, I could be just as stupid as Byng or Crandall, for all she knows, in which case I'd need something pretty damned obvious to make the point."

It was the first time he'd allowed himself to attach that particular adjective to those two paragons of tactical and strategic genius in front of anyone else. Under the circumstances, however, he doubted it was going to have any detrimental impact on the career which was about to come to a screeching halt. Sadako might very well be right about Gold Peak's reasons for appearing in such strength, and no reasonable board of inquiry would expect him to oppose his single understrength battlecruiser squadron and its screen to that kind of armada. Despite which, he was about to go down in history as the first Solarian League naval officer ever to surrender a Solarian-claimed star system to an enemy.

Well, not to *surrender* one, precisely, perhaps. But what he was actually going to do would be even worse, in some ways.

Assuming we can get away with it in the first place. Which doesn't seem all that damned likely, really, he reminded himself, looking at those acceleration numbers again. *At least the exercise schedule means we're starting with hot nodes, though, thank God.*

"I suppose we'd better get Commissioner Verrochio on the com," he said out loud.

❖   ❖   ❖

"What the hell do we do now?" Lorcan Verrochio demanded harshly.

"Assuming Thurgood's sensor reports are accurate, I don't see that we have a lot of *choice*, Lorcan," Junyan Hongbo replied tartly from the com on the sector governor's desk after a brief delay.

"The bastard could at least *try* to fight instead of just running away!"

"Why? What possible good could it do?" Hongbo asked bluntly. "We're talking about twenty-eight ships-of-the-wall, Lorcan. *Manty* ships-of-the-wall!" He shook his head. "Thurgood's ships would be toast against anybody's wallers, but against Manties—?"

"But he's just *running* for it!" Verrocchio half-wailed. "He's abandoning the entire star system!"

"Which is the smartest thing he could possibly do, under the circumstances," Hongbo shot back after another of those delays. "At least this way the Navy doesn't lose his *ships*, too."

Verrocchio started to say something else, then stopped, and his eyes narrowed suddenly. Unlike the sector governor, Hongbo wasn't in the capital city of Pine Mountain. For that matter, he wasn't even on the planet of Meyers. No, he was aboard Meyers One, the primary freight handling platform orbiting the planet. Or that was where he was supposed to be, anyway. But if he were on Meyers One, the com delay should be scarcely noticeable.

"Where are you, Junyan?" Verrocchio demanded.

"Why do you ask?" Hongbo responded.

"Just answer the damned question!"

"Well, as it happens," Hongbo replied after that same brief but discernible delay, "I was aboard *Wanderlust* discussing those shipping arrangements of yours when Commodore Thurgood gave the alarm. I'm afraid Captain Herschel was adamant about getting underway immediately, and since her impellers happened to be hot at the moment—"

Hongbo shrugged, and Verrocchio's jaw muscles

clenched as his teeth ground together. Captain Martina Herschel of the merchant vessel *Wanderlust* had been the sector governor's primary conduit for the clandestine movement of personal property acquired under... questionable circumstances for T-years. Hongbo had had some business of his own aboard Meyers One this afternoon, so Verrocchio had asked him to drop certain items off with Herschel before her scheduled departure.

A departure whose schedule had obviously been moved up substantially.

"Of course there wasn't time for you to get back aboard the station," he grated after a moment, and Hongbo shrugged again.

"The Captain was very insistent, Lorcan."

"I see."

Verrocchio glared at the vice commissioner, yet even as he did, he knew he would have done precisely the same thing in Hongbo's place. Of course, Hongbo was abandoning a sizable chunk of personal wealth and possessions, but like every other Frontier Security commissioner or vice commissioner—including Lorcan Verrochio—he'd squirreled away the majority of his assets elsewhere. And it was unlikely any of his colleagues or superiors were going to fault his conduct in running for it if the opportunity presented itself. It wasn't as if there were anything he could have accomplished by staying, especially if the system's naval defenders had already decided to hightail it. And the final responsibility for what happened here in the Meyers System and in the Madras Sector generally was Lorcan Verrocchio's, not his.

"Have a nice voyage," the sector governor said sarcastically, and cut the connection.

Bastard, he thought, burying his face in his hands. *Wonder how much he promised Herschel for his passage?*

He sat that way for several seconds, then straightened. Unlike Hongbo, he was expected to ride the ship down in flames in a situation like this. Or that was what the rulebook said, anyway. But no Solarian sector governor had ever actually found himself in "a situation like this" before, so when it came down to it...

Verrocchio's eyes narrowed. There hadn't been very much hyper-capable shipping in Meyers when the sensor platforms picked up the Manties' arrival, and Thurgood had ordered all of it to get underway and scatter towards the hyper limit as soon as possible. That was exactly what *Wanderlust* had done, but two other freighters had been in parking orbit at the same time, and he wondered suddenly if they'd been able to get *their* impellers online quickly enough to run for it. According to Thurgood, the Manties were still three hours out. Assuming they opted for a zero-zero rendezvous with the planet, that was. Which they had to be planning on, didn't they? But if either of those other two freighters *could* get their impellers up and running, it would be his duty as the Madras Sector's governor to see to the protection and orderly governance of the *rest* of the sector, wouldn't it? From one of the uncaptured and still-defiant star systems like, say...McIntosh. Which just happened to be fifty-plus light-years away from Meyers.

Of course it would!

He reached for his com again.

❖   ❖   ❖

"Sort of reminds you of cockroaches, doesn't it, Ma'am?" Captain Armstrong remarked, and Michelle Henke chuckled. Cockroaches were one of the Old Terran species which had become as ubiquitous as mankind itself, and she had to admit Armstrong's simile fitted.

Tenth Fleet—or most of it, at any rate—had made its alpha translation seventy-three minutes ago, a half-million kilometers outside the hyper limit and just over eleven light-minutes from the planet of Meyers. Since then, her command's closing velocity relative to the planet had risen to 23,576 KPS, and she'd traveled over fifty-three million kilometers. In just over twenty-seven more minutes, her superdreadnoughts would be making turnover and beginning their deceleration towards the planet.

In the meantime, every hyper-capable ship that *could* get underway, had. She wasn't especially surprised to see the Frontier Fleet detachment running hard for the hyper limit, and she didn't blame Commodore Francis Thurgood one bit. In fact, she'd expected no less out of him. She and Cynthia Lecter had made it their business to study every scrap of information they could dig up on him, and it was obvious he was no Byng or Crandall. She'd been confident he'd recognize his responsibility to rescue whatever he could from the wreck for future service, and given that they'd obviously caught him with hot impeller nodes for some reason—an exercise, perhaps?—he was doing precisely what she would have anticipated.

Too bad, she thought. *Takes a certain degree of moral courage for an officer who knows her duty to cut and run in the face of the enemy. Lots easier for a coward to make that decision, really. He deserves better than what's going to happen.*

"I assume Captain Morgan's staying in touch?" she asked now, glancing at Lieutenant Commander Edwards, her com officer.

"Yes, Ma'am," Edwards acknowledged with an evil grin. Bill Edwards, who'd spent a lot of time at BuWeaps with Admiral Sonja Hemphill, wasn't exactly a typical communications specialist. He was actually a lot more of a "shooter" than a technical weenie, and Michelle shook her head at him fondly.

"Bloodthirsty, aren't you?" His grin only grew broader, and she shook her head, then glanced at Commander Adenauer.

The dark-haired operations officer had lost a lot of family in the Yawata Strike, and it had taken her a long time to regain her lively sense of humor. Indeed, there were shadows behind her eyes even now. It hadn't affected her work, though, and she looked up and raised one eyebrow as she felt her admiral's gaze.

"Yes, Ma'am?"

"What's the latest on those merchies, Dominica?"

"I think just about everyone who's going to get her impellers online before we hit orbit already has, Ma'am." The ops officer twitched her head in the direction of the master plot. "The only one that's really got a chance to make it across the limit is that first one, the one that bolted the instant they picked us up inbound. Well, I suppose I should say the only one that *thinks* it's really got a chance to make it across the limit is probably that one."

Her lips twitched, and Michelle sighed.

"Bloodthirsty lunatics. I'm surrounded by blood-thirsty lunatics."

"In all fairness, Ma'am, I don't think '*lunatics*' is exactly the right word," Cynthia Lecter said respectfully.

"Oh, really? And what noun would you choose instead, Cindy?"

"I think *enthusiasts* would be the best way to describe them," the trim, blonde chief of staff replied.

Michelle considered the suggestion for a second or two, then nodded.

"Point taken," she acknowledged, and turned her attention back to the plot once more.

Thurgood's battlecruisers had been accelerating away from Meyers for sixty-five minutes, and they hadn't been wasting any time about it. In fact, they were accelerating at almost 4.8 KPS^2, their maximum military power, without the inertial compensator safety margin upon which SLN doctrine insisted. As a result, their velocity away from the planet was up to 18,712 KPS, and they'd traveled 36.5 million kilometers. Assuming constant velocities, Thurgood would reach the hyper limit on the far side of the primary twenty-six minutes before Michelle could, which meant his battlecruisers would be able to slip away into hyper before she brought him into her Mark 16s' effective powered envelope. She would have been able to get inside her Mark 23s' much longer powered envelope, however, and her SD(P)s would have made short work of his battlecruisers and lighter units under those circumstances. It would have required the units she committed to the attack to simply overfly the planet without decelerating, but she had far more firepower than she'd ever need to deal with Meyers.

The three merchantmen who'd broken away from the planet complicated the situation a bit more, but not enough to do Thurgood any good. They were slower, they'd gotten started later, and even though each of them had headed off in a different direction, her warships had ample acceleration advantage to run them all down. She could have diverted a single destroyer—or even a LAC from one of her carriers—to deal with each of them. For that matter, she could have sent a massive LAC strike screaming after Thurgood and brought him to action long before he reached the hyper limit. Of course, more people would probably get killed that way before Thurgood formally surrendered what was left of his command, but there was no doubt she could have done it if she'd wanted to.

There was a much simpler and more elegant way to do the same job, however.

"All right, Dominica," she said after a moment. "Update the merchies' course profiles. As soon as she's done that, Bill," she turned back to the communications officer, "pass all the tactical data on to Captain Morgan. Tell him I don't want any of those freighters getting out with news of our arrival."

❖　❖　❖

"Message from the Flag, Sir," Commander Frank Ukhtomskoy's com officer announced.

"Ah?" Ukhtomskoy turned his command chair towards HMS *Talon*'s com section. "Our marching orders, I presume?"

"Yes, Sir. Latest update on enemy movements and target assignments for the intercepts."

"Good." Ukhtomskoy nodded and looked at his

astrogator. "In that case, I suppose we should be going," he observed.

Thirty-two seconds later, the destroyer disappeared quietly into hyper-space 198.2 million kilometers from the star called Meyers.

❖   ❖   ❖

"That's it, Sir," Captain Wayne said quietly, taking the message board Lieutenant Commander Olaf Lister, Thurgood's communications officer, had just sent to the briefing room. "Colonel Trondheim's officially surrendered." The chief of staff shrugged and handed the board back to the flag bridge yeoman who'd delivered it. He twitched his head at the briefing room door, and the yeoman vanished as Wayne turned back to Thurgood.

"Not like he had a lot of choice once they dropped into orbit around the planet and demanded his surrender," the commodore observed. "In fact, if I'm surprised by anything, it's that it took that long for the Manties to find someone to do the surrendering!"

And that we actually got the chance to run for it, he added mentally, trying to feel grateful for his good fortune.

To be honest, he'd never expected the Manties to simply let him go, not with their acceleration advantage. They could easily have dropped a handful of cruisers into Meyers orbit and sent everything else after him, and he'd never had any illusions about what would have happened if they had. The fact that they'd opted to simply ignore him and continue on their profile to secure the capital planet had been an enormous relief, yet there was a part of him which almost . . . resented it.

That wasn't the right verb, and he knew it, but it came close. It was as if he and his ships were so sublimely unimportant that the Manty admiral couldn't even be bothered to send someone to squash them. Francis Thurgood had never been one of those Battle Fleet idiots, and he'd never felt any particular urge to die for the honor of the flag. The lives of the men and women under his command were far too important to waste doing stupid things. But still that sensation of being casually brushed aside...

Better that than being turned into glowing wreckage, he reminded himself. *Not that your career isn't going to get turned into wreckage when Old Terra finds out about this. Alonso y Yáñez will probably realize you did the right thing, but that prick Rajampet sure as hell won't. The civilians are going to be looking for scapegoats, too, and you can bet your bottom credit they aren't going to put any of the blame on Verrocchio. Hell, they'll probably turn him and Hongbo into martyrs! The courageous civilian administrators who stayed at their posts while the military cut and ran on them. Blech.*

"I suppose we should head back to Flag Bridge," he said out loud, pushing back from the table. Wayne and Commander Merriman followed him out of the briefing room, and he tried hard to shake free of the numb dejection which had flowed over him in the last three and three-quarters hours.

It had taken the Manties roughly three hours and twenty minutes to reach Meyers, and Trondheim had surrendered the planet to them as soon as they did. No doubt they'd been "discussing" his options with him throughout their approach. Of course, it had taken another twenty-five minutes for Trondheim's lightspeed message to overtake Thurgood's fleeing command. Which meant he'd been up to a base velocity of almost 79,000 KPS, and only 89.6 million kilometers from the hyper limit—and safety—when *Edgehill* received the confirming transmission.

Trondheim's career would be going down the toilet, too, he reflected. For that matter, plenty of other careers were going to get turned into mush right along with his before this rat fuck of a war was over. But at least *his* people were going to live to fight another—

His thoughts cut off abruptly as an alarm shrilled.

"Hyper footprint!" Captain Macpherson snapped. "Multiple hyper footprints at zero-zero-zero by zero-zero-two! Range eight-niner-point-seven million kilometers!"

Thurgood's breathing seemed to stop as the blood-red icons appeared on the master plot directly ahead of his battlecruisers. How—?

The range was still the next best thing to five light-minutes. It was going to be a while before they had any lightspeed sensor results, but gravitics were FTL, and he watched silently as a pale-faced Macpherson leaned over a sensor rating's shoulder, staring at the detailed information from CIC. The ops officer's eyes darted from side to side, absorbing the data, and then she straightened slowly.

"From the impeller signatures, CIC makes it at least six of those big battlecruisers of theirs, Sir. Looks like they've got four heavy cruisers and at least four light cruisers—or maybe those outsized destroyers—to back them."

"I see."

Thurgood looked back at her for a moment, then clasped his hands behind him and walked slowly over to the communications section. He paused behind Lieutenant Commander Lister, waiting for what he knew had to come.

No wonder they didn't chase us, his mind reflected in the still calm that followed utter disaster. *They didn't have to. All they had to do was send somebody back up into hyper to tell the people they'd left there where they had to go to intercept us. And all I managed to do was to build up enough velocity I can't possibly avoid running right into that fucking long-ranged missile basket of theirs!*

He felt his jaw muscles ache with the pressure of his clenched teeth and forced himself to relax them. No doubt those fleeing freighters were going to find *themselves* picked off, too, he thought. Which meant Verrocchio and Hongbo weren't going to manage to run out on their mess after all. That was something, at least.

"We have a message request, Commodore," Lister said quietly. "It's from a Rear Admiral Oversteegen."

"I've been expecting it, Olaf," Thurgood replied with a thin smile. "I suppose you'd better go ahead and put him through."

✦ Chapter Thirty-Four

MICHELLE HENKE ROSE BEHIND her desk as her day cabin's door opened. The man who stepped through it was of average height, with the dark hair and eyes which seemed to be the norm here on the planet of Meyers. He was well dressed, although the cut of his clothing was a T-year or two out of date by the latest Core World fashions, and he extended a well manicured hand as he approached her.

"Prime Minister Montview," she said, reaching out her own hand. His grip was surprisingly firm, not the perfunctory squeeze too many politicians had perfected from too many T-years of shaking voters' hands, and his dark eyes met hers.

"Admiral Gold Peak," he responded.

"Please, have a seat," she invited, reclaiming her hand and indicating the pair of armchairs arranged on either side of the coffee table.

"Thank you."

Montview accepted the invitation, and Chris Billingsley appeared as if by magic. Michelle's steward was resplendent in perfectly turned out mess dress

550

uniform, with a white towel over his left forearm which ought to have seemed out of keeping with his battered prizefighter's face but somehow didn't. He carried a tray of finger sandwiches, which he placed on the coffee table. Then he gathered up the silver coffee pot embossed with HMS *Artemis'* crossed-arrow coat of arms and poured two cups.

"Will there be anything else, Milady?" he inquired.

"Just make sure Alfredo has fresh celery, please, Chris," Michelle replied.

"Of course, Milady."

Billingsley bowed slightly to her and to her guest, then withdrew, pausing to check with the treecat arranged on the perch behind Michelle's desk. Master Sergeant Cognasso just happened to be the Marine sentry posted outside Michelle's cabin door, and Alfredo—celery stalk clutched in hand—watched her and the prime minister with apparent indifference.

Appearances, of course, could be deceiving.

"Thank you for coming, Prime Minister," Michelle said as the door closed behind Billingsley.

"It wasn't exactly as if attendance was discretionary, Admiral," Montview pointed out with a disarming smile. "Although the invitation was phrased with admirable courtesy, I thought."

"There was no point being impolite," Michelle responded with a smile of her own. Then her smile faded. "Of course, I'm afraid we've been rather less polite with some people than with you."

"I presume that refers to Commissioner Verrochio and Vice Commissioner Hongbo?" Montview inquired, and she nodded. "Ah." He nodded, then shrugged slightly. "Understandable, I suppose."

Michelle sat back with her coffee cup, studying him thoughtfully. Thomas Montview was officially the prime minister of King Lawrence IX, titular ruler of the Kingdom of Meyers, which covered about three quarters of the surface of the planet of Meyers. In fact, Lawrence Thomas and his entire family had been little more than figureheads ever since Frontier Security's arrival in the Meyers System. Still, the House of Thomas had provided a useful interface, and the Thomases had survived better than most local dynasties who found themselves engulfed by the protectorates system. They'd actually retained a sizable percentage of the family wealth, and everything Michelle and Cynthia Lecter had been able to find in the local system databases suggested that Lawrence and his parents and grandparents had done their best to mitigate the weight of the OFS yoke for the population of Meyers. They'd been active in philanthropic pursuits, and they'd given a great deal of support to public education out of their private coffers.

None of which meant they hadn't had to make their own accommodations with the Frontier Security system, and Montview, as Lawrence's prime minister, had been the primary local front man for Lorcan Verrochio's administration. It was apparent that he'd done quite well out of his position, but he was something of a cipher as far as Michelle and Lecter had been able to determine.

"I'm afraid the two of them—and especially Commissioner Verrocchio—took it rather less philosophically than that," she said now.

"I'm sure they did." Montview sipped his own coffee. "They had so much more to lose, after all. And

I feel certain their superiors back on Old Terra are going to have a few harsh words for them, as well." He smiled thinly. "The one thing you can depend upon is that everyone in OFS has a scapegoat ready and waiting should the need arise."

"I should take it, then, that you weren't too fond of Frontier Security?" Michelle asked lightly, watching Alfredo out of the corner of her eye.

"No one who's ever had the dubious privilege of being gathered to Frontier Security's protective bosom is 'too fond' of it." Montview's tone was as light as Michelle's own, but there was a measured bite buried in it. "The more closely you find yourself compelled to work with them, the less fond of them you become, however."

Alfredo waved his celery stalk casually, confirming Montview's sincerity. The fact that the prime minister didn't care for Frontier Security didn't automatically make him a paragon of virtue, but it was definitely a point in his favor.

"Well, Mr. Prime Minister, as it happens, we're not too fond of Frontier Security—or the Solarian League in general—at the moment, ourselves." Michelle shrugged. "I think we can all take it as a given that relations between the Star Empire and the League are going to get worse before they get better."

"Would you be terribly disappointed, Admiral Gold Peak, if I told you that didn't come as a huge surprise?" Montview inquired, and Michelle chuckled.

"Not at all, Mr. Prime Minister. I only mentioned it as a preface to what I really wanted to speak to you about."

She paused, head cocked, and he frowned thoughtfully. Then he shrugged.

"I would presume that what you're leading up to has to do with the long-term political situation here on Meyers," he said, and Michelle nodded. She wasn't really surprised by his comment—she'd already come to the conclusion he was no dummy—but she was pleased by his directness.

"Precisely," she agreed. "At the moment, I have no definitive instructions on political administration of territory captured—or liberated—from the Solarian League." Which, she refrained from mentioning, was because she had no instructions about capturing or liberating that territory in the first place. "Because of that," she continued, "I'm afraid I'm rather in the position of making things up as I go along. That gives me a certain degree of freedom, although it also obviously means any arrangements I might put in place would be subject to review by higher authority. On the other hand," she looked directly into Montview's eyes, "there aren't a great many 'higher authorities' in the Star Empire."

Montview sat back in his armchair, sipping coffee and regarding her thoughtfully. It was clear to Michelle that he'd done his homework on her just as thoroughly as she'd done hers on him. What she wasn't certain of was whether or not he realized she was effectively putting the honor of the House of Winton on the line. She couldn't be certain even Beth would honor every detail of any arrangement to which she committed the Star Empire, but she was positive her cousin would never betray or abandon anyone Michelle had agreed to support.

"I believe I appreciate your position, Milady," Montview said, and Michelle raised mental eyebrows as he addressed her as a member of the Manticoran peerage rather than by her naval rank. "Should I conclude from what you've just said that you're considering an arrangement which would involve my King?"

"I am," Michelle confirmed, leaning back in her own chair and resting her elbows on its arms to steeple her fingers in front of her. "Of course, the exact nature of that arrangement would depend on a great many factors."

"Factors such as . . . ?" Montview raised his eyebrows as he allowed his voice to trail off.

"At the moment, Mr. Prime Minister, no one outside the Meyers System knows what's happened here. No hyper-capable unit made it out, which means it will be some time—probably T-months, in fact—before anyone else realizes anything's happened at all. That gives us some time to work with. Unfortunately, we're in what you might call a . . . dynamic situation, and my military capabilities are a bit lopsided." Michelle showed her teeth briefly. "I've got oodles—that's a technical term, Mr. Prime Minister; it means lots and lots—of *naval* combat power, but I'm severely strapped for *ground* combat power."

Montview nodded gravely, although Michelle doubted that he truly realized just how short of ground troops she actually was. Colonel Liam Trondheim, the senior Gendarmerie officer present, had surrendered the system to her as soon as her ships entered Meyers planetary orbit. He hadn't had a great deal of choice about that, under the recognized interstellar laws of war. For that matter, Michelle had been perfectly willing to take out every Gendarmerie base on the planet from orbit (also as the interstellar laws of war permitted for planets which *didn't* surrender), and he seemed to realize that fact.

She rather regretted that Brigadier Yucel hadn't been here to do the surrendering herself. Everything she and Cynthia Lecter had been able to dig up on the brigadier suggested she was an ugly piece of work, even by the standards of the Solarian League Gendarmerie. On the other hand, according to Trondheim, one reason he'd been so quick to surrender was that Yucel had taken two full battalions of her best troops (although Michelle doubted Yucel's definition of "best troops" would have matched her own) off to the Mobius System. She didn't like to think about what someone like Yucel might have been doing with those troops, but she felt confident, somehow, that Sir Aivars Terekhov would experience no insurmountable difficulty in dealing with the brigadier.

Here in Meyers, however, Michelle was left with the problem that she simply didn't have the troop strength to garrison what she'd captured. The planet Meyers itself was home to 3.6 billion people. Another thirty-two thousand lived on the next planet out, Socrates, which was very like the Sol System's Mars but with a slightly thicker atmosphere. The Truman Belt was home to another 843,000 people, most committed to routine mining and other resource extraction. And then there were the two hundred thousand living on the moons of the gas giant Damien, mining the planetary atmosphere for hydrogen and rare gases.

That wasn't very many people by the standards of one of the League's Core Worlds, but it very nearly equaled the total population of the Manticore Binary System, and there was no way in the universe her own limited Marine strength could possibly hope to control them.

On the other hand, *Frontier Security* hadn't been able to ship in enough troops to actually garrison the system, either. The Sollies had been forced to rely on local police forces to maintain public order and enforce civil law. That was always the case, of course, but generally those local police forces took their cue from the OFS administration which had co-opted their services. That was one reason Michelle had dreaded what she'd find when they reached Meyers, given Yucel's reputation.

To her surprise, however, local law enforcement appeared to have avoided the brutality and repressiveness she'd anticipated. Partly that was because Yucel had been assigned to the Madras Sector fairly recently. Another part of it, she'd been forced to admit—grudgingly, grudgingly!—was probably due to Lorcan Verrochio and Junyan Hongbo. In fact, she suspected more to the vice commissioner than to Verrocchio, although it was early to be drawing that sort of conclusion. But even more of it, she thought—hoped—stemmed from the example of King Lawrence and his family.

Michelle Henke wasn't about to conclude that the Meyers police forces were miraculously free of the corruption which followed Frontier Security like a pestilence. But they clearly took their responsibility as the guardians of public order and safety seriously, and because they did, she was inclined to cut them a substantial amount of slack. The question was who they ultimately answered to.

"I anticipate receiving additional ground troops

as soon as they can be forwarded from the Talbott Quadrant," she continued. There was no need to tell him just how long "soon" might be. "In the meantime, however, we have to make do out of the forces currently available to me, and most of my ground personnel are trained as Marines—as combat troops—not law enforcement personnel. Under the circumstances, I think it would be to everyone's advantage to keep a trained and experienced police force on the job. Assuming, of course," she looked into Montview's eyes again, "that I could come to some sort of mutually acceptable arrangement with some local authority who could command that police force's loyalty and obedience."

"Actually, Milady," Montview said after a moment, "our law officers' formal oaths of office are sworn to the House of Thomas, not to the Solarian League or Frontier Security." It was his turn to show his teeth. "An unfortunate oversight on their part."

"Yes, it was," Michelle agreed.

It was also fairly standard operating procedure for OFS, however. The legal fiction that the Protectorates were still independent star systems simply "under the protection" of the beneficent Solarian League required local régimes. Those régimes were well aware of the fact that they actually possessed no authority of their own, yet the *forms* were important. Michelle sometimes thought that was due to the Solarian League's unhealthy worship of bureaucratic paperwork, but it was also a fig leaf which could be hauled out if some Solarian newsy muckraker started poking about. *Imperialism?* Oh, my, no! Perish the very thought! We're simply here as *advisers* to support yet another neobarb star system in its painful march towards truly representative and democratic government! See? We can't even give any direct orders to the local police force. They all have to go through the local, duly elected government.

"Should I take it, Mr. Prime Minister, that if I were to recognize—provisionally, of course; as I say, any decision I make would be subject to review by higher authority—King Lawrence as the local, legitimate head of state and charge him with creating a provisional government for the entire star system, he would be prepared to accept that responsibility under the protection of the Star Empire of Manticore?"

Montview's eyes flickered. For a moment, Michelle wondered why. Then it hit her.

"Forgive me." She shook her head. "That was clumsily phrased, especially in light of your star system's experience of *Frontier Security's* notion of 'protection.'" She shook her head again. "Allow me to clarify what I actually meant."

Montview took a slow sip of coffee, then set the cup on the saucer in his lap and nodded.

"While many of my decisions will be subject to review, Mr. Prime Minister, one thing I can tell you with absolute certainty at this time is that my Empress and her government have no intention of adding independent star systems forcibly to the Star Empire. Nor are we interested in controlling nominally independent star systems through puppet governments and protectorate arrangements. In fact, our recent expansion is going to leave us with some significant problems when it comes to integrating our new citizens into our existing political and economic system.

We still don't know how those problems are going to work out, although I'm optimistic that they *will* work out, but no one in the Star Empire's government is eager to add still more potential headaches to the list. Holding down forcibly annexed populations would probably rate pretty high on anyone's list of headaches, I'd think, and that doesn't even consider the fact that we literally cannot afford to fritter away the military resources we need against something the size of the League by tying them down on occupation duty just to keep our boot on the neck of someone who doesn't want us running their star system.

"Because of the nature of our conflict with the Solarian League, however, it's inevitable that we're going to find ourselves doing very much what we did here—taking star systems away from *Solarian* control. When that happens, we automatically assume a moral responsibility for the future well-being of those star systems. We don't want our actions to lead to wholesale violence, political instability, or the emergence of warlordism, and that means we can't simply pull back out as soon as the local Sollies surrender. For that matter, if we did any such thing, it would simply invite the Sollies to return to the vacuum we'd leave behind us.

"As I see it, that means our best course of action is to encourage the formation of stable system governments. *Independent* stable system governments. In many cases, that's going to be very difficult, for reasons I'm sure you understand." Michelle's brown eyes turned grim. "Frankly, Mr. Prime Minister, the Meyers System's been incredibly fortunate compared to the vast majority of protectorate systems. That's the reason you and I are having this conversation. I believe there's an excellent chance King Lawrence can form a genuine, popularly accepted government with our support, and I'm prepared to offer that support as long as he's committed to forming a government prepared to safeguard its citizens' fundamental civic rights and safety. I am *not* prepared to support him in the formation of any government which does not safeguard those rights and that safety."

She paused to let that last sentence sink in, then leaned forward, resting her elbows on her thighs and clasping her hands under her chin.

"Should King Lawrence be interested in forming such a government, and should he be prepared to demonstrate guarantees for his subjects' rights and safety, I'm prepared, provisionally, speaking for the Star Empire of Manticore, to acknowledge him as the rightful sovereign of the Meyers System, and to offer him a military and economic alliance with the Star Empire. We're *not* interested in policing, occupying, or owning your planets, Mr. Prime Minister. We *are* interested in depriving the Solarian League of a foothold here or elsewhere in the Madras Sector, and our experience has been that offering a potential ally a helping hand instead of an iron fist is the best way to achieve a stable, long-lasting relationship. You might want to study the relationship we've achieved with the Yeltsin System and the Protectorship of Grayson."

Montview sat silent, gazing into her eyes very intently for several seconds. Then he drew a deep breath and squared his shoulders.

"Obviously, I'll have to discuss this with His Majesty, Milady. I believe, however, that you'll discover this is no more than what he's always wished it had been within his power to accomplish. I don't say there won't be problems. Among other things, I expect the Damien Moons to argue in favor of independence from the Kingdom. That's where the most . . . recalcitrant of our people have relocated since Frontier Security's arrival. They haven't thought much of our 'inner world' softness and collaboration." He smiled briefly. "Hard to blame them, really, but I've often wondered if they realized how much that 'collaboration' of the King's had to do with Frontier Security's leaving them alone out there.

"Aside from that, I think the political equation would work itself out much more smoothly than you might have anticipated. I also think our local police forces would be extremely grateful if we could establish a clear-cut source of local authority as quickly as possible. At the moment, everyone's operating in something of a vacuum, and that means all of them are also looking over their shoulders, wondering what's going to happen if and when you and your ships pull out."

Michelle had gazed attentively at—and past—him while he was speaking. She'd watched Alfredo the entire time, and the treecat had sat upright on his perch, his full attention focused on Montview. Now he looked away from the prime minister, directly at Michelle, and nodded slowly.

"In that case, Mr. Prime Minister," Michelle said, "I think it would be a good thing if you could arrange a direct meeting between me and the King, don't you?"

Chapter Thirty-Five

"I THINK WE SHOULD have another little chat with Vice Commissioner Hongbo, Ma'am," Cynthia Lecter said.

"Not exactly the most enjoyable thing I could imagine doing," Michelle Henke replied dryly.

She reached out a long arm for the coffee carafe and replenished her cup. Then she sat back on her own side of the breakfast table, nursing the cup in both hands, and regarded her chief of staff through the wisp of steam rising from the black liquid. They'd been in the Meyers System for over two T-weeks now, and things had been going smoothly enough to make her nervous. In her experience, the calmer and more orderly things *seemed*, the more likely it was that something was lurking just beneath the surface to leap out and bite one on the posterior. And since Lecter was still wearing the intelligence officer's hat as well as the chief of staff's hat, she was the one responsible for digging under that surface and finding the lurker before it struck.

"I presume you have a specific reason for that

suggestion?" Michelle asked after a moment, and Lecter nodded.

"We're turning up some things I'd like to try on him." The chief of staff was a fidgeter, and she picked up her grapefruit spoon, twirling it between the thumb and first two fingers of her right hand while she spoke. "I think he could tell us a few things we'd really like to know."

"I'm sure he could be a fount of information on any number of subjects." Michelle shrugged and took a sip of coffee. "He was second in command of an entire protectorate sector. Somebody like that's bound to know where a lot of bodies are buried."

"I know." Lecter thumped the bowl of the spoon on the white breakfast tablecloth, drumming gently. "The thing is, we're picking up some suggestions that he might have what you could call a friendly relationship with Manpower and Mesa in general."

"And?" Michelle's eyes narrowed.

"I know that's hardly surprising." Lecter grimaced. "I sometimes think the *majority* of Frontier Security officials have 'friendly relationships' with Manpower. Hell, Ma'am, they've got 'friendly relationships' with *every* dirty transstellar! After all, it's the illegal transstellars—like Manpower and the rest of that bunch in Mesa—that pay the best when they manage to put somebody in their pocket."

"Exactly. So what is it about Hongbo that suggests we should pay special attention to him?"

"Well, with Kowalski helping to point the way, our friends here in Pine Mountain have managed to break into a lot of people's financial records. Specifically, they're well on their way to opening up virtually all of Hongbo's, Verrocchio's, Palgani's, and Kasomoulis' private little books, and there's some interesting reading in there."

"No! Really?" Michelle said dryly, and Lecter chuckled.

Saverio Palgani was—or had been, at any rate, prior to Tenth Fleet's arrival—the Meyers System manager for Brindle Star, Ltd., of Hirochi. His position in the sector capital meant he'd actually been in charge of all of Brindle Star's operations in the entire Madras Sector, which had made him a very big fish, indeed.

Theophilia Kasomoulis had fulfilled the same role for Newman & Sons, headquartered in the Core System of Eris, and Brindle Star and Newman & Sons had divided most of the Madras Sector between themselves as their private possession. Brindle Star controlled effectively the entire sector's interstellar shipping and financial transactions, while Newman & Sons controlled resource extraction and consumer manufacturing and distribution. Palgani and Kasomoulis were undoubtedly the two wealthiest individuals in the entire Meyers System, but Michelle had to admit they seemed to have been less rapacious than their counterparts in many another protectorate star system. Apparently they'd at least been enlightened enough to realize that while the sort of slash-and-burn exploitation practiced in other portions of the Verge might return a higher short-term profit, *long*-term profitability required at least a modicum of local prosperity.

Not that that made them any great paragons of virtue, she reminded herself.

Yeargin Kowalski, on the other hand, was a local businessman and banker. He'd had to deal with the transstellars, especially with Brindle Star, but he'd focused more on the more marginal deals too small to attract Palgani's attention. In some ways, Michelle supposed, Kowalski had followed in Brindle Star's wake, gleaning the predator's leftovers. Another way to look at it, though, was that he'd provided capital to a host of locally owned entrepreneurships which would have been completely squeezed out by the transstellars without him.

When Prime Minister Montview began constructing a genuine government, he'd needed a finance minister to replace the totally incompetent (and totally corrupt) crony Palgani had insisted hold that position in the "official" government. Kowalski had been on his short list from the outset, and nothing anyone had turned up in his background had disqualified him. In fact, he'd been a highly popular choice among those same local entrepreneurs, and there'd never been the least suggestion of dishonesty or corruption on his part.

Because of his dealings with Palgani and Kasomoulis, on the other hand, Kowalski had had a very good idea of where to start when it came to exhuming the transstellars' books. Not the official books which they'd kept primarily for tax assessment, shareholder earnings calculations, and writeoff purposes, but the *real* books, the ones which detailed every sordid detail of their actual operations.

Helen Sanderson, originally the Pine Mountain Police Department's second ranking officer, had been named to head the new Royal Police whose jurisdiction spanned the entire star system. Her immediate superior had been unavailable for the position, since he'd been under arrest at the time and was probably going to spend the next several T-years as a guest of the Meyers penal system. With Kowalski to guide her, and the enthusiastic support of Janice Hannover, a Meyers realtor and commercial farmer who'd been strong-armed into taking the position of attorney general, Sanderson had launched an aggressive probe of the entire "black economy."

Aside from providing a handful of computer techs to assist in the effort, Tenth Fleet had been perfectly happy to stand back and let the locals deal with their own dirty laundry. It was the last thing Michelle wanted to get involved in, yet they'd been sharing their findings with Lecter from the beginning, and Michelle had always realized Sanderson and Kowalski were almost certain to eventually unearth something with implications for her.

"All right," she said. "Give me the quick summary version."

"You want to hear about Palgani and Kasomoulis? Or just about Verrocchio and Hongbo?"

"Which do you think I should be hearing about?"

Lecter pondered for a moment, drumming more loudly with the grapefruit spoon until Michelle reached across and snatched it out of her hand with a glare. The chief staff looked at her for a moment, then grinned.

"Sorry about that," she said. "And as to your question, eventually I think you're going to be *very* interested in what we've discovered about Palgani and Kasomoulis. I know *I* wouldn't have believed how the hell much money they could siphon off." She shook her head. "I mean, we've always known the amounts have to be huge in any protectorate system, but these two—! Let's put it this way, neither of them was ever going to reach Klaus Hauptman levels, but both of them were—conservatively—multibillionaires. And the really neat thing about it is that it looks like a lot of what they squirreled away was illegal even under the letter of *Solly* law. Everybody knew they were doing it, of course, but it *was* illegal, and that means Hanover and Sanderson are in a perfect position to seize their ill-gotten gains, completely irrespective of what the Crown ultimately does about nationalizing Brindle Star and Newman and Sons' local assets."

The chief of staff's smile was positively seraphic, and Michelle chuckled evilly.

"You're right, I am going to want to hear all about that eventually. Or at least my nasty side is. The best way to deal with someone like those two is to leave them without a pot to piss in. I mean, a little prison time on top of it would be nice, but taking away all their toys is even better."

"I know."

Lecter smiled for a few more moments, but then the smile faded.

"I know," she repeated. "But aside from the fact that it looks like Brindle Star was probably carrying the occasional illicit cargo for Manpower and some of the other Mesan transstellars—they had a reciprocal agreement with Jessyk, for example—what Sanderson and Kowalski have turned up about them so far is less immediately important than what they're finding about Verrocchio and Hongbo. Especially Hongbo."

"You said that already—that Hongbo's a more important player from our perspective than Verrocchio," Michelle observed. "I find that a little surprising. Why buy the *vice* commissioner when you've already bought the *commissioner*?"

"That surprised me at first, too," Lecter admitted. "Then I got to thinking about it. How often have both of us seen someone else being the power behind the throne—especially in a bureaucratic relationship? From the looks of things, Hongbo's made quite a bit of his career on the basis of 'managing' Verrocchio. And I don't think he did all of that managing just for his superiors in the Office of Frontier Security, either."

"Ah?" Michelle took another sip of coffee and raised both eyebrows.

"Ah," Lecter said with a nod. Then she looked at the piece of silverware her admiral had taken away from her. "Can I please have my spoon back, Ma'am?" she said almost plaintively. "You know how much better I think when I've got something to do with my hands."

Michelle considered her forbiddingly for several moments.

"You can have it back if you *promise* not to drum with it," she said after a moment. "One *tap*, though, and—"

She drew the tip of her left thumb across her throat in a slicing motion and glowered at Lecter.

"I promise to be good, Ma'am."

"All right then." Michelle slid the spoon back across the table to her. "Now continue with your explanation."

Lecter recovered the spoon with a broad smile and started twirling it again, but her blue eyes were serious as she tipped back in her chair.

"Verrocchio's records were easier to break into than Hongbo's," she began. "The encryption wasn't as good, and apparently he only had two or three personal passwords that he reused a lot." She grimaced. "Hongbo, on the other hand, had top-flight encryption—by civilian Solly standards, at least—and he was a lot more inventive when it came to generating passwords. We still haven't gotten into some of his files, and at least one entire folder went up in smoke on us." She shook her head. "It looks to the computer geeks like he got some high-powered outside help. The kind of help that only makes itself available when you're hiding something *it* doesn't want found, either."

"And Verrocchio's records didn't have that level of sophistication?" Michelle asked thoughtfully.

"No, they didn't. Despite the fact that Verrocchio was dealing *directly* with Manpower, and that he'd been doing it long before the situation with Monica ever blew up in Sir Aivars' face. You'd have thought if Manpower was going to provide technical assistance to one of them, it would have provided it to both of them, wouldn't you?"

"Yes, you would. Unless, of course, one of them was dealing with someone a layer or two *up* from Manpower," Michelle said slowly.

"That's what got me interested in Hongbo," Lecter admitted. "More interested in him than in Verrocchio, I mean. And when I got interested in him, I put a team on Verrocchio's correspondence files, looking specifically for memos generated by Hongbo. Or sent by him to Hongbo, for that matter."

"That must have produced the odd petabyte," Michelle said dryly, considering the bureaucratic morass of the Solarian League's civil services.

"There *were* a bunch of them, Ma'am," Lecter agreed. "I had them filtered by date and also using strings like 'Monica' and 'Byng' or 'New Tuscany,' though. That reduced the overall sample in a hurry."

"All right, I'm with you so far." Michelle leaned back, sipping coffee, and reached for the last cinnamon bun.

"There was still a lot of garbage-in-garbage-out, Ma'am, but a pattern emerged. Back before Monica, or rather in the buildup *to* Monica, Hongbo was consistently pushing Verrocchio to be 'more proactive' even in his official memos. We've turned up a side file of private correspondence as well, and he's even more persistent there. There's no proof he knew everything Manpower and Technodyne were up to—no direct evidence he knew about Nordbrandt or Westman, for example—but it's obvious both of them *did* know about the battlecruisers Technodyne was supplying to Monica. And from their private correspondence, it's equally obvious both of them were scared to death when they saw what happened to those battlecruisers. You wouldn't believe how much time, effort, and bandwidth they spent—Verrocchio, especially—on proving to Frontier Security HQ back on Old Terra that whatever happened in Monica, it wasn't *their* fault! I suspect a few of the official memos they'd exchanged before it all went south on them got fed to the chip shredder at that point, as a matter of fact.

"But what's even more interesting to me is that Hongbo, who apparently had been carrying water for Manpower, at least to judge from the memos he was sending Verrocchio, put the brakes on big-time after Monica." The blonde-haired chief of staff shrugged, still twirling her spoon. "Nothing too surprising about that, I suppose, but then, just before Josef Byng and Sandra Crandall got sent out here, the tone of this correspondence shifts again. All of a sudden he's subtly encouraging Verrocchio to 'cooperate' with Byng. And if you read the official minutes of the meetings between Verrocchio, Hongbo, and Byng before New Tuscany—and between those two and Crandall, before she set off for Spindle—there's a definite subtext."

"Subtext?" Michelle repeated.

"Yes, Ma'am." Lecter nodded. "We've both been around enough bureaucrats, civilian and Navy alike, to know how it's done. The two of them—Verrocchio's the one taking point, but from my reading, Hongbo was probably the one who was actually steering—double-teamed Byng and probably Crandall into doing exactly what they did. Not only that, they maneuvered Byng and Crandall into making their decisions *against* Verrocchio's official recommendations."

She paused, and silence hovered for the better part of two minutes.

"You know any court of law would chuck that straight out the airlock," Michelle said at last, her tone mild. "I haven't looked at the memos myself, of course, but from what you've just said, it sounds like Mr. Verrocchio and Mr. Hongbo must be pretty good at the bureaucratic fan dance."

"I'm inclined to agree, Ma'am. Both of them covered themselves pretty well, at least in terms of ever coming right out in any official setting and saying anything someone could nail them for. And given what they *did* say, if I hadn't already been suspicious about Hongbo for other reasons, I probably would have simply accepted that Verrocchio, as Hongbo's boss, had to be making the decisions. And he clearly was the one making the *final* decisions. But it's increasingly apparent to me that he was dancing to Hongbo's piping. And there's another thing, too. There's a Mesan diplomat—a fairly senior trade attaché by the name of Ottweiler, Valery Ottweiler—whose name appears on Hongbo's calendar of appointments with an interesting frequency. There's no record of Ottweiler ever having had a private meeting with Verrocchio, but I've found over a dozen between him and *Hongbo*."

Lecter paused again, and Michelle considered her expression.

"You want to go ahead and let that other shoe drop now, Cindy?" she inquired.

"What other shoe?" Lecter asked innocently.

"The one that doesn't have anything to do with memos between Hongbo and Verrocchio. The one you found by following some kind of wild, totally illogical hunch." Michelle snorted. "I've known you a long time, you know, and that talent for being... creatively erratic is one reason I wanted you for my chief of staff. So spill it."

"Yes, Ma'am." Lecter grinned, but then she sobered. "Although, to be fair, it wasn't really following a hunch in this case. I just took all the names I'd come up with and threw them into the filters for all the records we've been breaking into. Including the Gendarmerie's."

"Oh?" Michelle cocked her head. "That sounds interesting."

"Oh, it was, Ma'am. It was! Because it would appear Brigadier Yucel didn't believe in keeping her nominal superiors fully apprised of her surveillance activities. In fact, she was bugging both Hongbo and Verrocchio. We haven't turned up anything especially incriminating in the official surveillance files on them—not yet, anyway—but we're getting into her more secure files now. The ones she kept for *herself*, not the official record. And yesterday evening, my cyber forensics team turned up at least two meetings that never officially happened—meetings between Verrocchio, Hongbo, Yucel herself, Ottweiler, Volkhart Kalokainos, Izrok Levakonic, Aldona Anisimovna, and Isabel Bardasano. And both of which happened here in Meyers, a couple of T-months before Technodyne offered all those battlecruisers to President Tyler."

Michelle straightened abruptly in her chair, her eyes very narrow, as those names registered. Volkhart Kalokainos was the eldest son of Heinrich Kalokainos, the CEO and majority stockholder of Kalokainos Shipping, one of the largest—and most violently anti-Manticoran—Solarian shipping houses. The late (and not particularly lamented) Izrok Levakonic had been the Technodyne executive who'd served as that transstellar's contact with President Roberto Tyler and the Monican Navy. Aldona Anisimovna had been the Mesan Alignment's contact in New Tuscany before Admiral Byng's disastrous confrontation with the Royal Manticoran Navy. And last but not least, as the pièce de résistance, there was Isabel Bardasano—the woman Jack McBryde had identified as the second in command of *all* of the Mesan Alignment's intelligence operations.

"My God, Cindy," she said after a moment, her tone considerably milder than she actually felt, "don't you think you could possibly have trotted that last little datum out first?"

"I could have," Lecter agreed. "But I wanted to lay out how we got from Point A to Point B. And I especially wanted to lay the groundwork for why I think Hongbo was more fully plugged into the Alignment than Verrocchio. I think both of them could probably give us a lot of really valuable information, but I also think Hongbo's going to be the richer vein if we can figure out how to mine him properly."

"I can see that," Michelle conceded. "Of course, there's a part of me that's inclined to just drag the bastard in and sweat it out of him. Somehow I'm not feeling all warm and gooey about Frontier Security at the moment. I think I can probably deal quite well with a few little human rights violations where these two scumbags are concerned."

"Never any of Duchess Harrington's Ballroom friends around when you need one, is there, Ma'am?" Lecter said wryly.

"I have no idea what you're talking about," Michelle said. "Besides, if we really needed someone to whistle up a Ballroom fanatic to loom threateningly in the background, we could probably ask Ensign Zilwicki to come up with one. Assuming we hadn't sent her off to Mobius with Aivars, that is."

"We could always bring in a *fake* fanatic," Lecter pointed out. "I've done a personnel search, and we've got better than thirty ex-genetic slaves, complete with tongue barcodes, assigned to the units we've got right here in Meyers. I'm sure any one of them—hell, *all* of them!— would be prepared to impersonate a Ballroom representative, show our OFS friends their tongues, and suggest it would be a good idea to tell us whatever we want to hear. In the most friendly possible way, of course."

"Tempting, Cindy. *Very* tempting," Michelle admitted. "In fact, that might be something to keep in reserve. Right now, though, I think we might try subtle first."

"*Subtle*, Ma'am?" Lecter repeated, regarding her admiral with a doubtful expression.

"I *have* been known to do subtle upon occasion," Michelle told her in quelling tones. "Not very often, I'll admit. And it's not my favorite way of getting things done. This isn't really a case that's suitable for shooting them all and letting God sort them out later, though, so I *think* I can restrain my homicidal inclinations as long as it's in a good cause."

"Yes, Ma'am. Never doubted it, Ma'am."

"I think you'd better let this one go before you get into *real* trouble, Captain," Michelle said repressively.

Lecter grinned at her, and Michelle shook her head. Then she continued.

"I've gotten pretty accustomed to working with Alfredo and Master Sergeant Cognasso," she pointed out. "And it's entirely possible that neither Hongbo nor Verrocchio have heard the reports about furry lie detectors yet. So if you happened to be able to prime me with the data you've pulled out of these hacked files of yours, and if I happened to invite those two estimable gentlemen in for a private chat—just me and my furry little pet, Alfredo, and possibly a Marine or two for security, like Cognasso—we could probably learn a lot."

"You mean by not confronting him directly? By just asking leading questions and letting Alfredo monitor his responses?"

"Maybe, but probably not." Michelle shook her head. "It's not like Alfredo can tell us what he's actually *thinking*; he can only tell us when he knows a two-leg is lying or telling the truth. I could probably nibble around the edges asking indirect questions, but if I'm really going to get confirmation, I'm going to have to go more directly to the heart of things. What I *can* do, though, is to let him think he's getting away with lying to me when he's not. I can probably pull a lot out of him that way—a lot more than we'd get voluntarily if he knew we were closing in on him."

"That's probably true, Ma'am," Lecter said. "On the other hand, and with all due respect, you're not really a trained interrogator."

"No, I'm not. And your point is—?"

"Do you think it might be better to let someone who *is* a trained interrogator ask the questions and work with Alfredo? Someone who might pick up on some of the body cues you might miss and use what she picks up to guide her follow-on questions?"

Michelle considered thoughtfully for a moment, then shrugged.

"You may have a point. In fact, you *do* have one. But I'm the one who's worked with Alfredo so far, and I'm not sure we've got anyone else in Tenth Fleet who can actually read treecat sign. Aside from me and Cognasso, at any rate, and I doubt he's a trained interrogator, either."

"No, that's true enough," Lecter acknowledged.

"I still think it's a good idea, though," Michelle said. "In fact, I think it's an excellent one. And workable, too."

"How, Ma'am?"

"Simple." Michelle shrugged again, this time with an evil smile. "We bug my cabin. We put in an audio-visual pickup without mentioning it to our guests. We park a trained interrogator in front of the monitors, and we give me a miniature earbug. The interrogator watches their expressions and body language, and if she sees anything, she passes it on to me over the earbug. Meanwhile, I ask the questions, and Alfredo sits on his perch behind my current victim and signs anything he picks up to me. What do you think?"

Lecter considered her reply. Michelle's suggestion did seem to cover most of the bases. And, possibly more to the point, Lecter knew her admiral. Michelle Henke was going to do this herself. That was already settled, cast in stone, as far as the Countess of Gold Peak was concerned. So—

"I'm not certain it's the absolutely best way to go about it, Ma'am, but I think it should work. In fact, it should work one hell of a lot better than any conventional interrogation technique I can come up with. And I'd really, really like to be able to find some additional confirmation of this Alignment's existence. A *Solly* confirmation, not just something manufactured out of our Manticoran paranoia."

"Oh, don't forget the part that's manufactured out of our Machiavellian Manticoran *imperialism*, either," Michelle said sourly. "Still, I take your point. And I agree."

"And best of all," Lecter's smile was every bit as evil as Michelle's had been, "if we do it right?" She chuckled. "The bastards won't even realize we're onto them until we hand them over for trial. I can hardly *wait* to see their expressions then."

◇ Chapter Thirty-Six

"SIT DOWN, MR. HONGBO."

Junyan Hongbo obeyed the command and settled into the chair facing the ebony-skinned woman in the black and gold uniform. He wasn't looking forward to this interview. In fact, he wasn't looking forward to just about anything that was likely to happen for the foreseeable future, and he found himself fervently wishing—again—that *Wanderlust* had managed to make it across the hyper limit in time after all.

Probably unreasonable to expect anything of the sort, he thought glumly. *After all, Herschel worked with Lorcan for years. Why should I have expected her to be any more competent than he was?*

He knew that thought was unfair, to Verrocchio as well as Captain Herschel, but he didn't much care at the moment.

The woman on the other side of the desk ignored him for several moments, letting him simmer in his own juices while she considered the data on her desk display. He could see its reflection in her eyes, and he wondered if it actually had anything at all to do with him or if it was simply window dressing. Whichever it might be, he told himself, it wasn't going to have any real effect on what he expected to be a most unpleasant interrogation. The only reason for her to be looking at it at this particular moment was to tweak his nerves a little tighter. He'd used the same technique himself more times than he could remember, and he was actually a bit surprised to discover that it was working *on* him just as well as it had ever worked *for* him.

I wonder if they've managed to crack my files yet? Bardasano swore no one could do it, and that if it looked like anyone was going to, the security protocols would scrub them back to the bare mollycirc. And they really were better than anything OFS had on tap. But Manty-proof? He grimaced mentally. *Not likely! They're going to get at least* something *out of them. The question is how much.*

At least he'd never been stupid enough to record anything likely to incriminate *him*. There was that handful of memos from Valery Ottweiler he'd tucked away as an insurance policy, but they only demonstrated what Ottweiler had asked him to pass on to Verrocchio on an official level. They didn't include any of Ottweiler's *un*official requests, and every one of them made it clear he himself had exercised no decision-making authority on the requests in question. He'd made damned sure there was nothing in his files that could link him to any of the more ... questionable decisions he'd helped guide Verrocchio into making.

Unfortunately, there was no way he could know what *Verrocchio* had been foolish enough to record. The possibility that he'd kept something that could lead back to Hongbo was unpleasantly high, although the vice commissioner could at least hope that if he had it would turn into a case of one man's word against another's. In the end, though, he knew the Manties were going to find at least something he'd dearly love for them *not* to find, and the best he could realistically hope for was that it would be one of his more minor peccadilloes.

And, of course, that they're willing to stop looking when they find it rather than turning over enough rocks to find something that isn't *minor,* he thought glumly. *And what do you think the odds of that are, Junyan? You're not exactly one of their favorite people in the entire universe.*

"Well, Mr. Hongbo," the woman behind the desk said finally, sitting back and folding her hands on the blotter in front of her, "you've been a rather busy fellow, haven't you?"

"I beg your pardon?" he replied stiffly, his expression carefully outraged.

"I said you've been rather busy," she repeated with a smile. "You and Commissioner Verrocchio both. All that running about discharging your little errands for people like Manpower and Technodyne." She shook her head. "I hate to think about all the time that took up. Time you could've spent so much more profitably on routine Frontier Security graft, embezzlement, and extortion."

"Admiral Gold Peak," he said coldly, "I am a vice commissioner in the service of the Office of Frontier Security and the Solarian League, not some minor functionary of one of your ragged 'Talbott Quadrant' system governments."

He straightened his spine, glaring at her, projecting his very best affronted senior bureaucrat image. There was no doubt in his mind that she was recording all of this, and eventually a copy of that recording was likely to find its way into Solarian channels. Under the circumstances, it behooved him to demonstrate the proper demeanor of a senior bureaucrat in hostile hands. That was particularly true given the search for scapegoats which would inevitably follow a disaster like this one. The last thing he needed was to provide ammunition for the people determined to make *him* the scapegoat by making any admissions of guilt or demonstrating any sign of weakness.

Of course, that was a long-term consideration, and there were shorter-term implications to his situation, as well. Like finding a way to fend off the immediate consequences if the Manties figured out just how instrumental he'd actually been in arranging events in the Talbott Quadrant.

Unfortunately, he didn't have much to work with. He recognized the weakness of his position as well as he was certain Gold Peak did, yet the only defense he *had* was to make it a matter of playing public roles against one another. He couldn't keep her from going wherever she wanted, but as long as he played *his* role and blustered strongly enough, he might at least slow her down. And he could always hope she'd be worried enough about setting precedents to hesitate about resorting to more rigorous techniques. After all, eventually *somebody* on the Manties' side was going to find himself in an analogous position. Hopefully Gold Peak would hesitate to give someone on the Solarian side an excuse for starting right out pulling fingernails and toenails.

Unfortunately, only a complete imbecile would think for one moment that the Solarian League was going to worry about precedents set by Manticore, and Gold Peak was no imbecile. Hongbo was glumly aware that Solarian arrogance—and especially that of Frontier Security and the Gendarmerie—was going to be sublimely confident it could do whatever it wanted without worrying about reprisals, and he never doubted the Manticoran admiral across the desk from him knew that as well as he did. Under the circumstances, he doubted somehow that someone who'd already displayed Gold Peak's . . . initiative was going to be fazed by any concerns about tender Solarian sensibilities when it came to something she really wanted to know about.

"I'm not answerable to you or to your 'Star Empire,' even in a private capacity, and certainly not in a public one!" he continued, putting as much bite into his voice as possible. "Your high-handed actions in this star system represent a flagrant violation of interstellar law, as you're very well aware. And your gross insult to the persons and offices of the Solarian League's official, legal representatives—and your bareknuckle aggression against the Solarian League Navy—is totally unacceptable. Believe me, you and your entire star nation will be held to account for your actions before this is over!"

He met her eyes levelly, refusing to flinch, letting her see the unbroken rock of his defiance.

And she laughed.

"Oh, very good, Mr. Hongbo!" She shook her head. "You actually sound as if you believe a single syllable you just said. That's amazing."

"I beg your pardon?" he repeated as icily as he

could. Which, to be honest, wasn't particularly icy at all. Her obvious amusement did not bode well.

"Yes, I'm sure you do. Beg my pardon, I mean." She smiled cheerfully. "Not too surprising for someone in your position. I'm pretty sure your superiors back in Old Chicago aren't going to be very happy with you or with Commissioner Verrocchio. No matter what else happens, they're bound to scapegoat the two of you, even for the things that weren't your fault. Of course, at the moment I haven't found anything that *wasn't* your fault, but I'm sure if we keep looking long enough we'll find *someone* else who screwed up almost as egregiously as you guys. I'm not a big fan of kicking someone when she's down, but the truth is that you and the Commissioner have shown an absolutely incredible talent for backing the wrong horse."

Hongbo felt himself wilt in his chair and forced his spine to stiffen. He managed to maintain eye contact, but he knew his effort to project defiance wasn't fooling her any more than it was fooling *him*.

"The two of you have made one…questionable decision after another from the moment you climbed into bed with Manpower and Technodyne and encouraged President Tyler in his little adventure in Talbott," she pointed out. "And that business with Admiral Byng and New Tuscany." She shook her head again. "Not the most shining moment of your career in public service, I'm afraid."

"I have no idea what you think you're talking about, Admiral," Hongbo retorted. "Admiral Byng, as you're very well aware, was a Battle Fleet officer operating under the authority of his own orders, not that of the Madras Sector's civilian officials."

"Oh?" She seemed to glance past him, making him acutely aware of the Marine master sergeant standing respectfully against the cabin bulkhead behind him. "So you're telling me you didn't deliberately encourage Admiral Byng's natural aggressiveness and arrogance in order to get him to New Tuscany?"

"I most certainly did not!" Hongbo snapped.

"And I take it you're also telling me you weren't being influenced by people like Valery Ottweiler or Aldona Anisimovna when you encouraged—or didn't, as the case may be—Admiral Byng and Admiral Crandall?"

"What? How dare you suggest anything of the sort!"

"It's not hard," she said mildly. "I open my mouth and the words come out. It's even easier when I'm pretty sure I'm being accurate. So, are you going to answer my question?"

"I was never unduly or improperly influenced by anyone—and especially not by the individuals you've just mentioned—in the discharge of my responsibilities!"

"Well, that's certainly a clear enough statement," she said. Her eyes refocused on his face, and she smiled again.

"The reason I asked those questions," she continued, "is that we've found records of over a dozen private meetings between you and Mr. Ottweiler since that whole business with Monica blew up. Given the degree of tension between the Star Empire and Mesa—and Manpower and Technodyne's demonstrated involvement with Monica—the number and frequency of those meetings inevitably leads us to wonder about the extent to which your own actions and the advice you gave Commissioner Verrocchio might have been influenced. I'm sure once we've cracked the encryption on your personal files—by the way, my people tell me it's a very good security package; congratulations—we'll have a much better picture of exactly what went on. A more fully developed one, I mean." She gave him yet another of those smiles, this one almost whimsical. "I'm afraid Commissioner Verrocchio's security wasn't quite as good as yours. We've gotten very good access on his side, although I am looking forward to seeing how the view from your side of the hill, as it were, meshes with his."

Hongbo kept his eyes from narrowing, but his brain raced. Was she telling him the truth when she implied they hadn't gotten access to his files yet? He could readily believe they'd cracked Verrocchio's already; the other man's approach to security had been as slovenly as his approach to anything else. But if all they had was the official, open record—which would have included his appointments calendar—and Verrocchio's private files, then Gold Peak actually *knew* very little, whatever she might *suspect*. Verrocchio certainly didn't have anything in written or recorded form from him that would indicate he'd been anything except a conduit for Ottweiler. And Ottweiler, as an accredited diplomat, had every right to be talking to Verrocchio or Hongbo.

"I would remind you, Admiral," he said, "that the files you're referring to are those of official representatives of the Solarian League. Violating them is an affront and an insult to the League, and one which will have very serious repercussions in the fullness of time."

"And Admiral Crandall's decision to attack the sovereign territory of the Star Empire doesn't come under the heading of the Solarian League's very best attempt at a 'serious repercussion,' Mr. Hongbo?" She looked at him quizzically. "Or did you have something even more serious—and possibly even effective, this time—in mind?"

"Whatever your temporary accomplishments may be, ultimately the League *is* going to win, Admiral," Hongbo replied. "You and your entire Star Empire might want to keep that in mind."

"I assure you that a proper regard for future consequences—for everyone—figures prominently in my thinking," Gold Peak assured him. "In the meantime, however, there are a few other minor matters I think need to be cleared up. For example, this business of you and Manpower's influence. Are you suggesting that if there was any improper influence on Manpower's part here in the Madras Sector, it was applied through Commissioner Verrocchio? That you yourself had nothing to do with it?"

"I have no way of knowing what someone else may or may not have said to Commissioner Verrocchio. I can assure you, however, that I never attempted to improperly influence the Commissioner on behalf of anyone, including Manpower."

"I see."

She picked up the stylus and made a note on the electronic pad at her elbow, then leaned back and crossed her legs.

"I'm sure you'll understand if I take your assurance with a grain of salt, Mr. Hongbo," she said. "After all, we wouldn't be having this conversation at all if there weren't a certain degree of tension between our mutual positions. You're the most senior Solarian representative I've had the opportunity to speak to, however, and I'm interested in getting your perspective on recent events. I'm sure by now you've heard at least rumors about my government's allegations against the Mesan Alignment. I'm curious. Did the Alignment ever come up in your meetings with Mr. Ottweiler?"

"No, it did not." Hongbo shook his head in clear disbelief. "I've never seen any evidence that the 'Mesan Alignment' is anything more than a figment of someone's overactive imagination, Admiral."

"I see." She made another note. "And you never met with anyone named Isabel Bardasano or Aldona Anisimovna?"

"Not personally, no," he replied. "I know a woman named Anisimovna was present here on Meyers at one time. In fact, now that I think about it, I may actually have encountered her, since she spent quite a bit of time with Mr. Ottweiler. As I understand it, she was a commercial representative for some private-sector interests in Mesa, and given Mr. Ottweiler's position as a member of the Mesan trade mission to the Madras Sector, I'm sure she had all sorts of legitimate reasons for meeting with him."

She made yet another note.

"So you had no involvement with Anisimovna or Bardasano in arranging President Tyler's involvement with Manpower and Technodyne?"

"I've already told you that. No, I did not."

"Or with Admiral Byng or Admiral Crandall's movements here in the Madras Sector and in the Talbott Quadrant?"

"No."

"Never had any reason to believe Ms. Anisimovna

was anything except—what was it you called her?—a commercial representative for *private*-sector interests?"

"Since I never directly discussed her activities here, I'm scarcely in a position to offer an opinion on that. Of course I had no reason to believe she was anything other than she and Mr. Ottweiler claimed she was."

"And you and Commissioner Verrocchio had no prior knowledge of Admiral Crandall's deployment to your sector?"

"Admiral Crandall was a *Battle Fleet* officer," Hongbo pointed out coldly. "She was deployed on a Battle Fleet training maneuver. Commissioner Verrocchio and I had no control over or influence upon the decision to send her to Madras."

"And you had no idea she was here prior to Admiral Byng's arrival?"

"None," he said firmly, allowing himself a faint stir of hopefulness. It wasn't really optimism, but from the sound of things, Gold Peak was on a fishing expedition. Was it possible she wasn't really after *him* at all, but rather looking for some evidence the 'Mesan Alignment' not only actually existed but had been actively involved in events in the region? He could see where the Manties would be eager for any outside evidence they could produce to support their allegations, and he wondered if he should allow himself to suggest that there *might*, just possibly, be some substance to them. He wouldn't have to say there was, wouldn't have to go out on any limbs, but suppose he allowed just a trace of genuine sounding doubt into his responses? It might well deflect her into chasing down that possibility. It might even (although the possibility was probably remote) convince her to cultivate him as a corroborating source rather than hammer him for his suspected involvement with Manpower.

Either way, at least they hadn't brought out the bright lights, the truncheons, and the fingernail-pullers. For the moment, Junyan Hongbo was willing to settle for that.

✧ ✧ ✧

"So what do you make of it?" Michelle Henke asked several hours later.

She and her staff sat around the briefing room table, where they'd just finished reviewing her notes and Alfredo's comments on the veracity and emotions of Vice Commissioner Hongbo during her conversation with him.

"I can't say there were a lot of surprises, Ma'am," Cynthia Lecter replied after a moment, and shrugged. "He lied every time you even implied *he'd* had anything to do with arranging events out here. No great surprise there. And we already knew he'd met with Anisimovna and Bardasano, courtesy of Brigadier Yucel."

"I'm inclined to agree, Ma'am," Dominica Adenauer said. "At the same time, though, we did get pretty positive confirmation that he knows Byng and Crandall *were* maneuvered into the region. And I know we're basically arguing from the fact that we know he lied about things, but it's pretty clear he was busy maneuvering Verrocchio into doing exactly what Anisimovna—or Ottweiler, at least—wanted Verrocchio to do. And, for that matter, he clearly figured Ottweiler was taking very specific marching orders from Anisimovna, and probably Bardasano. Now, I realize everybody's always regarded the Mesan government as basically a shill and a front for the transstellars in the Mesa System. But his responses to your questions about their relationship with Ottweiler certainly seem to indicate that Hongbo at least suspected this was more than a business-as-usual corrupt business deal."

"Granted," Lecter said. "But let's face it, Dominica, even if the Alignment never existed at all, the Mesa System would probably be plenty nervous about our frontiers getting this much closer to it. It's entirely possible Ottweiler really was acting for his government in this case, rather than for any clandestine organization."

"Except that in that case I would have anticipated the messengers between Ottweiler and the home system also being representatives of his government, Ma'am," Commander Edwards pointed out. Lecter looked at him, and he shrugged. "Why send people like Anisimovna and Bardasano, with no official connection to the Mesa System government at all? Unless those people had connections to something besides the Mesa System government that was really calling the shots? And if they weren't here representing a 'business-as-usual corrupt business deal,' then who *were* they representing?"

"That was one of the points that struck me most strongly, too," Michelle said with a nod. "And according to Alfredo, Hongbo registered a lot of uncertainty himself when it came to whether or not the Alignment existed. And here." She tapped one of her own notes on the display in front of her. "When I asked him about Levakonic and what Hongbo thought Technodyne was doing out here. Alfredo says that uncertainty quotient of his peaked really high when I suggested the Alignment might have seen this situation in Monica as an opportunity to get a closer look at our military hardware. I think our Mr. Hongbo's wondering whether or not he's been taking orders from the Alignment without realizing it for quite some time."

"Agreed, Ma'am," Lecter said. "And there's no question that we've clearly established that both Hongbo and Verrocchio have been squarely—and knowingly—in *somebody's* pocket from the very beginning. I think we've also established that Hongbo was really the primary contact point between Mesa and everything else going on in the Madras Sector. That was worthwhile in its own right, and it's going to help steer the investigators to the evidence they need. And I'll concede that Hongbo, at least, is coming to the conclusion the Alignment actually exists. But he wasn't able to give us a smoking gun. There's nothing in any of his responses, whether they were truthful or lies, that demonstrates any actual *knowledge* on his part that the Alignment is a reality and not just a figment of our imaginations."

"No, there isn't," Michelle acknowledged. "There is clear confirmation, though, that somebody in Mesa was pulling the strings out here. That everything we've been saying about outside involvement was justified, and that it was coming out of Mesa. Whether it was the Alignment or not is really beside the point, in that regard. Personally, I'm pretty damn sure it *was* the Alignment. But whether I'm right about that or not, I don't see any reason to think the string-pullers in Mesa are going to suddenly stop acting against our interests. And it's occurred to me that there's one place in the galaxy where we can probably find *proof* whether or not the Alignment exists."

Lecter's eyes widened with what might have been a touch of alarm, and Michelle smiled thinly.

"In my opinion, what we've already established from the files we've cracked, completely exclusive of anything Hongbo may have said to me or Alfredo may have picked up from his mind-glow is that some group in the Mesa System was directly behind the actions leading to the deaths of our personnel in New Tuscany. Moreover, *Ottweiler's* involvement means the Mesan *government* was involved. There's a phrase that describes an official government action hostile to the interests of and to the safety of the citizens of another government, people. It's called 'an act of war,' and that's precisely what the Mesa System has perpetrated against the Star Empire of Manticore."

Silence hovered for a moment. Then Lecter cleared her throat.

"I can't disagree with anything you just said, Ma'am," she said very carefully. "Can I ask where you're going with it, though?"

"Instead of just asking me whether or not I've lost my mind, you mean?" Michelle inquired with a smile which looked oddly impish.

"Far be it from me to put it in those terms, Ma'am."

"Oh, I'm sure." Michelle chuckled, but then her expression sobered.

"This isn't some impulsive decision on my part, Cindy." She let her gaze circle the table, meeting each of her staffers' eyes in turn. "I've been thinking about it ever since the Yawata Strike, and especially since Cachat and Zilwicki got home from Mesa. The Solarian League and the Star Empire are at war, and we got there because of someone else's machinations.

And while those idiots in Old Terra appear unwilling or unable to admit the possibility, whoever's behind all this obviously doesn't have the League's best interests at heart any more than she's looking out for ours. We've done our best to suggest that possibility to the Mandarins, but they've been too busy spinning the confrontation to consider our suggestions seriously. Of course, that's the best-case explanation for their actions. The worst-case explanation is that the bureaucrats calling the shots in Old Chicago know exactly what's going on and *they're* in the Alignment's pocket. I'm not quite paranoid enough to buy into that theory, though. If for no other reason because if they already controlled Kolokoltsov and his buddies that thoroughly, they'd have no need to set the League on a collision course with the Star Empire and the Republic."

She paused for a moment, as if allowing that to settle in, then shrugged.

"There's an old, old story about Alexander the Great back on old Earth, when he was a young man. When he was confronted by the Gordian knot that no one could untie, he solved the problem with a sword. I'm coming to the conclusion that what we have here isn't the Gordian knot, but a *Mesan* knot. And Tenth Fleet makes a pretty good sword when you think about it."

❖   ❖   ❖

Michelle Henke sat in her quarters once again, facing her com pickup. It was very quiet, quiet enough that Dicey's purring came clearly from under her desk where the enormous cat lay curled across her feet. She thought about moving the feet in question, but not very hard, and she smiled ruefully. The damned cat was finally establishing his ownership over her, as well as Billingsley, she realized.

She shook her head. Then the smile faded, and she considered the last couple of days.

From Commodore Thurgood's records, she knew that none of the Madras Sector's other star systems were even picketed. They were wide open, and she'd been considering the Gendarmerie's reports on the populations of those star systems. It was unlikely any of the other systems would be able to assume the functions of self-government as smoothly and effectively as Meyers had, yet even in the case of McIntosh there was clearly at least a hub around which a government could coalesce. That was actually one of the few points she'd been able to come up with in Lorcan Verrocchio's favor. He'd been venal, corrupt, and entirely too susceptible to being maneuvered by people like the Mesan Alignment. But he *hadn't* been willing to unleash Francisca Yucel on planetary populations if he'd had other options, and he'd permitted a degree of self-government—or self-*administration*, at least—that was rare in the Protectorates.

Dispatches from Baroness Medusa and Admiral Khumalo had arrived, authorizing her capture of Meyers. Of course, she'd already done it by the time authorization arrived, but it was good to know that so far at least her actions stood approved. And although her message requesting ground forces to bolster her Marine strength hadn't arrived when their dispatches were sent, they'd informed her they would be forwarding the first locally raised and equipped Guard battalions within the next T-month or so.

Bearing all of that in mind, she was confident she

could sweep up the rest of the Madras Sector with no more than destroyers and possibly a few cruisers. And that, of course, left her battlecruisers, her CLACs, and her superdreadnoughts for something else.

She intended to use them.

Her orders and operations plan had been drafted. Within the next ten hours ships would be departing from Meyers for every other system in the Madras Sector, and two hours after that, everything except a minimal security force of three LAC squadrons would depart Meyers itself. She'd already written the official dispatches to Spindle and to Manticore itself explaining her actions and intentions. Now there was one final message left to record, and she keyed the pickup.

"By the time you view this, Beth, I'm sure at least some of my professional colleagues are going to have cast a certain degree of doubt upon my alleged mental processes. In this instance, they may even have a point. But I think this is important—well, obviously I think that, or I wouldn't be doing it." She shook her head with a slight smile. "Trust me, I'm aware of the risks involved. I'm also aware that when you've already got a shooting war with the League on your hands, having someone dash off on her own and open yet another front may not be incredibly high on the list of your priorities. On the other hand, we *are* already at war with the League. Somehow I don't see my going calling on Mesa making that situation a lot worse. And the potential return, the chance to actually find proof of the Alignment's existence—not to mention the possibility of throwing a king-sized spanner into its works—strikes me as well worthwhile.

"The reason this is coming to you as a private

message, in addition to and unattached to my official dispatches, is that I want you to understand that I'm doing this on my own authority for a reason. I made it as clear as I could in the *official* record that I'm acting on my own. The reason for *this* message is to tell you that I did it that way deliberately to give you the option of disavowing my actions if that turns out to be necessary. Maybe I've been hanging around Honor too long, but this is something that needs doing, and if the price for my doing it is that you'll be forced to recall me or even court-martial me, it's worth it.

"Our family has a responsibility here, over and above my responsibility as an officer in your Navy. I intend to meet that responsibility.

"God bless, Beth. I love you."

Citizens ed. by John Ringo & Brian M. Thomsen
(trade pb) 978-1-4391-3347-7 • $16.00

Master of Epic SF
The Council War Series

There Will Be Dragons (pb) 0-7434-8859-8 • $7.99

Emerald Sea (pb) 1-4165-0920-8 • $7.99

Against the Tide (pb) 1-4165-2057-0 • $7.99

East of the Sun, West of the Moon
(pb) 1-4165-5518-87 • $7.99

Master of Real SF
The Troy Rising Series

Live Free or Die (hc) 1-4391-3332-8 • $26.00
(pb) 978-1-4391-3397-2 • $7.99

Citadel (hc) 978-1-4391-3400-9 • $26.00
(pb) 978-1-4516-3757-1 • $7.99

The Hot Gate (pb) 978-1-4516-3818-9 • $7.99

■ ■ ■

Von Neumann's War with Travis S. Taylor
(pb) 1-4165-5530-8 • $7.99

■ ■ ■

The Looking Glass Series

Into the Looking Glass (pb) 1-4165-2105-4 • $7.99

Vorpal Blade with Travis S. Taylor
(hc) 1-4165-2129-1 • $25.00
(pb) 1-4165-5586-2 • $7.99

Manxome Foe with Travis S. Taylor
(pb) 1-4165-9165-6 • $7.99

Claws That Catch with Travis S. Taylor
(hc) 1-4165-5587-0 • $25.00
(pb) 978-1-4391-3313-2 • $7.99

Master of Hard-Core Thrillers
The Kildar Saga

Ghost
(pb) 1-4165-2087-2 • $7.99

Kildar
(pb) 1-4165-2133-X • $7.99

Choosers of the Slain
(hc) 1-4165-2070-8 • $25.00
(pb) 1-4165-7384-4 • $7.99

Unto the Breach
(hc) 1-4165-0940-2 • $26.00
(pb) 1-4165-5535-8 • $7.99

A Deeper Blue
(hc) 1-4165-2128-3 • $26.00
(pb) 1-4165-5550-1 • $7.99

Tiger by the Tail with Ryan Sear
(hc) 978-1-4516-3856-1 • $25.00
(pb) 978-1-4767-3615-0 • $7.99

• • •

The Last Centurion
(hc) 1-4165-5553-6 • $25.00
(pb) 978-1-4391-3291-3 • $7.99

Master of Dark Fantasy

Princess of Wands
(hc) 1-4165-0923-2 • $25.00

Queen of Wands
(hc) 978-1-4516-3789-2 • $25.00
(pb) 978-1-4516-3917-9 • $7.99

Master of Bolos

The Road to Damascus with Linda Evans
(pb) 0-7434-9916-6 • $7.99

• • •

IT'S ALL ABOUT HONOR!

David Weber's Bestselling Honor Harrington series